GW00733946

RED EVE

PHIL.

RED EVE

The Essential Adventure Library

H. Rider Haggard

68-PHIL

To order additional copies of this book, contact:
Xlibris Corporation
1-888-795-4274
www.Xlibris.com
Orders@Xlibris.com

CONTENTS

INTRODUCTION

MURGH THE DEATH

They knew nothing of it in England or all the Western countries in those days before Crecy was fought, when the third Edward sat upon the throne. There was none to tell them of the doom that the East, whence come light and life, death and the decrees of God, had loosed upon the world. Not one in a multitude in Europe had ever even heard of those vast lands of far Cathay peopled with hundreds of millions of cold-faced yellow men, lands which had grown very old before our own familiar states and empires were carved out of mountain, of forest, and of savage-haunted plain. Yet if their eyes had been open so that they could see, well might they have trembled. King, prince, priest, merchant, captain, citizen and poor labouring hind, well might they all have trembled when the East sent forth her gifts!

Look across the world beyond that curtain of thick darkness. Behold! A vast city of fantastic houses half buried in winter snows and reddened by the lurid sunset breaking through a saw-toothed canopy of cloud. Everywhere upon the temple squares and open spaces great fires burning a strange fuel—the bodies of thousands of mankind. Pestilence was king of that city, a pestilence hitherto unknown. Innumerable hordes had died and were dying, yet innumerable hordes remained. All the patient East bore forth those still shapes that had been theirs to love or hate, and, their task done, turned to the banks of the mighty river and watched.

Down the broad street which ran between the fantastic houses advanced a procession toward the brown, ice-flecked river. First marched a company of priests clad in black robes, and carrying on poles lanterns of black paper, lighted, although the sun still shone. Behind marched another company of priests clad in white robes, and bearing white lanterns, also lighted. But at these none looked, nor did they listen to the dirges that they sang, for all eyes were fixed upon him who filled the centre space and upon his two companions.

The first companion was a lovely woman, jewel-hung, wearing false flowers in her streaming hair, and beneath her bared breasts a kirtle of white silk. Life and love embodied in radiance and beauty, she danced in front, looking about her with alluring eyes, and scattering petals of dead roses from a basket which she bore. Different was the second companion, who stalked behind; so thin, so sexless that none could say if the shape were that of man or woman. Dry, streaming locks of iron-grey, an ashen countenance, deep-set, hollow eyes, a beetling, parchment-covered brow; lean shanks half hidden with a rotting rag, claw-like hands which clutched miserably at the air. Such was its awful fashion, that of new death in all its terrors.

Between them, touched of neither, went a man, naked save for a red girdle and a long red cloak that was fastened round his throat and hung down from his broad shoulders. There was nothing strange about this man, unless it were perhaps the strength that seemed to flow from him and the glance of his icy eyes. He was just a burly yellow man, whose age none could tell, for the hood of the red cloak hid his hair; one who seemed to be far removed from youth, and yet untouched by time. He walked on steadily, intently, his face immovable, taking no heed.

Only now and again he turned those long eyes of his upon one of the multitude who watched him pass crouched upon their knees in solemn silence, always upon one, whether it were man, woman, or child, with a glance meant for that one and no other. And ever the one upon whom it fell rose from the knee, made obeisance, and departed as though filled with some inspired purpose.

Down to the quay went the black priests, the white priests, and the red-cloaked man, preceded by rose life, followed by ashen death. Through the funeral fires they wended, and the lurid sunset shone upon them all.

To the pillars of this quay was fastened a strange, high-pooped ship with crimson sails set upon her masts. The white priests and the black priests formed lines upon either side of the broad gangway of that ship and bowed as the red-cloaked man walked over it between them quite alone, for now she with the dead roses and she of the ashen countenance had fallen back. As the sun sank, standing on the lofty stern, he cried aloud:

"Here the work is done. Now I, the Eating Fire, I the Messenger, get me to the West. Among you for a while I cease to burn; yet remember me, for I shall come again."

As he spoke the ropes of the ship were loosened, the wind caught her crimson sails, and she departed into the night, one blood-red spot against its blackness.

The multitude watched until they could see her no longer. Then they flamed up with mingled joy and rage. They laughed madly. They cursed him who had departed.

"We live, we live, we live!" they cried. "Murgh is gone! Murgh is gone! Kill his priests! Make sacrifice of his Shadows. Murgh is gone bearing the curse of the East into the bosom of the West. Look, it follows him!" and they pointed to a cloud of smoke or vapour, in which terrible shapes seemed to move dimly, that trailed after the departing, red-sailed ship.

The black priests and the white priests heard. Without struggle, without complaint, as though they were but taking part in some set ceremony, they kneeled down in lines upon the snow. Naked from the waist up, executioners with great swords appeared. They advanced upon the kneeling lines without haste, without wrath, and, letting fall the heavy swords upon the patient, outstretched necks, did their grim office till all were dead. Then they turned to find her of the flowers who had danced before, and her of the tattered weeds who had followed after, purposing to cast them to the funeral flames. But these were gone, though none had seen them go. Only out of the gathering darkness from some temple or pagoda-top a voice spoke like a moaning wind.

"Fools," wailed the voice, "still with you is Murgh, the second

Thing created; Murgh, who was made to be man's minister. Murgh the Messenger shall reappear from beyond the setting sun. Ye cannot kill, ye cannot spare. Those priests you seemed to slay he had summoned to be his officers afar. Fools! Ye do but serve as serves Murgh, Gateway of the Gods. Life and death are not in your hands or in his. They are in the hands of the Master of Murgh, Helper of man, of that Lord whom no eye hath seen, but whose behests all who are born obey— yes, even the mighty Murgh, Looser of burdens, whom in your foolishness ye fear."

So spoke this voice out of the darkness, and that night the sword of the great pestilence was lifted from the Eastern land, and there the funeral fires flared no more.

CHAPTER I

THE TRYSTING-PLACE

On the very day when Murgh the Messenger sailed forth into that uttermost sea, a young man and a maiden met together at the Blythburgh marshes, near to Dunwich, on the eastern coast of England. In this, the month of February of the year 1346, hard and bitter frost held Suffolk in its grip. The muddy stream of Blyth, it is true, was frozen only in places, since the tide, flowing up from the Southwold harbour, where it runs into the sea between that ancient town and the hamlet of Walberswick, had broken up the ice. But all else was set hard and fast, and now toward sunset the cold was bitter.

Stark and naked stood the tall, dry reeds. The blackbirds and starlings perched upon the willows seemed swollen into feathery balls, the fur started on the backs of hares, and a four-horse wain could travel in safety over swamps where at any other time a schoolboy dared not set his foot.

On such an eve, with snow threatening, the great marsh was utterly desolate, and this was why these two had chosen it for their meeting place.

To look on they were a goodly pair—the girl, who was clothed in the red she always wore, tall, dark, well shaped, with large black eyes and a determined face, one who would make a very stately woman; the man broad shouldered, with grey eyes that were quick and almost fierce, long limbed, hard, agile, and healthy, one who had never known sickness, who looked as though the world were his own to master. He was young, but three-and-twenty that day, and his simple dress, a tunic of thick wool fastened round him with a leathern belt, to which hung a short sword, showed that his degree was modest.

The girl, although she seemed his elder, in fact was only in her twentieth year. Yet from her who had been reared in the hard school of that cruel age childhood had long departed, leaving her a ripened woman before her time.

This pair stood looking at each other.

"Well, Cousin Eve Clavering," said the man, in his clear voice, "why did your message bid me meet you in this cold place?"

"Because I had a word to say to you, Cousin Hugh de Cressi," she answered boldly; "and the marsh being so cold and so lonesome I thought it suited to my purpose. Does Grey Dick watch yonder?"

"Ay, behind those willows, arrow on string, and God help him on whom Dick draws! But what was that word, Eve?"

"One easy to understand," she replied, looking him in the eyes— "Farewell!"

He shivered as though with the cold, and his face changed.

"An ill birthday greeting, yet I feared it," he muttered huskily, "but why more now than at any other time?"

"Would you know, Hugh? Well, the story is short, so I'll let it out. Our great-grandmother, the heiress of the de Cheneys, married twice, did she not, and from the first husband came the de Cressis, and from the second the Claverings. But in this way or in that we Claverings got the lands, or most of them, and you de Cressis, the nobler stock, took to merchandise. Now since those days you have grown rich with your fishing fleets, your wool mart, and your ferry dues at Walberswick and Southwold. We, too, are rich in manors and land, counting our acres by the thousand, but yet poor, lacking your gold, though yonder manor"—and she pointed to some towers which rose far away above the trees upon the high land—"has many mouths to feed. Also the sea has robbed us at Dunwich, where I was born, taking our great house and sundry streets that paid us rent, and your market of Southwold has starved out ours at Blythburgh."

"Well, what has all this to do with you and me, Eve?"

"Much, Hugh, as you should know who have been bred to trade," and she glanced at his merchant's dress. "Between de Cressi and Clavering there has been rivalry and feud for three long generations. When we were children it abated for a while, since your father lent money to mine, and that is why they suffered us to grow up side by side. But then they quarrelled about the ferry that we had set in pawn, and your father asked his gold back again, and, not getting it, took the ferry, which I have always held a foolish and strife-breeding deed, since from that day forward the war was open. Therefore, Hugh, if we meet at all it must be in these frozen reeds or behind the cover of a thicket, like a village slut and her man."

"I know that well enough, Eve, who have spoken with you but twice in nine months." And he devoured her beautiful face with hungry eyes. "But of that word, 'Farewell'—"

"Of that ill word, this, Hugh: I have a new suitor up yonder, a fine French suitor, a very great lord indeed, whose wealth, I am told, none can number. From his mother he has the Valley of the Waveney up to Bungay town—ay, and beyond—and from his father, a whole county in Normandy. Five French knights ride behind his banner, and with them ten squires and I know not how many men-at-arms. There is feasting yonder at the manor, I can tell you. Ere his train leaves us our winter provender will be done, and we'll have to drink small beer till the wine ships come from France in spring."

"And what is this lord's name?"

"God's truth, he has several," she answered. "Sir Edmund Acour in England, and in France the high and puissant Count of Noyon, and in Italy, near to the city of Venice—for there, too, he has possessions which came to him through his grandmother—the Seigneur of Cattrina."

"And having so much, does he want you, too, as I have heard, Eve? And if so, why?"

"So he swears," she answered slowly; "and as for the reason, why, I suppose you must seek it in my face, which by ill-fortune has pleased his lordship since first he saw it a month ago. At the least he has asked me in marriage of my father, who jumped at him like a winter pike, and so I'm betrothed."

"And do you want him, Eve?"

"Ay, I want him as far as the sun is from the moon or the world from either. I want him in heaven or beneath the earth, or anywhere away from me."

At these words a light shone in Hugh's keen grey eyes.

"I'm glad of that, Eve, for I've been told much of this fine fellow—amongst other things that he is a traitor come here to spy on England. But should I be a match for him, man to man, Eve?" he asked after a little pause.

She looked him up and down; then answered:

"I think so, though he is no weakling; but not for him and the five knights and the ten squires, and my noble father, and my brother, and the rest. Oh, Hugh, Hugh!" she added bitterly, "cannot you understand that you are but a merchant's lad, though your blood be as noble as any in this realm—a merchant's lad, the last of five brothers? Why were you not born the first of them if you wished for Eve Clavering, for then your red gold might have bought me."

"Ask that of those who begot me," said Hugh. "Come now, what's in your mind? You're not one to be sold like a heifer at a faring and go whimpering to the altar, and I am not one to see you led there while I stand upon my feet. We are made of a clay too stiff for a French lord's fingers, Eve, though it is true that they may drag you whither you would not walk."

"No," she answered, "I think I shall take some marrying against my wish. Moreover, I am Dunwich born."

"What of that, Eve?"

"Go ask your godsire and my friend, Sir Andrew Arnold, the old priest. In the library of the Temple there he showed me an ancient roll, a copy of the charter granted by John and other kings of England to the citizens of Dunwich."

"What said this writing, Eve?"

"It said, among other things, that no man or maid of Dunwich can be forced to marry against their will, even in the lifetime of their parents."

"But will it hold to-day?"

"Ay, I think so. I think that is why the holy Sir Andrew showed it to me, knowing something of our case, for he is my confessor when I can get to him."

"Then, sweet, you are safe!" exclaimed Hugh, with a sigh of relief.

"Ay, so safe that to-morrow Father Nicholas, the French chaplain in his train, has been warned to wed me to my lord Acour—that is, if I'm there to wed."

"And if this Acour is here, I'll seek him out to-night and challenge him, Eve," and Hugh laid hand upon his sword.

"Doubtless," she replied sarcastically, "Sir Edmund Acour, Count of Noyon, Seigneur of Cattrina, will find it honour to accept the challenge of Hugh de Cressi, the merchant's youngest son. Oh, Hugh, Hugh! are your wits frozen like this winter marsh? Not thus can you save me."

The young man thought a while, staring at the ground and biting his lips. Then he looked up suddenly and said:

"How much do you love me, Eve?"

With a slow smile, she opened her arms, and next moment they were kissing each other as heartily as ever man and maid have kissed since the world began, so heartily, indeed, that when at length she pushed him from her, her lovely face was as red as the cloak she wore.

"You know well that I love you, to my sorrow and undoing," she said, in a broken voice. "From childhood it has been so between us, and till the grave takes one or both it will be so, and for my part beyond it, if the priests speak true. For, whatever may be your case, I am not one to change my fancy. When I give, I give all, though it be of little worth. In truth, Hugh, if I could I would marry you to-night, though you are naught but a merchant's son, or even—" And she paused, wiping her eyes with the back of her slim, strong hand.

"I thank you," he answered, trembling with joy. "So it is with me. For you and no other woman I live and die; and though I am so humble I'll be worthy of you yet. If God keeps me in breath you shall not blush for your man, Eve. Well, I am not great at words, so let us come to deeds. Will you away with me now? I think that Father

Arnold would find you lodging for the night and an altar to be wed at, and to-morrow our ship sails for Flanders and for France."

"Yes, but would your father give us passage in it, Hugh?"

"Why not? It could not deepen the feud between our Houses, which already has no bottom, and if he refused, we would take one, for the captain is my friend. And I have some little store set by; it came to me from my mother."

"You ask much," she said; "all a woman has, my life, perchance, as well. Yet there it is; I'll go because I'm a fool, Hugh; and, as it chances, you are more to me than aught, and I hate this fine French lord. I tell you I sicken at his glance and shiver when he touches me. Why, if he came too near I should murder him and be hanged. I'll go, though God alone knows the end of it."

"Our purpose being honest, the end will be good, Eve, though perhaps before all is done we may often think it evil. And now let's away, though I wish that you were dressed in another colour."

"Red Eve they name me, and red is my badge, because it suits my dark face best. Cavil not at my robe, Hugh, for it is the only dowry you will get with Eve Clavering. How shall we go? By the Walberswick ferry? You have no horses."

"Nay, but I have a skiff hidden in the reeds five miles furlongs off. We must keep to the heath above Walberswick, for there they might know your red cloak even after dark, and I would not have you seen till we are safe with Sir Arnold in the Preceptory. Mother of Heaven! what is that?"

"A peewit, no more," she answered indifferently.

"Nay, it is my man Dick, calling like a peewit. That is his sign when trouble is afoot. Ah, here he comes."

As he spoke a tall, gaunt man appeared, advancing towards them. His gait was a shambling trot that seemed slow, although, in truth, he was covering the ground with extraordinary swiftness. Moreover, he moved so silently that even on the frost-held soil his step could not be heard, and so carefully that not a reed stirred as he threaded in and out among their clumps like an otter, his head crouched down and his long bow pointed before him as though it were a spear. Half a minute more, and he was before them—a very strange man to see. His years were not so many, thirty perhaps, and yet his face looked quite old because of its lack of colouring, its thinness, and the hard lines that marked where the muscles ran down to the tight, straight mouth and up to the big forehead, over which hung hair so light that at a little distance he seemed ashen-grey. Only in this cold, rocky face, set very far apart, were two pale-blue eyes, which just now, when he chose to lift their lids that generally kept near together, as though he were half asleep, were full of fire and quick cunning.

Reaching the pair, this strange fellow dropped to his knee and raised his cap to Eve, the great lady of the Claverings—Red Eve, as they called her through that country-side. Then he spoke, in a low, husky voice:

"They're coming, master! You and your mistress must to earth unless you mean to face them in the open," and the pale eyes glittered as he tapped his great black bow.

"Who are coming, Dick? Be plain, man!"

"Sir John Clavering, my lady's father; young John, my lady's brother; the fine French lord who wears a white swan for a crest; three of the nights, his companions; and six—no seven—men-at-arms. Also from the other side of the grieve, Thomas of Kessland, and with him his marsh men and verderers."

"And what are they coming for?" he asked again. "Have they hounds, and hawk on wrist?"

"Nay, but they have swords and knife on thigh," and he let his pale eyes fall on Eve.

"Oh, have done!" she broke in. "They come to take me, and I'll not be taken! They come to kill you, and I'll not see you slain and live. I had words with my father this morning about the Frenchman and, I fear, let out the truth. He told me then that ere the Dunwich roses bloomed again she who loved you would have naught but bones to kiss. Dick, you know the fen; where can we hide till nightfall?"

"Follow me," said the man, "and keep low!"

Plunging into the dense brake of reeds, through which he glided like a polecat, Dick led them over ground whereon, save in times of hard frost, no man could tread, heading toward the river bank. For two hundred paces or more they went thus, till, quite near to the lip of the stream, they came to a patch of reeds higher and thicker than the rest, in the centre of which was a little mound hid in a tangle of scrub and rushes. Once, perhaps a hundred or a thousand years before, some old marsh dweller had lived upon this mound, or been buried in it. At any rate, on its southern side, hidden by reeds and a withered willow, was a cavity of which the mouth could not be seen that might have been a chamber for the living or the dead.

Thrusting aside the growths that masked it, Dick bade them enter and lie still.

"None will find us here," he said as he lifted up the reeds behind them, "unless they chance to have hounds, which I did not see. Hist! be still; they come!"

CHAPTER II

THE FIGHT BY THE RIVER

For a while Hugh and Eve heard nothing, but Grey Dick's ears were sharper than theirs, quick as these might be. About half a minute later, however, they caught the sound of horses' hoofs ringing on the hard earth, followed by that of voices and the crackle of breaking reeds.

Two of the speakers appeared and pulled up their horses near by in a dry hollow that lay between them and the river bank. Peeping between the reeds that grew about the mouth of the earth-dwelling, Eve saw them.

"My father and the Frenchman," she whispered. "Look!" And she slid back a little so that Hugh might see.

Peering through the stems of the undergrowth, set as it were in a little frame against the red and ominous sky, the eyes of Hugh de Cressi fell upon Sir Edmund Acour, a gallant, even a splendid-looking knight—that was his first impression of him. Broad shouldered, graceful, in age neither young nor old, clean featured, quick eyed, with a mobile mouth and a little, square-cut beard, soft and languid voiced, black haired, richly dressed in a fur robe, and mounted on a fine black horse, such was the man.

Staring at Acour, and remembering that he, too, loved Red Eve, Hugh grew suddenly ashamed. How could a mere merchant compare himself with this magnificent lord, this high-bred, many-titled favourite of courts and of fortune? How could he rival him, he who had never yet travelled a hundred miles from the place where he was born, save once, when he sailed on a trading voyage to Calais? As well might a hooded crow try to match a peregrine that swooped to snatch away the dove from beneath its claws. Yes, he, Hugh, was the grey crow, Eve was the dove whom he had captured, and yonder shifty-eyed Count was the fleet, fierce peregrine who soon would tear out his heart and bear the quarry far away. Hugh shivered a little as the thought struck him, not with fear for himself, but at the dread of that great and close bereavement.

The girl at his side felt the shiver, and her mind, quickened by love and peril, guessed its purport. She said nothing, for words were dangerous; only turning her beautiful face she pressed her lips upon her lover's hand. It was her message to him; thereby, as he knew well, humble as he might be, she acknowledged him her lord forever. I am with you, said that kiss. Have no fear; in life or in death none shall divide us. He looked at her with grateful eyes, and would have spoken had she not placed her hand upon his mouth and pointed.

Acour was speaking in English, which he used with a strong French accent.

"Well, we do not find your beautiful runaway, Sir John," he said, in a clear and cultivated voice; "and although I am not vain, for my part I cannot believe that she has come to such a place as this to meet a merchant's clerk, she who should company with kings."

"Yet I fear it is so, Sir Edmund," answered Sir John Clavering, a stout, dark man of middle age. "This girl of mine is very heady, as I give warning you will find out when she is your wife. For years she has set her fancy upon Hugh de Cressi; yes, since they were boy and girl together, as I think, and while he lives I doubt she'll never change it."

"While he lives—then why should he continue to live, Sir John?" asked the Count indifferently. "Surely the world will not miss a chapman's son!"

"The de Cressis are my kin, although I hate them, Sir Edmund. Also they are rich and powerful, and have many friends in high places. If this young man died by my command it would start a blood feud of which none can tell the end, for, after all, he is nobly born."

"Then, Sir John, he shall die by mine. No, not at my own hands, since I do not fight with traders. But I have those about me who are pretty swordsmen and know how to pick a quarrel. Before a week is out there will be a funeral in Dunwich."

"I know nothing of your men, and do not want to hear of their quarrels, past or future," said Sir John testily.

"Of course not," answered the Count. "I pray you, forget my words. Name of God! what an accursed and ill-omened spot is this. I feel as though I were standing by my own grave—it came upon me suddenly." And he shivered and turned pale.

Dick lifted his bow, but Hugh knocked the arrow aside ere he could loose it.

"To those who talk of death, death often draws near," replied Clavering, crossing himself, "though I find the place well enough, seeing the hour and season."

"Do you—do you, Sir John? Look at that sky; look at the river beneath which has turned to blood. Hark to the howl of the wind in the reeds and the cry of the birds we cannot see. Ay, and look at our shadows on the snow. Mine lies flat by a great hole, and yours rising against yonder bank is that of a hooded man with hollow eyes—Death himself as I should limn him! There, it is gone! What a fool am I, or how strong is that wine of yours! Shall we be going also?"

"Nay, here comes my son with tidings. Well, Jack, have you found your sister?" he added, addressing a dark and somewhat saturnine young man who now rode up to them from over the crest of the hollow.

"No, sir, though we have beat the marsh through and through, so that scarce an otter could have escaped us. And yet she's here, for Thomas of Kessland caught sight of her red cloak among the reeds, and what's more, Hugh de Cressi is with her, and Grey Dick too, for both were seen."

"I am glad there's a third," said Sir John drily, "though God save me from his arrows! This Grey Dick," he added to the Count, "is a wild, homeless half-wit whom they call Hugh de Cressi's shadow, but the finest archer in Suffolk, with Norfolk thrown in; one who can put a shaft through every button on your doublet at fifty paces—ay, and bring down wild geese on the wing twice out of four times, for I have seen him do it with that black bow of his."

"Indeed? Then I should like to see him shoot—at somebody else," answered Acour, for in those days such skill was of interest to all soldiers. "Kill Hugh de Cressi if you will, friend, but spare Grey Dick; he might be useful."

"Ay, Sir Edmund," broke in the young man furiously, "I'll kill him if I can catch him, the dog who dares to bring scandal on my sister's name. Let the Saints but give me five minutes face to face with him alone, with none to help either of us, and I'll beat him to a pulp, and hang what's left of him upon the nearest tree to be a warning to all such puppies."

"I note the challenge," said Sir Edmund, "and should the chance come my way will keep the lists for you with pleasure, since whatever this Hugh may be I doubt that from his blood he'll prove no coward. But, young sir, you must catch your puppy ere you hang him, and if he is in this marsh he must have gone to ground."

"I think so, too, Sir Edmund; but, if so, we'll soon start the badger. Look yonder." And he pointed to smoke rising at several spots half a mile or more away.

"What have you done, son?" asked Sir John anxiously.

"Fired the reeds," he said with a savage laugh, "and set men to watch that the game does not break back. Oh, have no fear, father! Red Eve will take no harm. The girl ever loved fire. Moreover, if she is there she will run to the water before it, and be caught."

"Fool," thundered Sir John, "do you know your sister so little? As like as not she'll stay and burn, and then I'll lose my girl, who, when all is said, is worth ten of you! Well, what is done cannot be undone, but if death comes of this mad trick it is on your head, not mine! To the bank, and watch with me, Sir Edmund, for we can do no more."

Ten minutes later, and the fugitives in the mound, peeping out from their hole, saw clouds of smoke floating above them.

"You should have let me shoot, Master Hugh," said Grey Dick, in his hard, dry whisper. "I'd have had these three, at least, and they'd have been good company on the road to hell, which now we must walk alone."

"Nay," answered Hugh sternly, "I'll murder none, though they strive to murder us, and these least of all," and he glanced at Eve, who sat staring out of the mouth of the hole, her chin resting on her hand. "You had best give in, sweetheart," he said hoarsely. "Fire is worse than foes, and it draws near."

"I fear it less," she answered. "Moreover, marriage is worse than either—sometimes."

Hugh took counsel with Grey Dick.

"This place will burn like tinder," he said, pointing to the dry reeds which grew thickly all about them, and to the masses of brushwood and other rubbish that had drifted against the side of the little mound in times of flood. "If the fire reaches us we must perish of flame, or smoke, or both."

"Ay," answered Dick, "like old witch Sarah when they burned her in her house. She screeched a lot, though some say it was her cat that screeched and she died mum."

"If we could get into the water now, Dick?"

He shook his ash-hued head.

"The pools are frozen. Moreover, as well die of heat as cold; I love not ice-water."

"What counsel, then, Dick?"

"You'll not take the best, master—to loose my bow upon them. That fine fellow did well to be afraid, for had you not knocked up my hand there'd be an arrow sticking in his throat by now. He was right, Death walked near to him."

"It must not be, Dick, unless they strike first. What else?"

"Perchance, when the smoke begins to trouble them, which it must soon, they'll move. Then we will run for the river; 'tis but fifty yards. The Lady Eve can swim like a duck, and so can you. The tide has turned, and will bear you to the point, and I'll hold the bank against any who try to follow, and take my chance. What say you of that plan, lady?"

"That it is good as another, or as bad," she answered indifferently.

"Let's bide where we are and do what we must when we must. Nay, waste no more breath, Hugh. I'll not yield and go home like a naughty child to be married. It was you who snatched away Grey Dick's shaft, not I; and now I'll save myself."

"Red Eve!—that's Red Eve!" muttered the henchman, with a dry chuckle of admiration. "The dead trouble neither man nor woman. Ah, she knows, she knows!"

After this there was silence for a while, save for the roar of the fire that ever drew more near.

Eve held her cloak pressed against her mouth to filter the smoke, which grew thick.

"It is time to move," said Hugh, coughing as he spoke. "By Heaven's grace, we are too late! Look!"

As he spoke, suddenly in the broad belt of reeds which lay between them and the river bank fire appeared in several places, caused doubtless by the flaming flakes which the strong wind had carried from behind the mound. Moreover, these new fires, burning up briskly and joining themselves together, began to advance toward the three in the hole.

"The wind has turned," said Dick. "Now it is fire, or water if you can get there. How do you choose to die?" and as he spoke he unstrung his bow and slipped it into its leathern case.

"Neither one way nor the other," answered Eve. "Some may die to-night, but we shall not."

Hugh leapt up and took command.

"Cover your faces to the eyes, and run for it," he said. "I'll go first, then you, Eve, and Dick behind. Make for the point and leap— the water is deep there."

They sprang to their feet and forward into the reeds. When they were almost at the edge of the fire a shout told them that they had been seen. Eve, the swift of foot, outpaced Hugh, and was the first to leap into that circle of tall flames. She was through it! They were all through it, scorched but unharmed. Thirty paces away was the little point of land where nothing grew, for the spring tides washed it, that jutted out into the waters of the Blythe, and, perhaps a hundred to their right, the Claverings poured down on them, foot and horse together.

Hugh caught his foot in a willow root and fell. Eve and Grey Dick sped onward unknowing. They reached the point above the water, turned, and saw. Dick slipped his bow from its case, strung it, and set an arrow on the string. Hugh had gained his feet, but a man who had come up sprang, and cast his arms about him. Hugh threw him to the ground, for he was very strong, and shook himself free. Then he drew the short and heavy sword that he wore, and, shouting out, "Make way!" to those who stood between him and the little promontory, started to run again.

These opened to the right and left to let him pass, for they feared the look in his eyes and the steel in his hand. Only young John Clavering, who had leapt from his horse, would not budge. As Hugh tried to push past him, he struck him in the face, calling out:

"We have caught the de Cressi thief! Take him and hang him!"

At the insult of the blow and words, Hugh stopped dead and turned quite white, whereupon the men, thinking that he was afraid, closed in upon him. Then in the silence the harsh, croaking voice of Grey Dick was heard saying:

"Sir John of Clavering, bid your people let my master go, or I will send an arrow through your heart!" and he lifted the long bow and drew it.

Sir John muttered something, thinking that this was a poor way to die, and again the men fell back, except one French knight, who, perhaps, did not catch or understand his words.

This man stretched out his hand to seize Hugh, but before ever it fell upon his shoulder the bow twanged and Acour's retainer was seen whirling round and round, cursing with pain. In the palm of his hand was an arrow that had sunk through it to the feathers.

"You are right; that knave shoots well," said the Count to Sir John, who made no answer.

Now again all fell back, so that Hugh might have run for it if he would. But his blood was up, and he did not stir.

"John Clavering," he said, addressing the young man, "just now, when I lay hid in yonder hole, I heard you say that if you had five minutes with me alone you'd beat me to a pulp and hang what was left of me on the nearest tree. Well, here I stand, and there's a tree. Having first tried to burn me and your sister, you have struck me in the face. Will you make good your words, or shall I strike you in the face and go my way? Nay, keep your dogs off me! Grey Dick yonder has more arrows."

Now a tumult rose, some saying one thing and some another, but all keeping an eye upon Grey Dick and his bent bow. At last Sir Edmund Acour rode forward, and in his polished, stately way said to John:

"Young sir, this merchant is in the right, and whatever his trade may be, his blood is as good as your own. After your brave words, either you should fight him or take back the blow you gave."

Then he leaned down and whispered into John's ear:

"Your sword is longer than his. Make an end of him and of all his trouble, lest men should laugh at you as an empty boaster."

Now John, who was brave and needed but little urging, turned to his father and said:

"Have I your leave to whip this fellow, sir?"

"You should have asked that before you struck him in the face," replied the knight. "You are a man grown. Do as best pleases you. Only if you take the blow, begone from Blythburgh."

Then Eve, who all this time had been listening, called out from where she stood above the river.

"Brother John, if you fight your cousin Hugh, who is my affianced husband, and fall, on your own head be it, for know, your blood shall not stand between him and me, since it was you who struck him, and not he you. Be warned, John, and let him go, lest he should send you farther than you wish to travel. And to you, Hugh, I say, though it is much to ask, if he throws down his sword, forget that unknightly blow and come thither."

"You hear," said Hugh shortly to John. "Now, because she is your sister, if it's your will I'll begone in peace."

"Ay," answered John, setting his thin lips, "because you are a coward, woman-thief, and seek to live that you may bring shame upon our House. Well, that will pass when you die presently!"

"John, John, boast not," cried Eve. "Who has shown you where you will sleep to-night?"

"Whether I shall live or die, God knows alone," said Hugh solemnly. "But what I seek to know is, should it chance to be your lot to die, whether your people or this Frenchman will set on me, or raise a blood-feud against me. Tell me now, Sir John Clavering."

"If you kill my son in combat à outrance, he being the challenger," answered the knight, "none shall lift hand against you for that deed if I can hold them back. But know that I have other cause of quarrel against you"—and he pointed to his daughter—"and that if you meddle more with her, who is not for you, certainly you shall die."

"And, young sir," broke in Sir Edmund, "I pray you to understand that this Lady Eve to-morrow becomes my wife with the will of her father and her kin; and that if you try to stand between us, although I may not fight you, seeing what I am and what you are, I'll kill you like a rat when and where I get the chance! Yes," he added, in a savage snarl, "I pledge my knightly honour that I will kill you like a rat, if I must follow you across the world to do so!"

"You will not have need to travel far if I have my will," answered the young man sternly, "since Red Eve is mine, not yours, and, living or dead, mine she will remain. As for your fine knightly honour, Sir Edmund Acour, Count de Noyon, Seigneur of Cattrina, what has a traitor to his King to do with honour, one who is here as a spy of Philip of France, as the poor merchant's lad knows well? Oh, take you hand from your sword, of which you say I am not worthy, and, since you say also that I have so many enemies, let me begin with a squire of my own degree."

Now at these bold words arose a clamour of voices speaking in French and English.

"What say you to this, Sir Edmund?" shouted Sir John Clavering above them all. "You are a great lord and a wealthy, beloved by me also as the affianced of my daughter, but I am a loyal Englishman who have no truck with traitors to my King."

"What say I?" asked Sir Edmund calmly. "I say that if this fellow can fight as well as he can lie, your son has but a poor chance with him. As you know well, I came hither from France to visit my estates, not to learn what strength his Grace of England, my liege lord, gathers for the new war with Philip."

"Enough," said Sir John; "though this is the first I have heard of such a war, for it would seem that you know more of King Edward's mind than I do. The light begins to fail, there is no time for talk. Stand clear, all men, and let these two settle it."

"Ay," croaked Grey Dick, "stand clear, all men, while my master cuts the throat of his cousin Clavering, since he who stands not clear shall presently lie straight!" and he tapped his terrible bow with his right hand, then instantly seized the string again.

The two were face to face. Round them on horse and on foot, at a distance perhaps of twenty paces, were gathered the Clavering men and the French Count's troop; for now all had come up from the far parts of the marsh. Only toward the river side the ring was open, whether because those who made it feared Grey Dick's arrows, or in order that he and Red Eve might see everything that chanced.

The pair were well matched, for though Hugh was the taller, John, his senior by a year, was thicker set and better trained in arms. But the sword of John was longer by a hand's breadth than that Hugh carried as a merchant, which was heavy, of such a make as the ancient Romans used, and sharpened on either edge. Neither of them wore armour, since Hugh had no right to do so, and John had not come out to fight.

They stood still for a moment in the midst of a breathless silence, the red light of the stormy sunset striking across them both. Everything was red, the smoke-clouds rising from the sullen, burning marsh, into which the fire was still eating far away; the waters of the Blythe brimful with the tide that had just turned toward the sea, the snow and ice itself. Even the triangle of wild swans brought by the hard weather from the northern lands looked red as they pursued their heavy and majestic flight toward the south, heedless of man and his affairs beneath.

Not long did these remain heedless, however, since, either to show his skill or for some other purpose of his own, Grey Dick lifted his bow and loosed an arrow, almost, it seemed, at hazard. Yet that arrow pierced the leader of the flock, so that down it came in wide circles, and in a last struggle hovered for a moment over the group of men, then fell among them with a thud, the blood from its pierced breast bespattering Sir Edmund Acour and John Clavering's black hair.

"An ill omen for those two, and especially for him who wears a white swan for a crest," said a voice. But at the moment none took much notice, except Grey Dick, who chuckled at the success of his shot, since all were intent on greater matters—namely, which of those two young men should die.

Sir John, the father, rode forward and addressed them.

"To the death without mercy to the fallen," he said grimly.

They bent their heads in answer.

"Now!" he cried, and reined back his horse.

"The first home thrust wins," whispered Acour to him, as he wiped the blood of the swan off his sleeve. "Thank God, your son's sword is the longer!"

Perhaps the pair heard this whisper, or, perhaps, being without mail, they knew that it was so. At least for a while they circled round and round each other, but out of reach.

Then at length John Clavering rushed in and thrust. Hugh sprang back before his point. Again he rushed and thrust and again Hugh sprang back. A third time and Hugh fairly ran, whereon a shout went up from the Claverings.

"The chapman's afraid!" cried one. "Give him a yard measure," shouted another; "he cannot handle steel!"

Eve turned her face, and her very eyes were sick with doubt.

"Is it true?" she gasped.

"Ay," answered Dick the Archer, "it's true that he draws him to the river bank! Those who wait will learn why. Oh, the swan! He sees not the swan!"

As he spoke, Hugh, in his retreat before another of John Clavering's rushes, struck his foot against the great dead bird, and staggered. John leapt upon him, and he went down.

"Is he pierced?" muttered Eve.

"Nay, missed," answered Dick, "by half an inch. Ah, I thought so!"

As the words left his lips Clavering fell sprawling on his back, for Hugh had caught his leg with his left arm and thrown him, so that they lay both together on the ground.

There they closed, rolling over each other, but too close to stab.

"Now good-night, John," said Dick, with his hoarse chuckle. "Throat him, master—throat him!"

The flurry in the snow was at an end. John lay on his back, de Cressi knelt on him and lifted his short sword.

"Do you yield?" men heard him say.

"Nay," answered Clavering. Then suddenly Hugh rose and suffered his adversary to do likewise.

"I'll not stick you like a hog!" he said, and some cried, "Well done!" for the act seemed noble. Only Acour muttered, "Fool!"

Next instant they were at it again, but this time it was Hugh who attacked and John who gave back right to the river's edge, for skill and courage seemed to fail him at once.

"Turn your head, lady," said Dick, "for now one must die." But Eve could not.

The swords flashed for the last time in the red light, then that of de Cressi vanished. Clavering threw his arms wide, and fell backward. A splash as of a great stone thrown into water, and all was done.

Hugh stood a moment on the river's bank, staring at the stream beneath; then he turned and began to walk slowly toward the dead swan.

Ere ever he reached it Sir John Clavering fell from his horse in a swoon, and a shout of rage went up from all his people.

"Kill him!" they yelled, and leapt forward.

Now Hugh understood, and ran for the point of land. One man, a Frenchman, got in front of him. He cut him down, and sped on.

"What now?" said Eve, as he joined them.

He did not answer, only pointed first to the Clavering folk and next to the water, showing that she must choose between the two.

"Swim for it!" growled Grey Dick. "I'll hold them back a while and then join you," and as he spoke his bow twanged.

For an instant Eve paused, then threw off her scarlet cloak.

"Remember, I slew your brother!" said Hugh hoarsely.

"I remember that he would have slain you," she answered; and leapt straight from the point into the icy flood, beneath which her head sank.

When it rose again there was another head beside it, that of dead John, who appeared for one moment, to be seen no more for ever, since ere morning the ocean had him.

Now Hugh leapt after her, and presently the pair of them were swimming side by side to the river's further shore. Then, as now, it was but a narrow stream. Yet they did not reach it easily, for, cumbered as they were with clothes, and numbed by the ice-cold water, the fierce tide caught them and carried them beyond the bend. There they were lost in the gathering darkness, so that most of those who watched believed that they had sunk and drowned. But it was not so, for after a long struggle they came safe to shore near to a clump of willows, and clambered over the frozen mud to the heath beyond.

"First fire, then water," said Hugh, in a mazed voice.

"You have missed out love and death," answered the girl—"a full feast for a day that is not done. But whither now?"

"To take sanctuary at the Preceptory and raise my kin. Forward, Eve, ere you freeze."

"I think there is that in me which will not freeze," she answered; and broke into a run.

Now night closed in, and the snow which had been threatening all day began to fall, making their path over the heath difficult.

"We need Grey Dick to guide us; but alack, I fear he is dead!" muttered Hugh.

"I think others will be dead, not Dick," she answered.

Just then they heard a footstep behind them.

Hugh wheeled round and drew his sword, but almost before it had left the scabbard a long figure glided out of the snow, and said:

"More to the left, master, more to the left, unless you would make your peace on Blythburgh bridge, where some would be glad to meet you."

"How went it?" asked Hugh shortly.

"Not well. I shot thrice and slew three men, two of the French knights, and Thomas of Kessland, against whom I had a score that now is settled. But the fourth time I missed."

"Who?" asked Eve between her teeth as she ran beside him.

"The Frenchman who means to marry you. When the others fell back he came at me on his horse as I was setting a fresh arrow, thinking to get me. I had to shoot quick, and aimed low for his heart, because in that light I could not make certain of his face. He saw, and jerked up the horses head, so that the shaft took it in the throat and killed the beast without hurting its rider. He was off in an instant and at me, with others, before I could draw again. So I thought it time to go, which I did, backward, as he thrust. Perhaps he thinks he killed me, as I meant he should, only when he looks at his sword he'll find it clean. That's all."

And again Grey Dick chuckled.

CHAPTER III

FATHER ANDREW

None were abroad in the streets of Dunwich on that bitter winter night when these three trudged wearily down Middlegate Street through the driving snow to the door of the grey Preceptory of the Knights Templar. In a window above the porch a light burned dimly, the only one to be seen in any of the houses round about, for by now all men were abed.

"'Tis Father Arnold's room," said Eve. "He sits there at his books. I'll knock and call him, but do you two go lay hold of the ring of the church door," and she nodded toward a grey pile that stood near by. "Then none can touch you, and how know we who may be in this house?"

"I'll go no step further," answered Hugh sullenly. "All this Temple ground is sanctuary, or at least we will risk it." And, seizing the knocker, he hammered at the door.

The light in the window vanished, and presently they heard a sound of creaking bolts. Then the door opened, revealing a tall man, white-bearded, ancient, and clad in a frayed, furred robe worn over a priest's cassock, who held a lantern in his hand.

"Who knocks?" he asked. "Does some soul pass that you disturb me after curfew?"

"Ay, Father Andrew," answered Hugh, "souls have passed, and souls are near to passing. Let us in, and we will tell you all."

Without waiting for an answer he entered with the others, pushed to the massive door and bolted it again.

"What's this? A woman?" said the old priest. "Eve of Clavering, by the Saints!"

"Yes," she answered calmly, though her teeth chattered; "Eve of Clavering, Eve the Red, this time with the blood of men, soaked with the waters of the Blythe, frozen with the snows of Dunwich Heath, where she has lain hid for hours with a furze bush for shelter. Eve who seeks shriving, a dry rag for her back, a morsel for her lips, and fire to warm her, which in the Name of Christ and of charity she prays you will not refuse to her."

So she spoke, and laughed recklessly.

Almost before she had finished her wild words the old man, who looked what he was, a knight arrayed in priestly robes, had run to a door at the end of the hall and was calling through it, "Mother Agnes! Mother Agnes!"

"Be not so hasty, Sir Andrew," answered a shrill voice. "A posset must have time to boil. It is meet now that you wear a tonsure that you who are no longer a centurion should forget these 'Come, and he cometh,' ways. When the water's hot—"

The rest of that speech was lost, for Father Arnold, muttering some word belonging to his "centurion" days, dived into the kitchen, to reappear presently dragging a little withered old woman after him who was dressed in a robe of conventual make.

"Peace, Mother Agnes, peace!" he said. "Take this lady, dry her, array her in your best gown, give her food, warm her, and bring her back to me. Short? What care I if the robe be short? Obey, or it will not be come, and he cometh, but go and she goeth, and then who will shelter one who talks so much?"

He thrust the pair of them through the kitchen door and, returning, led Hugh and Grey Dick up a broad oak stair to what had been the guest-hall of the Preceptory on its first floor.

It was a very great chamber where, before their Order was dispersed, all the Knights Templar had been wont to dine with those who visited them at times of festival. Tattered banners still hung among the cobwebs of the ancient roof, the shields of past masters with stately blazonings were carved in stone upon the walls. But of all this departed splendour but little could be seen, since the place was lit only by a single lamp of whale's oil and a fire that burned upon the wide stone hearth, a great fire, since Father Arnold, who had spent many years of his life in the East, loved warmth.

"Now, Hugh de Cressi," he said, "what have you done?"

"Slain my cousin, John of Clavering, Father, and perhaps another man."

"In fair fight, very fair fight," croaked Grey Dick.

"Who doubts it? Can a de Cressi be a murderer?" asked the priest. "And you, Richard the Archer, what have you done?"

"Shot a good horse and three bad men dead with arrows—at least they should be dead—and another through the hand, standing one against twenty."

"A gallant—I mean—an evil deed," broke in the old warrior priest, "though once it happened to me in a place called Damascus—but you both are wet, also. Come into my chamber; I can furnish you with garments of a sort. And, Richard, set that black bow of yours near the fire, but not too fire. As you should know well, a damp string is ill to draw with. Nay, fear not to leave it; this is sanctuary, and to make sure I will lock the doors."

Half an hour was gone by, and a very strange company had gathered round the big fire in the guest-chamber of the Temple, eating with appetite of such food as its scanty larder could provide for them. First there was Red Eve in a woollen garment, the Sunday wear of Mother Agnes for twenty years past and more, which reached but little below her knees, and was shaped like a sack. On her feet were no shoes, and for sole adornment her curling black hair fell about her shoulders, for so she had arranged it because the gown would not meet across her bosom. Yet, odd as it might be, in this costume Eve looked wonderfully beautiful, perhaps because it was so scant and the leathern strap about her waist caused it to cling close to her shapely form.

By her stood Hugh, wearing a splendid suit of chain armour. It had been Sir Andrew Arnold's in his warlike years, and now he lent it to his godson Hugh because, as he said, he had nothing else. Also, it may have crossed the minds of both of them that such mail as this which the Saracens had forged, if somewhat out of fashion, could still turn swordcuts.

Then there was Grey Dick, whose garments seemed to consist of a sack with holes in it tied round him with a rope, his quiver of arrows slung over it for ornament. He sat by the fire on a stool, oiling his black bow with a rind of the fat bacon that he had been eating.

All the tale had been told, and Father Arnold looked very grave indeed.

"I have known strange and dreadful stories in my time," he said, "but never, I think, one stranger or more dreadful. What would you do now, godson?"

"Take sanctuary for myself and Grey Dick because of the slaying of John Clavering and others, and afterward be married by you to Eve."

"Be married to the sister with the brother's blood upon your hands without absolution from the Church or pardon from the King; and you but a merchant's younger son and she to-night one of the greatest heiresses in East Anglia! Why, how may that be?"

"I blame him not," broke in Eve. "John, whom I never loved, strove to smoke us out like rats because he was in the pay of the Norman, my Lord of Acour. John struck Hugh in the face with his hand and slandered him with his tongue. John was given his life once, and afterwards slain in fair fight. Oh, I say, I blame him not, nor shall John's blood rise between him and me!"

"Yet the world will blame him, and you, too, Eve; yes, even those who love you both. A while must go by, say a year. At least I'll not marry you at once, and cannot, if I would, with both your fathers living and unadvised, and the sheriff waiting at the gate. Tell me now, do any know that you have entered here?"

"Nay," said Dick, looking up from his bow. "The hunt came after us, but I hid these two in a bush and led it away past Hinton to the Ipswich road, keeping but just ahead in the snow and talking in three voices. Then I gave them the slip and returned. They'll not guess that we have come to Dunwich for a while."

"And when they do even the boldest will not enter this holy sanctuary while the Church has terrors for men's souls. Yet, here you must not stay for long, lest in this way or in that your lives pay the price of it, or a bloody feud break out between the Claverings of Blythburgh and the de Cressis of Dunwich. Daughter Eve, get you to bed with old Agnes. You are so weary that you will not mind her snores. To-morrow ere the dawn I'll talk with you, and, meanwhile, I have words for Hugh. Nay, have no fear, the windows are all barred, and Archer Dick shall watch the door."

Eve went, unwillingly enough, although she could scarcely walk, flashing a good-night to her lover with her fine eyes. Presently Grey Dick also went to sleep, like a dog with one eye open, in the little ante-chamber, near to the great door.

"Now, Hugh," said Father Arnold, when they were left alone, "your case is desperate, for if you stay here certainly these Claverings will have your blood. Yet, if you can be got away safely, there is still a shaft that you may shoot more deadly than any that ever left Grey Dick's quiver. But yesterday I told you for your comfort—when we spoke of his wooing of Red Eve—that this Norman, for such he is, although his mother was English and he was English born, is a traitor to King Edward, whom he pretends to serve."

"Ay, and I said as much to him this afternoon when he prated to me of his knightly honour, and, though I had no time to take note of faces, I thought he liked it little who answered hotly that I was a liar."

"I am sorry, Hugh; it may put him on his guard, or perhaps he'll pay no heed. At least the words are said, and there's an end. Now hearken. I told neither you nor any one all the blackness of his treachery. Have you guessed what this Acour is here to do?"

"Spy out the King's power in these parts, I suppose."

"More than that"—and he dropped his voice to a whisper—"spy out a safe landing-place for fifty thousand Normans upon our Suffolk coast. They are to sail hither this coming summer and set the crown of England upon their Duke John, who will hold it as vassal to his sire, Philip of France."

"God's name! Is that true?"

"Ay, though in such a devil's business that Name is best left out. Look you, lad, I had warning from overseas, where, although I am now nothing but a poor old priest of a broken Order, I still have friends in high places. Therefore I watched and found that messengers were passing between Acour and France. One of these messengers, a priest, came a week ago to Dunwich, and spent the night in a tavern waiting for his ship to sail in the morning. The good wife who keeps that tavern—ask not her name—would go far to serve me. That night this priest slept sound, and while he slept a letter was cut from the lining of his cassock, and another without writing sewn there in place of it, so that he'll never know the difference till he reaches John of Normandy, and then not where he lost it. Stay, you shall see," and he went to the wall and from some secret place behind the hangings produced a writing, which he handed to Hugh, who looked at it, then gave it back to him, saying:

"Read it to me, Father, English I can spell out, but this French puzzles my eyes."

So he read, Hugh listening eagerly to every word:

My Lord Duke:

This by a faithful hand that you know to tell you all goes well with your Grace's business, and with that of your royal father. While pretending to hunt or hawk I have found three places along this seaboard at any one of which the army can land next summer with little resistance to fear, for though the land is rich in cattle and corn, the people are few.

These places of which I have made survey have deep water up to the beach. I will tell you of them more particularly when I return. Meanwhile I linger here for sundry reasons, which you know, hoping to draw those of whom you speak to me to your cause, which, God aiding me, I shall do, since he of England has wronged one of them and slighted the others, so that they are bitter against him, and ready to listen to the promises which I make in your name.

As an excuse for my long stay that has caused doubts in some quarters, I speak of my Suffolk lands which need my care. Also I court the daughter of my host here, the Knight of Clavering, a stubborn Englishman who cannot be won, but a man of great power and repute. This courtship, which began in jest, has ended in earnest, since the girl is very haughty and beautiful, and as she will not be played with I propose, with your good leave, to make her my wife. Her father accepts my suit, and when he and the brother are out of the way, as doubtless may happen after your army comes, she will have great possessions.

I thank your Grace for the promise of the wide English lands of which I spoke to you, and the title that goes with them. These I will do my best to earn, nor will I ask for them till I kneel before you when you are crowned King of England at Westminster, as I doubt not God will bring about before this year is out. I have made a map of the road by which your army should march on London after landing, and of the towns to be sacked upon the way thither. This, however, I keep, since although not one in ten thousand of these English swine can read French, or any other tongue, should it chance to be lost, all can understand a map. Not that there is any fear of loss, for who will meddle with a priest who carries credentials signed by his Holiness himself.

I do homage to your Grace. This written with my hand from Blythburgh, in Suffolk, on the twentieth day of February, 1346.
Edmund of Noyon.

Father Arnold ceased reading, and Hugh gasped out:
"What a fool is this knave-Count!"

"Most men are, my son, in this way or in that, and the few wise profit by their folly. Thus this letter, which he thought so safe, will save England to Edward and his race, you from many dangers, your betrothed from a marriage which she hates—that is, if you can get safe away with it from Dunwich."

"Where to, Father?"

"To King Edward in London, with another that I will write for you ere the dawn."

"But is it safe, Father, to trust so precious a thing to me, who have bitter enemies awaiting me, and may as like as not be crow's meat by to-morrow?"

Father Arnold looked at him with his soft and dreamy eyes, then said:

"I think the crow's not hatched that will pick your bones, Hugh, though at the last there be crows, or worms, for all of us."

"Why not, Father? Doubtless, this morning young John of Clavering thought as much, and now he is in the stake-nets, or food for fishes."

"Would you like to hear, Hugh, and will you keep it to yourself, even from Eve?"

"Ay, that I would and will."

"He'll think me mad!" muttered the old priest to himself, then went on aloud as one who takes a sudden resolution. "Well, I'll tell you, leaving you to make what you will of a story that till now has been heard by no living man."

"Far in the East is the great country that we call Cathay, though in truth it has many other names, and I alone of all who breathe in England have visited that land."

"How did you get there?" asked Hugh, amazed, for though he knew dimly that Father Arnold had travelled much in his youth, he never dreamed that he had reached the mystic territories of Cathay, or indeed that such a place really was except in fable.

"It would take from now till morning to tell, son, nor even then would you understand the road. It is enough to say that I went on a pilgrimage to Jerusalem, where our blessed Saviour died. That was the beginning. Thence I travelled with Arabs to the Red Sea, where wild men made a slave of me, and we were blown across the Indian Ocean to a beauteous island named Ceylon, in which all the folk are black.

"From this place I escaped in a vessel called a junk, that brought me to the town of Singapore. Thence at last, following my star, I came to Cathay after two years of journeyings. There I dwelt in honour for three more years, moving from place to place, since never before had its inhabitants seen a Western man, and they made much of me, always sending me forward to new cities. So at length I reached the greatest of them all, which is called Kambaluc, or Peking, and there was the guest of its Emperor, Timur.

"All the story of my life and adventures yonder I have written down, and any who will may read it after I am dead. But of these I have no time to speak, nor have they anything to do with you. Whilst I dwelt in Kambaluc as the guest of the Emperor Timur, I made study of the religion of this mighty people, who, I was told, worshipped gods in the shape of men. I visited a shrine called the Temple of Heaven, hoping that there I should see such a god who was named Tien, but found in it nothing but splendid emptiness.

"Then I asked if there was no god that I could see with my eyes, whereon the Emperor laughed at me and said there was such a god, but he counselled me not to visit him. I prayed him to suffer me to do so, since I, who worshipped the only true God, feared no other. Whereon, growing angry, he commanded some of his servants to 'take this fool to the house of Murgh and let him see whether his God could protect him against Murgh.' Having said this he bade me farewell, adding that though every man must meet Murgh once, few met him twice, and therefore he did not think that he should see me again.

"Now, in my heart I grew afraid, but none would tell me more of this Murgh or what was likely to happen to me at his hands. Still, I would not show any fear, and, strong in the faith of Christ, I determined to look upon this idol, for such I expected him to be.

"That night the servants of Timur bore me out of the city in a litter, and by the starlight I saw that we travelled toward a hill through great graveyards, where people were burying their dead. At the foot of the hill they set me down upon a road, and told me to walk up it, and that at dawn I should see the House of Murgh, whereof the gates were always open, and could enter there if I wished. I asked if they would wait for my return, whereon they answered, smiling, that if I so desired they would do so till evening, but that it seemed scarcely needful, since they did not suppose that I should return.

"'Do yonder pilgrims to the House of Murgh return?' asked their captain, pointing towards those graveyards which we had passed.

"I made no answer, but walked forward up a broad and easy road, unchallenged of any, till I came to what, even in that dim light, I could see was a great and frowning gateway, whereof the doors appeared to be open. Now, at first I thought I would pass this gateway at once and see what lay beyond. But from this I was held back by some great fear, for which I could find no cause, unless it were bred of what the Emperor and his servants had said to me. So I remembered their words—namely, that I should tarry till dawn to enter the house.

"There, then, I tarried, seated on the ground before the gateway, and feeling as though, yet alive, I had descended among the dead. Indeed, the silence was that of the dead. No voice spoke, no hound barked, no leaf stirred. Only far above me I heard a continual soughing, as though winged souls passed to and fro. Never in my life had I felt so much alone, never so much afraid.

"At length the dawn broke, and oh, glad was I to see its light, for fear lest I should die in darkness! Now I saw that I was on a hilltop where grew great groves of cedar trees, and that set amid them was a black-tiled temple, surrounded by a wall built of black brick.

"It was not a great place, although the gateway, which was surmounted by two black dragons of stone or iron, was very great, so great that a tall ship could have sailed through it and left its arch untouched.

"I kneeled down and prayed to the blessed Saints and the guardian angels to protect me. Then I arose, crossed myself to scare off all evil things by that holy sign, and set forward toward the mighty gateway. Oh, never, never till that hour had I understood how lowly a thing is man! On that broad road, travelling toward the awful, dragon-guarded arch, beyond which lay I knew not what, it seemed to me that I was the only man left in the world, I, whose hour had come to enter the portals of destruction.

"I passed into the cold shadow of the gateway, unchallenged by any watchman, and found myself in a courtyard surrounded by a wall also built of black brick, which had doors in it that seemed to be of dark stone or iron. Whither these doors led I do not know, since the wall cut off the sight of any buildings that may have lain beyond. In the centre of this courtyard was a pool of still, black water, and at the head of the pool a chair of black marble."

Sir Andrew paused, and Hugh said:

"A plain place for a temple, Father, without adornments or images. But perhaps this was the outer court, and the temple stood within."

"Ay, son, the plainest temple that ever I saw, who have seen many in all lands, though what was beyond it I do not know. And yet—terrible, terrible, terrible!—I tell you that those black walls and that black water were more fearsome to look on than any churchyard vault grim with bones, or a torture-pit where victims quiver out their souls midst shrieks and groanings. And yet I could see nothing of which to be afraid, and hear nothing save that soughing of invisible wings whereof I have spoken. An empty chair, a pool of water, some walls and doors, and, above, the quiet sky. What was there to fear in such things as these? Still, so greatly did I fear that I sank to my knees and began to pray once more, this time to the blessed Saviour himself, since I was sure that none else could help me.

"When I looked up again the chair was no longer empty. Hugh, a man sat in it, of whom I thought at first only one thing—that he must be very strong, though not bigger than other men. Strength seemed to flow from him. I should not have wondered if he had placed his hands upon the massive sides of that stone chair and torn it asunder."

"What was he like, Father? Samson or Goliath?"

"I never saw either, son, so cannot say. But what was he like? Oh, I cannot say that either, although still I see him in my heart. My mortal lips will not tell the likeness of that man, perhaps because he seemed to be like all men, and yet different from all. He had an iron brow, beneath which shone deep, cold eyes. He was clean-shaven, or perchance his face grew no hair. His lips were thick and still and his features did not change like those of other men. He looked as though he could not change; as though he had been thus for infinite ages, and yet remained neither young nor old. As for his dress, he wore a cloak of flaming red, such a cloak as your Eve loves to wear, and white sandals on his feet. There was no covering on his shaven head, which gleamed like a skull. His breast was naked, but across it hung one row of black jewels. From the sheen of them I think they must have been pearls, which are sometimes found of that colour in the East. He had no weapon nor staff, and his hands hung down on either side of the chair.

"For a long while I watched him, but if he saw me he took no note. As I watched I perceived that birds were coming to and leaving him in countless numbers, and thought that it must be their wings which made the constant soughing sound that filled all the still and dreadful air."

"What kind of birds were they, Father?"

"I am not sure, but I think doves; at least, their flight was straight and swift like to that of doves. Yet of this I am not sure either, since I saw each of them for but a second. As they reached the man they appeared out of nothingness. They were of two colours, snow-white and coal-black. The white appeared upon his right side, the black upon his left side. Each bird in those never-ceasing streams hovered for an instant by his head, the white over his right shoulder, the black over his left shoulder, as though they whispered a message to his ear, and having whispered were gone upon their errand."

"What was that errand, Father?"

"How can I know, as no one ever told me? Yet I will hazard a guess that it had to do with the mystery of life and death. Souls that were born into the world, and souls departing from the world, perchance, making report to one of God's ministers clothed in flesh.

But who can say? At least I watched those magic fowls till my eyes grew dizzy, and a sort of slumber began to creep into my brain.

"How long I stayed thus I do not remember, for I had lost all sense of time. In the end, however, I was awakened by a cold, soft voice, the sound of which seemed to flow through my veins like ice, that addressed me in our own rough English tongue, spoken as you and I learned it at our nurses' knees.

"'To what god were you praying just now, Andrew Arnold?'

"'Oh, sir,' I answered, 'how do you, who dwell in Cathay, where I am a stranger, know my language and my name?'

"He lifted his cold eyes and looked at me, and I felt them pierce into the depths of my soul. 'In the same way that I know your heart,' he said. 'But do not ask questions. Answer them, that I may learn whether you are a true man or a liar.'

"'I was praying to Christ,' I faltered, 'the Saviour of us all.'

"'A great God, Andrew Arnold, and a pure, though His followers are few in the world as yet. But do you think that He can save you from Me, as you were asking Him to do?'

"'He can save my soul,' I replied, plucking up courage, who would not deny the Lord even in a devil's den.

"'Ah! your soul. Well, I have nothing to do with souls, except to count them as they pass through my dominion, and you are quite right to pray to one of the lords of that into which you go. Now, man, what is your business with me, and why do you visit one of whom you are so much afraid?'

"'O Murgh!' I began, then ceased, for I knew not what to answer.

"'So they have told you my name? Now I will tell you one of its meanings. It is "Gate of the Gods." Why did you dare to visit Gate of the Gods? You fear to answer. Listen! You came forth to see some painted idol, or some bedizened priest muttering rites he does not understand to that which is not; and lo! you have found that which is behind all idols and all priests. You sought an incensed and a golden shrine and you have found only the black and iron portals which every man must pass but which few desire to enter until they are called. Well, you are young and strong, come try a fall with Murgh, and when he has thrown you, rise and choose which of those ways you will,' and he swept his hand toward the doors around him. 'Then forget this world and enter into that which you have chosen.'

"Now, because I could not help myself, I rose from my knees and advanced, or was drawn toward that dreadful man. As I came he, too, rose from his chair, stretching out his arms as a wrestler does, and I knew that within the circle of those arms lay my death. Still I, who in my youth was held brave, went on and rushed, striving to clasp him. Next moment, before ever I touched him—oh, well was it for me that I touched him not!—some strength seized me and whirled me round and round as a dead leaf is whirled by the wind, and tossed me up and cast me down and left me prone and nerveless.

"'Rise,' said the cold voice above me, 'for you are unhurt.'

"So I rose, and felt even then that I who thought that every bone in my body must be broken, was stronger than I had ever been before. It was as though the lamp which had burnt low was filled suddenly with a new and purer oil.

"'Man,' said mine adversary, and I thought that in his cold eyes there was something like a smile, 'did you think to touch Murgh and live? Did you think to wrestle with him as in a book of one of your prophets a certain Jacob wrestled with an angel, and conquered—until it was his turn to pass the Gate of the Gods?'

"Now I stared at this dweller in Cathay, who spoke my tongue and knew the tale of Jacob in the ancient Book, then answered:

"'Sir Murgh, or Sir Gate, or whatever your name may be, I thought to do nothing. You drew me to you, you challenged me and, since by the rule of my Order I may refuse no challenge from one who is not a Christian, I came on to do my best. But before ever I laid hand on you I was cast down by a wind. That is all the story, save that it has pleased you to let me live, who evidently could have slain me, for which I thank you.'

"'You are wrong, Sir Andrew,' he answered, 'I did not draw you to me. Men come to Murgh at their appointed hour; Murgh does not come to them. You sought him before your hour, and therefore he refused you. Yet you will meet him again, as all flesh must when its hour comes, and because you are bold and have not cringed before my strength, for your comfort I will show you when and how. Stand by me, but lay no hand on me or my robe, and look into my glass while for a moment, for your sake, I stay the stream of time and show you what lies beneath its foam that blinds the eyes of men.'

"He waved his arms and the black doves and the white doves ceased to appear and disappear, and the eternal soughings of their wings was silent. He pointed to the water at his feet and I saw, not a picture, but a scene so real that I could have sworn it was alive about me. Yes, those who took part in it stood in front of me as though the pool were solid ground that their feet pressed. You were one of them, son, you were one of them," and the old knight paused, supporting himself against the mantel-shelf as though that recollection overcame him.

"What did you see?" whispered Hugh.

"By God's holy name, I saw the Blythburgh Marshes deep in snow that was red, blood-red with the light of sunrise. Oh! I could not be mistook, and there ran the wintry river, there the church tower soared, there were the frowning, tree-clad banks. There was the rough moorland over which the east wind piped, for the dead bracken bent before it, and not twenty paces from me leaped a hare, disturbed suddenly from its form by a hungry fox, whose red head peeped through the reeds. Yes, yes, I saw the brute's white teeth gleam as it licked its disappointed lips, and I felt glad that its prey had beaten it! When you look upon that scene, Hugh, as one day you shall, remember the hare and the head of the hungry fox, and by these judge my truth."

"A fox and a hare!" broke in Hugh. "I'd show you such to-morrow; was there no more?"

"Ay, much. For instance, a hollow in the Marsh, an open grave, and an axe; yes, an axe that had delved it where the bog was soft beneath the snow. Grey Dick held the axe in one hand and his black bow in the other, while Red Eve, your Eve, stood at its edge and stared into it like one in a dream. Then at the head of the grave an old, old man clad in mail beneath his priestly robes, and that man myself, Hugh, grown very ancient, but still myself, and no other.

"And at the foot of the grave you, Hugh de Cressi, you and no other, wayworn and fierce, but also clad in mail, and wearing a knight's crest upon your shield. You with drawn sword in hand, and facing you, also with drawn sword, rage and despair on his dark face, a stately, foreign-looking man, whom mine eyes have never seen, but whom I should know again midst a million, a man who, I think, was doomed to fill the grave.

"Lastly, standing on a little mound near to the bank of the swirling river, where jagged sheets of ice ground against each other like the teeth of the wicked in hell, strangely capped and clad in black, his arms crossed upon his breast and a light smile in his cold eyes, he who was called Murgh in Cathay, he who named himself Gateway of the Gods!

"For a moment I saw, then all was gone, and I found myself—I know not why—walking toward the mighty arch whereon sat the iron dragons. In its shadow I turned and looked back. There at the head of the pool the man was seated in his chair, and to right and to left of him came the black doves and the white doves in countless multitudes, all the thousands of them that had been stayed in their flight pouring down upon him at once—or so I thought. They wheeled about his head, they hid his face from me, and I—I departed into the shadow of the arch, and I saw him and them no more."

CHAPTER IV

THE PENANCE

The tale was done, and these two stood staring at one another from each side of the glowing hearth, whose red light illumined their faces. At length the heavy silence was broken by Sir Andrew.

"I read your heart, Hugh," he said, "as Murgh read mine, for I think that he gave me not only strength, but something of his wisdom also, whereby I was able to win safe back to England and to this hour to walk unharmed by many a pit. I read your heart, and in its book is written that you think me mad, one who pleases his old age with tales of marvel that others told him, or which his own brain fashioned."

"Not so, Father," answered Hugh uneasily, for in truth some such thoughts were passing through his mind. "Only—only the thing is very strange, and it happened so long ago, before Eve and I were born, before those that begot us were born either, perchance."

"Yes; more than fifty years ago—it may be sixty—I forget. In sixty years the memory plays strange tricks with men, no doubt, so how can I blame you if you believe—what you do believe? And yet, Hugh," he went on after a pause, and speaking with passion, "this was no dream of which I tell you. Why do you suppose that among all those that have grown up about me I have chosen you out to love, you and your Eve? Not because a chance made me your godsire and her my pupil. I say that from your infancy your faces haunted me. Ay, and when you had turned childhood's corner and once I met the pair of you walking hand in hand, then of a sudden I knew that it was you two and no others whom that god or devil had showed to me standing by the open grave upon the banks of Blythe. I knew it of Dick the

Archer also, and can I be mistaken of such a man as that who has no fellow in England? But you think I dreamed it all, and perhaps I should not have spoken, though something made me speak. Well, in a day to come you may change your mind, since whatever dangers threaten you will not die yet, Hugh. Tell me now, what is this Frenchman like who would marry Eve? I have never seen him."

Hugh, who was glad to get back to the things of earth, described Acour as best he could.

"Ah!" said Sir Andrew. "Much such a man as stood face to face with you by the grave while Murgh watched; and you are not likely to be friends, are you? But I forgot. You have determined that it was but a dream and now you are wondering how he who is called Gate of the Gods in Cathay could come to Blythburgh. Well, I think that all the world is his garden, given to him by God, but doubtless that's only another face of my dream whereof we'll speak no more—at present. Now for your troubles, which are no dream. Lie you down to sleep on the skin of that striped beast. I killed it in Cathay—in my day of dreams, and now it shall serve for yours, from which may the dead eyes of John Clavering be absent! I go forth to seek your father and to arrange certain matters. With Grey Dick at the door you'll be safe for a while, I think. If not, here's a cupboard where you may hide." And, drawing aside the arras, he showed him a certain secret place large enough to hold a man, then left the room.

Hugh laid himself upon the skin of the beast, which had been a tiger, though he did not know it by that name. So weary was he that not all he had gone through that day or even the old warrior-priest's marvellous tale, in which he and Eve played so wonderful a part, could keep his eyes from closing. Presently he was fast asleep, and so remained until, four hours later, something disturbed him, and he awoke to see Sir Andrew writing at a desk.

"Rise, my son," said the old priest without looking up from his paper. "Early as it is you must be stirring if you would be clear of Dunwich by daybreak and keep a whole skin. I have set a taper in my sleeping-closet yonder, and there you'll find water to wash with and a stool to kneel on for your prayers, neither of which neglect, since you have blood on your hands and great need for Heaven's help."

So Hugh arose, yawning, and stumbled heavily to the chamber, for he was still faint with sleep, which would not leave him till he had plunged his head into a basin of icy water. This done, he knelt and prayed as he had been bidden, with a very earnest heart, and afterward came back to the guest-hall.

Seeing folk gathered there as he entered he laid hand on sword, not his own with which he had killed his cousin, but a long and knightly weapon that Sir Andrew had given him with the armour. Drawing it, he advanced boldly, for he thought that his enemies might have found him out, and that his best safety lay in courage. Thus he appeared in the ring of the lamplight clad in gleaming steel and with raised weapon.

"What, son!" asked a testy voice which he knew for that of his own father, "is it not enough to have killed your cousin? Would you fall on your brothers and me also, that you come at us clad in mail and with bare steel in hand?"

Hearing these words Hugh sheathed the sword, and, advancing toward the speaker, a handsome, portly man, who wore a merchant's robe lined with rich fur, sank to his knee before him.

"Your pardon, my father," he said. "Sir Andrew here will have told you the story; also that I am not to blame for this blood-shedding."

"I think you need to ask it," replied Master de Cressi, "and if you and that lean henchman of yours are not to blame, then say who is?"

Now a tall, slim figure glided up to them. It was Eve, clothed in her own robe again, and beautiful as ever after her short rest.

"Sir, I am to blame," she said in her full, low voice. "My need was sore and I sent a messenger to Hugh bidding him meet me in the Blythburgh Marsh. There we were set on, and there John Clavering, my brother, smote Hugh in the face. Would you, a de Cressi, have had him take the blow and yield me up to the Frenchman?"

"By God and my forefathers, no! least of all from one of your stock—saving your presence," answered the merchant. "In truth, had he done so, dead or living from that day I would have called him no son of mine. Yet, Red Eve, you and he and your love-makings have brought much trouble on me and my House. Look now what it means. A feud to the death between our families of which no man can foresee the end. Moreover, how can you marry, seeing that a brother's blood runs between you?"

"It is on John's head," she answered sadly, "not on Hugh's hand. I warned him, and Hugh spared him once. What more could we do?"

"I know not, Eve; I only know what you have done, you and Hugh and Grey Dick. Four dead and two wounded, that's the bill I must discharge as best I may. Doubtless too soon there will be more to follow, whether they be Claverings or de Cressis. Well, we must take things as God sends them, and leave Him to balance the account.

"But there is no time to lose if Hugh's neck is to escape a halter. Speak you, Father Andrew, who are wise and old, and have this matter in hand. Oh! Hugh, Hugh, you were born a fighter, not a merchant like your brethren," and he pointed to three young men who all this while had stood silently behind him looking upon their youngest brother with grave disapproval. "Yes, the old Norman blood comes out in you, and the Norman mail suits you well," he added with a flash of pride, "and so there's an end—or a beginning. Now, Sir Andrew, speak."

"Master de Cressi," said the old priest, "your son Hugh rides to London on an errand of mine which I think will save his neck from that halter whereof you spoke but now. Are those four mounted men that you promised me ready to companion him?"

"They will be within an hour, Father, but not before, since six good horses cannot be laid hands on in the dead of night, being stabled without the gates. But what is this message of yours, and to whom does Hugh go?"

"To his Grace Edward the King, none less, Geoffrey de Cressi, with that which shall earn pardon for him and Dick the Archer, or so I believe. As for what it is I may not tell you or any man. It has to do with great matters of State that are for the King's ear alone; and I charge you, every one, on your honour and your safety, to make no mention of this mission without these walls. Do you swear, Geoffrey de Cressi, and you, his sons?"

Then one by one they swore to be secret as the grave; and Eve swore also, though of her he had sought no promise. When this was finished Sir Andrew asked if any of his brothers accompanied Hugh, saying that if so they must arm.

"No," answered Master de Cressi, "one of the family is enough to risk as well as four of our best servants. My sons bide here with me, who may need their help, though they are not trained to arms."

"Perhaps it is as well," said Sir Andrew drily, "though were I their age—well, let that be. Now, son Hugh, before you eat do you and Eve come with me into the church."

At these words Hugh flushed red with joy, and opened his lips to speak.

"Nay, nay," broke in Sir Andrew, with a frown; "for a different purpose to that which is in your mind. Man, is this a time for marrying and giving in marriage? And if it were, could I marry you who are stained with new-shed blood? 'Tis that you both may be absolved from the guilt of that blood and learn the penance which God decrees to you through the mouth of me, His unworthy minister, in payment of its shedding. Thus you, son, may go forth upon your great adventure with a clean heart, and you, daughter, may await what shall befall with a quiet mind. Say, are you willing?"

Now they bowed their heads and answered that they were, though Eve whispered to Hugh that she misdoubted her of this talk of penance.

"So do I," he replied, beneath his breath, "but he is a merciful confessor and loves us. From some it might be harder."

They passed down the stairs, followed by Master de Cressi and his sons, into the entrance hall, where Grey Dick stood watching by the door.

"Whither go they?" he asked of Sir Andrew, "for their road is mine."

"To confession at God's altar," answered the old priest. "Do you come also, Richard?"

"Oh!" he replied, "I hoped it had been to breakfast. As for

confession I have naught upon my soul save that I shot too low at the Frenchman."

"Bide where you are, O man of blood," said Sir Andrew sternly: "and pray that a better mood be given to you before it is too late."

"Ay, Father," he answered unabashed. "I'll pray, and it is as well that one should wait to watch the door lest you should all presently become men of blood against your will."

Turning to the right, Sir Andrew led them down steps to a passage underground that joined the Temple to the Church of the Holy Virgin and St. John. It was but short, and at the end of it they found a massive door which he unbolted, and, passing this door, entered the great building, whereof the silence and the icy cold struck them like blows. They had but two lanterns between them, one of which Master de Cressi and his elder sons took with them to the nave of the church. Bearing the other, Sir Andrew departed into the vestry, leaving Hugh and Eve seated together in the darkness of the chancel stalls.

Presently his light reappeared in the confessional, where he sat robed, and thither at his summons went first Hugh and then Eve. When their tales were told, those who watched in the nave of the splendid building—which, reared by the Knights Templar, was already following that great Order to decay and ruin—saw the star of light he bore ascend to the high altar. Here he set it down, and, advancing to the rail, addressed the two shadowy figures that knelt before him.

"Son and daughter," he said, "you have made confession with contrite hearts, and the Church has given you absolution for your sins. Yet penance remains, and because those sins, though grievous in themselves, were not altogether of your own making, it shall be light. Hugh de Cressi and Eve Clavering, who are bound together by lawful love between man and woman and the solemn oath of betrothal which you here renew before God, this is the penance that I lay upon you by virtue of the authority in me vested as a priest of Christ: Because between you runs the blood of John Clavering, the cousin of one of you and the brother of the other, slain by you, Hugh de Cressi, in mortal combat but yester eve, I decree and enjoin that for a full year from this day you shall not be bound together as man and wife in the

holy bonds of matrimony, nor converse after the fashion of affianced
lovers. If you obey this her command, faithfully, then by my mouth
the Church declares that after the year has gone by you may lawfully
be wed where and when you will. Moreover, she pronounces her solemn
blessing on you both and her dreadful curse upon any and upon all
who shall dare to sunder you against your desires, and of this blessing
and this curse let all the congregation take notice."

Now Hugh and Eve rose and vanished into the darkness. When
they had gone the priest celebrated a short mass, but two or three
prayers and a blessing, which done, all of them returned to the
Preceptory as they had come.

Here food was waiting for them, prepared by the old Sister Agnes.
It was a somewhat silent meal of which no one ate very much except
Grey Dick, who remarked aloud that as this might be his last breakfast
it should be plentiful, since, shriven or unshriven, it was better to die
upon a full stomach.

Master de Cressi called him an impious knave. Then he asked
him if he had plenty of arrows, because if not he would find four
dozen of the best that could be made in Norwich done up in a cloak
on the grey horse he was to ride, and a spare bow also.

"I thank you for the arrows, Master, but as for the bow, I use
none but my own, the black bow which the sea brought to me and
death alone shall part from me. Perchance both will be wanted, since
the Claverings will scarcely let us out of the sanctuary if they can help
it. Still, it is true they may not know where we lie hid, and that is our
best chance of eating more good breakfasts this side the grave."

"A pest on your evil talk," said de Cressi with an uneasy laugh, for
he loved Hugh best of all his sons and was afraid of him. "Get through
safely, man, and though I like not your grim face and bloody ways you
shall lose little by it. I promise you," he added in a whisper, "that if
you bring my boy safe home again, you shall not want for all your life;
ay, and if there is need, I'll pay your blood-scot for you."

"Thank you, master, thank you. I'll remember, and for my part
promise you this, that if he does not return safe, Dick the Archer

never will. But I think I'll live to shoot more than your four dozen of arrows."

As he spoke there came a knock upon the outer door and every one sprang up.

"Fear not," said Sir Andrew; "doubtless it will be the men with the horses. I'll go look. Come you with me, Richard."

Presently he returned, saying that it was so, and that Master de Cressi's servants were waiting with the beasts in the courtyard. Also that they brought tidings that some of the Clavering party were now at the Mayor's house, rousing him from his sleep, doubtless to lay information of the slayings and ask for warrant to take those who wrought them, should they be in the borough.

"Then we had best be going," said Hugh, "since soon they will be here with or without their warrant."

"Ay," answered Sir Andrew. "Here are the papers. Take them, Hugh, and hide them well; and if any accident should befall you, try to pass them on to Richard that they may be delivered into the King's hands at Westminster. Say that Sir Andrew Arnold sends you on business that has to do with his Grace's safety, and neither of you will be refused a hearing. Then act as he may command you, and maybe ere long we shall see you back at Dunwich pardoned."

"I think it is the Claverings and their French lord who need pardon, not I," said Hugh. "But be that as it may, what of Eve?"

"Fear not for Eve, son, for here she bides in sanctuary until the Frenchman is out of England, or perchance," he added grimly, "under English soil."

"Ay, ay, we'll guard the maid," broke in Master de Cressi. "Come! to saddle ere you be trapped."

So they descended to a back entrance, and through it into the courtyard, where the four armed men waited with six good horses, one of them Hugh's own. Here he bade farewell to his brothers, to his father, who kissed him on the brow, and to Sir Andrew, who stretched his hand above his head in blessing. Then he turned to Eve and was about to embrace her even before that company, when Sir Andrew looked at him, and, remembering the penance that had been laid upon him, he but pressed her hand, whispering:

"God be with you, sweetheart!"

"He is with us all, but I would that you could be with me also," she answered in the same low voice. "Still, man must forth to battle and woman must wait and watch, for that is the world's way. Whate'er befalls, remember that dead or living I'll be wife to no man but you. Begone now ere my heart fails me, and guard yourself well, remembering that you bear in your breast not one life, but two."

Then Hugh swung himself to the saddle of which Grey Dick had already tested the girths and stirrup leathers. In another minute the six of them were clattering over the stones of Middlegate Street, while the burgesses of Dunwich peeped from their window places, wondering what knight with armed men rode through their town thus early.

Just as the grey dawn broke they passed the gate, which, there being peace in the land, was already open. Fifteen minutes later they were on the lonely Westleton Heath, where for a while naught was to be heard save the scream of the curlew and the rush of the wings of the wild-duck passing landward from the sea. Presently, however, another sound reached their ears, that of horses galloping behind them. Grey Dick pulled rein and listened.

"Seven, I think, not more," he said. "Now, master, do you stand or run, for these will be Clavering horses?"

Hugh thought for a moment. His aim was not to fight, but to get through to London. Yet if he fled the pursuers would raise the country on them as they came, so that in the end they must be taken, since those who followed would find fresh horses.

"It seems best to stand," he said.

"So say I," answered Grey Dick; and led the way to a little hillock by the roadside on which grew some wind-bent firs.

Here they dismounted and gave their horses into the keeping of one man, while Grey Dick and the others drew their bows from the cases and strung them. Scarcely had they done so when the mist, lifting in the morning breeze, showed them their pursuers—seven of them, as Dick had said—headed by one of the French knights, and riding scattered, between two and three hundred yards away. At the same moment a shout told them that they had been seen.

"Hark now all!" said Hugh. "I would shed no more blood if it may be so, who have earned enough of penance. Therefore shoot at the horses, not at the riders, who without them will be helpless. And let no man harm a Clavering unless it be to save his own life."

"Poor sport!" grunted Grey Dick.

Nevertheless, when the Norman knight who led came within two hundred yards, shouting to them in French to surrender, Dick lifted his great bow, drew and loosed carelessly, as though he shot at hazard, the others holding their bows till the Claverings were nearer. Yet there was little of hazard when Grey Dick shot, save to that at which he aimed. Away rushed the arrow, rising high and, as it seemed, bearing somewhat to the left of the knight. Yet when it drew near to that knight the wind told on it and bent it inward, as he knew it would. Fair and full it struck upon the horse's chest, piercing through to the heart, so that down the poor beast came, throwing its rider to the ground.

"A good shot enough," grumbled Grey Dick. "Still, it is a shame to slay nags of such a breed and let the rogues who ride them go."

But his companions only stared at him almost in awe, while the other Clavering men rode on. Before they had covered fifty paces, again the great bow twanged, and again a horse was seen to rear itself up, shaking the rider from its back, and then plunge away to die. Now Hugh's serving-men also lifted their bows, but Grey Dick hissed:

"Leave them to me! This is fine work, and you'd muddle it!"

Ere the words had ceased to echo another horse was down.

Then, as those who remained still came on, urged by the knight who ran shouting behind them, all loosed, and though some arrows went wide, the end of it was that ere they reached the little mound every Clavering horse was dead or sore wounded, while on the heath stood or lay seven helpless men.

"Now," said Grey Dick, "let us go and talk with these foot-soldiers."

So they went out, all of them, except he who had the horses, and

Hugh called aloud that the first man of the Claverings who lifted a bow or drew a sword should die without mercy. And he pointed to Grey Dick, who stood beside him, arrow on string.

The Claverings began to talk together excitedly.

"Throw down your weapons!" commanded Hugh.

Still they hesitated. Then, without further warning Dick sent an artful arrow through the cap of one of them, lifting it from his head, and instantly set another shaft to his string. After this, down went the swords and bows.

"Daggers and knives, too, if it please you, masters!"

Then these followed.

Now Hugh spoke a word to his men, who, going to the dead and dying horses, took from them the stirrup-leathers and bridle-reins and therewith bound the Claverings back to back. But the French knight, in acknowledgment of his rank, they trussed up by himself, having first relieved him of his purse by way of fine. As it chanced, however, Hugh turned and saw them in the act.

"God's truth! Would you make common thieves of us?" he said angrily. "Their weapons and harness are ours by right of war, but I'll hunt the man who steals their money out of my company."

So the purse was restored. When it was safe in the knight's pouch again Hugh saluted him, begging his pardon that it should have been touched.

"But how are you named, sir?" he added.

"Sir Pierre de la Roche is my name," replied the knight sadly, and in French.

"Then, Sir Pierre de la Roche," said Hugh, "here you and your people must bide until some come to set you free, which, as this place is lonely and little crossed in winter, may be to-day or may be to-morrow. When at length you get back to Blythburgh Manor, however, or to Dunwich town, I trust it to your honour to declare that Hugh de Cressi has dealt well with you. For whereas he might have slain you every one, as you would have slain him and his if you could, he has harmed no hair of your heads. As for your horses, these, to his sorrow, he was obliged to kill lest they should be used to ride him down. Will you do this of your courtesy?"

"Ay," answered the knight, "since to your gentleness we owe our lives. But with your leave I will add that we were overcome not by men, but by a devil"—and he nodded toward Grey Dick—"since no one who is only man can have such hellish skill in archery as we saw yesterday, and now again this morning. Moreover," he went on, contemplating Dick's ashen hair and cold eyes set wide apart in the rocky face, like to those of a Suffolk horse, "the man's air shows that he is in league with Satan."

"I'll not render your words into our English talk, Sir Pierre," replied Hugh, "lest he of whom you speak should take them amiss and send you where you might learn them false. For know, had he been what you say, the arrow that lies in your horse's heart would have nailed the breastplate to your own. Now take a message from me to your lord, Sir Edmund Acour, the traitor. Tell him that I shall return ere long, and that if he should dare to attempt ill toward the Lady Eve, who is my betrothed, or toward my father and brethren, or any of my House, I promise, in Grey Dick's name and my own, to kill him or those who may aid him as I would kill a forest wolf that had slunk into my sheepfold. Farewell! There is bracken and furze yonder where you may lie warm till some pass your way. Mount, men!"

So they rode forward, bearing all the Clavering weapons with them, which a mile or two further on Grey Dick hid in an empty fox's earth where he knew he could find them again. Only he kept the French knight's beautiful dagger that was made of Spanish steel, inlaid with gold, and used it to his life's end.

Here it may be told that it was not until thirty-six hours had gone by, as Hugh learned afterward, that a countryman brought this knight and his companions, more dead than alive, to Dunwich in his wain. As he was travelling across Westleton Heath, with a load of corn to be ground at the Dunwich mill, it seemed that he heard voices calling feebly, and guided by them found these unhappy men half buried in the snow that had fallen on that day, and so rescued them from death.

But when Sir Edmund Acour knew the story of their overthrow and of the message that Hugh had sent to him, he raved at them, and especially at Sir Pierre de la Roche, saying that the worst of young de Cressi's crimes against him was that he had left such cowardly hounds alive upon the earth. So he went on madly till Sir John Clavering checked him, bidding him wait to revile these men until he, and not his horse, had met Grey Dick's arrows and Hugh de Cressi's sword.

"For," he added, "it may happen then that you will fare no better than they have done, or than did John, my son."

On the morning of the third day after they left Dunwich, having been much delayed by foul weather and fouler roads, Hugh de Cressi and his company came at length to London. They had suffered no further adventure on their way for, though the times were rough and they met many evil-looking fellows, none ventured to lift hand against six men so well armed and sturdy. Guided by one of their number who had often been to London on Master de Cressi's business, they rode straight to Westminster. Having stabled their horses at an inn near by, and cleaned the mire of the road from their mail and garments, they went up to the palace, where Hugh told his errand to an officer whom he found on duty at the gate.

"Then it is a fool's errand," said the captain, "seeing that his Grace rode yesterday to his castle at Windsor to hunt and revel, and will be gone eight days at the least."

"Then to Windsor I must follow," answered Hugh.

CHAPTER V

GREY DICK SHOWS HIS ARCHERY

So sorely did the horses need rest, that Hugh and his people could not ride from London till the following morning, and evening was closing in before they found themselves drawing near the gate of Windsor Castle. In the market-place of the little town they pulled rein, while one of them went to search for a good inn at which they might lie, for the place seemed to be very full of people. Suddenly, as they stood there, wondering at the mighty, new-built keep which towered above them, a trumpet was blown and from round a corner appeared a gay procession of noble-looking men, and with them some ladies, who carried hawk on wrist, all mounted on splendid horses.

Now, the people who had gathered to study the strangers or tout for their custom, took off their bonnets and bent low, saying: "The King! The King! God save him!"

"Which is his Grace?" asked Hugh of one of them, whereon the man pointed to a royal-eyed and bearded knight, still in early middle life, who rode toward him, talking to a gallant youth at his side.

Now a thought came into Hugh's mind that the present time is always the best time to strike. Leaping from his horse, he advanced bowing, and stood in the pathway of the King. Seeing this, two of the fine Court lords spurred their horses and rode straight at him, thinking to drive him back. But he held his ground, for their insolence made him angry, and, catching the bridle of one of the horses, threw it on its haunches so sharply that the knight who rode it rolled from his saddle into the mire, whereupon every one laughed. In a moment he was on his feet again, and shouting:

"Out of the road, jackanapes, dressed in your grandfather's mail, unless you would stop there in the stocks. Do you know whose path you block?"

"That of his Grace," answered Hugh, "for whom I have a message that he will be glad to hear, and, popinjay, this for yourself; were it not for his presence it is you who should stop upon the road till you were carried thence."

Now, noting this disturbance, the King spoke to the youth at his side, who came forward and said, in a pleasant, courteous voice, addressing Hugh:

"Sir, why do you make trouble in these streets, and tumble the good Sir Ambrose Lacey from his horse with such scant ceremony?"

"Sir," answered Hugh, "because the good Sir Ambrose tried to ride his horse over me for no offence save that I would deliver a message to his Grace, which he will wish to hear."

"This is scarcely a time for the giving of messages," replied the young man, "but what is your name, and who sends the message? I am the Prince Edward," he added modestly, "so you may speak to me without fear."

"My name is Hugh de Cressi, your Highness, and I am sent by the Reverend Father Sir Andrew Arnold, of Dunwich, and have followed his Grace from Westminster, whither I and my men rode first."

Now, the Prince went to the King and spoke to him, and, returning presently, said:

"My father says that he knows both the names you give well enough and holds them dear. He bids that you and your people should follow him to the castle, where you will be entertained, with your horses. Sir Ambrose," he added, "the King desires that you should forget your choler, since he saw what passed, and deems that this young stranger did well to check your horse. Follow on, Hugh de Cressi, the officers will show you where you and your men may lodge."

So Hugh obeyed, and rode with the rest of the train and his folks through the gates of Windsor Castle. Nor did they do so unobserved, since many of the Court had no love for Sir Ambrose, and were glad to see him tumbled in the mire.

HIL

After they had stabled their beasts, as Hugh, followed by Grey Dick, was advancing toward a hall which he was told that he might enter, an officer came up.

"His Grace desires your presence before you sup," he said.

Pointing to Grey Dick, at whom the officer looked doubtfully, Hugh asked that he might accompany him, as he had much to do with the message. After some argument they were led through various passages to a chamber, at the door of which the officer wished to take away Dick's bow. But he would not give it up.

"The bow and I do not part," he said, in his croaking voice, "for we are husband and wife, and live and sleep together as the married should."

As Dick spoke the door was opened, and Prince Edward appeared.

"And do you eat together also, good fellow?" he asked, having overheard the talk.

"Ay, sir, we feed full together," replied Dick grimly; "or so thought some on Blythburgh Marsh a few days gone."

"I should like to hear that tale," said the Prince. "Meanwhile, since both my father and I love archers, let him pass with his bow. Only keep his arrows lest it should happen to grow hungry here."

Then they entered the chamber, led by the Prince. It was a fine place, with a vaulted stone roof and windows of coloured glass, that looked like the chancel of a church. Only at the head of it, where the altar should have been, was a kind of dais. On this dais were set some high-backed oaken chairs with many lanterns behind them in which burned tapers that, together with a great wood fire, gave light to the chamber.

In one of these chairs sat a gracious lady, who was embroidering something silken in a frame. This was Queen Philippa, and talking to her stood the tall King, clad in a velvet robe lined with fur. Behind, seated at a little table on which lay parchments, was a man in a priest's robe, writing. There was no one else in the room.

Hugh and Dick advanced to the foot of the dais, and stood there bowing.

"Who are these?" asked the King of the Prince. "Oh, I remember, the man who overthrew Sir Ambrose and said he had a message!"

"Ay, Sire," answered the Prince; "and this dust-coloured fellow is his servant, who will not part with his bow, which he calls his wife and says he sleeps with."

"I would all Englishmen did the same," broke in the King. "Say, man, can you shoot straight?"

"I know not, Sire," replied Grey Dick, "but perhaps straighter than most, for God, Who withheld all else from me, gave me this gift. At least, if I be not made drunk overnight, I'll match myself against any man at this Court, noble or simple, and stake twenty angels on it."

"Twenty angels! Have you so much, fellow?"

"Nay, Sire, nor more than one; but as I know I shall win, what does that matter?"

"Son," said the King, "see that this man is kept sober to-night, and to-morrow we will have a shooting match. But, sirrah, if you prove yourself to be a boaster you shall be whipped round the walls, for I love not tall words and small deeds. And now, young Master de Cressi, what is this message of yours?"

Hugh thrust his hand into his bosom, and produced a sealed packet which was addressed to "His Grace King Edward of England, sent from Andrew Arnold, priest, by the hand of Hugh de Cressi."

"Can you read?" the King asked of Hugh when he had spelt out this superscription.

"Ay, Sire; at least if the writing be that of Sir Andrew Arnold, for he was my master."

"A learned one and a brave, Hugh de Cressi. Well, break seal; we listen."

Hugh obeyed, and read as follows:

"Your Grace:
"Mayhap, Sire, you will remember me, Andrew Arnold, late master of the Templars in this town of Dunwich, in whose house, by your warrant for certain services rendered to your grandsire, your sire, and to yourself, I still dwell on as a priest ordained. Sire, the bearer of this, Hugh de Cressi, my godchild, is the son of Geoffrey de

Cressi, of this town, the great wool-merchant, with whom your Highness has had dealings—"

"In truth I have!" interrupted the King, with a laugh. "Also I think the account is still open—against myself. Well, it shall be paid some day, when I have conquered France. Forward!"

"Sire, this Hugh is enamoured of Eve Clavering, daughter of Sir John Clavering of Blythburgh, a cousin of his House, a very beauteous maiden, commonly known as Red Eve, and she in turn is enamoured of and betrothed to him—"

Here Queen Philippa suddenly became interested.

"Why is the lady called Red Eve, sir?" she asked in her soft voice. "Because her cheeks are red?"

"No, Madam," answered Hugh, blushing; "because she always loves to wear red garments."

"Ah, then she is dark!"

"That is so, Madam; her eyes and hair are black as ash-buds."

"God's truth! Lady," interrupted King Edward, "is this young man's message of the colour of the eyes of his mistress, which, without doubt, being in love, he describes falsely? On with the letter!"

"Out of this matter," continued Hugh, "rose a feud yesterday, during which Hugh de Cressi killed his cousin John, fighting à outrance, and his servant, Richard the Archer, who accompanies him, commonly known as Grey Dick, slew three men with as many arrows, two of them being Normans whose names are unknown to us, and the third a grieve to Sir John Clavering, called Thomas of Kessland. Also, he killed a horse, and when another Frenchman tried to grasp his master, sent a shaft through the palm of his hand."

"By St. George," said the King, "but here is shooting! Were they near to you, Grey Dick?"

"Not so far away, Sire. Only the light was very bad, or I should have had the fourth. I aimed low, Sire, fearing to miss his skull, and he jerked up his horse's head to take the arrow."

"A good trick! I've played it myself. Well, let us have done with the letter, and then we'll come to archery."

"Sire," read on Hugh, "I ask your royal pardon to Hugh de Cressi and Richard the Archer for these slayings, believing that when you have read these letters it will be granted."

"That remains to be seen," muttered the King.

"Sire, Sir Edmund Acour, who has lands here in Suffolk, Count de Noyon in Normandy, and Seigneur of Cattrina in Italy—"

"I know the man," exclaimed Edward to the Queen, "and so do you. A handsome knight and a pleasant, but one of whom I have always misdoubted me."

"—Is also enamoured of Eve Clavering, and with her father's will seeks to make her his wife, though she hates him, and by the charter of Dunwich, of which she is a citizen, has the right to wed whom she will."

"It is well there are not many such charters. The old story—brave men done to death for the sake of a woman who is rightly named Red Eve," mused the King.

"My Liege, I pray that you will read the letter herein enclosed. Hugh de Cressi will tell you how it came to my hand, since I lack time to write all the story. If it seems good to your Grace, I pray you scotch this snake while he is in your garden, lest he should live to sting you when you walk abroad. If it please you to give your royal warrant to the bearer of this letter, and to address the same to such of your subjects in Dunwich as you may think good, I doubt not but that men can be found to execute the same. Thus would a great and traitorous plot be brought to nothing, to your own glory and the discomfiture of your foes in France, who hope to lay their murderous hands upon the throne of England. "Your humble servant and subject, "Andrew Arnold."

"What's this?" exclaimed the King starting from his seat. "To lay hands upon the throne of England! Quick with the other letter, man!"

"I was charged that it is for your Grace's eye alone," said Hugh as he unfolded the paper. "Is it your pleasure that I read it aloud, if I can, for it is writ in French?"

"Give it me," said the King. "Philippa, come help me with this crabbed stuff."

Then they withdrew to the side of the dais, and, standing under a lantern, spelled out Sir Edmund Acour's letter to the Duke of Normandy, word by word.

The King finished the letter, and, still holding it in his hand, stood for a minute silent. Then his rage broke out.

"'He of England,'" he quoted. "That's your husband, Edward, Lady, who is to be overthrown and killed 'that Philip's son may take his seat and be crowned King at Westminster,' which God is to bring about before this year is out. Yes; and my cities are to be sacked and my people slain, and this French dog, Edmund Acour, who has sworn fealty to me, is to be rewarded with wide English lands and high English titles. Well, by God's blood I swear that, dead or living, he shall be lifted higher than he hopes, though not by Normandy or my brother of France! Let me think! Let me think! If I send men-at-arms he'll hear of it and slip away. Did not good old Sir Andrew call him a snake? Now, where's this girl, Red Eve?"

"In sanctuary, Sire, at the Temple Church in Dunwich," answered Hugh.

"Ah, and she's a great heiress now, for you killed her brother, and Acour, although he has wide possessions in sundry lands, was ever a spendthrift and deep in debt. No, he'll not leave unless he can get the girl; and old Sir Andrew will guard her well with the power of the Church, and with his own right arm if need be, for he's still more knight than priest. So there's no hurry. Tell me all you know of this story, Hugh de Cressi, omitting nothing, however small. Nay, have no fear, if you can vouch for your fellow there, all of us in this chamber are loyal to England. Speak out, man."

So Hugh began and told of the de Cressis and the Claverings and their feud, and of how he and Eve had always loved each other. He told of their meeting in the reeds of Blythburgh Fen, and of the death of John de Clavering at his hand and of the others at the hand of Grey Dick, and of the escape of Acour from the fourth arrow. He told how he and Eve had swum the Blyth in flood though the ice cut them, and hid on the moor while Grey Dick led the Claverings astray, and came at last safe to sanctuary. He told how Acour's letter had been won

from his messenger by Sir Andrew's loyal guile. He told of the penance
that Sir Andrew had laid upon them because of the new-shed blood of
John Clavering, of the flight from Dunwich and the shooting of the
horses of the Clavering men, and of their ride to London and to
Windsor. He told everything, save only the tale of what Sir Andrew
had seen in the House of Murgh in far Cathay.

When at last he had finished, and though it was long none there
grew weary of that story, the King turned to the clerk, and said:

"Brother Peter, make out a full pardon to Hugh de Cressi of
Dunwich and Richard Archer his servant for all slayings or other
deeds wrought by them contrary to our general peace. Draw it wide,
and bring the same to me for execution ere I sleep to-night. Make out
a commission also to the Mayor of Dunwich—nay, I'll think that
matter over and instruct you further. Hugh de Cressi, you have our
thanks, and if you go on as you have begun you shall have more ere
long, for I need such men about me. You also, strange and death-like
man named Grey Dick, shall not lack our favour if it proves that you
can shoot but half as well as you have boasted, and, unless you lie,
both of you, as it seems that you have done. And now to supper,
though in truth this news does not kindle appetite. Son, see that this
gentleman is well served, and that none mock him more about the
fashion of his armour, above all Sir Ambrose, for I'll not suffer it.
Plate and damascene do not make a man, and this, it seems, was
borrowed from as brave, ay, and as learned, a knight as ever bestrode a
horse in war. Come, Lady," and taking the Queen by the hand, he left
the chamber.

That evening Hugh ate his food seated among the knights of the
Household at a high table in the great hall, at the head of which, for
the King supped in private, was placed the young Prince Edward. He
noted that now none laughed at him about the fashion of his mail or
his country ways. Indeed, when after supper Sir Ambrose Lacey came
to him and asked his pardon for the talk that he had used to him in
the Windsor street—he was sure that some word had been sent round
that his business had brought him favour with the King and that he
must be treated with all courtesy. Several of those who sat round him

tried to discover what that business was. But of this he would say nothing, parrying their questions with others about the wars in France, and listening with open ears to the tales of great deeds done there.

"Ah, would that I could see such things!" he said.

To which one of them answered:

"Well, why not? There'll be chance enough ere long, and many of us would be glad of a square built like you."

Now, at lower tables, in that vast hall, Hugh's servants, and with them Grey Dick, sat among the men-at-arms of the King's Guard, who were all chosen for their courage, and skill in archery. These soldiers, noting the strange-faced, ashen-haired fellow who ate with his bow resting on the bench beside him, inquired about him from the other Dunwich men, and soon heard enough to cause them to open their eyes. When the ale had got hold of them they opened their mouths also, and, crowding round Dick, asked if it were true that he could shoot well.

"As well as another," he answered, and would say no more.

Then they looked at his bow, and saw that it was old-fashioned, like his master's mail, and of some foreign make and wood, but a mighty weapon such as few could handle and hold straight. Lastly, they began to challenge him to a match upon the morrow, to which he answered, who also had been drinking ale and was growing angry, that he'd give the best of them five points in fifty.

Now they mocked, for among them were some famous archers, and asked at what range.

"At any ye will," answered Grey Dick, "from twelve score yards down to one score yards. Now trouble me no longer, who if I must shoot to-morrow would sleep first and drink no more of your strong ale that breeds bad humours in one reared upon dyke water."

Then, seizing his bow, he glided away in his curious stoat-like fashion to the hole where he had been shown that he should sleep.

"A braggart!" said one.

"I am not so sure," answered a grizzled captain of archers, who had fought in many wars. "Braggarts make a noise, but this fellow only spoke when we squeezed him and perhaps what came out of those thin lips was truth. At least, from his look I'd sooner not find him against me bow to bow."

Then they fell to betting which of them would beat Grey Dick by the heaviest points.

Next morning about nine o'clock the King sent a messenger to Hugh, bidding him and his servant Richard wait upon them. They went with this messenger, who led them to a little chamber, where his Grace sat, attended only by the clerk, Brother Peter, and a dark-browed minister, whose name he never learned.

"Hugh de Cressi and Richard Archer," said Edward, motioning to the minister to hand Hugh a parchment to which hung a great seal, "here is the pardon which I promised you. No need to stay to read it, since it is as wide as Windsor Keep, and woe betide him who lifts hand against either of you for aught you may have done or left undone in the past contrary to the laws of our realm. Yet remember well that this grace runs not to the future. Now that matter is ended, and we come to one that is greater. Because of the faith put in you by our loyal and beloved subject, Sir Andrew Arnold, your godsire, and because we like the fashion of you, Hugh de Cressi, and hold you brave and honest, it has pleased us to give you a commission under which we direct the Mayor of Dunwich and all true and lawful men of that town and hundred to aid you in the taking or, if need be, in the slaying of our subject, Sir Edmund Acour, Count of Noyon and Seigneur of Cattrina. We command you to bring this man before us alive or dead, that his cause may be judged of our courts and the truth of the matter alleged against him by the Reverend Father Sir Andrew Arnold therein determined. Nevertheless, we command you not to wound or kill the said knight unless he resists the authority of us by you conveyed and you cannot otherwise hold him safe from escaping from out this our realm. This commission you will presently go forth to execute, keeping its tenor and your aim secret until the moment comes to strike, and, as you perform your duty, of which you will return and make report to us, so shall we judge and reward you. Do you understand?"

HIL

"Sire," answered Hugh, bowing, "I understand, and I will obey to my last breath."

"Good! When the parchments are engrossed my officer here will read them to you and explain aught that may need it. Meanwhile, we have an hour or two during which your horses can eat, for there are no fresh beasts here to give you, and it is best, to avoid doubts, that you should return as you came, only showing your powers if any should attempt to arrest you. So let us have done with these heavy matters, and disport us for a while. This servant of yours has made a common boast that he will outshoot any of our picked archers, and now we are ready to go forth and put him to the proof of the butts. Let him know, however, that, notwithstanding our words of yesterday, we shall not hold him to blame if he fails, since many a man of higher degree promises more at night than he can perform in the morning."

"Sire, I'll do my best. I can no more," said Grey Dick. "Only I pray that none may be suffered to hang about or pester me at the butts, since I am a lonely man who love not company when I use my art."

"That shall be so," said the King. "And now to the sport."

"The sport!" grumbled Grey Dick, when he and Hugh were alone together. "Why, it is other sport we should be seeking, with Acour and his knaves for targets. Go to the King, master, and show him that while we linger here the Frenchman may slip away, or work more and worse treasons."

"I cannot, Dick; the parchments are not written out, and his Grace is bent upon this pleasure match. Moreover, man, all these archers here—yes, and their betters also—would say that you had fled because you were an empty boaster who dared not face the trial."

"They'd say that, would they?" snarled Grey Dick. "Yes, they'd say that, which would be bitter hearing for you and me. Well, they shall not say it. Yet I tell you, master," he added in a burst of words, "although I know not why, I'd rather bear their scorn and be away on the road to Dunwich."

"It may not be, Dick," replied Hugh, shaking his head doubtfully. "See, here they come to fetch us."

In a glade of the forest of Windsor situated near to the castle and measuring some twenty-five score yards of open level ground, stood Grey Dick, a strange, uncouth figure, at whom the archers of the guard laughed, nudging each other. In his bony hand, however, he held that at which they did not laugh, namely, the great black bow, six feet six inches long, which he said had come to him "from the sea," and was fashioned, not of yew, but of some heavy, close-grained wood, grown perhaps in Southern or even in far Eastern lands. Still, one of them, who had tried to draw this bow to his ear and could not, said aloud that "the Suffolk man would do naught with that clumsy pole." Whereat, Grey Dick, who heard him, grinning, showing his white teeth like an angry dog.

Near by, on horseback and on foot, were the King, the young Prince Edward, and many knights and ladies; while on the other side stood scores of soldiers and other folk from the castle, who came to see this ugly fellow well beaten at his own game.

"Dick," whispered Hugh, "shoot now as you never shot before. Teach them a lesson for the honour of Suffolk."

"Let me be, master," he grumbled. "I told you I would do my best."

Then he sat himself down on the grass and began to examine his arrows one by one, to all appearance taking no heed of anything else.

Presently came the first test. At a distance of five score yards was set a little "clout," or target, of white wood, not more than two feet square. This clout had a red mark, or eye, three inches across, painted in its centre, and stood not very high above the sward.

"Now, Richard," said the King, "three of the best archers that we have about us have been chosen to shoot against you and each other by their fellows. Say, will you draw first or last?"

"Last, Sire," he answered, "that I may know their mettle."

Then a man stepped forward, a strong and gallant looking fellow, and loosed his three arrows. The first missed the clout, the second pierced the white wood, and the third hit the red eye.

The clout having been changed, and the old one brought to the

King with the arrows in it, the second man took his turn. This time all three of the arrows hit the mark, one of them being in the red. Again it was changed, and forth came the great archer of the guard, a tall and clear-eyed man named Jack Green, and whom, it was said, none had ever beaten. He drew, and the arrow went home in the red on its left edge. He drew again, and the arrow went home in the red on its right edge. He drew a third time, and the arrow went home straight in the very centre of the red, where was a little black spot.

Now a great laugh went up, since clearly the Suffolk man was beaten ere ever he began.

"Your Dick may do as well; he can do no better," said the King, when the target was brought to him.

Grey Dick looked at it.

"A boon, your Grace," said Dick. "Grant that this clout may be set up again with the arrows fast. Any may know them from mine since they are grey, whereas those I make are black, for I am a fletcher in my spare hours, and love my own handiwork."

"So be it," said the King, wondering; and the clout was replaced upon its stand.

Now Grey Dick stretched himself, looked at the clout, looked at his bow, and set a black-winged arrow on the string. Then he drew, it seemed but lightly and carelessly, as though he thought the distance small. Away flew the shaft, and sank into the red a good inch within the leftmost arrow of Jack Green.

"Ah," said the onlookers, "a lucky shot indeed!"

Again he drew, and again the arrow sank into the red, a good inch within the rightmost shot of Jack Green.

"Oh!" said the onlookers, "this man is an archer; but Jack's last he cannot best, let the devil help him how he will."

"In the devil's name, then, be silent!" wheezed Grey Dick, with a flash of his half-opened eye.

"Ay, be silent—be silent!" said the King. "We do not see such shooting every day."

Now Dick set his foot apart and, arrow on string, thrice he lifted his bow and thrice let it sink again, perhaps because he felt some breath of wind stir the still air. A fourth time he lifted, and drew, not as he had before, but straight to the ear, then loosed at once.

Away rushed the yard-long shaft, and folk noted that it scarcely seemed to rise as arrows do, or at least not half so high. It rushed, it smote, and there was silence, for none could see exactly what had happened. Then he who stood near the target to mark ran forward, and screamed out:

"By God's name, he has shattered Jack Green's centre arrow, and shot clean through the clout!"

Then from all sides rose the old archer cry, "He, He! He, He!" while the young Prince threw his cap on high, and the King said:

"Would that there were more such men as this in England! Jack Green, it seems that you are beaten."

"Nay," said Grey Dick, seating himself again upon the grass, "there is naught to choose between us in this round. What next, your Grace?"

Only Hugh, who watched him, saw the big veins swell beneath the pale skin of his forehead, as they ever did when he was moved.

"The war game," said the King; "that is, if you will, for here rough knocks may be going. Set it out, one of you."

Then a captain of the archers explained this sport. In short it was that man should stand against man clad in leather jerkins, and wearing a vizor to protect the face, and shoot at each other with blunt arrows rubbed with chalk, he who first took what would have been a mortal wound to be held worsted.

"I like not blunted arrows," said Grey Dick; "or, for the matter of that, any other arrows save my own. Against how many must I play? The three?"

The captain nodded.

"Then, by your leave, I will take them all at once."

Now some said that this was not fair, but in the end Dick won his point, and those archers whom he had beaten, among them Jack Green, were placed against him, standing five yards apart, and blunted arrows served out to all. Dick set one of them on the string, and laid the two others in front of them. Then a knight rode to halfway between them, but a little to one side, and shouted: "Loose!"

As the word struck his ear Dick shot with wonderful swiftness, and almost as the arrow left the bow flung himself down, grasping another as he fell. Next instant, three shafts whistled over where he had stood. But his found its mark on the body of him at whom he had aimed, causing the man to stagger backward and throw down his bow, as he was bound to do, if hit.

Next instant Dick was up again and his second arrow flew, striking full and fair before ever he at whom it was aimed had drawn.

Now there remained Jack Green alone, and, as Dick set the third arrow, but before he could draw, Jack Green shot.

"Beat!" said Dick, and stood quite still.

At him rushed the swift shaft, and passed over his shoulder within a hairbreadth of his ear. Then came Dick's turn. On Jack Green's cap was an archer's plume.

"Mark the plume, lords," he said, and lo! the feather leapt from that cap.

Now there was silence. No one spoke, but Dick drew out three more arrows.

"Tell me, captain," he said, "is your ground marked out in scores; and what is the farthest that any one of you has sent a flighting shot?"

"Ay," answered the officer, "and twenty score and one yard is the farthest, nor has that been done for many a day."

Dick steadied himself, and seemed to fill his lungs with air. Then, stretching his long arms to the full, he drew the great bow till the horns looked as though they came quite close together, and loosed. High and far flew that shaft; men's eyes could scarcely follow it, and all must wait long before a man came running to say where it had fallen.

"Twenty score and two yards!" he cried.

"Not much to win by," grunted Dick, "though enough. I have done twenty and one score once, but that was somewhat downhill."

Then, while the silence still reigned, he set the second arrow on the string, and waited, as though he knew not what to do. Presently, about fifty paces from him, a wood dove flew from out a tree and, as such birds do at the first breath of spring, for the day was mild and sunny, hovered a moment in the air ere it dipped toward a great fir where doubtless it had built for years. Never, poor fowl, was it destined to build again, for as it turned its beak downward Dick's shaft pierced it through and through and bore it onward to the earth.

Still in the midst of a great silence, Dick took up his quiver and emptied it on the ground, then gave it to the captain of the archers, saying:

"And you will, step sixty, nay, seventy paces, and set this mouth upward in the grass where a man may see it well."

The captain did so, propping the quiver straight with stones and a bit of wood. Then, having studied all things with his eyes, Dick shot upward, but softly. Making a gentle curve, the arrow turned in the air as it drew near the quiver, and fell into its mouth, striking it flat.

"Ill done," grumbled Dick; "had I shot well, it should have been pinned to earth. Well, yon shadow baulked me, and it might have been worse."

Then he unstrung his bow, and slipped it into its case.

Now, at length, the silence was broken, and in good earnest. Men, especially those of Dunwich, screamed and shouted, hurling up their caps. Jack Green, for all jealousy was forgotten at the sight of this wondrous skill, ran to Dick, clasped him in his arms, and, dragging the badge from off his breast, tried to pin it to his rough doublet. The young Prince came and clapped him on the shoulder, saying:

"Be my man! Be my man!"

But Dick only growled, "Paws off! What have I done that I have not done a score of times before with no fine folk to watch me? I shot to please my master and for the honour of Suffolk, not for you, and because some dogs keep their tails too tightly curled."

"A sulky fellow," said the Prince, "but, by heaven, I like him!"

Then the King pushed his horse through the throng, and all fell back before his Grace.

"Richard Archer," he said, "never has such marksmanship as yours been seen in England since we sat upon the throne, nor shall it go unrewarded. The twenty angels that you said you would stake last night shall be paid to you by the treasurer of our household. Moreover, here is a gift from Edward of England, the friend of archers, that you may be pleased to wear," and taking his velvet cap from off his head, the King unpinned from it a golden arrow of which the barbed head was cut from a ruby, and gave it to him.

"I thank you, Sire," said Dick, his pale skin flushing with pride and pleasure. "I'll wear it while I live, and may the sight of it mean death to many of your enemies."

"Without doubt it will, and that ere long, Richard, for know you that soon we sail again for France, whence the tempest held us back, and it is my pleasure that you sail with us. Therefore I name you one of our fletchers, with place about our person in our bodyguard of archers. Jack Green will show you your quarters, and instruct you in your duties, and soon you shall match your skill against his again, but next time with Frenchmen for your targets."

"Sire," said Dick, very slowly, "take back your arrow, for I cannot do as you will."

"Why, man? Are you a Frenchman?" asked the King, angrily, for he was not wont to have his favours thus refused.

"My mother never told me so, Sire, although I don't know for certain who my father may have been. Still, I think not, since I hate the sight of that breed as a farmer's dog hates rats. But, Sire, I have a good master, and do not wish to change him for one who, saving your presence, may prove a worse, since King's favour on Monday has been known to mean King's halter on Tuesday. Did you not promise to whip me round your walls last night unless I shot as well as I thought I could, and now do you not change your face and give me golden arrows?"

At these bold words a roar of laughter went up from all who heard them, in which the King himself joined heartily enough.

"Silence!" he cried presently. "This yeoman's tongue is as sharp as his shafts. I am pierced. Let us hear whom he will hit next."

"You again, Sire, I think," went on Dick, "because, after the fashion of kings, you are unjust. You praise me for my shooting, whereas you should praise God, seeing that it is no merit of mine, but a gift He gave me at my birth in place of much which He withheld. Moreover, my master there," and he pointed to Hugh, "who has just done you better service than hitting a clout in the red and a dow beneath the wing, you forget altogether, though I tell you he can shoot almost as well as I, for I taught him."

"Dick, Dick!" broke in Hugh in an agony of shame. Taking no heed, Dick went on imperturbably: "And is the best man with a sword in Suffolk, as the ghost of John Clavering knows to-day. Lastly, Sire, you send this master of mine upon a certain business where straight arrows may be wanted as well as sharp swords, and yet you'd keep me here whittling them out of ashwood, who, if I could have had my will, would have been on the road these two hours gone. Is that a king's wisdom?"

"By St. George!" exclaimed Edward, "I think that I should make you councillor as well as fletcher, since without doubt, man, you have a bitter wit, and, what is more rare, do not fear to speak the truth as you see it. Moreover, in this matter, you see it well. Go with Hugh de Cressi on the business which I have given him to do, and, when it is finished, should both or either of you live, neglect not our command to rejoin us here, or—if we have crossed the sea—in France. Edward of England needs the service of such a sword and such a bow."

"You shall have them both, Sire," broke in Hugh, "for what they are worth. Moreover, I pray your Grace be not angry with Grey Dick's words, for if God gave him a quick eye, He also gave him a rough tongue."

"Not I, Hugh de Cressi, for know, we love what is rough if it be also honest. It is smooth, false words of treachery that we hate, such words as are ever on the lips of one whom we send you forth to bring to his account. Now to your duty. Farewell till we meet again, whether it be here or where all men, true or traitors, must foot their bill at last."

CHAPTER VI

THE SNARE

About noon of the day on which Hugh and his company had ridden for London, another company entered Dunwich—namely, Sir John Clavering and many of his folk, though with him were neither Sir Edmund Acour nor any of his French train. Sir John's temper had never been of the best, for he was a man who, whatever his prosperity, found life hard and made it harder for all those about him. But seldom had he been angrier than he was this day, when his rage was mingled with real sorrow for the loss of his only son, slain in a fight brought about by the daughter of one of them and the sister of the other and urged for honour's sake by himself, the father of them both.

Moreover, the marriage on which he had set his heart between Eve and the glittering French lord whose future seemed so great had been brought to naught, and this turbulent, hot-hearted Eve had fled into sanctuary. Her lover, too, the youngest son of a merchant, had ridden away to London, doubtless upon some mission which boded no good to him or his, leaving a blood feud behind him between the wealthy de Cressis and all the Clavering kin.

There was but one drop of comfort in his cup. By now, as he hoped, Hugh and his death's-head, Grey Dick, a spawn of Satan that all the country feared, and who, men said, was a de Cressi bastard by a witch, were surely slain or taken by those who followed upon their heels.

Sir John rode to the Preceptory and hammered fiercely on its oaken door. Presently it was opened by Sir Andrew Arnold himself, who stood in the entrance, grey and grim, a long sword girt about his loins and armour gleaming beneath his monkish robe.

"What would you, Sir John Clavering, that you knock at this holy house thus rudely?" he asked.

"My daughter, priest, who, they say, has sheltered here."

"They say well, knight, she has sheltered here beneath the wings of St. Mary and St. John. Begone and leave her in peace."

"I make no more of such wings than if they were those of farmyard geese," roared the furious man. "Bring her or I will pluck her forth."

"Do so," replied Sir Andrew, "if you live to pass this consecrated sword," and he laid his hand upon its hilt. "Take with her also the curse of the Mother of God, and His beloved Apostle, and that of the whole Church of Christ, by me declared upon your head in this world and upon your soul in the world to come. Man, this is sanctuary, and if you dare to set foot within it in violence, may your body perish and your soul scorch everlastingly in the fires of hell. And you," he added, raising his voice till it rang like a trumpet, addressing the followers of Sir John, "on you also let the curse of excommunication fall. Now slay me and enter if you will, but then every drop of blood in these veins shall find a separate tongue and cry out for vengeance on you before the judgment seat of God, where presently I summon you to meet me."

Then he crossed himself, drew the great sword, and, holding it in his left hand, stretched out his right toward them in malediction.

The Clavering men heard and saw. They looked at each other, and, as though by common consent, turned and rode away, crossing themselves also. In truth, they had no stomach for the curse of the Church when it was thundered forth from the lips of such a monk as Sir Andrew Arnold, who, they knew well, had been one of the greatest and holiest warriors of his generation, and, so said rumour, was a white wizard to boot with all the magic of the East at his command.

"Your men have gone, Sir John," said the old priest; "will you follow them or will you enter?"

Now fear drove out the knight's rage and he spoke in another voice.

"Sir Andrew, why do you bring all these wrongs upon me? My boy is dead at the hand of Hugh de Cressi, your godson, and he has robbed me of my daughter, whom I have affianced to a better and a nobler man. Now you give her sanctuary and threaten me with the curse of the Church because I would claim her, my own flesh and blood; ay, and my heiress too to-day. Tell me, as one man to another, why do you do these things?"

"And tell me, Sir John Clavering, why for the sake of pelf and of honours that you will never harvest do you seek to part those who love each other and whom God has willed to bring together? Why would you sell your child to a gilded knave whom she hates? Nay, stop me not. I'd call him that and more to his face and none have ever known me lie. Why did you suffer this Frenchman or your dead son, or both of them, to try to burn out Hugh de Cressi and Red Eve as though they were rats in rubbish?"

"Would you know, Father? Then I'll tell you. Because I wish to see my daughter set high among lords and princes and not the wife of a merchant's lad, who by law may wear cloth only and rabbit fur. Because, also, I hate him and all his kin, and if this is true of yesterday, how much more true is it now that he has killed my son, and by the arrows of that wolf-man who dogs his heels, slain my guests and my grieve. Think not I'll rest till I have vengeance of him and all his cursed House. I'll appeal to the King, and if he will not give me justice I'll take it for myself. Ay, though you are old, I tell you you shall live to see the de Cressi vault crowded with the de Cressi dead."

Sir Andrew hid his eyes for a moment with his hand, then let it fall and spoke in a changed voice.

"It comes upon me that you speak truth, Sir John, for since I met a certain great Master in the East, at times I have a gift of foresight. I think that much sorrow draws near this land; ay, and others. I think that many vaults and many churchyards, too, will ere long be filled with dead; also that the tomb of the Claverings at Blythburgh will soon be opened. Mayhap the end of this world draws near to all men, as surely it draws near to you and me. I know not—yet truth was in your lips just now, and in mine as well, I think. Oh, man, man!" he went on after a pause, "appeal not unto the world's Cæsar lest Cæsar render different judgment to that which you desire. Get you home, and on your knees appeal unto God to forgive you your proud, vengeance-seeking heart. Sickness draws near to you; death draws near to you, and after death, hell—or heaven. I have finished."

As he heard these words Sir John's swarthy face grew pale and for a little while his rage died down. Then it flared up again.

"Don't dream to frighten me with your spells, old wizard," he said. "I'm a hale man yet, though I do lose my breath at times when my mind is vexed with wrongs, and I'll square my own account with God without your help or counsel. So you'll not give me my daughter?"

"Nay, here she bides in sanctuary for so long as it shall please her."

"Does she in truth? Perhaps you married her to this merchant fellow ere he rode this morning."

"Nay, Sir John, they betrothed themselves before the altar and in presence of his kin, no more. Moreover, if you would know, because of your son's blood which runs between them I, after thought and prayer, speaking in the name of the Church, swore them to this penance—that for a year from yesterday they should not wed nor play the part of lovers."

"I thank you, priest, for this small grace," answered Sir John, with a bitter laugh, "and in my turn I swear this, that after the year they shall not wed, since the one of them will be clay and the other the wife of the man whom I have chosen. Now, play no tricks on me, lest I burn this sanctuary of yours about your head and throw your old carcass to roast among the flames."

Sir Andrew made no reply, only, resting his long sword on the threshold, he leant upon its hilt, and fixed his clear grey eyes upon Clavering's face. What Sir John saw in those eyes he never told, but it was something which scared him. At least that shortening of the breath of which he had spoken seemed to take a hold of him, for he swayed upon his horse as though he were about to fall, then, recovering, turned and rode straight for Blythburgh.

It was the second night after that day when Sir Andrew had looked John Clavering in the eyes.

Secretly and in darkness those three whom Grey Dick had killed were borne into the nave of Blythburgh church and there laid in the grave which had been made ready for them. Till now their corpses had been kept above ground in the hope that the body of John Clavering the younger might be added to their number. But search as they would upon seashore and river-bank, nothing of him was ever seen again. This funeral was celebrated in the darkness, since neither Sir John nor Acour desired that all men should see three bodies that had been slain by one archer, aided by a merchant's lad, standing alone against a score, and know, to say naught of the wounded, that there was yet another to be added to the tale. Therefore they interred them by night with no notice of the ceremony.

It was a melancholy scene. The nave of the great church, lighted only with the torches borne by the six monks of the black Augustines from the neighbouring priory of St. Osyth; the candles, little stars of light, burning far away upon the altar; the bearers of the household of the Claverings and the uncoffined corpses lying on their biers by the edge of the yawning graves; the mourners in their mail; the low voice of the celebrating priest, a Frenchman, Father Nicholas, chaplain to Acour, who hurried through the Latin service as though he wished to be done with it; the deep shadows of the groined roof whereon the rain pattered—such were the features of this interment. It was done at last, and the poor dead, but a few days before so full of vigour and of passion, were left to their last sleep in the unremembered grave. Then the mourners marched back to the manor across the Middle Marsh and sought their beds in a sad silence.

Shortly after daybreak they were called from them again by the news that those who had followed Hugh de Cressi had returned. Quickly they rose, thinking that these came back with tidings of accomplished vengeance, to find themselves face to face with seven starved and miserable men who, all their horses being dead, had walked hither from Dunwich.

The wretched story was learned at length, and then followed that violent scene, which has been told already, when Acour cursed his followers as cowards, and Clavering, sobered perhaps by the sadness of the midnight burial or by the memory of Arnold's words, reproved him. Lastly, stung by the taunts that were heaped upon them, Sir Pierre de la Roche gave Hugh's message—that if they lifted hand against his love or his House he would kill them like ravening wolves, "which I think he certainly will do, for none can conquer him and his henchman," he added shortly.

Then Sir John's rage flared up again like fire when fresh fuel is thrown on ashes. He cursed Hugh and Grey Dick; he cursed his daughter; he even cursed Acour and asked for the second time how it came about that he who had brought all this trouble on him was given the evil name of traitor.

"I know not," answered Sir Edmund fiercely, and laying his hand upon his sword, "but this I know, that you or any man will do well not to repeat it if you value life."

"Do you threaten me?" asked Sir John. "Because, if so, you will do well to begone out of this house of shame and woe lest you be borne out feet first. Nay, nay, I forgot," he added slowly, clasping his head in his hands, "you are my daughter's affianced, are you not, and will give her high place and many famous titles, and her son shall be called Clavering, that the old name may not die but be great in England, in France, and in Italy. You must bide to marry her, lest that cuckoo, Hugh de Cressi, that cuckoo with the sharp bill, should creep into my nest. I'll not be worsted by a stripling clad in merchant's cloth who slew my only son. Take not my words ill, noble Noyon, for I am overdone with grief for the past and fear for the future. You must bide to marry her by fair means or by foul. Draw her from the sanctuary and marry her whether she say you yea or nay. You have my leave, noble Noyon," and so speaking he swayed and fell prone upon the floor.

At first they thought that he was dead. But the chaplain, Nicholas, who was a leech, bled him, and he came to himself again, although he still wandered in his talk and lay abed.

Then Acour and Nicholas took counsel together.

"What is to be done?" said Sir Edmund, "for I am on fire for this maid, and all her scorn and hate do but fan my flame. Moreover, she is now very rich, for that old hot-head cannot live long. His violent humours will kill him, and, as you know, Father, although I have great possessions, my costs are large and I have still greater debts. Lastly, shall de Noyon and his knights be worsted by a wool-merchant's younger son, a mere 'prentice lad, and his henchman, a common archer of the fens? Show me how to get her, Nicholas, and I'll make an abbot of you yet. This sanctuary, now? will it hold? If we stormed the place and took her, would the Holy Father give us absolution, do you think?"

"No, my lord," answered the fox-faced Nicholas. "The Church is great because the Church is one, and what the priest does the Pope upholds, especially when that priest is no mean man. This holy monk, Sir Andrew Arnold, has reputation throughout Europe, and, though he seems so humble, because of his wisdom is in the counsel of many great men whose fathers or grandfathers were guided by him long ago. Commit what crime you will, dip yourself to the lips in blood, and you may find forgiveness, but touch not an ancient and acknowledged sanctuary of the Church, since for this offence there will be none."

"What then, Nicholas? Must I give up the chase and fly? To speak truth, things seem to threaten me. Why has that Hugh twice called me traitor? Have any of my letters fallen into strange hands, think you? I have written several, and you know my mission here."

"It is possible, lord; all things are possible, but I think not. I think that he only draws the bow at a hazard, which is more than Grey Dick does," he added with a chuckle. "These brute English hate us French, whom they know to be their masters in all that makes a man, and traitor to their fool king is the least of the words they throw at us."

"Well, priest, my mother was English, as my wife will be. Therefore stay your tongue on that matter and tell me how I am to make her my wife," answered Acour haughtily.

The chaplain cringed and bowed, rubbing his thin hands together.

"I thought you wished to speak of the English, my lord, otherwise

I should not have ventured—but as to the lady Eve, something comes to me. Why does she stay in sanctuary who herself has committed no crime? Is it not, such is her madness, because she would be out of reach of you and your endearments? Now if she believed you gone far enough away, let us say to France, and knew that her father lay ill, why then—" and he paused.

"You mean that she might come out of sanctuary of her own accord?"

"Yes, lord, and we might set a springe to catch this bird so rare and shy, and though she'd flutter, flutter, flutter, and peck, peck, peck, what could she do when you smoothed her plumage with your loving hand, and a priest was waiting to say the word that should cause her to forget her doubts and that merchant bumpkin?"

"Ah, Nicholas, you have a good wit, and if all goes well you shall certainly be an abbot. But would her father, do you think—"

"Lord, that beef-eating knight is in such a rage that he would do anything. What did he say just before the stroke took him? That you were to marry her by fair means or by foul. Yes, and he told me an hour ago that if only he knew she was your wife, he would die happy. Oh, you have his warrant for anything you do to bring about this end. Still there is no need to tell him too much lest it should cause his good name to be aspersed by the vulgar. Many, it seems, love this Red Eve for her high spirit, and are friends to the de Cressis, an open-handed race who know how to bind folk to them. Listen how it must be done."

That day it was given out that Sir Edmund Acour, those of his knights who remained alive and all his following were about to leave for London and lay their cause before the King, having learned that Hugh de Cressi had gone thither to prejudice his Grace on his own behalf. It was added, moreover, that they would not return to Suffolk, but proposed when they had found justice or the promise of it, to take ship at Dover for France. Next morning, accordingly, they rode away from Blythburgh Manor and passed through Dunwich with much pomp, where the citizens of that town, who were friends of the de Cressis, stared at them with no kind eyes. Indeed, one of these as they crossed the market-place called to them to be careful not to meet Hugh de Cressi and Grey Dick upon their journey, lest there should be more midnight burials and men-at-arms turned into foot-soldiers, whereat all about him laughed rudely.

But Acour did not laugh. He ground his teeth and said into the ear of Nicholas:

"Register this vow for me, priest, that in payment for that jest I'll sack and burn Dunwich when our army comes, and give its men and children to the sword and its women to the soldiers."

"It shall be done, lord," answered the chaplain, "and should your heart soften at the appointed time I'll put you in memory of this solemn oath."

At the great house of the Mayor of Dunwich Sir Edmund drew rein and demanded to see him. Presently this Mayor, a timid, uncertain-looking man, came in his robes of office and asked anxiously what might be the cause of this message and why an armed band halted at his gate.

"For no ill purpose, sir," answered Acour, "though little of justice have I found at your hands, who, therefore, must seek it at the Court of my liege lord, King Edward. All I ask of you is that you will cause this letter to be delivered safely to the lady Eve Clavering, who lies in sanctuary at the Preceptory of St. Mary and St. John. It is one of farewell, since it seems that this lady who, by her own will and her father's, was my affianced, wishes to break troth, and I am not a man who needs an unwilling bride. I'd deliver it myself only that old knave, half priest and half knight, but neither good—"

"You'd best speak no ill of Sir Andrew Arnold here," said a voice in the crowd.

"Only the master of the Preceptory," went on Acour, changing his tone somewhat, "might take fright and think I wished to violate his sanctuary if I came there with thirty spears at my back."

"And no fool either," said the voice, "seeing that they are French spears and his is an English sanctuary."

"Therefore," continued Acour, "I pray you, deliver the letter.

Perchance when we meet again, Master Mayor," he added with a venomous glance of his dark eyes, "you will have some boon to ask of me, and be sure I'll grant it—if I can."

Then without waiting for an answer, for the mob of sturdy fishermen, many of whom had served in the French wars, looked threatening, he and his following rode away through the Ipswich gate and out on to the moorlands beyond, which some of them knew but too well.

All the rest of that day they rode slowly, but when night came, having halted their horses at a farm and given it out that they meant to push on to Woodbridge, they turned up a by-track on the lonely heath, and, unseen by any, made their through the darkness to a certain empty house in the marshes not far from Beccles town. This house, called Frog Hall, was part of Acour's estate, and because of the ague prevalent there in autumn, had been long unattended. Nor did any visit it at this season of the year, when no cattle grazed upon these salt marshes.

Here, then, he and his people lay hid, cursing their fortunes, since, notwithstanding the provisions that they had conveyed thither in secret, the place was icy cold in the bitter, easterly winds which tore over it from the sea. So lonely was it, also, that the Frenchmen swore that their comrades slain by Grey Dick haunted them at nights, bidding them prepare to join the number of the dead. Indeed, had not Acour vowed that he would hang the first man who attempted to desert, some of them would have left him to make the best of their way back to France. For always as they crouched by the smoking hearth they dreamed of Grey Dick and his terrible arrows.

Sir Edmund Acour's letter came safely into the hands of Eve, brought to her by the Mayor himself. It read thus:

Lady,

You will no more of me, so however much you should live to ask it, I will have no more of you. I go hang your merchant lout, and afterward away to France, who wish to have done with your cold Suffolk, where you may buy my lands cheap if you will. Yet, should Master Hugh de Cressi chance to escape me, I counsel you to marry him, for I can wish you no worse fate, seeing what you will be, than to remember what you might have been. Meanwhile it is my duty as a Christian to tell you, in case you should desire to speak to him ere it be too late, that your father lies at the point of death from a sickness brought on by his grief at the slaying of his son and your cruel desertion of him, and calls for you in his ravings. May God forgive you, as I try to do, all the evil that you have wrought, which, perhaps, is not done with yet. Unless Fate should bring us together again, for as aught I know it may, I bid you farewell forever. Would that I had never seen your face, but well are you named Red Eve, who, like the false Helen in a story you have never heard, were born to bring brave men to their deaths. Again farewell, De Noyon.

"Who is this Helen?" asked Eve of Sir Andrew when the letter had been read.

"A fair Grecian, daughter, over whom nations fought when the world was young, because of her beauty."

"Ah, well! she did not make herself beautiful, did she? and, perchance, was more sinned against than sinning, since women, having but one life to live, must follow their own hearts. But this Helen has been dead a long while, so let her rest, if rest she may. And now it seems that Acour is away and that my father lies very sick. What shall I do? Return to him?"

"First I will make sure that the Frenchman has gone, and then we will see, daughter."

So Sir Andrew sent out messengers who reported it to be true that Acour had ridden straight to London to see the King and then sail for Dover. Also they said that no Frenchmen were left at Blythburgh save those who would never leave the place again, and that Sir John Clavering lay sick in his bed at the manor.

"God fights for us!" said Sir Andrew with a little laugh. "This Acour's greeting at Court may be warmer than he thinks and at the least you and Dunwich are well rid of him. Though I had sooner that you stayed here, to-morrow, daughter, you shall ride to Blythburgh. Should your father die, as I think he will ere long, it might grieve you in the after years to remember that you had bid him no farewell. If he recovers or is harsh with you it will be easy for you to seek sanctuary again."

CHAPTER VII

THE LOVE PHILTRE

So it came about that on the morrow Eve and Sir Andrew, accompanied only by a single serving man, fearing no guile since it seemed certain that the Frenchmen were so far away, rode across the moor to Blythburgh. At the manor-house they found the drawbridge up. The watchman at the gate said also that his orders were to admit none, for the Frenchmen being gone, there were but few to guard the place.

"What, good fellow," asked Eve, "not even the daughter of the house who has heard that her father lies so sick?"

"Ay, he lies sick, lady," the man replied, "but such are his orders. Yet if you will bide here a while, I'll go and learn his mind."

So he went and returned presently, saying that Sir John commanded that his daughter was to be admitted, but that if Sir Andrew attempted to enter he should be driven back by force.

"Will you go in or will you return with me?" asked her companion of Eve.

"God's truth!" she answered, "am I one to run away from my father, however bad his humour? I'll go in and set my case before him, for after all he loves me in his own fashion and when he understands will, I think, relent."

"Your heart is your best guide, daughter, and it would be an ill task for me to stand between sire and child. Enter then, for I am sure that the Saints and your own innocence will protect you from all harm. At the worst you can come or send to me for help."

So they parted, and the bridge having been lowered, Eve walked boldly to her father's sleeping chamber, where she was told he lay. As she approached the door she met several of the household leaving it with scared faces, who scarcely stayed to salute her. Among these were two servants of her dead brother John, men whom she had never liked, and a woman, the wife of one of them, whom she liked least of all.

Pushing open the door, which was shut behind her, she advanced toward Sir John, who was not, as she had thought, in bed, but clad in a furred robe and standing by the hearth, on which burnt a fire. He watched her come, but said no word, and the look of him frightened her somewhat.

"Father," she said, "I heard that you were sick and alone—"

"Ay," he broke in, "sick, very sick here," and he laid his hand upon his heart, "where grief strikes a man. Alone, too, since you and your fellow have done my only son to death, murdered my guests, and caused them to depart from so bloody a house."

Now Eve, who had come expecting to find her father at the point of death and was prepared to plead with him, at these violent words took fire as was her nature.

"You know well that you speak what is not true," she said. "You and your Frenchmen strove to burn us out of Middle Marsh; my brother John struck Hugh de Cressi as though he were a dog and used words toward him that no knave would bear, let alone one better born than we are. Moreover, afterward once he spared his life, and Grey Dick, standing alone against a crowd, did but use his skill to save us. Is it murder, then to protect our honour and to save ourselves from death? And am I wrong to refuse to marry a fine French knave when I chance to love an honest man?"

"And, pray, am I your father, girl, that you dare to scold at me thus?" shouted Sir John, growing purple with wrath. "If I choose a husband for you, by what right do you refuse him, saying that you love a Dunwich shop-boy? Down on your knees and beg my pardon, or you shall have the whipping you have earned."

Now Eve's black eyes glittered dangerously.

"Ill would it go with any man who dared to lay a hand upon me," she said, drawing herself up and grasping the dagger in her girdle.

"Yes, very ill, even though he were my own father. Look at me and say am I one to threaten? Ay, and before you answer bear in mind that there are those at my call who can strike hard, and that among them I think you'll find the King of England."

She paused.

"What hellish plot is this that you hatch against me?" asked Sir John, with some note of doubt in his voice. "What have I to fear from my liege lord, the King of England?"

"Only, sir, that you consort with and would wed me to one who, although you may not know it, has, I am told, much to fear from him, so much that I wonder that he has ridden to seek his Grace's presence. Well, you are ill and I am angered and together we are but as steel and flint, from the meeting of which comes fire that may burn us both. Therefore, since being better than I thought, you need me not and have only cruel words for greeting, I'll bid you farewell and get me back to those who are kindlier. God be with you, and give you your health again."

"Ah!" said or rather snarled Sir John, "I thought as much and am ready for the trick. You'd win back to sanctuary, would you, and the company of that old wizard, Andrew Arnold, thence to make a mock of me? Well, not one step do you take upon that road while I live," and pushing past her he opened the door and shouted aloud.

Apparently the men and woman whom Eve had met in the passage were still waiting there, for instantly they all reappeared.

"Now, fellows," said Sir John, "and you, Jane Mell, take this rebellious girl of mine to the chamber in the prisoners' tower, whence I think she'll find it hard to fly to sanctuary. There lock her fast, feeding her with the bread and water of affliction to tame her proud spirit, and suffering none to go near her save this woman, Jane Mell. Stay, give me that bodkin which she wears lest she, who has learned bloody ways of late, should do some of you or herself a mischief."

As he spoke one of the men deftly snatched the dagger from Eve's girdle and handed it to Sir John who threw it into the farthest corner of the room. Then he turned and said:

"Now, girl, will you go, or must you be dragged?"

She raised her head slowly and looked him in the eyes. Mad as he was with passion there was something in her face that frightened him.

"Can you be my father?" she said in a strained, quiet voice. "Oh! glad am I that my mother did not live to see this hour."

Then she wheeled round and addressed the men.

"Hearken, fellows. He who lays a finger on me, dies. Soon or late assuredly he dies as he would not wish to die. Yes, even if you murder me, for I have friends who will learn the truth and pay back coin for coin with interest a hundredfold. Now I'll go. Stand clear, knaves, and pray to God that never again may Red Eve cross the threshold of her prison. Pray also that never again may you look on Hugh de Cressi's sword or hear Grey Dick's arrows sing, or face the curse of old Sir Andrew."

So proud and commanding was her mien and so terrible the import of her words, that these rough hinds shrank away from her and the woman hid her face in her hands. But Sir John thundered threats and oaths at them, so that slowly and unwillingly they ringed Eve round. Then with head held high she walked thence in the midst of them.

The prisoners' chamber beneath the leads of the lofty tower was cold and unfurnished save for a stool and a truckle-bed. It had a great door of oak locked and barred on the outer side, with a grille in it through which the poor wretch within could be observed. There was no window, only high up beneath the ceiling were slits like loopholes that not a child could have passed. Such was the place to which Eve was led.

Here they left her. At nightfall the door was opened and Jane Mell entered, bearing a loaf of bread and a jug of water, which she set down upon the floor.

"Would you aught else?" she asked.

"Ay, woman," answered Eve, "my thick red woollen cloak from my chamber, and hood to match. Also water to wash me, for this place is cold and foul, and I would die warm and clean."

"First I must get leave from my lord your father," said the woman in a surly voice.

"Get it then and be swift," said Eve, "or leave it ungotten; I care little."

Mell went and within half an hour returned with the garments, the water and some other things. Setting them down without a word she departed, locking and bolting the door behind her.

While there remained a few rays of light to see by, Eve ate and drank heartily, for she needed food. Then having prayed according to her custom, she laid herself down and slept as a child sleeps, for she was very strong of will and one who had always taught herself to make the best of evil fortune. When she woke the daws were cawing around the tower and the sun shone through the loopholes. She rose refreshed and ate the remainder of her bread, then combed her hair and dressed herself as best she could.

Two or three hours later the door was opened and her father entered. Glancing at him she saw that little sleep had visited him that night, for he looked old and very weary, so weary that she motioned to him to sit upon the stool. This he did, breathing heavily and muttering something about the steepness of the tower stairs. Presently he spoke.

"Eve," he said, "is your proud spirit broken yet?"

"No," she answered, "nor ever will be, living or dead! You may kill my body, but my spirit is me, and that you will never kill. As God gave it so I will return it to Him again."

He stared at her, with something of wonder and more of admiration in his look.

"Christ's truth," he said, "how proud I could be of you, if only you'd let me! I deem your courage comes from your mother, but she never had your shape and beauty. And now you are the only one left, and you hate me with all your proud heart, you, the heiress of the Claverings!"

"Whose estate is this," she answered, pointing to the bare stone walls. "Think you, my father, that such treatment as I have met with at your hands of late would breed love in the humblest heart? What devil drives you on to deal with me as you have done?"

"No devil, girl, but a desire for your own good, and," he added with a burst of truth, "for the greatness of my House after I am gone, which will be soon. For your old wizard spoke rightly when he said that I stand near to death."

"Will marrying me to a man I hate be for my good and make your House great? I tell you, sir, it would kill me and bring the Claverings to an end. Do you desire also that your broad lands should go to patch a spendthrift Frenchman's cloak? But what matters your desire seeing that I'll not do it, who love another man worth a score of him; one, too, who will sit higher than any Count of Noyon ever stood."

"Pish!" he said. "'Tis but a girl's whim. You speak folly, being young and headstrong. Now, to have done with all this mummer's talk, will you swear to me by our Saviour and on the welfare of your soul to break with Hugh de Cressi once and forever? For if so I'll let you free, to leave me if you will, and dwell where it pleases you."

She opened her lips to answer, but he held up his hand, saying:

"Wait ere you speak, I have not done. If you take my offer I'll not even press Sir Edmund Acour on you; that matter shall stand the chance of time and tide. Only while you live you must have no more to do with the man who slew your brother. Now will you swear?"

"Not I," she answered. "How can I who but a few days ago before God's altar and His priest vowed myself to this same Hugh de Cressi for all his life?"

Sir John rose from the stool and walked, or, rather, tottered to the door.

"Then stay here till you rot," he said quite quietly, "for I'll give you no burial. As for this Hugh, I would have spared him, but you have signed his death-warrant."

He was gone. The heavy door shut, the bars clanged into their sockets. Thus these two parted, for when they met once more no word passed between them; and although she knew not how these things would end, Eve felt that parting to be dreadful. Turning her face to the wall, for a while she wept, then, when the woman Mell came with her bread and water, wiped away her tears and faced her calmly. After all, she could have answered no otherwise; her soul was pure of sin, and, for the rest, God must rule it. At least she would die clean and honest.

That night she was wakened from her sleep by the clatter of horses' hoofs on the courtyard stones. She could hear no more because a wind blew that drowned all sound of voices. For a while a wild hope had filled her that Hugh had come, or perchance Sir Andrew, with the Dunwich folk, but presently she remembered that this was foolish, since these would never have been admitted within the moat. So sighing sadly she turned to rest again, thinking to herself that doubtless her father had called in some of his vassal tenants from the outlying lands to guard the manor in case it should be attacked.

Next morning the woman Jane Mell brought her better garments to wear, of her best indeed, and, though she wondered why they were sent, for the lack of anything else to do she arrayed herself in them, and braided her hair with the help of a silver mirror that was among the garments. A little later this woman appeared again, bearing not bread and water, but good food and a cup of wine. The food she ate with thankfulness, but the wine she would not drink, because she knew that it was French and had heard Acour praise it.

The morning wore away to noon, and again the door opened and there stood before her—Sir Edmund Acour himself, gallantly dressed, as she noticed vaguely, in close-fitting tunic of velvet, long shoes that turned up at the toes and a cap in which was set a single nodding plume. She rose from her stool and set her back against the wall with a prayer to God in her heart, but no word upon her lips, for she felt that her best refuge was silence. He drew the cap from his head, and began to speak.

"Lady," he said, "you will wonder to see me here after my letter to you, bidding you farewell, but you will remember that in this letter I wrote that Fate might bring us together again, and it has done so through no fault or wish of mine. The truth is that when I was near to London I heard that danger awaited me there on account of certain false accusations, such danger that I must return again to Suffolk and seek a ship at some eastern port. Well, I came here last night, and learned that you were back out of sanctuary and also that you had quarrelled with your father who in his anger had imprisoned you in this poor place. An ill deed, as I think, but in truth he is so distraught with grief and racked with sickness that he scarce knows what he does."

Now he paused, but as Eve made no answer went on:

"Pity for your lot, yes, and my love for you that eats my heart out, caused me to seek your father's leave to visit you and see if perchance I could not soften your wrath against me."

Again he paused and again there was no answer.

"Moreover," he added, "I have news for you which I fear you will think sad and which, believe me, I pray you, it pains me to give, though the man was my rival and my enemy. Hugh de Cressi, to whom you held yourself affianced, is dead."

She quivered a little at the words, but still made no answer, for her will was very strong.

"I had the story," he continued, "from two of his own men, whom we met flying back to Dunwich from London. It seems that messengers from your father reached the Court of the King before this Hugh, telling him of the slaying in Blythburgh Marsh. Then came Hugh himself, whereon the King seized him and his henchman, the archer, and at once put them on their trial as the murderers of John Clavering, of my knights, and Thomas of Kessland, which they admitted boldly. Thereon his Grace, who was beside himself with rage, said that in a time of war, when every man was needed to fight the French, he was determined by a signal example to put a stop to the shedding of blood in these private feuds. So he ordered the merchant to the block, and his henchman, the archer, to the gallows, giving them but one hour to make their peace with God. Moreover," he went on, searching her cold impassive face with his eyes, "I did not escape his wrath, for he gave command that I was to be seized wherever I might be found and cast into prison till I could be put upon my trial, and my knights with me. Of your father's case he is considering since his only son has been slain and he holds him in regard. Therefore it is that I am obliged to avoid London and take refuge here."

Still Eve remained silent, and in his heart Acour cursed her stubbornness.

"Lady," he proceeded, though with somewhat less assurance—for now he must leave lies and get to pleading, and never did a suit seem more hopeless, "these things being so through no fault of mine whose hands are innocent of any share in this young man's end, I come to pray of you, the sword of death having cut all your oaths, that you will have pity on my love and take me as your husband, as is your father's wish and my heart's desire. Let not your young life be swallowed up in grief, but make it joyous in my company. I can give you greatness, I can give you wealth, but most of all I can give you such tender adoration as never woman had before. Oh! sweet Eve, your answer," and he cast himself upon the ground before her, and, snatching the hem of her robe, pressed it to his lips.

Then at length Eve spoke in a voice that rang like steel:

"Get you gone, knave, whose spurs should be hacked from your heels by scullions. Get you gone, traitor and liar, for well I know that Hugh de Cressi is not dead, who had a certain tale to tell of you to the King of England. Get you back to the Duke of Normandy and there ask the price of your betrayal of your liege lord, Edward, and show him the plans of our eastern coast and the shores where his army may land in safety."

Acour sprang to his feet and his face went white as ashes. Thrice he strove to speak but could not. Then with a curse he turned and left the chamber.

"The hunt's up," said Father Nicholas when he had heard all this tale a little later, "and now, lord, I think that you had better away to France, unless you desire to stop without companions in the church yonder."

"Ay, priest, I'll away, but by God's blood, I'll take that Red Eve with me! For one thing she knows too much to leave her behind. For a second I mean to pay her back, and for a third, although you may think it strange, I'm mad for her. I tell you she looked wondrous standing with her back against that wall, her marble face never wincing when I told her all the lie about young de Cressi's death—which will be holy truth when I get a chance at him—watching me out of those great, dark eyes of hers."

"Doubtless, lord, but how did she look when she called you knave and traitor? I think you said those were her wicked words. Oh!" he added with a ring of earnestness in his smooth voice, "let this Red Eve be. At bed or board she's no mate for you. Something fights at her side, be it angel or devil, or just raw chance. At the least she'll prove your ruin unless you let her be."

"Then I'll be ruined, Nicholas, for I'll not leave her, for a while, at any rate. What! de Noyon, whom they call Danger of Dames, beaten by a country girl who has never seen London or Paris! I'd sooner die."

"As well may chance if the country lad and the country archer come back with Edward's warrant in their pouch," answered the priest, shrugging his lean shoulders. "Well, lord, what is your plan?"

"To carry her off. Can't we manage nine stone of womanhood between us?"

"If she were dead it might be done, though hardly—over these Suffolk roads. But being very much alive with a voice to scream with, hands to fight with, a brain to think with and friends who know her from here to Yarmouth, or to Hull, and Monsieur Grey Dick's arrows pricking us behind perchance—well, I don't know."

"Friend," said Acour, tapping him on the shoulder meaningly, "there must be some way; there are always ways, and I pray you to hunt them out. Come, find me one, or stay here alone to explain affairs, first to this Dick whom you have so much upon the brain, and afterward to Edward of England or his officers."

Father Nicholas looked at the great Count's face. Then he looked at the ground, and, having studied it a while without result, turned his beady eyes to the heavens, where it would seem that he found inspiration.

"I am a stranger to love, thank the Saints," he said, "but, as you know, lord, I am a master leech, and amongst other things have studied certain medicines which breed that passion in the human animal."

"Love philtres?" queried Acour doubtfully.

"Yes, that kind of thing. One dose, and those who hate become enamoured, and those who are enamoured hate."

"Then in God's or Satan's name, give her one. Only be careful it is the right sort, for if you made a mistake so that she hated me any more than she does at present, I know not what would happen. Also if you kill her I'll dig a sword point through you. How would the stuff work?"

"She'll seem somewhat stupid for a while, perhaps not speak, but only smile kindly. That will last twelve hours or so, plenty of time for you to be married, and afterward, when the grosser part of the potion passes off leaving only its divine essence, why, afterward she'll love you furiously."

"A powerful medicine, truly, that can change the nature of woman. Moreover, I'd rather that she loved me—well, as happy brides do. Still I put up with the fury provided it be of the good kind. And now how is it to be done?"

"Leave that to me, lord," said Nicholas, with a cunning smile. "Give me a purse of gold, not less than ten pieces, for some is needed to melt in the mixture, and more to bribe that woman and others. For the rest, hold yourself ready to become a husband before sunset to-morrow. Go see Sir John and tell him that the lady softens. Send men on to King's Lynn also to bid them have our ship prepared to sail the minute we appear, which with good fortune should be within forty-eight hours from now. Above all, forget not that I run great risk to soul and body for your sake and that there are abbeys vacant in Normandy. Now, farewell, I must to my work, for this medicine takes much skill such as no other leech has save myself. Ay, and much prayer also, that naught may hinder its powerful working."

"Prayer to the devil, I think," said his master looking after him with a shrug of his shoulders. "God's truth! if any one had told me three months gone that de Noyon would live to seek the aid of priests and potions to win a woman's favour, I'd have named him liar to his face. What would those who have gone before her think of this story, I wonder?"

Then with a bitter laugh he turned and went about his business, which was to lie to the father as he had lied to the daughter. Only in this second case he found one more willing to listen and easier to deceive.

On the following morning, as it chanced, Eve had no relish for the food that was brought to her, for confinement in that narrow place had robbed her of her appetite. Also she had suffered much from grievous fear and doubt, for whatever she might say to Acour, how could she be sure that his story was not true? How could she be sure that her lover did not, in fact, now lie dead at the headsman's hands? Such things often happened when kings were wroth and would not listen. Or perhaps Acour himself had found and murdered him, or hired others to do the deed. She did not know, and, imprisoned here without a friend, what means had she of coming at the truth? Oh! if only she could escape! If only she could speak with Sir Andrew for one brief minute, she, poor fool, who had walked into this trap of her own will.

She sent away the food and bade the woman Mell bring her milk, for that would be easy to swallow and give her sustenance. After some hours it came, Mell explaining that she had been obliged to send for it to the farmsteading, as none drank milk in the manor-house. Being thirsty, Eve took the pitcher and drained it to the last drop, then threw it down, saying that the vessel was foul and made the milk taste ill.

The woman did not answer, only smiled a little as she left the chamber, and Eve wondered why she smiled.

A while later she grew very sleepy, and, as it seemed to her, had strange dreams in her sleep. She dreamed of her childhood, when she and Hugh played together upon the Dunwich shore. She dreamed of her mother, and thought dimly that she was warning her of something. She heard voices about her and thought that they were calling her to be free. Yes, and followed them readily enough, or so it seemed in her dream, followed them out of that hateful prison, for the bolts clanged behind her, down stairs and into the courtyard, where the sun's light almost blinded her and the fresh air struck her hot brow like ice. Then there were more voices, and people moving to and fro and the drone of a priest praying and a touch upon her hand from which she shrank. And oh! she wished that dream were done, for it was long, long. It wearied her, and grasped her heart with a cold clutch of fear.

CHAPTER VIII

TOO LATE

It was past three o'clock on this same day when Eve had drunk the milk and some hours after she began to dream, that Hugh de Cressi and his men, safe and sound but weary, halted their tired horses at the door of the Preceptory of the Templars in Dunwich.

"Best go on to his worship the Mayor and serve the King's writ upon him, master," grumbled Grey Dick as they rode up Middlegate Street. "You wasted good time in a shooting bout at Windsor against my will, and now you'll waste more time in a talking match at Dunwich. And the sun grows low, and the Frenchmen may have heard and be on the wing, and who can see to lay a shaft at night?"

"Nay, man," answered Hugh testily, "first I must know how she fares."

"The lady Eve will fare neither better nor worse for your knowing about her, but one with whom you should talk may fare further, for doubtless his spies are out. But have your way and leave me to thank God that no woman ever found a chance to clog my leg, perhaps because I was not born an ass."

It is doubtful if Hugh heard these pungent and practical remarks, for ere Dick had finished speaking them, he was off his horse, and hammering at the Preceptory door. Some while passed before any answer came, for Sir Andrew was walking in the garden beyond the church, in no happy mind because of certain rumours that had reached him, and the old nun Agnes, spying armed men and not knowing who they were, was afraid to open. So it came about that fifteen minutes or more went by before at length Hugh and his godsire stood face to face.

"How is Eve and where? Why is she not with you, Father?" he burst out.

"One question at a time, son, for whose safe return I thank God. I know not how she is, and she is not with me because she is not here. She has returned to her father at Blythburgh."

"Why?" gasped Hugh. "You swore to keep her safe."

"Peace, and you shall learn," and as shortly as he could he told him.

"Is that all?" asked Hugh doubtfully, for he saw trouble in Sir Andrew's face.

"Not quite, son. Only to-day I have learned that Acour and his folk never went to London, and are back again at Blythburgh Manor."

"So much the better, Father, for now I have the King's warrant addressed to the Mayor and all his Grace's subject in Dunwich, to take these Frenchmen, living or dead."

"Ah! But I have learned also that her father holds Eve a prisoner, suffering her to speak with none, and—one lamb among those wolves— Oh! God! why didst Thou suffer my wisdom to fail me? Doubtless for some good purpose—where is my faith? Yet we must act. Hie, you there," he called to one of the men-at-arms, "go to Master de Cressi's house and bid him meet us by the market-cross mounted and armed, with all his sons and people. And, you, get out my horse. Mother Agnes, bring my armour, since I have no other squire! We'll go to the Mayor. Now, while I don my harness, tell me all that's passed, wasting no words."

Another half-hour almost had gone by before Hugh met his father, two of his brothers and some men riding into the market-place. They greeted in haste but thankfulness, and something of the tale was told while they passed on to the house of the Mayor, who, as they thought, had already been warned of their coming by messengers. But here disappointment awaited them, for this officer, a man of wealth and honour, was, as it chanced, absent on a visit to Norwich, whence it was said that he would not return for three full days.

"Now what shall we do?" asked Sir Andrew, his face falling. "It is certain that the burgesses of Dunwich will not draw sword in an unknown quarrel, except upon the direct order of their chief, for there is no time to collect them and publish the King's warrant. It would seem that we must wait till to-morrow and prepare tonight."

"Not I," answered Hugh. "The warrant is to me as well as to the Mayor. I'll leave it with his clerk, which is good delivery, and away to Blythburgh Manor on the instant with any who will follow me, or without them. Come, Dick, for night draws on and we've lost much time."

Now his father tried to dissuade him, but he would not listen, for the fear in his heart urged him forward. So the end of it was that the whole party of them—thirteen men in all, counting those that Master de Cressi brought, rode away across the heath to Blythburgh, though the horses of Hugh's party being very weary, not so fast as he could have wished.

Just as the sun sank they mounted the slope of the farther hill on the crest of which stood the manor-house backed by winds.

"The drawbridge is down, thanks be to God!" said Sir Andrew, "which shows that no attack is feared. I doubt me, son, we shall find Acour flown."

"That we shall know presently," answered Hugh.

"Now, dismount all and follow me."

They obeyed, though some of them who knew old Sir John's temper seemed not to like the business. Leaving two of their people with the horses, they crossed the bridge, thinking to themselves that the great house seemed strangely silent and deserted. Now they were in the outer court, on one side of which stood the chapel, and still there was no one to be seen. Dick tapped Hugh upon the shoulder, pointing to a window of this chapel that lay in the shadow, through which came a faint glimmering of light, as though tapers burned upon the altar.

"I think there's a burying yonder," he whispered, "at which all men gather."

Hugh blanched, for might it not be Eve whom they buried? But Sir Andrew, noting it, said:

"Nay, nay, Sir John was sick. Come, let us look."

The door of the chapel was open and they walked through it as quietly as they could, to find the place, which was not very large, filled with people. Of these they took no heed, for the last rays of the sunlight flowing through the western window, showed them a scene that held their eyes.

A priest stood before the lighted altar holding his hands in benediction over a pair who kneeled at its rail. One of these wore a red cloak down which her dark hair streamed. She leaned heavily against the rail, as a person might who is faint with sleep or with the ardour of her orisons. It was Red Eve, no other!

At her side, clad in gleaming mail, kneeled a knight. Close by Eve stood her father, looking at her with a troubled air, and behind the knight were other knights and men-at-arms. In the little nave were all the people of the manor and with them those that dwelt around, every one of them intently watching the pair before the altar.

The priest perceived them at first just as the last word of the blessing passed his lips.

"Why do armed strangers disturb God's house?" he asked in a warning voice.

The knight at the altar rails sprang up and turned round. Hugh saw that it was Acour, but even then he noted that the woman at his side, she who wore Eve's garment, never stirred from her knees.

Sir John Clavering glared down the chapel, and all the other people turned to look at them. Now Hugh and his company halted in the open space where the nave joined the chancel, and said, answering the priest:

"I come hither with my companions bearing the warrant of the King to seize Edmund Acour, Count de Noyon, and convey him to London, there to stand his trial on a charge of high treason toward his liege lord, Edward of England. Yield you, Sir Edmund Acour."

At these bold words the French knights and squires drew their swords and ringed themselves round their captain, whereon Hugh and his party also drew their swords.

"Stay," cried old Sir Andrew in his ringing voice. "Let no blood be shed in the holy house of God. You men of Suffolk, know that you harbour a foul traitor in your bosoms, one who plots to deliver you to the French. Lift no hand on his behalf, lest on you also should fall the vengeance of the King, who has issued his commands to all his officers and people, to seize Acour living or dead."

Now a silence fell upon the place, for none liked this talk of the King's warrant, and in the midst of it Hugh asked:

"Do you yield, Sir Edmund Acour, or must we and the burgesses of Dunwich who gather without seize you and your people?"

Acour turned and began to talk rapidly with the priest Nicholas, while the congregation stared at each other. Then Sir John Clavering, who all this while had been listening like a man in a dream, suddenly stepped forward.

"Hugh de Cressi," he said, "tell me, does the King's writ run against John Clavering?"

"Nay," answered Hugh, "I told his Grace that you were an honest man deceived by a knave."

"Then what do you, slayer of my son, in my house? Know that I have just married my daughter to this knight whom you name traitor, and that I here defend him to the last who is now my kin. Begone and seek elsewhere, or stay and die."

"How have you married her?" asked Hugh in a hollow voice. "Not of her own will, surely? Rise, Eve, and tell us the truth."

Eve stirred. Resting her hands upon the altar rails, slowly she raised herself to her feet and turned her white face toward him.

"Who spoke?" she said. "Was it Hugh that Acour swore is dead? Oh! where am I? Hugh, Hugh, what passes?"

"Your honour, it seems, Eve. They say you are married to this traitor."

"I married, and in this red robe! Why, that betokens blood, as blood there must be if I am wed to any man save you," and she laughed, a dreadful laugh.

"In the name of Christ," thundered old Sir Andrew, "tell me, John Clavering, what means this play? Yonder woman is no willing wife. She's drugged or mad. Man, have you doctored your own daughter?"

"Doctored my daughter? I! I! Were you not a priest I'd tear out your tongue for those words. She's married and of her own will. Else would she have stood silent at this altar?"

"It shall be inquired of later," Hugh answered coldly. "Now yield you, Sir Edmund Acour, the King's business comes first."

"Nay," shouted Clavering, springing forward and drawing his sword; "in my house my business comes first. Acour is my daughter's husband and so shall stay till death or Pope part them. Out of this, Hugh de Cressi, with all your accursed chapman tribe."

Hugh walked toward Acour, taking no heed. Then suddenly Sir John lifted his sword and smote with all his strength. The blow caught Hugh on the skull and down he fell, his mail clattering on the stones, and lay still. With a whine of rage, Grey Dick leapt at Clavering, drawing from his side the archer's axe he always wore. But old Sir Andrew caught and held him in his arms.

"Vengeance is God's, not ours," he said. "Look!"

As he spoke Sir John began to sway to and fro. He let fall his murdering sword, he pressed his hands upon his heart, he threw them high. Then suddenly his knees gave beneath him; he sank to the floor a huddled heap and sat there, resting against the altar rail over which his head hung backward, open mouthed and eyed.

The last light of the sky went out, only that of the tapers remained. Eve, awake at last, sent up shriek after shriek; Sir Andrew bending over the two fallen men, the murderer and the murdered, began to shrive them swiftly ere the last beat of life should have left their pulses. His father, brothers, and Grey Dick clustered round Hugh and lifted him. The fox-faced priest, Nicholas, whispered quick words into the ears of Acour and his knights. Acour nodded and took a step toward Eve, who just then fell swooning and was grasped by Grey Dick with his left hand, for in his right he still held the axe.

"No, no," hissed Nicholas, dragging Sir Edmund back, "life is more than any woman." Then some one overset the tapers, so that the place was plunged in gloom, and through it none saw Acour and his train creep out by the chancel door and hurry to their horses, which waited saddled in the inner yard.

The frightened congregation fled from the nave with white faces, each seeking his own place, or any other that was far from Blythburgh Manor. For did not their dead master's guilt cling to them, and would they not also be held guilty of the murder of the King's officer, and swing for it from the gallows? So it came about that when at last lights were brought Hugh's people found themselves alone.

"The Frenchmen have fled!" cried Grey Dick. "Follow me, men," and with most of them he ran out and began to search the manor, till at length they found a woman who told them that thirty minutes gone Acour and all his following had ridden through the back gates and vanished at full gallop into the darkness of the woods.

With these tidings, Dick returned to the chapel.

"Master de Cressi," said Sir Andrew when he had heard it, "back with some of your people to Dunwich and raise the burgesses, warning them that the King's wrath will be great if these traitors escape the land. Send swift messengers to all the ports; discover where Acour rides and follow him in force and if you come up with him, take him dead or living. Stop not to talk, man, begone! Nay, bide here, Richard, and those who rode with you to London, for Acour may return again and some must be left to guard the lady Eve and your master, quick or dead."

De Cressi, his two sons and servants went, and presently were riding for Dunwich faster than ever they rode before. But, as it proved, Acour was too swift for them. When at length a messenger galloped into Lynn, whither they learned that he had fled, it was to find that his ship, which awaited him with sails hoisted, had cleared the port three hours before, with a wind behind her which blew straight for Flanders.

"Ah!" said Grey Dick when he heard the news, "this is what comes of wasting arrows upon targets which should have been saved for traitors' hearts! With those three hours of daylight in hand we'd have ringed the rogues in or run them down. Well, the devil's will be done; he does but spare his own till a better day."

But when the King heard the news he was very wroth, not with Hugh de Cressi, but with the burgesses of Dunwich, whose Mayor, although he was blameless, lost his office over the matter. Nor was there any other chosen afterward in his place, as those who read the records of that ancient port may discover for themselves.

When Master de Cressi and his people were gone, having first searched the great manor-house and found none in it save a few serving-men and women, whom he swore to put to death if they disobeyed him, Grey Dick raised the drawbridge. Then, all being made safe, he set a watch upon the walls and saw that there was wood in the iron cradle on the topmost tower in case it should be needful to light the beacon and bring aid. But it was not, since the sun rose before any dared to draw near those walls, and then those that came proved to be friendly folk from Dunwich bearing the ill news that the Frenchmen were clean away.

About midnight the door of the chamber in which Sir Andrew knelt by a bed whereon lay Hugh de Cressi opened and the tall Eve entered, bearing a taper in her hand. For now her mind had returned to her and she knew all.

"Is he dead, Father?" she asked in a small, strange voice; then, still as any statue, awaited the answer that was more to her than life.

"Nay, daughter. Down on your knees and give thanks. God, by the skill I gained in Eastern lands, has stayed the flow of his life's blood, and I say that he will live."

Then he showed her how her father's sword had glanced from the short hood of chain-mail which he had given Hugh, stunning him, but leaving the skull unbroken. Biting into the neck below, it had severed the outer vein only. This he had tied with a thread of silk and burned with a hot iron, leaving a scar that Hugh bore to his death, but staunching the flow of blood.

"How know you that he will live?" asked Eve again, "seeing that he lies like one that is sped."

"I know it, daughter. Question me no more. As for his stillness, it is that which follows a heavy blow. Perhaps it may hold him fast many days, since certainly he will be sick for long. Yet fear nothing; he will live."

Now Eve uttered a great sigh. Her breast heaved and colour returned to her lips. She knelt down and gave thanks as the old priest-knight had bidden her. Then she rose, took his hand and kissed it.

"Yet one more question, Father," she said. "It is of myself. That knave drugged me. I drank milk, and, save some dreams, remember no more till I heard Hugh's voice calling. Now they tell me that I have stood at the altar with de Noyon, and that his priest read the mass of marriage over us, and—look! Oh! I never noted it till now—there is a ring upon my hand," and she cast it on the floor. "Tell me, Father, according to the Church's law is that man my—my husband?"

Sir Andrew's eloquent dark eyes, that ever shadowed forth the thoughts which passed within him, grew very troubled.

"I cannot tell you," he answered awkwardly after thinking a while. "This priest, Nicholas, though I hold him a foul villain, is doubtless still a priest, clothed with all the authority of our Lord Himself, since the unworthiness of the minister does not invalidate the sacrament. Were it otherwise, indeed, few would be well baptized or wed or shriven. Moreover, although I suspect that himself he mixed the draught, yet he may not have known that you were drugged, and you stood silent, and, it would appear, consenting. The ceremony, alas! was completed; I myself heard him give the benediction. Your father assisted thereat and gave you to the groom in the presence of a congregation. The drugging is a matter of surmise and evidence which may not be forthcoming, since you are the only witness, and where is the proof? I fear me, daughter, that according to the Church's law you are de Noyon's lawful wife—"

"The Church's law," she broke in; "how about God's law? There lies the only man to whom I owe a bond, and I'll die a hundred deaths before any other shall even touch my hand. Ay, if need be, I'll kill myself and reason out the case with St. Peter in the Gates."

"Hush! hush! speak not so madly. The knot that the Church ties it can unloose. This matter must to his Holiness the Pope; it shall be my business to lay it before him; yea, letters shall go to Avignon by the first safe hand. Moreover, it well may happen that God Himself will free you, by the sword of His servant Death. This lord of yours, if indeed he be your lord, is a foul traitor. The King of England seeks his life, and there is another who will seek it also ere very long," and he glanced at the senseless form of Hugh. "Fret not yourself overmuch, daughter. Be grateful rather that matters are no worse, and that you remain as you always were. Another hour and you might have been snatched away beyond our finding. What is not ended can still be mended. Now go, seek the rest you need, for I would not have two sick folk on my hands. Oh, seek it with a thankful heart, and forget not to pray for the soul of your erring father, for, after all he loved you and strove for your welfare according to his lights."

"It may be so," answered Eve, "and I'll pray for him, as is my duty. I'll pray also that I may never find such another friend as my father showed himself to me."

Then she bent for a moment over Hugh, stretching out her hands above him as though in blessing, and departed as silently as she had come.

Three days went by before Hugh found his mind again, and after that for two weeks he was so feeble that he must lie quite still and scarcely talk at all. Sir Andrew, who nursed him continually with the help of Grey Dick, who brought his master possets, bow on back and axe at side but never opened his grim mouth, told his patient that Eve was safe and sound, but that he must not see her until he grew strong again.

So Hugh strove to grow strong, and, nature helping him, not in vain. At length there came a day when he might rise from his bed, and sit on a bench in the pleasant spring sunshine by the open window. Walk he could not, however, not only on account of his weakness, but because of another hurt, now discovered for the first time, which in the end gave him more trouble than did the dreadful and dangerous blow of Clavering's sword. It seemed that when he had fallen suddenly beneath that murderous stroke all his muscles relaxed as though he were dead, and his left ankle bent up under him, wrenching its sinews in such a fashion that for the rest of his life he walked a little lame. Especially was this so in the spring season, though whether because he had received his hurt at that time or owing to the quality of the air none could ever tell him.

Yet on that happy day he thought little of these harms, who felt the life-blood running once more strongly through his veins and who awaited Eve's long-promised advent. At length she came, stately, kind and beautiful, for now her grief and terror had passed by, leaving her as she was before her woes fell upon her. She came, and in Sir Andrew's presence, for he would not leave them, the tale was told.

Hugh learned for the first time all the truth of her imprisonment and of her shameful drugging. He learned of the burying of Sir John Clavering and of her naming as sole heiress to his great estates. To these, however, Acour had not been ashamed to submit some shadowy claim, made "in right of his lawful wife, Dame Eve Acour, Countess de Noyon," which claim had been sent by him from France addressed to "all whom it might concern." He learned of the King's wrath at the escape of this same Acour, and of his Grace's seizure of that false knight's lands in Suffolk, which, however, proved to be so heavily mortgaged that no one would grow rich upon them.

Lastly he learned that King Edward, in a letter written by one of his secretaries to Sir Andrew Arnold and received only that morning, said that he held him, Hugh de Cressi, not to blame for Acour's escape. It commanded also that if he recovered from his wound, for the giving of which Sir John Clavering should have paid sharply if he had lived, he and the archer, his servant, should join him either in England or in France, whither he purposed shortly to proceed with all his host. But the Mayor and men of Dunwich he did not hold free of blame.

The letter added, moreover, that the King was advised that Edmund Acour on reaching Normandy had openly thrown off his allegiance to the crown of England and there was engaged in raising forces to make war upon him. Further, that this Acour alleged himself to be the lawfully married husband of Eve Clavering, the heiress of Sir John Clavering, a point upon which his Grace demanded information, since if this were true he purposed to escheat the Clavering lands. With this brief and stern announcement the letter ended.

"By God's mercy, Eve, tell me, are you this fellow's wife?" exclaimed Hugh.

"Not so," she answered. "Can a woman who is Dunwich born be wed without consent? And can a woman whose will is foully drugged out of her give consent to that which she hates? Why, if so there is no justice in the world."

"'Tis a rare jewel in these evil days, daughter," said Sir Andrew with a sigh. "Still fret not yourself son Hugh. A full statement of the case, drawn by skilled clerks and testified to by many witnesses, has gone forward already to his Holiness the Pope, of which statement true copies have been sent to the King and to the Bishops of Norwich and of Canterbury. Yet be warned that in such matters the law ecclesiastic moves but slowly, and then only when its wheels are greased with gold."

"Well," answered Hugh with a fierce laugh, "there remains another law which moves more swiftly and its wheels are greased with vengeance; the law of the sword. If you are married, Eve, I swear that before very long you shall be widowed or I dead. I'll not let de Noyon slip a second time even if he stands before the holiest altar in Christendom."

"I'd have killed him in the chapel yonder," muttered Grey Dick, who had entered with his master's food and not been sent away. "Only," he added looking reproachfully at Sir Andrew, "my hand was stayed by a certain holy priest's command to which, alack, I listened."

"And did well to listen, man, since otherwise by now you would be excommunicate."

"I could mock at that," said Dick sullenly, "who make confession in my own way, and do not wish to be married, and care not the worth of a horseshoe nail how and where I am buried, provided those I hate are buried first."

"Richard Archer, graceless wight that you are," said Sir Andrew, "I say you stand in danger of your soul."

"Ay, Father, and so the Frenchman, Acour, stood in danger of his body. But you saved it, so perhaps if there is need at the last, you will do as much for my soul. If not it must take its chance," and snatching at the dish-cover angrily, he turned and left the chamber.

"Well," commented Sir Andrew, shaking his head sadly, "if the fellow's heart is hard it is honest, so may he be forgiven who has something to forgive like the rest of us. Now hearken to me, son and daughter. Wrong, grievous and dreadful, has been done to you both. Yet, until death or the Church levels it, a wall that you may not climb stands between you, and when you meet it must be as friends—no more."

"Now I begin to wish that I had learned in Grey Dick's school," said Hugh. But whatever she thought, Eve set her lips and said nothing.

CHAPTER IX

CRECY FIELD

It was Saturday, the 26th of August, in the year 1346. The harassed English host—but a little host, after all, retreating for its life from Paris—had forced the passage of the Somme by the ford which a forgotten traitor, Gobin Agache by name, revealed to them. Now it stood at bay upon the plain of Crecy, there to conquer or to die.

"Will the French fight to-day, what think you?" asked Hugh of Grey Dick, who had just descended from an apple-tree which grew in the garden of a burnt-out cottage. Here he had been engaged on the twofold business of surveying the disposition of the English army and in gathering a pocketful of fruit which remained upon the tree's topmost boughs.

"I think that these are very good apples," answered Dick, speaking with his mouth full. "Eat while you get the chance, master, for, who knows, the next you set your teeth in may be of the kind that grew upon the Tree of Life in a very old garden," and he handed him two of the best. Then he turned to certain archers, who clustered round with outstretched hands, saying: "Why should I give you my apples, fellows, seeing that you were too lazy to climb and get them for yourselves? None of you ever gave me anything when I was hungry, after the sack of Caen, in which my master, being squeamish, would take no part. Therefore I went to bed supperless, because, as I remember you said, I had not earned it. Still, as I don't want to fight the French with a bellyache, go scramble for them."

Then, with a quick motion, he flung the apples to a distance, all save one, which he presented to a tall man who stood near, adding:

"Take this, Jack Green, in token of fellowship, since I have nothing else to offer you. I beat you at Windsor, didn't I, when we shot a match before the King? Now show your skill and beat me and I'll say 'thank you.' Keep count of your arrows shot, Jack, and I'll keep count of mine, and when the battle is over, he who has grassed most Frenchmen shall be called the better man."

"Then I'm that already, lad," answered the great yeoman with a grin as he set his teeth in the apple. "For, look you, having served at Court I've learned how to lie, and shall swear I never wasted shaft, whereas you, being country born, may own to a miss or two for shame's sake. Or, likelier still, those French will have one or both of us in their bag. If all tales are true, there is such a countless host of them that we few English shall not see the sky for arrows."

Dick shrugged his shoulders and was about to answer when suddenly a sound of shouting deep and glad rose from the serried companies upon their left. Then the voice of an officer was heard calling:

"Line! Line! The King comes!"

Another minute and over the crest of a little rise appeared Edward of England clad in full armour. He wore a surtout embroidered with the arms of England and France, but his helm hung at his saddle-bow that all might see his face. He was mounted, not on his war steed, but on a small, white, ambling palfrey, and in his hand he bore a short baton. With him came two marshalls, gaily dressed, and a slim young man clad from head to foot in plain black armour, and wearing a great ruby in his helm, whom all knew for Edward, Prince of Wales.

On he rode, acknowledging the cheering of his soldiers with smiles and courtly bows, till at length he pulled rein just in front of the triple line of archers, among whom were mingled some knights and men-at-arms, for the order of battle was not yet fully set. Just then, on the plain beneath, riding from out the shelter of some trees and, as they thought, beyond the reach of arrows, appeared four splendid French knights, and with them a few squires. There they halted, taking stock, it would seem, of the disposition of the English army.

"Who are those that wear such fine feathers?" asked the King.

"One is the Lord of Bazeilles," answered a marshall. "I can see the monk upon his crest, but the blazons of the others I cannot read. They spy upon us, Sire; may we sally out and take them?"

"Nay," answered Edward, "their horses are fresher than ours; let them go, for pray God we shall see them closer soon."

So the French knights, having stared their full, turned and rode away slowly. But one of their squires did otherwise. Dismounting from his horse, which he left with another squire to hold, he ran forward a few paces to the crest of a little knoll. Thence he made gestures of contempt and scorn toward the English army, as he did so shouting foul words, of which a few floated to them in the stillness.

"Now," said Edward, "if I had an archer who could reach that varlet, I'll swear that his name should not be forgotten in England. But alas! it may not be, for none cam make an arrow fly true so far."

Instantly Grey Dick stepped forward.

"Sire, may I try?" he asked, stringing his great black bow as he spoke.

"Who are you?" said the King, "who seem to have been rolled in ashes and wear my own gold arrow in your cap? Ah! I remember, the Suffolk man who showed us all how to shoot at Windsor, he who is called Grey Dick. Yes, try, Grey Dick, try, if you think that you can reach so far. Yet for the honour of St. George, man, do not miss, for all the host will see Fate riding on your shaft."

For one moment Dick hesitated. Such awful words seemed to shake even his iron nerve.

"I've seen you do as much, Dick," said the quiet voice of Hugh de Cressi behind him. "Still, judge you."

Then Dick ground his heels into the turf and laid his weight against the bow. While all men watched breathless, he drew it to an arc, he drew it till the string was level with his ear. He loosed, then, slewing round, straightened himself and stared down at the earth. As he said afterward, he feared to watch that arrow.

Away it sped while all men gazed. High, high it flew, the sunlight glinting on its polished barb. Down it came at length, and the King muttered "Short!" But while the word passed his lips that shaft seemed to recover itself, as though by magic, and again rushed on. He of the foul words and gestures saw it coming, and turned to fly. As he leapt forward the war arrow struck him full in the small of the back, just where the spine ends, severing it, so that he fell all of a heap like an ox beneath the axe, and lay a still and huddled shape.

From all the English right who saw this wondrous deed there went up such a shout that their comrades to the left and rear thought for a moment that battle had been joined. The King and the Prince stared amazed. Hugh flung his arms about Dick's neck, and kissed him. Jack Green cried:

"No archer, but a wizard! Mere man could not have sent a true shaft so far."

"Then would to heaven I had more such wizards," said the King. "God be with you, Grey Dick, for you have put new heart into my and all our company. Mark, each of you, that he smote him in the back, smote him running! What reward would you have, man?"

"None," answered Dick in a surly voice. "My reward is that, whatever happens, yon filthy French knave will never mock honest English folk again. Or so I think, though the arrow barely reached him. Yet, Sire," he added after a pause, "you might knight my master, Hugh de Cressi, if you will, since but for him I should have feared to risk that shot."

Then turning aside, Dick unstrung his bow, and, pulling the remains of the apple out of his pouch, began to munch it unconcernedly.

"Hugh de Cressi!" said the King. "Ah! yes, I mind me of him and of the rogue, Acour, and the maid, Red Eve. Well, Hugh, I am told you fought gallantly at Blanche-Tague two days gone and were among the last to cross the Somme. Also, we have other debts to pay you. Come hither, sir, and give me your sword."

"Your pardon, my liege," said Hugh, colouring, "but I'll not be knighted for my henchman's feats, or at all until I have done some of my own."

"Ah, well, Master Hugh," said the King, "that's a right spirit. After the battle, perhaps, if it should please God that we live to meet again in honour. De Cressi," he added musingly, "why this place is called Crecy, and here, I think, is another good omen. At Crecy shall de Cressi gain great honour for himself and for St. George of England. You are luck bringers, you two. Let them not be separated in the battle, lest the luck should leave them. See to it, if it please you, my lord of Warwick. Young de Cressi can draw a bow; let him fight amongst the archers and have liberty to join the men-at-arms when the time comes. Or stay; set them near my son the Prince, for there surely the fight will be hottest.

"And now, you men of England, whatever your degree, my brothers of England, gentle and simple, Philip rolls down upon us with all the might of France, our heritage which he has stolen, our heritage and yours. Well, well, show him to-day, or to-morrow, or whenever it may be, that Englishmen put not their faith in numbers, but in justice and their own great hearts. Oh, my brothers and my friends, let not Edward, whom you are pleased to serve as your lawful King, be whipped off the field of Crecy and out of France! Stand to your banners, stand to your King, stand to St. George and God! Die where you are if need be, as I will. Never threaten and then show your backs like that knave the archer shot but now. Look, I give my son into your keeping," and he pointed to the young Prince, who all this while sat upon his horse upright and silent. "The Hope of England shall be your leader, but if he flies, why then, cut him down, and fight without him. But he'll not fly and you'll not fly; no, you and he together will this day earn a name that shall be told of when the world is grey with age. Great is the chance that life has given you; pluck it, pluck it from the land of opportunity and, dead or living, become a song forever in the mouths of men unborn. Think not of prisoners; think not of ransoms and of wealth. Think not of me or of yourselves, but think of England's honour, and for that strike home, for England watches you to-day."

"We will, we will! Fear not, King, we will," shouted the host in answer.

With a glad smile, Edward took his young son's hand and shook it; then rode away followed by his marshals.

"De Cressi," he said, as he passed Hugh, "the knave Acour, your foe and mine, is with Philip of France. He has done me much damage, de Cressi, more than I can stop to tell. Avenge it if you can. Your luck is great, you may find the chance. God be with you and all. My lords, farewell. You have your orders. Son Edward, fare you well, also. Meet me again with honour, or never more."

It was not yet noon when King Edward spoke these words, and long hours were to go by before the battle joined. Indeed, most thought that no blow would be struck that day, since it was known that Philip had slept at Abbeville, whence for a great army the march was somewhat long. Still, when all was made ready, the English sat them down in their ranks, bows and helmets at side, ate their mid-day meal with appetite, and waited whatever fate might send them.

In obedience to the King's command Hugh and Grey Dick had been attached to the immediate person of the Prince of Wales, who had about him, besides his own knights, a small band of chosen archers and another band of men-at-arms picked for their strength and courage. These soldiers were all dismounted, since the order had gone forth that knight and squire must fight afoot, every horse having been sent to the rear, for that day the English expected to receive charges, not to make them. This, indeed, would have been impossible, seeing that all along their front the wild Welsh had laboured for hours digging pits into which horses might plunge and fall.

There then the Prince's battle sat, a small force after all, perhaps twelve hundred knights and men-at-arms, with three or four thousand archers, and to their rear, as many of the savage, knife-armed Welsh who fought that day under the banner of their country, the red Dragon of Merlin. Grey Dick's place was on the extreme left of the archer bodyguard, and Hugh's on the extreme right of that of the men-at-arms, so that they were but a few yards apart and could talk together. From time to time they spoke of sundry things, but mostly of home, for in this hour of danger through which both of them could hardly hope to live, even if one did, their thoughts turned thither, as was but natural.

"I wonder how it fares with the lady Eve," said Hugh, with a sigh, for of her no news had come to him since they had parted some months before, after he recovered from the wound which Clavering gave him.

"Well enough, doubtless. Why not?" replied Dick. "She is strong and healthy, she has many friends and servants to guard her and no enemy there to harm her, for her great foe is yonder," and he nodded towards Abbeville. "Oh, without doubt well enough. It is she who should wonder how it fares with us. Let us hope that, having naught else to do, she remembers us in her prayers, since in such a case even one woman's prayers are worth something, for does not a single feather sometimes turn the scale?"

"I think that Eve would rather fight than pray," answered Hugh, with a smile, "like old Sir Andrew, who would give half his remaining days to sit here with us this afternoon. Well, he is better where he is. Dick, that knave Acour sent only insolent words in answer to my challenge, which I despatched to him by the knight I took and spared at Caen."

"Why should he do more, master? He can find plenty of ways of dying without risking a single combat with one whom he has wronged and who is therefore very dangerous. You remember his crest, master— a silver swan painted on his shield. I knew it, and that is why I shot that poor fowl just before you killed young Clavering on the banks of Blythe, to teach him that swans are not proof against arrows. Watch for the swan crest, master, when the battle joins, and so will I, I promise you."

"Ay, I'll watch," said Hugh grimly. "God help all swans that come my way. Let us pray that this one has not taken wing, for if so I, too, must learn to fly."

Thus they talked of these and other things amongst the hum of the great camp, which was like to that of bees on a lime-tree in summer, and whilst they talked the blue August sky became suddenly overcast. Dense and heavy clouds hid up its face, a cold and fitful wind began to blow, increasing presently to a gale which caused the planted standards, blazoned with lions rampant and with fleurs-de-lis, and the pennons of a hundred knights set here and there among the long battle lines, first to flap and waver and then to stand out straight as though they were cut of iron.

A word of command was called from rank to rank.

"Sheath bows!" it said, and instantly thousands of slender points were lifted and sank again, vanishing into the leathern cases which the archers bore.

Scarcely were these snug when the storm broke. First fell a few heavy drops, to be followed by such a torrent that all who had cloaks were glad to wear them. From the black clouds above leapt lightnings that were succeeded by the deep and solemn roll of thunder. A darkness fell upon the field so great that men wondered what it might portend, for their minds were strained. That which at other times would have passed without remark, now became portentous. Indeed, afterward some declared that through it they had seen angels or demons in the air, and others that they had heard a voice prophesying woe and death, to whom they knew not.

"It is nothing but a harvest tempest," said Dick presently, as he shook the wet from him like a dog and looked to the covering of his quiver. "See, the clouds break."

As he spoke a single red ray from the westering sun shot through a rift in the sky and lay across the English host like a sword of light, whereof the point hung over the eastern plain. Save for this flaming sword all else was dark, and silent also, for the rain and thunder had died away. Only thousands of crows, frightened from the woods, wheeled to and fro above, their black wings turning to the redness of blood as they crossed and recrossed that splendid path of light, and their hoarse cries filling the solemn air with clamour. The sight and sounds were strange, nor did the thickest-headed fellow crouched upon Crecy's fateful plain ever forget them till his dying day.

The sky cleared by slow degrees, the multitudes of crows wheeled off toward the east and vanished, the sun shone out again in quiet glory.

"Pray God the French fight us to-day," said Hugh as he took off his cloak and rolled it up.

"Why, master?"

"Because, Dick, it is written that the rain falls on the just and the unjust; and the unjust, that is the French, or rather the Italians whom they hire, use these new-fangled cross-bows which as you know cannot be cased like ours, and therefore stretch their strings in wet."

"Master," remarked Dick, "I did not think you had so much wit—that is, since you fell in love, for before then you were sharp enough. Well, you are right, and a little matter like that may turn a battle. Not but what I had thought of it already."

Hugh was about to answer with spirit, when a sound of distant shouting broke upon their ears, a very mighty sound, and next instant some outposts were seen galloping in, calling: "Arm! Arm! The French! The French!"

Suddenly there appeared thousands of cross-bow men, in thick, wavering lines, and behind them the points of thousands of spears, whose bearers as yet were hidden by the living screen of the Italian archers. Yes, before them was the mighty host of France glittering in the splendid light of the westering sun, which shone full into their faces.

The irregular lines halted. Perhaps there was something in the aspect of those bands of Englishmen still seated in silence on the ground, with never a horse among them, that gave them pause. Then, as though at a word of command, the Genoese cross-bow men set up a terrific shout.

"Do they think to make us run at a noise, like hares?" said Hugh contemptuously.

But Grey Dick made no answer, for already his pale eyes were fixed upon the foe with a stare that Hugh thought was terrible, and his long fingers were playing with the button of his bow-case. The Genoese advanced a little way, then again stood and shouted, but still the English sat silent.

A third time they advanced and shouted more loudly than before, then began to wind up their cross-bows.

From somewhere in the English centre rose a heavy, thudding sound which was new to war. It came from the mouths of cannons now for the first time fired on a field of battle, and at the report of them the Genoese, frightened, fell back a little. Seeing that the balls fell short and did but hop toward them slowly, they took courage again and began to loose their bolts.

"You're right, master," exclaimed Grey Dick in a fierce chuckle, "their strings are wet," and he pointed to the quarrels that, like the cannon balls, struck short, some within fifty paces of those who shot them, so that no man was hurt.

Now came a swift command, and the English ranks rose to their feet, uncased their bows and strung them all as though with a single hand. A second command and every bow was bent. A third and with a noise that was half hiss and half moan, thousands of arrows leapt forward. Forward they leapt, and swift and terrible they fell among the ranks of the advancing Genoese. Yes, and ere ever one had found its billet, its quiver-mate was hastening on its path. Then—oh! the sunlight showed it all—the Genoese rolled over by scores, their frail armour bitten through and through by the grey English arrows. By scores that grew to hundreds, that grew till the poor, helpless men who were yet unhurt among them wailed out in their fear, and, after one short, hesitant moment, surged back upon the long lines of men-at-arms behind.

From these arose a great shout: "Trahison! Trahison! Tuez! Tuez!" Next instant the appalling sight was seen of the chivalry of France falling upon their friends, whose only crime was that their bow-strings were wet, and butchering them where they stood. So awful and unexpected was this spectacle that for a little while the English archers, all except Grey Dick and a few others cast in the same iron mould, ceased to ply their bows and watched amazed.

The long shafts began to fly again, raining alike upon the slaughterers and the slaughtered. A few minutes, five perhaps, and this terrible scene was over, for of the seven thousand Genoese but a tithe remained upon their feet, and the interminable French lines, clad in sparkling steel and waving lance and sword, charged down upon the little English band.

"Now for the feast!" screamed Grey Dick. "That was but a snack to sharp the appetite," and as he said the words a gorgeous knight died with his arrow through the heart.

It came, the charge came. Nothing could stop it. Down went man and horse, line upon line of them swept to death by the pitiless English arrows, but still more rushed on. They fell in the pits that had been dug; they died beneath the shafts and the hoofs of those that followed, but still they struggled on, shouting: "Philip and St. Denis!" and waving their golden banner, the Oriflamme of France.

The charge crept up as a reluctant, outworn wave creeps to a resisting rock. It foamed upon the rock. The archers ceased to shoot and drew their axes. The men-at-arms leapt forward. The battle had joined at last! Breast to breast they wrestled now. Hugh's sword was red, and red was Grey Dick's axe. Fight as they would, the English were borne back. The young Prince waved his arm, screaming something, and at that sight the English line checked its retreat, stood still, and next plunged forward with a roar of:

"England and the Prince!"

That assault was over. Backward rolled the ride of men, those who were left living. After them went the dark Welsh. Their commanders ordered them to stand; the Earl of Warwick ordered them to stand. The Prince himself ordered them to stand, running in front of them, only to be swept aside like a straw before a draught of wind. Out they broke, grinning and gnashing their teeth, great knives in their hands.

The red Dragon of Merlin which a giant bore led them on. It sank, it fell, it rose again. The giant was down, but another had it. They scrambled over the mass of dead and dying. They got among the living beyond. With eerie screams they houghed the horses and, when the riders fell, hacked open the lacings of their helms, and, unheeding of any cries for mercy, drove the great knives home. At length all were dead, and they returned again waving those red knives and singing some fierce chant in their unknown tongue.

The battle was not over yet. Fresh horses of Frenchmen gathered out of arrow range, and charged again under the banners of Blois, Alencon, Lorraine, and Flanders. Forward they swept, and with them came one who looked like a king, for he wore a crown upon his helm. The hawk-eyed Dick noted him, and that his bridle was bound to those of the knights who rode upon his either side. On them he rained shafts from his great black bow, for Grey Dick never shot without an aim, and after the battle one of his marked arrows was found fixed in the throat of the blind king of Bohemia.

This second charge could not be stayed. Step by step the English knights were beaten back; the line of archers was broken through; his guard formed round the Prince, Hugh among them. Heavy horses swept on to them. Beneath the hoofs of one of these Hugh was felled, but, stabbing it from below, caused the poor beast to leap aside. He gained his feet again. The Prince was down, a splendid knight—it was the Count of Flanders—who had sprung from his horse, stood over him, his sword point at his throat, and called on him to yield. Up ran Robert Fitzsimmon, the standard bearer, shouting:

"To the son of the King! To the son of the King!"

He struck down a knight with the pole of his standard. Hugh sprang like a wild-cat at Louis of Flanders, and drove his sword through his throat. Richard de Beaumont flung the great banner of Wales over the Prince, hiding him till more help came to beat back the foe. Then the Prince struggled from the ground, gasping:

"I thank you, friends," and once more the French retreated. The Welsh banner rose again and that danger was over.

The Earl of Warwick ran up. Hugh noted that his armour was covered with blood.

"John of Norwich," he cried to an aged knight, who stood leaning on his sword, "take one with you, away to the King and pray him for aid. The French gather again; we are outworn with blows; the young Prince is in danger of his life or liberty. Begone!"

Old John's eyes fell on Hugh.

"Come with me, you Suffolk man," he said, and away they went.

"Now what would you give," he gasped as they ran, "to be drinking a stoup of ale with me in my tower of Mettingham as you have done before this red day dawned? What would you give, young Hugh de Cressi?"

"Nothing at all," answered Hugh. "Rather would I die upon this field in glory than drink all the ale in Suffolk for a hundred years."

"Well said, young man," grunted John. "So do I think would I, though I have never longed for a quart of liquor more."

They came to a windmill and climbed its steep stairs. On the top stage, amid the corn sacks stood Edward of England looking through the window-places.

"Your business, Sir John?" he said, scarcely turning his head.

The old knight told it shortly.

"My son is not dead and is not wounded," replied the King, "and I have none to send to his aid. Bid him win his spurs; the day shall yet be his. Look," he added, pointing through the window-place, "our banners have not given back a spear's throw, and in front of them the field is paved with dead. I tell you the French break. Back, de Norwich! Back, de Cressi, and bid the Prince to charge!"

Some one thrust a cup of wine into Hugh's hand. He swallowed it, glancing at the wild scene below, and presently was running with Sir John toward the spot where they saw the Prince's banner flying. They came to Warwick and told him the King's answer.

"My father speaks well," said the Prince. "Let none share our glory this day! My lord, form up the lines, and when my banner is lifted thrice, give the word to charge. Linger not, the dark is near, and either France or England must go down ere night."

Forward rolled the French in their last desperate onset; horse and foot mingled together. Forward they rolled almost in silence, the arrows playing on their dense host, but not as they did at first, for many a quiver was empty. Once, twice, thrice the Prince's banner bowed and lifted, and as it rose for the third time there rang out a shout of:

"Charge for St. George and Edward!"

Then England, that all these long hours had stood still, suddenly hurled herself upon the foe. Hugh, leaping over a heap of dead and dying, saw in front of him a knight who wore a helmet shaped like a wolf's head and had a wolf painted upon his shield. The wolf knight charged at him as though he sought him alone. An arrow from behind— it was Grey Dick's—sank up to the feathers in the horse's neck, and down it came. The rider shook himself clear and began to fight. Hugh was beaten to his knee beneath a heavy blow that his helm turned. He rose unhurt and rushed at the knight, who, in avoiding his onset, caught his spur on the body of a dead man and fell backward.

Hugh leapt on to him, striving to thrust his sword up beneath his gorget and make an end of him.

"Grace!" said the knight in French, "I yield me."

"We take no prisoners," answered Hugh, as he thrust again.

"Pity, then," said the knight. "You are brave, would you butcher a fallen man? If you had tripped I would have spared you. Show mercy, some day your case may be mine and it will be repaid to you."

Hugh hesitated, although now the point of his sword was through the lacing of the gorget.

"For your lady's sake, pity," gasped the knight as he felt its point.

"You know by what name to conjure," said Hugh doubtfully. "Well, get you gone if you can, and pray for one Hugh de Cressi, for he gives you your life."

The knight seemed to start, then struggled to his feet, and, seizing a loose horse by the bridle, swung himself to the saddle and galloped off into the shadows.

"Master," croaked a voice into Hugh's ear, "I've seen the swan! Follow me. My arrows are all gone, or I'd have shot him."

"God's truth! show him to me," gasped Hugh, and away they leapt together.

Soon they had outrun even the slaughtering Welsh, and found themselves mingled with fugitives from the French army. But in the gathering twilight none seemed to take any note of them. Indeed every man was engaged in saving his own life and thought that this was the purpose of these two also. Some three hundred yards away certain French knights, mounted, often two upon one horse, or afoot, were flying from that awful field, striking out to the right in order to clear themselves of the cumbering horde of fugitives. One of these knights lagged behind, evidently because his horse was wounded. He turned to look back, and a last ray from the dying sun lit upon him.

"Look," said Dick; and Hugh saw that on the knight's shield was blazoned a white swan and that he wore upon his helmet a swan for a crest. The knight, who had not seen them, spurred his horse, but it would not or could not move. Then he called to his companions for help, but they took no heed. Finding himself alone, he dismounted, hastily examined the horse's wound, and, having unbuckled a cloak from his saddle, cast down his shield in order that he might run more lightly.

"Thanks to God, he is mine," muttered Hugh. "Touch him not, Dick, unless I fall, and then do you take up the quarrel till you fall."

So speaking he leapt upon the man out of the shadow of some thorns that grew there.

"Lift your shield and fight," said Hugh, advancing on him with raised sword. "I am Hugh de Cressi."

"Then, sir, I yield myself your prisoner," answered the knight, "seeing that you are two and I but one."

"Not so. I take no prisoners, who seek vengeance, not ransom, and least of all from you. My companion shall not touch you unless I fall. Swift now, the light dies, and I would kill you fighting."

The knight picked up his shield.

"I know you," he said. "I am not he you think."

"And I know you," answered Hugh. "Now, no words, of them there have been enough between us," and he smote at him.

For two minutes or more they fought, for the armour of both was good, and one was full of rage and the other of despair. There was little fine sword-play about this desperate duel; the light was too low for it. They struck and warded, that was all, while Grey Dick stood by and watched grimly. Some more fugitives came up, but seeing that blows passed, veered off to the left, for of blows they had known enough that day. The swan knight missed a great stroke, for Hugh leapt aside; then, as the Frenchman staggered forward, struck at him with all his strength. The heavy sword, grasped in both hands, for Hugh had thrown aside his shield, caught his foe where neck joins shoulder and sank through his mail deep into the flesh beneath. Down he went. It was finished.

"Unlace his helm, Dick," grasped Hugh. "I would see his face for the last time, and if he still lives—"

Dick obeyed, cutting the lashings of the helm.

"By the Saints!" he said presently in a startled voice, "if this be Sir Edmund Acour he has strangely changed."

"I am not Acour, lord of Noyon," said the dying man in a hollow voice. "Had you given me time I would have told you so."

"Then, in Christ's name, who are you?" asked Hugh, "that wear de Noyon's cognizance?"

"I am Pierre de la Roche, one of his knights. You have seen me in England. I was with him there, and you made me prisoner on Dunwich heath. He bade me change arms with him before the battle, promising me great reward, because he knew that if he were taken, Edward of England would hang him as a traitor, whereas me they might ransom. Also, he feared your vengeance."

"Well, of a truth, you have the reward," said Dick, looking at his ghastly wound.

"Where then is Acour?" gasped Hugh.

"I know not. He fled from the battle an hour ago with the King of France, but I who was doomed would not fly. Oh, that I could find a priest to shrive me!"

"Whither does he fly?" asked Hugh again.

"I know not. He said that if the battle went against us he would seek his castle in Italy, where Edward cannot reach him."

"What armour did he wear?" asked Dick.

"Mine, mine—a wolf upon his shield, a wolf's head for crest."

Hugh reeled as though an arrow had passed through him.

"The wolf knight, Acour!" he groaned. "And I spared his life."

"A very foolish deed, for which you now pay the price," said Dick, as though to himself.

"We met in the battle and he told me," said de la Roche, speaking very slowly, for he grew weak. "Yes, he told me and laughed. Truly we are Fate's fools, all of us," and he smiled a ghastly smile and died.

Hugh hid his face in his hands and sobbed in his helpless rage.

"The innocent slain," he said, "by me, and the guilty spared—by me. Oh, God! my cup is full. Take his arms, man, that one day I may show them to Acour, and let us be going ere we share this poor knight's fate. Ah! who could have guessed it was thus that I and Sir Pierre should meet and part again."

CHAPTER X

THE KING'S CHAMPION

Back over that fearful field, whereof the silence was broken only by the groans of the wounded and the dying, walked Hugh and Grey Dick. They came to the great rampart of dead men and horses that surrounded the English line, and climbed it as though it were a wall. On the further side bonfires had been lit to lighten the darkness, and by the flare of them they saw Edward of England embracing and blessing his son, the Black Prince, who, unhelmeted, bowed low before him in his bloodstained mail.

"Who were they besides, Sir Robert Fitzsimmon and Richard de Beaumont who helped you when you were down, my son?" asked the King.

The Prince looked about him.

"I know not, Sire. Many, but here is one of them," and he pointed to Hugh, who just then appeared within the circle of the firelight. "I think that he slew the Count Louis of Flanders."

"Ah!" said the King, "our young merchant of Dunwich—a gallant man. Kneel you down, merchant of Dunwich."

Hugh knelt, and the King, taking the red sword from his hand, struck him with it on the shoulder, saying:

"Rise, Sir Hugh de Cressi, for now I give you that boon which your deathfaced servant asked before the battle. You have served us, or rather England well, both of you. But whose armour is that the archer carries, Sir Hugh?"

"Sir Edmund Acour's, lord de Noyon, Sire, only, alack! another man was within the armour."

"Your meaning?" said the King briefly, and in few words Hugh told the tale.

"A strange story, Sir Hugh. It would seem that God fought against you in this matter. Also I am wroth; my orders were that none of my men should sally out, though I fear me that you are not the only one who has broken them, and for your great deeds I forgive you."

"Sire," said Hugh, dropping to his knee again, "a boon. This de Noyon, your enemy and mine, has cheated and mocked me. Grant to me and my servant, Richard the archer, permission to follow after him and be avenged upon him."

"What is this you ask, Sir Hugh? That you and your brave henchman should wander off into the depths of France, there to perish in a dungeon or be hanged like felons? Nay, nay, we need good men and have none to spare for private quarrels. As for this traitor, de Noyon, and his plot, that egg is broken ere it was hatched, and we fear him no more. You follow me, Sir Hugh, and your servant with you, whom we make a captain of our archers. Until Calais is taken, leave not our person for any cause, and ask no more such boons lest you lose our favour. Nay, we have no more words for you since many others seek them. Stand back, Sir Hugh! What say you, my lord of Warwick? Ay, it is a gruesome task, but let the Welshmen out, those wounded will be well rid of their pain, and Christ have mercy on their souls. Forget not when it is finished to gather all men that they may give thanks to God for His great mercies."

Well nigh a year had gone, for once again the sun shone in the brazen August heavens. Calais had fallen at last. Only that day six of her noblest citizens had come forth, bearing the keys of the fortress, clad in white shirts, with ropes about their necks, and been rescued from instant death at the hands of the headsman by the prayer of Queen Philippa.

In his tent sat Hugh de Cressi, who, after so much war and hardship, looked older than his years, perhaps because of a red scar across the forehead, which he had come by during the siege. With him was his father, Master de Cressi, who had sailed across from

Dunwich with a cargo of provisions, whereof, if the truth were known, he had made no small profit. For they were sold, every pound of them, before they left the ship's hold, though it is true the money remained to be collected.

"You say that Eve is well, my father?"

"Aye, well enough, son. Never saw I woman better or more beautiful, though she wears but a sad face. I asked her if she would not sail with me and visit you. But she answered: 'Nay, how can I who am another man's wife? Sir Hugh, your son, should have killed the wolf and let the poor swan go. When the wolf is dead, then, perchance, I will visit him. But, meanwhile, say to him that Red Eve's heart is where it always was, and that, like all Dunwich, she joys greatly in his fame and is honoured in his honour.' Moreover, to Grey Dick here, she sends many messages, and a present of wines and spiced foods for his stomach and of six score arrows made after his own pattern for his quiver."

"But for me no gift, father?" said Hugh.

"Nothing, son, save her love, which she said was enough. Also, in all this press of business and in my joy at finding you safe I had almost forgotten it, there is a letter from the holy Father, Sir Andrew. I have it somewhere in my pouch amid the bills of exchange," and he began to hunt through the parchments which he carried in a bag within his robe.

At length the letter was found. It ran thus:

> To Sir Hugh de Cressi, knight, my beloved godson:
> With what rejoicings I and another have heard of your knightly deeds through the letters that you have sent to us and from the mouths of wounded soldiers returned from the war, your honoured father will tell you. I thank God for them, and pray Him that this may find you unhurt and growing ever in glory.
>
> My son, I have no good news for you. The Pope at Avignon, having studied the matter, (if indeed it ever reached his own ears) writes by one of his secretaries to

say that he will not dissolve the alleged marriage between the Count of Noyon and the lady Eve of Clavering until the parties have appeared before him and set out their cause to his face. Therefore Eve cannot come to you, nor must you come to her while de Noyon lives, unless the mind of his Holiness can be changed. Should France become more quiet, so that English folk can travel there in safety, perchance Eve and I will journey to Avignon to lay her plaint before the Holy Father. But as yet this seems scarcely possible. Moreover, I trust that the traitor, Acour, may meet his end in this way or in that, and so save us the necessity. For, as you know, such cases take long to try, and the cost of them is great. Moreover, at the Court of Avignon the cause of one of our country must indeed be good just now when the other party to it is of the blood of France.

Soon I hope to write to you again, who at present have no more to say, save that notwithstanding my years I am well and strong, and would that I sat with you before the walls of Calais. God's blessing and mine be on you, and to Richard the archer, greetings. Dunwich has heard how he shot the foul-tongued Frenchman before the great battle closed, and the townsfolk lit a bonfire on the walls and feasted all the archers in his honour.

Andrew Arnold.

"I have found another letter," said Master de Cressi, when Hugh had finished reading, "which I remember Sir Andrew charged me to give to you also," and he handed him a paper addressed in a large, childish hand.

Hugh broke its silk eagerly, for he knew that writing.

"Hugh," it began simply, "Clement the Pope will not void my false marriage unless I appear before him, and this as yet I cannot do because of the French wars. Moreover, he sets the curse of the Church upon me and any man with whom I shall dare to re-marry until this be done. For myself I would defy the Church, but not for you or for children that might come to us. Moreover, the holy father, Sir Andrew, forbids it, saying that God will right all in His season and that we must not make Him wroth. Therefore, Hugh, lover you are, but husband you may not be while de Noyon lives or until the Pope gives his dispensation of divorce, which latter may be long in winning, for the knave de Noyon has been whispering in his ear. Hugh, this is my counsel: Get you to the King again and crave his leave to follow de Noyon, for if once you twain can come face to face I know well how the fray will end. Then, when he is dead, return to one who waits for you through this world and the next.

> "Hugh, I am proud of your great deeds. No longer can they mock you as 'the merchant's son,' Sir Hugh. God be with you, as are my prayers and love.
> "Eve Clavering."
> "I forgot to tell you that Sir Andrew is disturbed in heart. He looks into a crystal which he says he brought with him from the East, and swears he sees strange sights there, pictures of woe such as have not been since the beginning of the world. Of this woe he preaches to the folk of Dunwich, warning them of judgment to come, and they listen affrighted because they know him to be a holy man who has a gift from God. Yet he says that you and I, Eve, need fear nothing. May it be so, Hugh.—E."

Now when he had thought awhile and hidden up Eve's letter, Hugh turned to his father and asked him what were these sermons that Sir Andrew preached.

"I heard but one of them, son," answered Master de Cressi, "though there have been three. By the Holy Mother! it frightened me so much that I needed no more of that medicine. Nor, to tell truth, when I got home again could I remember all he said, save that it was of some frightful ill which comes upon the world from the East and will leave it desolate."

"And what think folk of such talk, father?"

"Indeed, son, they know not what to think. Most say that he is mad; others say that he is inspired of God. Yet others declare that he is a wizard and that his familiar brings him tidings from Cathay, where once he dwelt, or perchance, from hell itself. These went to the bishop, who summoned Sir Andrew and was closeted with him for three hours. Afterward he called in the complainers and bade them cease their scandal of wizardry, since he was sure that what the holy Father said came from above and not from below. He added that they would do well to mend their lives and prepare to render their account, as for his part he should also, since the air was thick with doom. Then he gave his benediction to the old knight and turned away weeping, and since that hour none talk of wizardry but all of judgment. Men in Dunwich who have quarrelled from boyhood, forgive each other and sing psalms instead of swearing oaths, and I have been paid debts that have been owing to me for years, all because of these sermons."

"An awesome tale, truly," said Hugh. "Yet like this bishop I believe that what Sir Andrew says will come to pass, for I know well that he is not as other men are."

That night, by special leave, Hugh waited on the King, and with him Grey Dick, who was ever his shadow.

"What is it now, Sir Hugh de Cressi?" asked Edward.

"Sire, after the great battle, nigh upon a year ago, you told me that I must serve you till Calais fell. I have served as best I could and Calais has fallen. Now I ask your leave to go seek my enemy—and yours—Sir Edmund Acour, Count de Noyon."

"Then you must go far, Sir Hugh, for I have tidings that this rogue who was not ashamed to wear another man's armour, and so save himself from your sword, is away to Italy this six months gone, where, as the Seigneur de Cattrina, he has estates near Venice. But tell me how things stand. Doubtless that Red Eve of yours—strangely enough I thought of her at Crecy when the sky grew so wondrous at nightfall—is at the bottom of them."

"That is so, Sire," and he told him all the tale.

"A strange case truly, Sir Hugh," said the King when he had heard it out. "I'll write to Clement for you both, but I doubt me whether you and your Eve will get justice from him, being English. England and Englishmen find little favour at Avignon just now, and mayhap Philip has already written on behalf of de Noyon. At the best His Holiness will shear you close and keep you waiting while he weighs the wool. No, Red Eve is right: this is a knot soonest severed by the sword. If you should find him, de Noyon could scarce refuse to meet you, for you shall fight him as the champion of our cause as well as of your own. He's at Venice, for our Envoy there reported it to me, trying to raise a fresh force of archers for the French.

"You have leave to go, Sir Hugh, who deserve much more, having served us well," went on the King. "We'll give you letters to Sir Geoffrey Carleon, who represents us there, and through him to the Doge. Farewell to you, Sir Hugh de Cressi, and to you, Captain Richard the Archer. When all this game is played, return and make report to us of your adventures, and of how de Noyon died. The Queen will love to hear the tale, and your nuptials and Red Eve's shall be celebrated at Westminster in our presence, for you have earned no less. Master Secretary, get your tools, I will dictate the letters. After they are signed to-morrow, see them into the hands of Sir Hugh, with others that I will give him for safe carriage, for alas I have creditors at Venice. Make out an open patent also to show that he and this captain travel as our messengers, charging all that do us service to forward them upon their journey."

Three days later Hugh and Grey Dick, in the character of royal messengers from the King of England to the Doge of Venice, took passage in a great vessel bound for Genoa with a cargo of wool and other goods. On board this ship before he sailed Hugh handed to his father letters for Eve and for Sir Andrew Arnold. Also he received from him money in plenty for his faring, and bills of exchange upon certain merchants of Italy, which would bring him more should it be needed.

Their parting was very sad, since the prophecies of Sir Andrew had taken no small hold upon Master de Cressi's mind.

"I fear me greatly, dear son," he said, "that we part to meet no more. Well, such is the lot of parents. They breed those children that heaven decrees to them; with toil and thought and fears they rear them up from infancy, learning to love them more than their own souls, for their sakes fighting a hard world. Then the sons go forth, north and south, and the daughters find husbands and joys and sorrows of their own, and both half forget them, as is nature's way. Last of all those parents die, as also is nature's way, and the half forgetfulness becomes whole as surely as the young moon grows to full. Well, well, this is a lesson that each generation must learn in turn, as you will know ere all is done. Although you are my youngest, I'll not shame to say I have loved you best of all, Hugh. Moreover, I've made such provision as I can for you, who have raised up the old name to honour, and who, as I hope, will once more blend the de Cressis and the Claverings, the foes of three generations, into a single House."

"Speak not so, father," answered Hugh, who was moved almost to tears. "Mayhap it is I who shall die, while you live on to a green old age. At least know that I am not forgetful of your love and kindness, seeing that after Eve you are dearer to me than any on the earth."

"Ay, ay, after Eve and Eve's children. Still you'll have a kind thought for me now and then, the old merchant who so often thwarted you when you were a wayward lad—for your own good, as he held. For what more can a father hope? But let us not weep before all these stranger men. Farewell, son Hugh, of whom I am so proud. Farewell, son Hugh," and he embraced him and went across the gangway, for the sailors were already singing their chanty at the anchor.

"I never had a father than I can mind," said Grey Dick aloud to himself, after his fashion, "yet now I wish I had, for I'd like to think on his last words when there was nothing else to do. It's an ugly world as I see it, but there's beauty in such love as this. The man for the maid and the maid for the man—pish! they want each other. But the father and the mother—they give all and take nothing. Oh, there's beauty in such love as this, so perhaps God made it. Only, then, how did He also make Crecy Field, and Calais siege, and my black bow, and me the death who draws it?"

The voyage to Genoa was very long, for at this season of the year the winds were light and for the most part contrary. At length, however, Hugh and Dick came there safe and sound. Having landed and bid farewell to the captain and crew of the ship, they waited on the head of a great trading house with which Master de Cressi had dealings.

This signor, who could speak French, gave them lodging and welcomed them well, both for the sake of Hugh's father and because they came as messengers from the King of England. On the morrow of their arrival he took them to a great lord in authority, who was called a Duke. This Duke, when he learned that one was a knight and the other a captain archer of the English army and that they both had fought at Crecy, where so many of his countrymen—the Genoese bowmen—had been slain, looked on them somewhat sourly.

Had he known all the part they played in that battle, in truth his welcome would have been rough. But Hugh, with the guile of the serpent, told him that the brave Genoese had been slain, not by the English arrows, for which even with their wet strings they were quite a match (here Dick, who was standing to one side grinned faintly and stroked the case of his black bow, as though to bid it keep its memories to itself), but by the cowardly French, their allies. Indeed Hugh's tale of that horrible and treacherous slaughter was so moving that the Duke burst into tears and swore that he would cut the throat of every Frenchman on whom he could lay hands.

After this he began to extol the merits of the cross-bow as against the long arm of the English, and Hugh agreed that there was much in what he said. But Grey Dick, who was no courtier, did not agree. Indeed, of a sudden he broke in, offering in his bad French to fight any cross-bow man in Genoa at six score yards, so that the Duke might learn which was the better weapon. But Hugh trod on his foot and explained that he meant something quite different, being no master of the French tongue. So that cloud passed by.

The end of it was that this Duke, or Doge, whose name they learned was Simon Boccanera, gave them safe conduct through all his dominion, with an order for relays of horses. Also he made use of

them to take a letter to the Doge of Venice, between which town and
Genoa, although they hated each other bitterly, there was at the
moment some kind of hollow truce. So having drunk a cup of wine
with him they bade him farewell.

Next morning the horses arrived, and with them two led beasts
to carry their baggage, in charge of a Genoese guide. So they departed
on their long ride of something over two hundred English miles,
which they hoped to cover in about a week. In fact, it took them ten
days, for the roads were very rough and the pack-beasts slow. Once,
too, after they had entered the territory of Venice, they were set on in
a defile by four thieves, and might have met their end had not Grey
Dick's eyes been so sharp. As it was he saw them coming, and, having
his bow at hand, for he did not like the look of the country or its
inhabitants, leaped to earth and shot two of them with as many arrows,
whereon the other two ran away. Before they went, however, they
shot also and killed a pack-beast, so that the Englishmen were obliged
to throw away some of their gear and go on with the one that remained.

At length, on the eleventh afternoon, they saw the lovely city of
Venice, sparkling like a cluster of jewels, set upon its many islands
amid the blue waters of the Adriatic. Having crossed some two miles
of open water by a ferry which plied for the convenience of travellers,
they entered the town through the western gate, and inquired as best
they could (for now they had no guide, the Genoese having left them
long before) for the house of Sir Geoffrey Carleon, the English Envoy.
For a long while they could make no one understand. Indeed, the
whole place seemed to be asleep, perhaps because of the dreadful heat,
which lay over it like a cloud and seemed to burn them to the very
bones.

Perplexed and outworn, at last Hugh produced a piece of gold
and held it before a number of men who were watching them idly,
again explaining in French that he wished to be led to the house of the
English ambassador. The sight of the money seemed to wake their
wits, for two or three of the fellows ran forward quarrelling with each
other, till one of them getting the mastery, seized Hugh's tired horse

by the bridle and dragged it down a side street to the banks of a broad canal.

Here he called something aloud, and presently two men appeared rowing a large, flat-bottomed punt from a dock where it was hidden. Into this boat the horses and pack-beast were driven, much against their will. Hugh and Dick having followed them, the three Italians began to punt them along the canal, which was bordered with tall houses. A mile or so farther on it entered another canal, where the houses were much finer and built in a style of which they had never seen the like, with beautiful and fantastic arches supported upon pillars.

At length to their great joy they came opposite to a house over the gateway of which, stirless in the still air, hung a flag whereon were blazoned the leopards of England. Here the boatmen, pulling in their poles, save one to which they made the punt fast in mid-stream, showed by their gestures that they desired to be paid. Hugh handed the piece of gold to the man who had led them to the boat, whereon he was seized with a fit of uncontrollable fury. He swore, he raved, he took the piece of gold and cast it down on the bilge-boards, he spat on it and his two companions did likewise.

"Surely they are mad," said Hugh.

"Mad or no, I like not the looks of them," answered Dick. "Have a care, they are drawing their knives," and as he spoke one of the rogues struck him in the face; while another strove to snatch away the pouch that hung at his side.

Now Grey Dick awoke, as it were. To the man who had tried to take his pouch he dealt such a buffet that he plunged into the canal. But him who had struck him he seized by the arm and twisted it till the knife fell from his hand. Then gripping his neck in an iron grasp he forced him downward and rubbed his nose backward and forward upon the rough edge of the boat, for the Italian was but as a child to him when he put out his strength.

In vain did his victim yell for mercy. He showed him none, till at length wearying of the game, he dealt him such a kick that he also flew over the thwarts to join his fellow-bully in the water.

Then seeing how it had gone with his companions who, sorely

damaged, swam to the farther side of the canal and vanished, the third man, he whom they had first met, sheathed his knife. With many bows and cringes he pulled up the pole and pushed the punt to the steps of the house over which the flag hung, where people were gathering, drawn by the clamour.

"Does Sir Geoffrey Carleon dwell here?" asked Hugh in a loud voice, whereon a gentleman with a pale face and a grizzled beard who appeared to be sick, for he was leaning on a staff, hobbled from out the porch, saying:

"Ay, ay, that is my name. Who are you that make this tumult at my gates? Another turbulent Englishman, I'll be bound."

"Ay, sir, an Englishman called Sir Hugh de Cressi, and his companion, Richard the Archer, whom these rogues have tried to rob and murder, messengers from his Grace King Edward."

Now Sir Geoffrey changed his tone.

"Your pardon if I spoke roughly, Sir Hugh, but we poor Envoys have to do with many rufflers from our own land. Enter, I pray you. My servants will see to your gear and horses. But first, what is the trouble between you and these fellows?"

Hugh told him briefly.

"Ah!" he said, "a common trick with foreigners. Well for you that night had not fallen, since otherwise they might have rowed you up some back waterway and there done you to death. The canals of Venice hide the traces of many such foul deeds. Mother of Heaven!" he added, "why, this boatman is none other than Giuseppe, the noted bravo," and he turned and in Italian bade his servants seize the man.

But Giuseppe had heard enough. Springing into the water he swam like a duck for the farther bank of the canal, and, gaining it, ran swiftly for some alley, where he vanished.

"He's gone," said Sir Geoffrey, "and as well hunt with a lantern for a rat in a sewer as for him. Well, we have his boat, which shall be sent to the magistrate with letters of complaint. Only, Sir Hugh, be careful to wear mail when you walk about at night, lest that villain and his mates should come to collect their fare with a stiletto. Now, enter and fear not for your goods. My folk are honest. God's name!

how fearful is this heat. None have known its like. Steward, give me your arm."

An hour later and Hugh, clad in fresh garments of sweet linen, bathed and shaved, sat at table in a great, cool room with Sir Geoffrey and his lady, a middle-aged and anxious-faced woman, while Grey Dick ate at a lower board with certain of the Envoy's household.

"I have read the letters which concern the business of his Grace the King," said Sir Geoffrey, who was toying languidly with some Southern fruits, for he would touch no meat. "They have to do with moneys that his Grace owes to great bankers of this city but does not yet find it convenient to discharge. I have seen their like before, and to-morrow must deal with them as best I may—no pleasant business, for these usurers grow urgent," and he sighed. "But," he added, "the King says that you, Sir Hugh de Cressi, whom he names his 'brave, trusty and most well beloved knight and companion in war,'" and he bowed courteously to Hugh, "have another business which he commands me to forward by every means in my power, and that without fail. What is this business, Sir Hugh?"

"It is set out, Sir Geoffrey, in a letter from his Grace to the Doge of Venice, which I am to ask you to deliver. Here it is. Be pleased to read it, it is open."

The Envoy took the letter and read it, lifting his eyebrows as he did so.

"By St. Mark,—he's the right saint to swear by in Venice"—he exclaimed when he had finished, "this is a strange affair. You have travelled hither to offer single combat to Edmund Acour, Count of Noyon and Seigneur of Cattrina. The Doge is urged by his friendship to the throne of England to bring about this combat to the death, seeing that de Noyon has broken his oath of homage, has plotted to overthrow King Edward, has fought against him and that therefore you are his Grace's champion as well as the avenger of certain private wrongs which you will explain. That's the letter. Well, I think the Doge will listen to it, because he scarce dare do otherwise who wishes no quarrel with our country just now when it is victorious. Also this de Noyon, whom we call Cattrina here, has allied himself with certain great men of the Republic, with whom he is connected by blood, who are secret enemies to the Doge. Through them he strives to stir up trouble between Venice and England, and to raise mercenaries to serve the flag of France, as did the Genoese, to their sorrow. Therefore I think that in the Doge you will find a friend. I think also that the matter, being brought forward with such authority, the Seigneur de Cattrina will scarcely care to refuse your challenge if you can show that you have good cause for quarrel against him, since in such affairs the Venetians are punctilious. But now tell me the tale that I may judge better."

So Hugh told him all.

"A strange story and a good cause," said Sir Geoffrey when he had done. "Only this Cattrina is dangerous. Had he known you came to Venice, mayhap you had never lived to reach my house. Go armed, young knight, especially after the sun sinks. I'll away to write to the Doge, setting out the heads of the matter and asking audience. The messenger shall leave ere I sleep, if sleep I may in this heat. Bide you here and talk with my lady, if it so pleases you, for I would show you my letter ere we bid good-night, and the thing is pressing. We must catch Cattrina before he gets wind of your presence in Venice."

CHAPTER XI

THE CHALLENGE

How long is it since you have seen England, Sir Hugh?" asked Dame Carleon languidly.

"Some eighteen months, lady, although in truth it seems more, for many things have happened to me in that time."

"Eighteen months only! Why, 'tis four long years since I looked upon the downs of Sussex, which are my home, the dear downs of Sussex, that I shall see never again."

"Why say you so, lady, who should have many years of life before you?"

"Because they are done, Sir Hugh. Oh, in my heart I feel that they are done. That should not grieve me, since my only child is buried in this glittering, southern city whereof I hate the sounds and sights that men call so beautiful. Yet I would that I might have been laid at last in the kind earth of Sussex where for generations my forbears have been borne to rest," and suddenly she began to weep.

"What ails you, lady? You are not well?"

"Oh, I know not. I think it is the heat or some presage of woe to come, not to me only, but to all men. Look, nature herself is sick," and she led him to the broad balcony of the chamber and pointed to long lines of curious mist which in the bright moonlight they could see creeping toward Venice from the ocean, although what wind there was appeared to be off land.

"Those fogs are unnatural," she went on. "At this season of the year there should be none, and these come, not from the lagoons, but up from the sea where no such vapours were ever known to rise. The physicians say that they foretell sickness, whereof terrible rumours have for some time past reached us from the East, though none know whether these be true or false."

"The East is a large place, where there is always sickness, lady, or so I have heard."

"Ay, ay, it is the home of Death, and I think that he travels to us thence. And not only I, not only I; half the folk in Venice think the same, though why, they cannot tell. Listen."

As she spoke, the sound of solemn chanting broke upon Hugh's ear. Nearer it grew, and nearer, till presently there emerged from a side street a procession of black monks who bore in front of them a crucifix of white ivory. Along the narrow margin which lay between the houses and the canal they marched, followed by a great multitude of silent people.

"It is a dirge for the dead that they sing," said Dame Carleon, "and yet they bury no man. Oh! months ago I would have escaped from this city, and we had leave to go. But then came orders from the King that we must bide here because of his creditors. So here we bide for good and all. Hush! I hear my husband coming; say nothing of my talk, it angers him. Rest you well, Sir Hugh."

"Truly that lady has a cheerful mind," grumbled Grey Dick, when she had gone, leaving them alone upon the balcony. "Ten minutes more of her and I think I should go hang myself, or squat upon these stones and howl at the moon like a dog or those whimpering friars."

Hugh made no answer, for he was thinking of his father's tale of the prophecies of Sir Andrew Arnold, and how they grew sad in Dunwich also. In truth, like Lady Carleon, he found it in his heart to wish that he too were clear of Venice, which he had reached with so much toil.

"Bah!" he said presently, "this place stinks foully. It puts me in mind of some woman, most beauteous indeed, but three days dead. Let us go in."

On the following morning, while they sat at breakfast, there came a messenger from the Doge of Venice, whose name Hugh learned was

Andrea Dandolo, bearing a letter sealed with a great seal. This letter, when opened, was found to be from some high officer. It stated that the Doge would hold a Court at noon, after which it was his pleasure to receive the English knight who came as a messenger from the mighty monarch, King Edward, and to talk with him on matters set out in the letter of Sir Geoffrey Carleon. The writing added that the Seigneur of Cattrina, who in France was known as the Count de Noyon and in England as Sir Edmund Acour, would be present at the Court and doubtless ready to answer all questions that might be put to him.

"Then at last we shall come face to face," said Hugh, with a fierce laugh.

"Yes, master," put in Dick, "but you've done that several times before and always ended back to back. Pray the Saints such may not be the finish of this meeting also."

Then he turned and went to clean his master's armour, for in this martial dress, notwithstanding the great heat, Hugh determined to appear before the Doge. It was good armour, not that, save for the sword, which Sir Arnold had given him, whereat the Court at Windsor had laughed as out of date, but mail of a newer fashion, some of it, from the bodies of knights who fell at Crecy, after which battle such wares had been cheap.

Still, Dick could have wished that it had been better for so fine an occasion, seeing that it was marked with many a battle dint and that right across the Cressi cognizance, which Hugh had painted on his shield after he was knighted—a golden star rising from an argent ocean—was a scar left by the battle-axe of a Calais man-at-arms. Moreover Hugh, or rather Dick, took with him other armour, namely, that of the knight, Sir Pierre de la Roche, whom Hugh had killed at Crecy thinking that he was Edmund Acour, whose mail Pierre wore.

For the rest, Dick clad himself in his uniform of a captain of archers of King Edward's guard, wearing a green tunic over his mail shirt, and a steel-lined cap from which rose a heron's plume, pinned thereto with his Grace's golden arrow.

All being ready they started in a painted barge, accompanied by

Sir Geoffrey Carleon, who wore his velvet robe of office, and grumbled at its weight and warmth. A row of some fifteen minutes along the great canal brought them to a splendid portal upon the mole, with marble steps. Hence they were conducted by guards across a courtyard, where stood many gaily dressed people who watched them curiously, especially Grey Dick, whose pale, sinister face caused them to make a certain sign with their fingers, to avert the evil eye, as Sir Geoffrey explained to them. Leaving this courtyard they went up more steps and along great corridors into the finest apartment that they had ever seen. It was a glitter of gold and marble, and rich with paintings.

Here on a kind of throne sat the Doge Dandolo, an imperial-looking man, magnificently attired. Guards stood like statues behind him, while in front, talking together and moving from place to place, were gathered all the great nobles of Venice, with their beauteous ladies. From time to time the Doge summoned one or other of these, who was called to him by a black-robed secretary. Advancing with bows the courtier talked to him a while, then was dismissed by a gracious motion of the hand.

As the Englishmen entered this hall a herald called their names thus from a written slip of paper:

"The Cavalier Geoffrey Carleon, Ambassador of England. The Cavalier Hugh de Cressi, Messenger from the King of England, and the Captain Richard Archer, his companion."

Now all talk was hushed and every eye turned to scan these strangers of whose business, it would seem, something was already known.

"A fine man," said one lady to another of Hugh, "but why does he come here in dinted armour?"

"Oh! he is English and the English are barbarians who like to be ready to cut some one's throat," answered her companion. "But Holy Jesus! look at the long fellow with the death's head who walks behind him, and carries his luggage in a sack. His face makes my back creep."

Fortunately neither Hugh nor Dick understood these and other such sayings which Sir Geoffrey repeated to them afterward and therefore walked on with their host unconcerned. Once, however, Grey Dick nudged his master and whispered in his ear:

"Be glad, our man is here. It is he who mocks us to those popinjays. Nay, turn not to look; you will see plenty of his sweet face presently."

Now they stood before the chair of state, from which the Doge rose, and advanced two steps to greet the Ambassador of England. When these courtesies were over Sir Geoffrey presented Hugh to him, to whom he bowed, and Dick, whose salute he acknowledged with a wave of his jewelled hand. Afterward they talked, all crowding round to listen, Sir Geoffrey himself, who spoke Italian well, acting as the interpreter.

"You come hither, Cavalier de Cressi," said the Doge, "on behalf of his royal Grace, King Edward, who speaks of you in his letter in terms of which any knight may well be proud. We understand that this captain with you is your companion," and he glanced curiously at Dick out of the corners of his dark eyes, adding, "If those are gifts which he bears in that leathern sack and the long case in his hand, let our servants relieve him of them."

"Let his servants leave me alone," growled Grey Dick when this was translated. "Say to this fine lord, Sir Knight, that the gifts in the sack are not for him, and that which the case scatters he would scarcely care to have."

Sir Geoffrey made some explanation in a low voice, and with a smile the Doge waved the matter by, then said:

"Will the noble cavalier be so good as to set out his business, unless it is for our private ear alone?"

Hugh answered that it was for the public ear of all Venice, and especially for that of the lord who was called Sir Edmund Acour in England, the Count de Noyon in France, and the Seigneur of Cattrina in Italy.

"Will you pleased to point out this lord to us," said the Doge, glancing at the gorgeous throng which was gathered behind them.

"I cannot, illustrious Doge," answered Hugh, "that is, with certainty. As it chances I have seen his face but twice—once in a marsh when I had other things to think of who must watch my enemy's sword, and once at eve in the corner of a dark chapel, where he had just gone through the rite of marriage with a lady whom he had drugged, which lady was my affianced wife. Often afterward I sought to see that face, especially in the great fray of Crecy, but failed, in a case which with your leave I will narrate to you."

Now when all that company understood the meaning of these outspoken words, they swayed to and fro and whispered like reeds in an evening wind. Presently above this whispering a soft yet penetrating voice was heard to say:

"If this English knight desires to study the poor face of Acour, de Noyon, and Cattrina, he who owns it is much honoured and prays your Excellency's leave to wait upon his pleasure."

So saying a tall and noble-looking man, who wore the badge of a white swan worked in pearls upon his rich tunic, stepped forward out of the ring of courtiers and bowed, first to the Doge and next to Hugh.

De Cressi looked at his handsome face with its quick dark eyes and little, square-cut, black beard, and answered:

"I thank you, Sir Edmund Acour, for I take it you are he. Now I shall never forget you again, for though a man may shift his armour he cannot change his countenance"—a saying at which de Noyon coloured a little and looked down uneasily.

"Cavalier de Cressi, he whom you seek is before you; we ourselves vouch for his identity," said the Doge. "Now be pleased to set out your case."

"My private case I thrust to one side," answered Hugh, Sir Geoffrey interpreting all the time, "for it is a matter between this Count, a certain lady and myself, and can wait. That which I have to lay before you, Illustrious, has to do with my master the King of England, as whose champion I am here to-day. I accuse this lord of the three names of black treachery to his august liege, Edward, all details of which treason I am prepared to furnish, and on behalf of that most puissant monarch I challenge him to single combat, as I am empowered and commissioned to do."

"Why should I fight the King of England's bravoes?" inquired

Acour in a languid voice of those who stood about him, a question at which they laughed.

"If the charge of treason is not sufficient," went on Hugh, "I'll add to it one of cowardice. At the battle of Crecy, as a man here will bear me witness," and he pointed to Dick, "I overcame in single combat a knight who wore upon his shield the cognizance of a wolf and on his helm a wolf's head, which were the arms of Sir Pierre de la Roche. At this knight's prayer I spared his life, for that day we took no prisoners, and let him go. Afterward I fought with another knight carrying the cognizance of a white swan, the arms of the Count de Noyon, and slew him in fair and single fight. But before he died he told me that he bore that armour by command of his lord, the Count de Noyon, and that the said Count fought that day in his mail because he feared the vengeance of the King of England and my own. Thus it came about that the Wolf who fought paid the price for the Swan who fled away, hid in the armour of his friend, whom he left to die for him."

There followed a great silence, for all those noble lords and ladies who thought little of treason, which to most of them was a very familiar thing, were not a little stirred by this tale of cowardice and false arms. The Doge said:

"Noble Cattrina, you have heard the story of the English knight. What do you answer to it?"

"Only that it is a lie, Illustrious, like everything else that he has told us," replied Acour with a shrug of his broad shoulders.

"You said that you had a witness, Cavalier de Cressi," said the Doge. "Where is he?"

"Here," answered Hugh. "Stand forward, Dick, and tell what you saw."

Dick obeyed, and in his low, rasping voice, with more detail than Hugh had given, set out the story of those two combats at Crecy, of the sparing of the wolf knight and the slaying of the swan knight.

"What say you now, noble Cattrina?" asked the Doge.

"I say that the man lies even better than his master," answered Acour coolly, and all the Court laughed.

"Illustrious," said Hugh, "doubtless you have some herald at your Court. I pray that he may fetch his book and tell us what are the arms of de Noyon and Cattrina, with all their colourings and details."

The Doge beckoned to an officer in a broidered tabard, who with bows, without needing to fetch any book, described the crest and arms of Cattrina in full particular. He added that, to his knowledge, these were borne by no other family or man in Italy, France, or England.

"Then you would know them if you saw them?" said Hugh.

"Certainly, cavalier. On it I stake my repute as a herald."

Now while all wondered what this talk might mean, the Doge and Acour most of any, although the latter grew uneasy, fearing he knew not what, Hugh whispered to Dick. Then Dick loosed the mouth of the leather sack he carried, and out of it tumbled on to the marble floor a whole suit of blood-stained armour.

"Whence came these?" asked Hugh of Dick.

"Off the body of the night, Sir Pierre de la Roche, whom you slew at Crecy. I stripped him of them myself."

"Whose crest and cognizance are these, herald?" asked Hugh again, lifting the helm and shield and holding them on high that all might see.

The herald stepped forward and examined them.

"Without doubt," he said slowly, "they are those of the lord of Cattrina. Moreover," he added, "five years ago I limned yonder swan upon this very shield with my own hand. I did it as a favour to Cattrina there, who said that he would trust the task to none but an artist."

Now the silence grew intense, so much so that the rustle of a lady's dress sounded loud in the great hall.

"What say you now, my lord of Cattrina?" asked the Doge.

"I say that there is some mistake, Illustrious. Even if there were none," he added slowly, "for their own good and lawful purposes knights have changed armour before to-day."

"There is no mistake!" cried Hugh in a ringing voice. "This signor of so many names is a signor of many coats also, which he can change to save his skin. He wore that of Sir Pierre de la Roche to protect himself from the vengeance of the King of England and of the English squire whom he had wronged. He took mercy from the hand of that squire, who, as he knew well, would have shown him none had he guessed the truth. He left the poor knight, whom he had bribed to be his double, to die beneath that same squire's hand who thought him named de Noyon. Therefore the blood of this de la Roche is on his head. Yet these are small matters of private conduct, and one that is greater overtops them. This false lord, as Sir Edmund Acour, swore fealty to Edward of England. Yet while he was bound by that sacred oath he plotted to depose Edward and to set up on his throne the Duke of Normandy.

"The King of England learned of that plot through me, and gave me charge to kill or capture the traitor. But when we came face to face in a consecrated church where I thought it sacrilege to draw sword, he, who had just done me bitter wrong, stayed not to answer the wrong. He slunk away into the darkness, leaving me felled by a treacherous blow. Thence he fled to France and stirred up war against his liege lord under the Oriflamme of King Philip. Now that this banner is in the dust he has fled again to Venice, and here, as I have heard, broods more mischief. Once, when after the sack of Caen I sent him my challenge, he returned to me an insolent answer that he did not fight with merchants' sons—he who could take mercy from the hand of a merchant's son.

"Now that for deeds done a King has made me knight, and now that this King under his seal and sign has named me his champion, in your presence, Illustrious, and in that of all your Court, I challenge Cattrina again to single combat to the death with lance and sword and dagger. Yes, and I name him coward and scullion if he refuses this, King Edward's gage and mine," and drawing the gauntlet from his left hand, Hugh cast it clattering to the marble floor at de Noyon's feet.

A babel of talk broke out in the great hall, and with it some vivas and clapping of hands, for Hugh had spoken boldly and well; moreover, the spectators read truth in his grey eyes. A dark figure in priest's robe—it was that of Father Nicholas, the secretary who had brewed

Red Eve's potion—glided up to Cattrina and whispered swiftly in his ear. Then the Doge lifted his hand and there was silence.

"My lord of Cattrina," he said, "Sir Hugh de Cressi, speaking as the champion of our ally, the King of England, has challenged you to single combat à outrance. What say you?"

"I, Illustrious?" he answered in his rich voice, drawling out his words like one who is weary. "Oh, of course, I say that if yon brawler wishes to find a grave in fair Venice, which is more than he deserves, I am not the man to thwart him, seeing that his cut-throat King—"

"As the ambassador of that King I protest," broke in Sir Geoffrey. "It is an insult that such a word should be used before me."

"I accept the protest of his Excellency, who forgot his noble presence," replied Cattrina bowing back. "Seeing that his King, who is not a cut-throat"—here a titter of laughter went through the company, though it was evident from the frown upon his face that the Doge liked the jest ill—"has chosen to make a knight of this de Cressi. Or so he says, which will show you, friends all, how hard it must be to find gentlemen in England."

Again the company tittered, though Dick's grey face turned scarlet and he bit upon his pale lip until the blood ran.

"As you accept the challenge," broke in the Doge shortly, "cease from gibes, my lord, which more befit an angry woman's mouth than that of one whose life is about to be put to hazard, and take up the gage of his Grace of England."

Cattrina looked round and bade a page who waited on his person obey the Doge's command, saying:

"Your pardon, most Illustrious, if I do not touch that glove myself, as it seems somewhat foul. I think it must have served its owner in his useful labours at the dyer's vat before his master made him noble."

Now it was Hugh's turn to colour, but when he understood the insult Grey Dick could contain himself no more.

"Ay, Sir Cheat and Traitor," he said in his hissing voice. "The vat in which it has been dipped was that of the life-blood of your dupe, Sir Pierre de la Roche, and of many a nobler Norman. Oh, did we not stand where we do I'd thrust it down your false throat, and with it twist out your slanderous tongue."

"Peace, peace!" cried the Doge, while those present who understood English translated Dick's wild words to their neighbours, and Cattrina laughed mockingly at the success of his sneer. "Have I not said that such words are unseemly? Ah! I thought it; well, my lord, you have brought it on yourself."

For while he spoke, the page, a mincing young man tied up with bows and ribbon like a woman, had lifted the glove. Holding it between his thumb and forefinger, he returned it to Hugh with a low, mock bow, being careful as he did so, as all might see, to tread upon Dick's foot and hustle him. Next moment two things happened. The first was that, dropping his cased bow, Grey Dick seized that young in his iron grip and hurled him into the air so that he fell heavily on the marble floor and lay there stunned, the blood running from his nose and mouth. The second was that, seizing his gauntlet, Hugh strode to where Cattrina stood, and struck him with it across the face, saying:

"Let your lips kiss what your fingers are too fine to touch."

With an oath Cattrina drew his sword and out flashed Hugh's in answer, as he cried:

"Ay, here and now if you will! Here and now!"

Then the Guard rushed in and forced them apart.

"Is this a place for brawling?" cried Dandolo in wrath, adding: "Yet I cannot blame the Englishmen overmuch, seeing that they were sore affronted, as I saw with my eyes and heard with my ears. Be silent, my lord of Cattrina. After your fashion you make trouble at my Court. And—hearken all—blood so hot had best be quickly cooled lest one or other of these knights should take a fever. Moreover, the noble Cattrina has but to-day asked my leave to ride from Venice to-morrow, having urgent business at Avignon at the Court of Pope Clement. So I decree that this combat à outrance shall take place in our presence on the Campo del Marte to-morrow, three hours before noon, ere the sun grows too hot. To all the details of the combat our heralds will attend forthwith. Officer, take soldiers and escort the Ambassador and the Champion of his Grace of England, together with this Captain of Archers, back to their own door. Set guards there and see that none molest them by word or deed under pain of fine and strait imprisonment. Sir Geoffrey Carleon, your requests are granted; be pleased to write it to the most puissant Edward, whom you serve, and for this time fare you well. Why, what is it, Captain Ambrosio?" he added irritably, addressing a raw-boned, lantern-jawed giant of a man clad in the splendid uniform of the Guard who stepped before his throne and saluted.

"Most Illustrious," said Ambrosio, in bad, guttural Italian, "my mother was a Swiss."

"Then congratulations to the Swiss, Ambrosio, but what of it?"

"Very Illustrious," replied the captain in his hollow voice, "the Swiss are brave and do not swallow insults. That lad whom the Englishman kicked, or smote, or tossed like a bull," and he pointed to the poor page, who, still senseless, was being carried from the hall, "is my youngest brother, who resembles our Venetian father somewhat more than I do."

"We see it, we see it. Indeed are you sure that the father was—" and the Doge checked himself. "The point, captain; we would dine."

"Illustrious, I would avenge my brother and myself on the Englishman, whom I will beat to a jelly," said the giant. "I crave leave to fight him to-morrow when the lord Cattrina fights his master," and advancing toward Grey Dick he made as though he would pull his nose.

"What is it he wants?" asked Grey Dick, staring up at the great fellow with a look in his eyes that caused Ambrosio to cease flourishing his fists.

The challenge was translated to him, and its reason. "Oh," said Dick, "tell him I am much obliged and that I will fight him with the bow or with the axe and dagger, or with all three. Then we will see whether he beats me to a jelly, or whether I cut him into collops, who, as I think, needs shortening."

Now the Captain Ambrosio consulted with his friends, who with much earnestness prayed him have nothing to do with arrows. They pointed out that there his bulk would put him at a disadvantage, especially in dealing with an English archer who had an eye like a snake and a face like that of death itself.

In short, one and all they recommended the battle-axe and the dagger as his most appropriate weapons—since his adversary refused swords. The battle-axe with which to knock him down, as he could easily do, being so strong, and the dagger with which to finish him.

When this was explained to Grey Dick he assented to the proposal with a kind of unholy joy that was almost alarming to those who saw it. Moreover, as neither of them had gauntlets to throw down or pick up, he stretched out his hand to seal the bargain, which, incautiously enough, the huge, half-breed Swiss accepted.

Dick's grasp, indeed, was so firm and long that presently the giant was observed first to move uneasily, secondly to begin to dance and thirdly to shout out with pain.

"What is the matter?" asked his friends.

"The matter is," he groaned, as Dick let go, "that this son of Satan has a blacksmith's vise in place of a hand," and he showed his great fingers, from beneath the nails of which the blood was oozing.

His Venetian companions of the Guard looked at them, then they looked at Grey Dick and gave him a wide berth. Also Ambrosio said something about having offered to fight a man and not a fiend. But it was too late to retract, for the Doge, taking, as was natural, no share in this small matter, had already left his throne.

Then, escorted by Sir Geoffrey and the city Guards, Hugh and Grey Dick passed through that splendid company away home to dinner, Dick carrying his bow-case in one hand and the sack of armour which de Noyon had not thought fit to claim in the other.

In the midst of dead silence, they departed, for now no one seemed to find either of them a fit subject for jest. Indeed there were some who said, as they watched the pair pass the door, that Cattrina and the giant would do well to consult a lawyer and a priest that night.

CHAPTER XII

THE MAN FROM THE EAST

In a great, cool room of his splendid Venetian palace, Sir Edmund Acour, Seigneur of Cattrina sat in consultation with the priest Nicholas. Clearly he was ill at ease; his face and his quick, impatient movements showed it.

"You arrange badly," he said in a voice quite devoid of its ordinary melodious tones. "Everything goes wrong. How is it you did not know that this accursed Englishman and his Death's-head were coming here? What is the use of a spy who never spies? Man, they should have been met upon the road, for who can be held answerable for what brigands do? Or, at the least, I might have started for Avignon two days earlier."

"Am I omnipotent, lord, that I should be held able to read the minds of men in far countries and to follow their footsteps?" asked the aggrieved Nicholas. "Still it might have been guessed that this bulldog of a Briton would hang to your heels till you kick out his brains or he pulls you down. Bah! the sight of that archer, who cannot miss, always gives me a cold pain in the stomach, as though an arrow-point were working through my vitals. I pity yonder poor fool of a Swiss to-morrow, for what chance has he against a fish-eyed wizard?"

"Ten thousand curses on the Swiss!" said Acour. "He thrust himself into the affair and will deserve all he gets. I pity myself. You know I am no coward, as not a few have learned before to-day, but I have little luck against this Englishman. I tell you that there at Crecy I went down before him like a ninepin, and he spared my life. My God! he spared my life, being a fool like all his breed. And now the tale is known against me and that of the changed armour, too. Why could not de la Roche die without speaking, the faithless hound whom I had fed so well! So, so, regrets are vain; de Cressi is here, and must be faced or I be shamed."

"You may be killed as well as shamed," Nicholas suggested unpleasantly. "It is certain that either you or that Englishman will die to-morrow, since he's set for no fancy tilting with waving of ladies' kerchiefs and tinsel crowns of victory, and so forth. Merchant bred or not, he is a sturdy fighter, as we all learned in France. Moreover, his heart is full with wrong, and the man whose quarrel is just is always to be feared."

"A pest on you!" snarled Cattrina. "Have you the evil eye that you then croak disaster in my ears? Look you, priest, I must come through this game unharmed. Death is a companion I do not seek just yet, who have too much to live for—power and wealth and high renown, if my plans succeed; and as you should know, they are well laid. Moreover, there is that English girl, Red Eve, my wife, from whose sweet side you made me flee. I tell you, Nicholas, I burn for her and had rather taste her hate than the love of any other woman on the earth. Now, too, the Pope has summoned me to Avignon, and her also, to lay our causes before him. Being bold, mayhap she will come, for his Holiness has sent her safe-conduct under his own hand. Nor has he mentioned—for I saw a copy of the brief—that the same business will take me to Avignon about this time. Well, if she comes she will not go away again alone; the French roads are too rough for ladies to travel unescorted. And if she does not come, at least our marriage will be declared valid and I'll take her when and where I can, and her wealth with her, which will be useful."

"Only then, lord, you must not die, nor even be wounded, to-morrow. It is the Englishman who should die, for whatever the Pope may decree I think that while de Cressi lives the slumbrous eyes of that Eve of yours will find a way to charm you to a sleep that has no wakening. She is not a fair-haired toy that weeps, forgets and at last grows happy in her babe. She's a woman to make men or break them. Oh, when her sense came back to her, for a flash she looked me cold yonder in that English chapel, and it seemed to me that God's curse was in her stare."

"You've caught the terror, Nicholas, like so many just now in Venice. Why, to-day I've not met a man or woman who is not afraid of something, they know not what—save the Englishman and his death's-head. I think 'tis the unwholesome air of this strange season, and all the signs and omens we hear of on every side that conjure vapours to the brain."

"Yes, I've the terror," said Nicholas with something like a groan. "Every sin I ever did—and most of them have been for you, lord— seems to haunt my sleep. Yes, and to walk with me when I wake, preaching woe at me with fiery tongues that repentance or absolution cannot quench or still."

"Yet, Nicholas, I think that you must add one more to their count, or a share of it, which should weigh light among so many. Either I or de Cressi must pack for our last journey, and if we meet face to face to-morrow, how know I that it will be de Cressi? Better far that we should not meet."

"Lord, lord, you cannot fly! He is King Edward's champion, so proclaimed before all whose names are written in the Golden Book of Venice. He would cry your shame in every Court, and so would they. There's not a knight in Europe but would spit upon you as a dastard, or a common wench but would turn you her back! You cannot fly!"

"Nay, fool, but he can die—and before to-morrow. What makes your brain so dull, Nicholas? It is not its wont."

"Ah, I see—not flight, murder. I had forgotten; it is not a usual sauce to a banquet of honour even in Italy, and therefore, perhaps, the safer to serve. But how is it to be done? Poison? He is in Carleon's house; Carleon has faithful servants. Though perhaps a basket of rare fruits—but then he might not eat them; those Englishmen live mostly on half-raw meat. The signora would probably eat them, and the others."

"Nay, no more of your drugs; your skill in them is too well known. Come, these men have been watched since they set foot in Venice. Have they offended none besides myself and the Swiss?"

A look of intelligence crept into the eyes of Nicholas.

"Now that you mention it, lord, they have. There is a certain boatman and bravo called Giuseppe. With him and his mates they quarrelled about their fare and threw them into the canal in front of the ambassador's house, just because they drew a knife or two. A woman I know told me of it. He's a great villain, this Giuseppe, who would do anything for ten pieces, also revengeful and a hater of cold water."

"Send for him, Nicholas, or send this woman to him—that may be safer. Ten pieces! I'll pay him fifty."

"Ay, lord, but the Englishman may not give him a chance. Only fools would go out walking in Venice along after dark if they should happen to have enemies here, and the house is watched by the Doge's Guards. Yet one can try. Fortune loves the brave, and Englishmen are very great fools. They might stroll abroad to see the moon rise over the Adriatic."

"Try, Nicholas, try as you never tried before. Succeed, too, lest you and I should part company and you never be named abbot after all."

The afternoon of the day of their reception by the Doge was well filled for Hugh and Dick. Scarcely had they eaten with their host when the Marshal and his officers arrived with the articles of the Morrow's combat very fully drawn up, each of which must be considered with the help of Sir Geoffrey Carleon, lest they should hide some trick, before they confirmed them with their signatures. Not that Hugh was over-anxious about the details. As he said to Sir Geoffrey, all he sought was to come face to face with his enemy, even if he had but a club for a weapon.

At length these articles were signed and the Marshal departed with his fee, for they must be paid for as though they were a legal document. Next Hugh must try various horses from Sir Geoffrey's stable, and choose one of them as his war steed for the morrow, since the beast he had ridden to Venice was in no condition to bear a full-armed knight. In the end he selected a grey gelding, quiet of temperament and rather heavy of build, which it was reported had been used by its former owner in several tournaments and there borne itself handsomely. This done, well or ill, his armour must be seen to, and Dick's also, such as it was; his lance tested, and all their other weapons sharpened on a whetstone that Sir Geoffrey borrowed. For this was a task that Grey Dick would leave to no other hand.

At length all was prepared as well as possible in such haste, and they went to supper with Lady Carleon, who, now she understood that they were to fight for their lives on the morrow, was more mournful even than she had been on the previous night. When at last she asked what they desired as to their funerals and if they had any tokens to be sent to friends in England, Hugh, whose thoughts were already sad enough, could bear no more of it. So he rose, saying that he would seek Sir Geoffrey, who was already in his cabinet engaged upon a letter to King Edward descriptive of these events and other business. But when they were out of the room he said that he must have fresh air or he would faint, which was not strange, seeing that heat prevailed on this night in Venice of an intensity unknown there at this season of the year.

"Whither shall we go?" asked Dick, mopping his brow. "Guards stand at the door and, I doubt, will not let us pass."

"I wish to see the place where we are to fight to-morrow," answered Hugh, "so as to form my judgment of it, if only we may come there."

At this moment an English lad of Sir Geoffrey's household chanced to pass by, having come to ask as to the feeding of the horse which Hugh should ride. Dick caught him by the arm and asked whether he could get them out of the house secretly, so that the Guards would not see them, and conduct them to the spot called the Place of Arms, where they understood they were to fight.

The lad, whose name was David Day, replied somewhat doubtfully that he could do so by a back door near the kitchen, and guide them also, but that they must protect him from the anger of Sir Geoffrey. This Hugh promised to do. So presently they started, carrying their weapons, but wearing no mail because of the intense heat, although

Dick reminded his master how they had been told that they should not venture forth without body armour.

"I have a sword and you have bow and axe," answered Hugh, "so we'll risk it. In leather-lined mail we should surely melt."

So they put on some light cloaks made of black silk, with hoods to them, such as the Venetians wore at their masques, for David knew where these were to be found. Slipping out quite unobserved by the kitchen door into a little courtyard, they passed into an unlighted back street through a postern gate whereof the lad had the key. At the end of the street they came to a canal, where David, who talked Italian perfectly, hailed a boat, into which they entered without exciting remark. For this sharp youth pointed to their cloaks and told the boatman that they were gallants engaged upon some amorous adventure.

On they rowed down the silent lanes of water, through the slumbrous city of palaces, turning here, turning there, till soon they lost all knowledge of the direction in which they headed. At length David whispered to them that they drew near the place where they must land. Everybody seemed to speak in a whisper that heavy night, even the folk, generally so light of heart and quick of tongue, who sat on the steps or beneath the porticoes of their houses gasping for air, and the passers-by on the rivas or footwalks that bordered the canals. At a sign from David the boat turned inward and grated against the steps of a marble quay. He paid the boatman, who seemed to have no energy left to dispute the fare, telling him in the same low voice that if he cared to wait he might perhaps row them back within an hour or so. Then they climbed steps and entered a narrow street where there was no canal, on either side of which stood tall houses or dark frowning gateways.

Just as they stepped into the shadow of this street they heard the prow of another boat grate against the marble steps behind them and caught the faint sound of talk, apparently between their rower and others in the second boat.

"Forward, Sir Hugh," said Day a little nervously. "This part of

Venice has no good name, for many wicked deeds are done here, but soon we shall be through it."

So they stepped out briskly, and when they were about half-way down the street heard other steps behind them. They turned and looked back through the gloom, whereon the sound of the following steps died away. They pushed on again, and so, unless the echo deceived them, did those quick, stealthy steps. Then, as though by common consent, though no one gave the word, they broke into a run and gained the end of the street, which they now saw led into a large open space lit by the light of the great moon, that broke suddenly through the veil of cloud or mist. Again, as though by common consent, they wheeled round, Hugh drawing his sword, and perceived emerging from the street six or seven cloaked fellows, who, on catching sight of the flash of steel, halted and melted back into the gloom.

"Who follow us so fast?" asked Hugh.

"Thieves, I think," answered David, even more nervously than before, adding, "but if so, we are safe from them here."

"Yes, sure enough," said Grey Dick, "for I can shoot by moonlight," and, drawing the black bow from its case, which he threw to the lad to carry, he strung it, after which they saw no more of their pursuers.

Having waited a while, they began to examine the spot where they found themselves, which Day told them was that Place of Arms where they must fight on the morrow. It was large and level, having been used as a drilling ground for generations. Perhaps it measured four hundred yards square, and almost in the centre of it rose a stand of painted timber roofed with canvas, and ornamented with gilded flagstaffs, from which hung banners. On this stand, David said, the Doge and nobles would take their seats to see the fray, for in front of it the charging knights must meet.

They walked up and down the course taking note of everything, and especially of how the sun would shine upon them and the foothold of the soil, which appeared to be formed of fine, trodden sand.

"I ask no better ground to fight on," said Hugh at length, "though it is strange to think," he added with a sigh, "that here within a dozen hours or so two men must bid the world farewell."

"Ay," answered Dick, who alone seemed untouched by the melancholy of that night. "Here will die the knave with three names and the big fool of a half-bred Swiss, and descend to greet their ancestors in a place that is even hotter than this Venice, with but a sorry tale to tell them. By St. George! I wish it were nine of the clock to-morrow."

"Brag not, Dick," said Hugh with a sad smile, "for war is an uncertain game, and who knows which of us will be talking with his ancestors and praying the mercy of his Maker by this time to-morrow night?"

Then, having learned all they could, they walked across the ground to the quay that bordered it on the seaward side. Here, as they guessed from the stone pillars to which ships were made fast, was one of the harbours of Venice, although as it happened none lay at that quay this night. Yet, as they looked they saw one coming in, watched curiously by groups of men gathered on the wall.

"Never knew I vessel make harbour in such a fashion," exclaimed Dick presently. "See! she sails stern first."

Hugh studied her and saw that she was a great, decked galley of many oars, such as the Venetians used in trading to the East, high-bowed and pooped. But the strange thing was that none worked these oars, which, although they were lashed, swung to and fro aimlessly, some yet whole and some with their blades broken off and their shafts bundles of jagged splinters. Certain sails were still set on the ship's mast, in tatters for the most part, though a few remained sound, and it was by these that she moved, for with the moonrise a faint wind had sprung up. Lastly, she showed no light at peak or poop, and no sound of officer's command or of boatswain's whistle came from her deck. Only slowly and yet as though of set purpose she drifted in toward the quay.

Those who watched her, sailors such as ever linger about harbours seeking their bread from the waters, though among these were mingled people from the town who had come to this open place to escape the heat, began to talk together affrightedly, but always in the dread whisper that was the voice of this fearful knight. Yes, even the hoarse-throated sailormen whispered like a dying woman.

"She's no ship," said one, "she's the wraith of a ship. When I was a lad I saw such a craft in the Indian seas, and afterward we foundered, and I and the cook's mate alone were saved."

"Pshaw!" answered another, "she's a ship right enough. Look at the weed and barnacles on her sides when she heaves. Only where in Christ's name are her crew?"

"Yes," said a third, "and how could she win through all the secret channels without a pilot?"

"What use would be a pilot," said a fourth, "if there are none to work the rudder and shift the sails? Do I not know, who am of the trade?"

"At least she is coming straight to the quay," exclaimed a fifth, "though what sends her Satan alone knows, for the tide is slack and this wind would scarce move a sponge boat. Stand by with the hawser, or she'll swing round and stave herself against the pier."

So they talked, and all the while the great galley drifted onward with a slow, majestic motion, her decks hid in shadow, for a sail cut off the light of the low moon from them. Presently, too, even this was gone, for the veil of cloud crept again over the moon's face, obscuring everything.

Then of a sudden a meteor blazed out in the sky, such a meteor as no living man had ever seen in Venice, for the size of it was that of the sun. It seemed to rise out of the ocean to the east and to travel very slowly across the whole arc of the firmament till at last it burst with a terrible noise over the city and vanished. While it shone, the light it gave was that of mid-day, only pale blue in colour, turning all it touched to a livid and unnatural white.

It showed the placid sea and fish leaping on its silver face half-a-mile or more away. It showed the distant land with every rock and house and bush. It showed the wharf and the watchers on it; among them Hugh noted a man embracing his sweetheart, as he thought under cover of the cloud. But most of all it showed that galley down to her last rope and even the lines of caulking on her deck. Oh, and now they saw the rowers, for they lay in heaps about the oars. Some of them even hung over these limply, moving to and fro as they swung, while others were stretched upon the benches as though they slept. They were dead—all dead; the wind following the meteor and blowing straight on shore told them that they were certainly all dead. Three hundred men and more upon that great ship, and all dead!

Nay, not all, for now on the high poop stood a single figure who seemed to wear a strange red head-dress, and about his shoulders a black robe. Straight and silent he stood, a very fearful figure, and in his hand a coil of rope. The sight of him sent those watchers mad. They ceased from their whisperings, they raved aloud.

"It is Satan!" they shouted, "Satan, who comes to drag the folk of Venice down to hell. Kill him ere he lands. Kill him!"

Even Grey Dick went mad like a dog when he meets a ghost. His pale hair rose upon his head, his cold, quiet eyes started. He set an arrow on the string of the black bow, drew it to his ear and loosed at the figure on the poop. But that arrow never left the string; it shattered to flinders where it was and fell tinkling to the marble floor. Only the barb of it turned and wounded Grey Dick in the chin, yes, and stuck there for a while, for his right arm was numbed so that he could not lift his hand to pull it forth.

"Truly, I have shot at the Fiend and hit that at which I did not aim," muttered Grey Dick, and sat himself down on a post of the quay to consider the matter. Only, as it seemed to him, he who stood on the poop of the ship not ten yards away smiled a little.

Unheeding of the clamour, this man upon the poop suddenly lifted the coil of rope and threw it shoreward. It was a thick and heavy rope, with a noose at its end, so heavy that none would have believed that one mortal could handle it. Yet it shot from him till it stood out stiff as an iron bar. Yes, and the noose fell over one of the stone posts on the quay, and caught there. Now the rope grew straighter still, stretching and groaning like a thing in pain as it took the weight of the great, drifting ship. She stayed; she swung round slowly and ranged herself broadside on against the quay as a berthed ship does. Then down the ladder on her side came the Man. Deliberately he set his white-sandalled feet upon the quay, advanced a few paces into the full light of the bright moon and stood still as though to suffer himself to be seen of every eye.

Truly he was worth the seeing. Hugh noted his garments first, and particularly the head-dress, which caught his glance and held it, for never had he known such a one before. It was a cap fitting tight to the skull, only running across the crown of it was a stiff raised ridge, of leather perhaps, jagged and pointed something like the comb of a cock. This comb, of brilliant red, was surmounted at its highest point by a ball of black of the size of a small apple. The cap itself was yellow, except its lowest band, which stood out from it and was also black. In the centre of this band upon the forehead glowed a stone like a ruby.

Such was the head-dress. The broad shoulders beneath were covered with a cape of long and glossy fur blacker than coal, on to either shoulder of which drooped ear-rings made of rings of green stone which afterward Hugh came to know was jade. The cape of fur, which hung down to the knees and was set over a kind of surplice of yellow silk, was open in front, revealing its wearer's naked bosom that was clothed only with row upon row of round gems of the size of a hazel nut. These like the fur were black, but shone with a strange and lustrous sheen. The man's thick arms were naked, but on his hands he wore white leather gloves made without division like a sock, as though to match the white sandals on his feet.

This was the Man's attire. Now for him who wore it. He was tall, but not taller than are many other men; he was broad, but not broader than many other men, and yet he looked stronger than all the men in the world. On his brow, which was prominent, smooth black hair parted in the middle was plastered back as that of women sometimes is, making hard lines against the yellow skin below. He had very thin eyebrows that ran upward on either side of a bow-shaped wrinkle in the centre of his forehead. The eyes beneath were small and pale— paler even than those of Grey Dick—yet their glance was like the points of thrusting swords. With those little eyes alone he seemed to smile, for the rest of his countenance did not move. The nose was long and broad at the end with wide spreading nostrils and a deep furrow on either side. The mouth was thin-lipped and turned downward at the corners, and the chin was like a piece of iron, quite hairless, and lean as that of a man long dead.

There he stood like some wild vision of a dream, smiling with those small unblinking eyes that seemed to take in all present one by one. There he stood in the moonlit silence, for the mob was quiet enough now for a little while, that yet was not silence because of a soughing noise which seemed to proceed from the air about his head.

Then suddenly the tumult broke out again with its cries of "Kill the devil! Tear the wizard to pieces! Death is behind him! He brings death! Kill, kill, kill!"

A score of knives flashed in the air, only this time Grey Dick set no arrow on his string. Their holders ran forward; then the Man lifted his hand, in which was no weapon, and they stopped.

Now he spoke in a low voice so cold that, to Hugh's excited fancy, the words seemed to tinkle like falling ice as one by one they came from his lips. He spoke in Italian—perfect Italian of Venice— and young Day, whose teeth where chattering with fear, translated his words.

"Is this your welcome to a stranger," he said, "the companions of whose voyage have unhappily met with misfortune?" Here with a faint motion of his fingerless glove he indicated the dead who lay all about the decks of that fatal ship. "Would you, men of Venice, kill a poor, unarmed stranger who has travelled to visit you from the farthest East and seen much sorrow on his way?"

"Ay, we would, sorcerer!" shouted one. "Our brothers were in that ship, which we know, and you have murdered them."

"How did you learn Italian in the farthest East?" asked another.

Then for the second time, like hounds closing in on a stag at bay, they sprang toward him with their poised knives.

Again he lifted his hand, again the semi-circle halted as though it must, and again he spoke.

"Are there none here who will befriend a stranger in a strange land? None who are ashamed to see a poor, unarmed stranger from the East done to death by these wolves who call themselves children of the white Christ of Mercy?"

Now Hugh touched Dick upon the shoulder.

"Rise and come," he said, "it is our fate"; and Dick obeyed.

Only after he had translated the Man's words, David fell down flat upon the quay and lay there.

They stepped to the yellow-capped Man and stood on each side of him, Hugh drawing his sword and Dick the battle-axe that he carried beneath his robe of silk.

"We will," said Hugh shortly, in English.

"Now there are three of us," went on the Man. "The stranger from the East has found defenders from the West. On, defenders, for I do not fight thus," and he folded his arms across his broad breast and smiled with the awful eyes.

Hugh and Dick knew no Italian, yet they both of them understood, and with a shout leaped forward toward those hungry knives. But their holders never waited for them. Some sudden panic seized them all, so that they turned and ran—ran straight across the wide Place of Arms and vanished into the network of narrow streets by which it was surrounded.

CHAPTER XIII

MURGH'S ARROW

Hugh and Dick came back. Something seemed to call them back, although no blow had been struck. The Man stood where they had left him, staring at nothing in particular. Apparently he was engaged in meditation.

"Thanking his gods because they have saved him from sudden death," muttered Grey Dick. "If he's got any gods!" he added doubtfully.

Now the three, or rather the four of them, for David Day had recovered, and once more stood upon his feet from time to time glancing at the stranger's costume with a frightened eye, were left alone upon the great place with no company save the shipful of dead behind them and the wild, white moon above. The silence that, save for the soughing sound for which they could not account, was intense, oppressed them, as also did the heat.

Grey Dick coughed, but the Man took no notice. Then he dropped his axe with a clatter on the marble flooring of the quay and picked it up again, but still the Man took no notice. Evidently his Eastern imperturbability was not to be disturbed by such trifles. What was worse, or so thought Dick, his master Hugh had fallen into a very similar mood. He stood there staring at the Man, while the Man stared over or through him—at nothing in particular.

Grey Dick felt aggrieved. An arrow had burst to pieces unaccountably in his bow, numbing his arm and wounding him on the chin, and now he was outpaced at his own game of cold silence. He grew angry and dug David in the ribs with his elbow.

"Tell that foreigner," he said, "that my master and I have saved his life. Those Italian cut-throats have run away, and if he is a gentleman he should say 'thank you.'"

David hesitated, whereon Dick gave him another dig, harder than the first, and asked if he heard what he said. Then David obeyed, addressing the Man as "Most Illustrious" as though he were the Doge, and ending his speech with a humble apology in case he should have interrupted his pious thanksgiving.

The Man seemed to awake. Taking no notice of Day, he addressed himself to Dick, speaking in English and using just that dialect of it to which he, Dick, had been accustomed from his childhood in the neighbourhood of Dunwich. Not even the familiar Suffolk whine was forgotten.

"You and your master have saved my life, have you?" he said. "Well, neighbour, why did you try to save my life by shooting at me with that great black bow of yours, which I see is made of Eastern woods?" He stared at the case in which it was now again hidden as though tanned leather were no obstacle to his sight; then went on: "Do not answer: I will tell you why. You shot at me because you were afraid of me, and fear is ever cruel, is it not? Only something happened to your arrow, something that has never happened to any arrow of yours before. Oh, yes, you have saved me from the Italian cut-throats, and being a gentleman I thank you very much. Only why did the arrow burst in your bow?" and he smiled with those dreadful eyes of his.

Now, feeling overwhelmed for the second time that night, Grey Dick sat himself down upon a quay post. It was clear to him that to argue with this person in a yellow cap who talked Suffolk so well was quite useless. Why, then, waste breath which was probably his last?

Everybody seemed to be falling into meditation again, when the Man, shifting his head slowly, began to consider Hugh.

"What is your name and which is your country, O my second saviour?" he asked, still speaking in English. Only now the English was of a different and more refined sort to that which he had used when he addressed Dick; such English, for instance, as came from the lips of Sir Geoffrey Carleon or from those of the lords of Edward's Court.

"I am Sir Hugh de Cressi of Dunwich, in the county of Suffolk, in England," answered Hugh slowly.

"England. I have heard of England, and Dunwich; I have heard of Dunwich. Indeed, I travel thither, having an appointment with an old friend in that town."

Now a light came into Hugh's bewildered face, but he said nothing.

"I seem to have touched some chord of recollection in your mind, O my saviour of Dunwich," said the Man. "Look at me and tell me, who am I?"

Hugh looked, and shook his head.

"I never saw you before, nor any one at all like you," he answered.

"No, no; you never saw me, though I have been very near to you once or twice. Yet, your pardon, look again."

Hugh obeyed, and this time, for a second only, perceived that the Man's head was surrounded by a multitude of doves. Two endless lines of doves, one line black and the other line white, stretched from his right shoulder and from his left shoulder, till miles away they melted into the lofty gloom of the sky that was full of the soughing sound of their wings.

Now he knew, and for the first time in his life fell upon his knees to a man, or to what bore the semblance of man.

"You are named Murgh, Gate of the Gods," he said. "Murgh, whom old Sir Andrew saw in that courtyard over which the iron dragons watch in the country called Cathay, that courtyard with the pool of water and the many doors."

"Ay," answered the Man in a new voice, a great voice that seemed to fill the air like the mutter of distant thunder. "I am Murgh, Gateway of the Gods, and since you have striven to defend Murgh, he who is the friend of all men, although they know it not, will above all be your friend and the friend of those you love."

He stretched out his long arms and laid his white-gloved hands for an instant, one of them upon Hugh's head and one on the shoulder of Grey Dick, who sat upon the pillar of stone.

Hugh muttered, "I thank you," not knowing what else to say. But in his heart he wondered what kind of friendship this mighty and awful being would show to him and his. Perhaps he might hold that the truest kindness would be to remove him and them from the miseries of a sinful world.

If Murgh read his thoughts he only answered them with that smile of his cold eyes which was more awful than the frown of any mortal man. Turning his head slowly he began to contemplate Dick sitting on his stone.

"If I had a son," he said, "by that face of yours you might be he."

"Perchance," answered Dick, "since I never knew for certain who my father was. Only I have always heard that Life begets, not Death."

"Death! You honour me with a great name. Well, life and death are one, and you and I are one with the moon and the stars above us, and many other things and beings that you cannot see. Therefore the begetter and the begotten are one in the Hand that holds them all."

"Ay," answered Dick, "and so my bow and I are one: I've often thought it. Only you nearly made me one with my own arrow, which is closer kinship than I seek," and he touched the cut upon his chin. "Since you are so wise, my father, or my son, tell me, what is this Hand that holds them all?"

"Gladly. Only if I do, first I must ask you to die, then—say in a minute or two—you shall know."

Dick peered at him doubtfully, and said:

"If that be so, I think I'll wait for the answer, which I am sure to learn soon or late."

"Ah! Many men have thought the same, and you have sent some to seek it, have you not, being so good an archer. For instance, that was a long shaft you shot before Crecy fray at the filthy fool who mocked your English host. Doubtless now he knows the answer to your riddle."

"Who told you of that?" asked Dick, springing up.

"A friend of mine who was in the battle. He said also that your name was Richard the Archer."

"A friend! I believe that you were there yourself, as, if you are Death, you may well have been."

"Perhaps you are right, Richard. Have I not just told you that we all are one; yes, even the slayer and the slain. Therefore, if my friend— did you call him Death?—was there, I was there, if you were there I was there and it was my hand that drew yonder great black bow of yours and my eye that guided the straight shaft which laid the foulmouthed jester low. Why, did you not say as much yourself when your master here bade farewell to his father in the ship at Calais? What were the words? Oh, I remember them. You wondered how One I may not name," and he bowed his solemn head, "came to make that black bow and yours and you 'the death that draw it.'"

Now at length Grey Dick's courage gave out.

"Of no man upon earth am I afraid," he said. "But from you, O god or devil, who read the secret hearts of men and hear their secret words, my blood flows backward as it did when first my eyes fell on you. You would kill me because I dared to shoot at you. Well, kill, but do not torture. It is unworthy of a knight, even if he took his accolade in hell," and he placed his hands before his eyes and stood before him with bent head waiting for the end.

"Why give me such high names, Richard the Fatherless, when you have heard two humbler ones? Call me Murgh, as do my friends. Or call me 'The Gate,' as do those who as yet know me less well. But talk not of gods or devils, lest suddenly one of them should answer you. Nay, man, have no fear. Those who seek Death he often flees, as I think he flees from you to-night. Yet let us see if we cannot send a longer shaft, you and I, than that which we loosed on Crecy field. Give me the bow."

Dick, although he had never suffered living man to shoot with it before, handed him the black bow, and with it a war shaft, which he drew from his quiver.

"Tell me, Archer Dick, have you any enemy in this town of Venice? Because if so we might try a shot at him."

"One or two, Gate Murgh," answered Dick, "Still whatever your half of me may do, my bit of you does not love to strike down men by magic in the dark."

"Well said and better thought. Then bethink you of something that belongs to an enemy which will serve as well for a test of shooting. Ah! I thank you, well thought again. Yes, I see the mark, though 'tis far, is it not? Now set your mind on it. But stay! First, will you know this arrow again?"

"Surely," answered Dick, "I made it myself. Moreover, though two of the feathers are black, the third is white with four black spots and a little splash of brown. Look on it, Sir Hugh; it cannot be mistook."

Hugh looked and nodded; speak he could not for the life of him.

Then Murgh began to play a little with the bow, and oh! strange and dreadful was the music that came from its string beneath the touch of his gloved fingers. It sang like a harp and wailed like a woman, so fearfully indeed that the lad Day, who all this while stood by aghast, stopped his ears with his fingers, and Hugh groaned. Then this awful archer swiftly set the arrow on the string.

"Now think with your mind and shoot with your heart," he said in his cold voice, and, so saying, drew and loosed as though at a hazard.

Out toward Venice leaped the shaft with a rushing sound like to that of wings and, as it seemed to the watchers, light went with it, for it travelled like a beam of light. Far over the city it travelled, describing a mighty arc such as no arrow ever flew before, then sank down and vanished behind some palace tower.

"A very good bow," said the shooter, as he handed it back to Dick. "Never have I used a better, who have used thousands made of many a substance. Indeed, I think that I remember it. Did you chance to find it years ago by the seashore? Yes? Well, it was a gift of mine to a famous archer who died upon a ship. Nay, it is not strained; I can judge of the breaking strength of a bow. Whether or no I can judge of the flight of an arrow you will learn hereafter. But that this one flew fast and far cannot be doubted since—did you watchers note it?—its speed made it shine like fire. This is caused by the rubbing of the air when aught travels through it very quickly. This night you have seen a meteor glow in the same fashion, only because the air fretted it in its passage. In the East, whence I come, we produce fire just so. And now let us be going, for I have much to do to-night, and would look upon this fair Venice ere I sleep. I'll lead the way, having seen a map of the town which a traveller brought to the East. I studied it, and now it comes back to my mind. Stay, let that youth give me his garment," and he pointed to David Day, who wore a silk cloak like the others, "since my foreign dress might excite remark, as it did but now."

In a moment Day had stripped himself of his light silk-hooded gown, and in another moment it was on the person of Murgh, though how it got there, when they came to think of it afterward, none could remember. Still, the yellow and red head-dress, the coal-black silky furs, the yellow skirt, the gleaming pearls, all vanished beneath it. Nothing remained visible except the white fingerless gloves—why were they fingerless, and what lay beneath them? Hugh wondered— and the white shoes.

Forward they went across the Place of Arms, past the timber stand ornamented with banners, which Murgh stayed to contemplate for an instant, until they came to the mouth of the street up which men had followed them, apparently with evil intent.

"Sir Murgh," said Hugh, stepping forward, "you had best let me and my companion Grey Dick walk first down this place, lest you should come to harm. When we passed it a while ago we thought that we heard robbers behind us, and in Venice, as we are told, such men use knives."

"Thank you for your warning, Sir Hugh," and even beneath the shadow of the silk hood Hugh thought that he saw his eyes smile, and seeing, remembered all the folly of such talk.

"Yet I'll risk these robbers. Do you two and the lad keep behind me," he added in a sterner voice.

So they advanced down the narrow street, the man called Murgh going first, Hugh, Grey Dick and the lad following meekly behind him. As they entered its shadows a low whistle sounded, but nothing happened for a while. When they had traversed about half its length, however, men, five or six of them in all, darted out of the gloom of a gateway and rushed at them. The faint light showed that they were masked and gleamed upon the blue steel of the daggers in their hands. Two of these men struck at Murgh with their knives, while the others tried to pass him, doubtless to attack his companions, but failed. Why they failed Hugh and Dick never knew. All they saw was that Murgh stretched out his white-gloved hands, and they fell back.

The men who had struck at him fell back also, their daggers dropping to the ground, and fled away, followed by their companions, all except one whom Murgh had seized. Hugh noted that he was a tall, thin fellow, and that, unlike the rest, he had drawn no weapon, although it was at his signal that the other bravoes had rushed on. This man Murgh seemed to hold with one hand while with the other he ripped the mask off his face, turning him so that the light shone on him.

Hugh and Dick saw the face and knew it for that of the priest who had accompanied Acour to England. It was he who had drugged Red Eve and read the mass of marriage over her while she was drugged.

"Who are you?" asked Murgh in his light, cold voice. "By your shaven head a priest, I think—one who serves some God of love and mercy. And yet you come upon this ill errand as a captain of assassins. Why do you seek to do murder, O Priest of the God of mercy?"

Now some power seemed to drag the answer from Father Nicholas.

"Because I must," he said. "I have sold myself and must pay the price. Step leads to step, and he who runs may not stop upon them."

"No, priest Nicholas, since ever they grow more narrow and more steep. Yet at the foot of them is the dark abyss, and, Murderer Nicholas, you have reached the last of all your steps. Look at me!" and with one hand he threw back the hood.

Next instant they saw Nicholas rush staggering down the street, screaming with terror as he went. Then, as all the bravoes had gone, they continued their march, filled with reflections, till they came to the little landing-stage where they had left the boat. It was still there though the boatman had gone.

"Let us borrow this boat," said Murgh. "As from my study of the map I know these water-paths, I will be steersman and that tongue-tied lad shall row and tell me if I go wrong. First I will take you to the house where I think you said you lodged, and thence to go seek friends of my own in this city who will show me hospitality."

They glided on down the long canals in utter silence that was broken only by the soft dipping of the oars. The night was somewhat cooler now, for the bursting of the great meteor seemed to have cleared the air. Or perhaps the gentle breeze that had sprung up, blowing from the open sea, tempered its stifling heat.

So it came about that although it grew late many people were gathered on the rivas or on the balconies of the fine houses which they passed, for the most part doubtless discussing the travelling star that had been seen in the sky. Or perhaps they had already heard rumours of the strange visitor who had come to Venice, although, however fast such news may fly, this seemed scarcely probable. At the least there they were, men and women, talking earnestly together, and about them the three Englishmen noted a strange thing.

As their boat slipped by, some influence seemed to pass from it to the minds of all these people. Their talk died out, and was succeeded by a morne and heavy silence. They looked at it as though wondering why a sight so usual should draw their eyes. Then after a few irresolute moments the groups on the footpaths separated and went their ways without bidding each other good night. As they went many of them made the sign with their fingers that these Italians believed could avert evil, which gave them the appearance of all pointing at the boat or its occupants. Those in the balconies did the same thing and disappeared through the open window-places.

More than any of the wonderful things that he had done, perhaps, this effect of the Eastern stranger's presence struck terror and foreboding to Hugh's heart.

At length they came to the end of that little street where they had hired the boat, for, although none had told him the way, thither their dread steersman brought them without fault. The lad David laid down his oars and mounted the steps that led to the street, which was quite deserted, even the bordering houses being in darkness.

"Hugh de Cressi and Richard the Fatherless," said Murgh, "you have seen wonderful things this night and made a strange friend, as you may think by chance, although truly in all the wide universe there is no room for such a thing as chance. Now my counsel to you and your companion is that you speak no word of these matters lest you should be set upon as wizards. We part, but we shall meet again twice more, and after many years a third time, but that third meeting do not seek, for it will be when the last grains of sand are running from the glass. Also you may see me at other times, but if so, unless I speak to you, do not speak to me. Now go your ways, fearing nothing. However great may seem your peril, I say to you—fear nothing. Soon you will hear ill things spoken of me, yet"—and here a touch of human wistfulness came into his inhuman voice—"I pray you believe them not. When I am named Murgh the Fiend and Murgh the Sword, then think of me as Murgh the Helper. What I do is decreed by That which is greater than I, and if you could understand it, leads by terrible ways to a goal of good, as all things do. Richard the Archer, I will answer the riddle that you asked yourself upon the ship at Calais. The Strength which made your black bow an instrument of doom made you who loose its shafts and me who can outshoot you far. As the arrow travels whither it is sent, and there does its appointed work, so do you travel and so do I, and many another thing, seen and unseen; and therefore I told you truly that although we differ in degree, yet we are one. Yes, even Murgh the Eating Fire, Murgh the Gate, and that bent wand of yours are one in the Hand that shaped and holds us both."

Then divesting himself of the long robe which he had borrowed from the lad, he handed it to Hugh, and, taking the oars, rowed away clad in his rich, fantastic garb which now, as at first, could be seen by all. He rowed away, and for a while the three whom he had left behind heard the soughing of the innumerable wings that went ever with him, after which came silence.

Silence, but not for long, for presently from the borders of the great canal into which his skiff must enter, rose shouts of fear and rage, near by at first, then farther and farther off, till these too were lost in silence.

"Oh! Sir Hugh!" sobbed poor David Day, "who and what is that dreadful man?"

"I think his name is Death," answered Hugh solemnly, while Dick nodded his head but said nothing.

"Then we must die," went on David in his terror, "and I am not fit to die."

"I think not," said Hugh again. "Be comforted. Death has passed us by. Only be warned also and, as he bade you, say nothing of all that you have heard and seen."

"By Death himself, I'll say nothing for my life's sake," he replied faintly, for he was shaking in every limb.

Then they walked up the street to the yard door. As they went Hugh asked Dick what it was that he had in his mind as a mark for the arrow that Murgh had shot, that arrow which to his charmed sight had seemed to rush over Venice like a flake of fire.

"I'll not tell you, master," answered Dick, "lest you should think me madder than I am, which to-night would be very mad indeed. Stay, though, I'll tell David here, that he may be a witness to my folly," and he called the young man to him and spoke with him apart.

Then they unlocked the courtyard gate and entered the house by the kitchen door, as it chanced quite unobserved, for now all the servants were abed. Indeed, of that household none ever knew that they had been outside its walls this night, since no one saw them go or return, and Sir Geoffrey and his lady thought that they had retired to their chamber.

They came to the door of their room, David still with them, for the place where he slept was at the end of this same passage.

"Bide here a while," said Dick to him. "My master and I may have a word to say to you presently."

Then they lit tapers from a little Roman lamp that burned all night in the passage and entered the room. Dick walked at once to the window-place, looked and laughed a little.

"The arrow has missed," he said, "or rather," he added doubtfully, "the target is gone."

"What target?" asked Hugh wearily, for now he desired sleep more than he had ever done in all his life. Then he turned, the taper in his hand, and started back suddenly, pointing to something which hung upon his bed-post that stood opposite to the window.

"Who nails his helm upon my bed?" he said. "Is this a challenge from some knight of Venice?"

Dick stepped forward and looked.

"An omen, not a challenge, I think. Come and see for yourself," he said.

This is what Hugh saw: Fixed to the post by a shaft which pierced it and the carved olivewood from side to side, was the helm that they had stripped from the body of Sir Pierre de la Roche; the helm of Sir Edmund Acour, which Sir Pierre had worn at Crecy and Dick had tumbled out of his sack in the presence of the Doge before Cattrina's face. On his return to the house of Sir Geoffrey Carleon he had set it down in the centre of the open window-place and left it there when they went out to survey the ground where they must fight upon the morrow.

Having studied it for a moment, Dick went to the door and called to David.

"Friend," he said, standing between him and the bed, so that he could see nothing, "what was it that just now I told you was in my mind when yonder Murgh asked me at what target he should shoot with my bow on the Place of Arms?"

"A knight's helm," answered David, "which stood in the window of your room at the ambassador's house—a knight's helmet that had a swan for its crest."

"You hear?" said Dick to Hugh; "now come, both of you, and see. What is that which hangs upon the bed-post? Answer you, David, for perchance my sight is bewitched."

"A knight's helm," answered David, "bearing the crest of a floating swan and held there by an arrow which has pierced it through."

"What was the arrow like which I gave this night to one Murgh, master?" asked Dick again.

"It was a war shaft having two black feathers and the third white but chequered with four black spots and a smear of brown," answered Hugh.

"Then is that the same arrow, master, which this Murgh loosed from more than a mile away?"

Hugh examined it with care. Thrice he examined it, point and shaft and feathers. Then in a low voice he answered:

"Yes!"

CHAPTER XIV

AT THE PLACE OF ARMS

Notwithstanding all that has been told, Hugh and Dick never slept more soundly than they did that night, nor was their rest broken by any dreams. At half past five in the morning—for they must be stirring early—David came to call them. He too, it seemed, had slept well. Also in the light of day the worst of his fear had left him.

"I am wondering, Sir Hugh," he said, looking at him curiously, "whether I saw certain things last night down yonder at the Place of Arms and in the boat, or whether I thought I saw them."

"Doubtless you thought you saw them, David," answered Hugh, adding with meaning, "and it is not always well to talk of things we think that we have seen."

The lad, who was sharp enough, nodded. But as he turned to hand Hugh some garment his eye fell upon the swan-crested helm that was still nailed by the long war-shaft with two black feathers and one white to the carved olivewood post of the bed.

"It must have been a mighty arm that shot this arrow, Sir Hugh," he said reflectively, "which could pierce a casque of Milan steel from side to side and a hardwood post beyond. Well for the owner of the helm that his head was not inside of it."

"Very well, and a very mighty arm, David. So mighty that I should say nothing about it for fear lest it should set another arrow upon another string and shoot again."

"God's truth, not I!" exclaimed David, "and for your comfort, sir, know that none saw us leave this house or reënter it last night."

Then Hugh and Dick clothed themselves and saw to their weapons and mail, but this they did not don as yet, fearing lest the weight of it should weary them in that great heat. Although the day was so young, this heat was terrible, more oppressive indeed than any they had yet known in Venice.

When they were ready David left them to see to the horse which de Cressi would ride in his combat with Cattrina. Hugh, as became a God-fearing knight whom Sir Andrew Arnold had instructed from childhood, crossed himself, knelt down and said his prayers, which that morning were long and earnest. Indeed he would have confessed himself also if he could, only there was no priest at hand who knew his language, Sir Geoffrey's chaplain being away. After watching him a while even Grey Dick, whose prayers were few, followed his example, kneeling in front of his bow as though it were an image that he worshipped. When they had risen again, he said:

"You grieve that there is none to shrive us, master, but I hold otherwise, since when it was told what company we kept last night absolution might be lacking. This would weigh on you if not on me, who, after what I have learned of Father Nicholas and others, love but one priest, and he far away."

"Yet it is well to have the blessings of Holy Church ere such a business as ours, Dick; that is, if it can be come by."

"Mayhap, master. But for my part I am content with that of Murgh, which he gave us, you may remember, or so I understood him. Moreover, did he not teach that he and all are but ministers of Him above? Therefore I go straight to the head of the stair," and he nodded toward the sky. "I am content to skip all those steps which are called priests and altars and popes and saints and such-like folk, living or dead. If Murgh's wisdom be true, as I think, these are but garnishings to the dish which can well be spared by the hungry soul."

"That may be," Hugh answered dubiously, for his faith in such matters was that of his time. "Yet were I you, Dick, I'd not preach that philosophy too loud lest the priests and popes should have something to say to it. The saints also, for aught I know, since I have always heard that they love not to be left out of our account with heaven."

"Well, if so," answered Dick, "I'll quote St. Murgh to them, who is a very fitting patron for an archer." Then once again he glanced at the helm and the arrow with something not unlike fear in his cold eye.

Presently they went down to the eating chamber where they had been told that breakfast would be ready for them at seven of the clock. There they found Sir Geoffrey awaiting them.

"I trust that you have slept well, Sir Hugh," he said. "You were a wise knight to go to rest so early, having before you such a trial of your strength and manhood, and, so to speak, the honour of our King upon your hands."

"Very well indeed; thank you, sir," answered Hugh. "And you?"

"Oh, ill, extremely ill. I do not know what is the matter with me or Venice either, whereof the very air seems poisoned. Feel the heat and see the haze! It is most unnatural. Moreover, although in your bed doubtless you saw it not, a great ball of fire blazed and burnt over the city last night. So bright was it that even in a darkened room each of us could see the colour of the other's eyes. Later, too, as I watched at the window, there came a thin streak of flame that seemed to alight on or about this very house. Indeed I thought I heard a sound as of iron striking upon iron, but could find no cause for it."

"Wondrous happenings, sir," said Grey Dick. "Glad am I that we were not with you, lest the sight of them should have made us fearful on this morning of combat."

"Wondrous happenings indeed, friend Richard," said Sir Geoffrey excitedly, "but you have not heard the half of them. The herald, who has just been here with the final articles of your fray signed by the Doge and Cattrina, has told me much that I can scarce believe. He says that the great galley from this port which is called Light of the East drifted up to the quay at the Place of Arms last night on her return voyage from Cyprus, filled with dead and with no living thing aboard her save the devil himself in a yellow robe and a many-hued head-dress like a cock's-comb with a red eye. He swears that this fiend landed and that the mob set on him, whereon two, some say three, other devils clad in long black gowns appeared out of the water and drove them back. Also, it seems that this same cock's-combed Satan stole a boat and rowed about the city afterward, but now none can find him, although they have got the boat."

"Then they should be well satisfied," said Hugh, "since its owner has lost nothing but the hire, which with Satan at the oars is better than might be hoped. Perhaps he was not there after all, Sir Geoffrey."

"I know not, but at least the galley Light of the East is there, for ever since the dawn they have been taking the dead out of her to bury them. Of these they say things too terrible to repeat, for no doctor can tell of what sickness they died, never having seen its like. For my part I pray it may not be catching. Were I the Doge I would have towed her out to sea and scuttled her, cargo and all. Well, well, enough of these wild tales, of which God alone knows the truth. Come, eat, if you can in this heat. We must be on the Place of Arms by half-past eight. You and the captain go thither in my own boat, Sir Hugh; your horse David Day takes on presently. Now, while you breakfast, I'll explain to you these articles, one by one, for they are writ in Italian, which you cannot read. See you forget them not. These Venetians are punctilious of such forms and ceremonies, especially when the case is that of combat to the death, which is rare among them."

The articles, which were lengthy, had been read, and the breakfast, or so much as they could eat of it, consumed. At last Hugh, accompanied by a Venetian squire of high birth sent by the Doge to bear his casque and other armour, stood in the vestibule waiting for the ambassador's barge of state. With him was Grey Dick, accompanied by no one and carrying the mail shirt in which he was to fight, like a housewife's parcel beneath his arm, although he wore bow on back, axe and dagger at side and iron cap upon his head.

Presently, while they lingered thus, out from a side-door appeared Lady Carleon, clothed in a white garment such as women wear when their dressing is half done, down which her grey hair hung dishevelled.

"I am come thus unkempt, Sir Hugh," she said, "for, not feeling well, I could not rise early, to bid you good-bye, since I am sure that we shall not meet again. However much that black-browed Doge may press it, I cannot go down yonder to see my countrymen butchered in this heat. Oh! oh!" and she pressed her hand upon her heart.

"What's the matter, madam?" asked Hugh anxiously.

"A pain in my breast, that is all, as though some one drove a dagger through me. There, there, 'tis gone."

"I thank you for your goodness, Lady Carleon," said Hugh when she was herself again; then paused, for he knew not what to add.

"Not so, Sir Hugh, not so; 'tis for your sakes in truth since you remember you never told me what you would wish done—afterward. Your possessions also—where are they to be sent? Doubtless you have money and other things of value. Be sure that they shall be sealed up. I'll see to it myself, but—how shall I dispose of them?"

"Madame, I will tell you when I return," said Hugh shortly.

"Nay, nay, Sir Hugh; pray do not return. Those who are gone had best keep gone, I think, who always have had a loathing of ghosts. Therefore, I beg you, tell me now, but do not come back shining like a saint and gibbering like a monkey at dead of night, because if you do I am sure I shall not understand, and if there is an error, who will set it straight?"

Hugh leaned against a marble pillar in the hall and looked at his hostess helplessly, while Sir Geoffrey, catching her drift at length, broke in:

"Cease such ill-omened talk, wife. Think you that it is of a kind to give brave men a stomach in a fight to the end?"

"I know not, Geoffrey, but surely 'tis better to have these matters settled, for, as you often say, death is always near us."

"Ay, madam," broke in Grey Dick, who could bear no more of it, "death is always near to all of us, and especially so in Venice just now. Therefore, I pray you tell me—in case we should live and you should die, you and all about you—whether you have any commands to give as to what should be done with your gold and articles of value, or any messages to leave for friends in England."

Then, having uttered this grim jest, Dick took his master by the arm and drew him through the door.

Afterward, for a reason that shall be told, he was sorry that it had

ever passed his lips. Still in the boat Sir Geoffrey applauded him,
saying that his lady's melancholy had grown beyond all bearing, and
that she did little but prate to him about his will and what colour of
marble he desired for his tomb.

After a journey that seemed long to Hugh, who wished to have
this business over, they came to the Place of Arms. Their route there,
however, was not the same which they had followed on the previous
night. Leaving the short way through the low part of the town
untraversed, they rowed from one of the canals into the harbour itself,
where they were joined by many other boats which waited for them
and so on to the quay. Hugh saw at once that the death ship, Light of
the East, was gone, and incautiously said as much to Sir Geoffrey.

"Yes," he answered, "one of my rowers tells me that they have
towed her to an island out at sea, since the stench from her holds was
more than could be borne. But how did you know that she lay at this
particular quay, Sir Hugh?"

"I thought you said so," he answered carelessly, adding, to change
the subject: "Look, our fray will not lack for spectators," and he pointed
to the thousands gathered upon the great tilting-ground.

"No, no, all Venice will be there, for these people love a show,
especially if there be death in it."

"Mayhap they will see more of him than they wish before all is
done," muttered Grey Dick, pausing from the task of whetting his
axe's edge with a little stone which he carried in his pouch. Then he
replaced the axe in its hanger, and, drawing Hugh's sword from its
sheath, began to give some final touches to its razor edge, saying:
"Father Sir Andrew Arnold blessed it, which should be enough, but
Milan steel is hard and his old battle blade will bite none the worse for
an extra sharpening. Go for his throat, master, go for his throat, the
mail is always thinnest there."

"God above us, what a grim man!" exclaimed Sir Geoffrey, and so
thought all in that boat and in those around them. At least they
looked at Dick askance as he whetted and whetted, and then, plucking
out one of the pale hairs from his head, drew it along the edge of the
steel, which severed it in twain.

"There! That'll do," said Grey Dick cheerfully, as he returned the long sword to its sheath, "and God help this Cattrina, I say, for he comes to his last battle. That is, unless he runs away," he added after reflection.

Now they landed and were received by heralds blowing trumpets, and conducted through a great multitude of people with much pomp and ceremony to a pavilion which had been pitched for them, where they must arm and make ready.

This then they did, helped or hindered by bowing squires whose language they could not understand.

At length, when it lacked but a quarter to the hour of nine, David Day led Hugh's horse into the wide entrance of the pavilion, where they examined its armour, bridle, selle and trappings.

"The beast sweats already," said Hugh, "and so do I, who, to tell truth, dread this heat more than Cattrina's sword. Pray that they get to the business quickly, or I shall melt like butter on a hot plate."

Then his lance was given to him, a lance that was sharp and strong. When they had been tested by them both, Hugh mounted the grey and at the agreed signal of a single blast upon a trumpet, walked it slowly from the pavilion, Dick going at his side on foot.

At their coming a shout went up from the assembled thousands, for in truth it seemed, as Sir Geoffrey had said, as though all the folk in Venice were gathered on that place. When they had finished shouting the people began to criticise, finding much in the appearance of this pair that moved their ready wit. Indeed there was little show about them, for Hugh's plain armour, which lacked all ornament or inlay, was worn with war and travel, and his horse came along as soberly as if it were going out to plough. Nor was there anything fine about the apparel of Grey Dick, who wore a loose chain shirt much out of fashion—it was that which Sir Andrew had given to Hugh—an iron cap with ear-pieces, and leather buskins on his legs. In his hand was his axe, heavy but not over large; at his side hung a great knife, and on his back was the long black bow and a quiver of arrows.

Thus arrayed, taking no heed of the jests and chatter of the multitude, they were led to the front of the bedecked timber stand which they had seen on the previous night. In the centre of this stand, occupying a kind of tribune, sat the Doge Dandolo in state, and with him many nobles and captains, while to right and left the whole length of the course, for the stand was very long, were packed a countless number of the best-born men and women in Venice. These, however, were but a tithe of the spectators, who encircled the Place of Arms in one serried horde which was kept back by a line of soldiers.

Arriving in front of the Doge's tribune, the pair halted and saluted him, whereon he and his escort rose and saluted them in turn. Then another trumpet blew and from a second pavilion at the other end of the course appeared Cattrina, wearing a splendid suit of white armour, damascened in gold, with a silver swan upon the helm and a swan painted on his shield.

"Very fine, isn't it?" said Grey Dick to his master, "only this time I hope he's inside the steel. Ask to see his face before you fight, master."

On came Cattrina on a noble black horse, which pawed and caracoled notwithstanding the heat, while after him strode a gigantic figure also clad from top to toe in white mail, who fiercely brandished a long-handled battle-axe.

"Ambrosio!" said Dick. "Now I ought to feel as much afraid as though that fellow wore a yellow cap and fur cape and pearls like another warrior whom we met last night. Yet, to speak the truth, I believe he has the fainter heart of the two. Also if he swings that chopper about so much he'll grow tired."

To the multitude, however, the gallant appearance of this pair, whom they looked on as the champions of Venice against foreigners, appealed not a little. Amidst clapping of hands and "evvivas!" they advanced to the Doge's tribune and there made their salutations, which the Illustrious acknowledged as he had those of the Englishmen.

Then the heralds intervened and again all the articles of combat were read and translated, although to these, of which they were weary, Hugh and Dick listened little. Next they were asked if they had any objections to make and with one voice answered, "None." But on the same question being put to their adversaries, the Swiss, Ambrosio, said that he with whom he must fight appeared to be armed with a bow, which was against the articles. Thereon Dick handed the bow and quiver to David, bidding him guard them until he asked for them again as he would his own life. In the event of his death, however, David was to give them to Sir Hugh, or if they both should die, to his own master, Sir Geoffrey. All of these things David promised to do.

Next followed a long discussion as to whether the four of them were to fight in pairs, Cattrina and Ambrosio against Hugh and Dick simultaneously, or whether Ambrosio was to fight alone with Dick, and Cattrina with Hugh. Upon Cattrina and Ambrosio being asked their wishes, the former said that he desired to fight alone, as he feared lest the English archer, if he overcame Ambrosio, should turn on him also, or perhaps hamstring his horse.

Then the Englishmen were asked what they wished, and replied that they did not care how it was arranged, being ready to fight either together or separately, as the Doge might decree.

The end of it was that after long consultations with sundry experts in such matters, the Most Illustrious decided that the Captains Ambrosio and Richard the Archer should first engage on foot, and when that business was settled the two knights should take their place in the arena.

So the end of it was that more than half an hour after the combat should have begun, Dick and the gigantic Ambrosio found themselves standing face to face waiting for the signal to engage, the Swiss shouting threats and defiance and Grey Dick grinning and watching him out of his half-shut eyes.

At length it came in the shape of a single blast upon a trumpet. Now seeing that Dick stood quite still, not even raising his axe, the Swiss advanced and struck a mighty blow at him, which Dick avoided by stepping aside. Recovering himself, again Ambrosio struck. This blow Dick caught upon his shield, then, as though he were afraid, began to retreat, slowly at first, but afterward faster till his walk broke into a run.

At this sight all that mighty audience set up a hooting. "Coward!

Dog! Pig of an Englishman!" they yelled; and the louder they yelled the more quickly did Grey Dick run, till at last even Hugh grew puzzled wondering what was in his mind and hoping that he would change it soon. So the audience hooted, and Grey Dick ran and the giant Swiss lumbered along after him, bellowing triumphantly and brandishing his battle-axe, which, it was noted, never seemed to be quite long enough to reach his flying foe.

When this had gone on for two or three minutes, Grey Dick stumbled and fell. The Swiss, who was following fast, likewise tripped and fell over him heavily, whereon the multitude shouted:

"Foul play! A dirty, foreign trick!"

In an instant Dick was up again, and had leapt upon the prostrate Swiss, as all thought, to kill him. But instead the only thing he did was to get behind him and kick him with his foot until he also rose. Thereat some laughed, but others, who had bets upon their champion, groaned.

Now the Swiss, having lost his shield in his fall, rushed at Dick, grasping his axe with both hands. As before, the Englishman avoided the blow, but for the first time he struck back, catching the giant on the shoulder though not very heavily. Then with a shout of "St. George and England!" he went in at him.

Hither and thither sprang Dick, now out of reach of the axe of the Swiss and now beneath his guard. But ever as he sprang he delivered blow upon blow, each harder than the last, till there appeared scars and rents in the fine white mail. Soon it became clear that the great Swiss was overmatched and spent. He breathed heavily, his strokes grew wild, he over-balanced, recovered himself, and at last in his turn began to fly in good earnest.

Now after him went Dick, battering at his back, but, as all might see, with the flat of his axe, not with its edge. Yes, he was beating him as a man might beat a carpet, beating him till he roared with pain.

"Fight, Ambrosio, fight! Don't fly!" shouted the crowd, and he tried to wheel round, only to be knocked prostrate by a single blow upon the head which the Englishman delivered with the hammer-like back of his axe.

Then Dick was seen to kneel upon him and cut the lashings of his helmet with his dagger, doubtless to give the coup de grâce, or so they thought.

"Our man is murdered!" yelled the common people, while those of the better sort remained shamed and silent.

Dick rose, and they groaned, thinking that all was done. But lo! stooping down he helped the breathless Swiss, whom he had disarmed, to his feet. Then, taking him by the nape of the neck, which was easy, as his helmet was off, with one hand, while in the other he held his bared knife, Dick thrust him before him till they reached the tribune of the Doge.

"Be pleased to tell the Illustrious," he said, to Sir Geoffrey, "that this braggart having surrendered, I spared his life and now return him to his brother the Page quite unharmed, since I did not wish to wound one who was in my power from the first. Only when he gets home I pray that he will look at his back in a glass and judge which of us it is that has been 'beaten to a pulp.' Let him return thanks also to his patron saint, who put pity in my heart, so that I did not cut him into collops, as I promised. For know, sir, that when I walked out yonder it was my purpose to hew off his hands and shorten him at the knees. Stay—one word more. If yonder boaster has more brothers who really wish to fight, I'll take them one by one and swear to them that this time I'll not give back a step unless I'm carried."

"Do you indeed yield and accept the Englishman's mercy?" asked the Doge in a stern voice.

The poor Ambrosio, making no answer, blundered forward among the crowd and there vanished, and this was the last that Dick ever saw or heard of him. But, although he waited there a while, feeling the edge of his axe and glaring about him, none of the captain's companions came forward to accept his challenge.

At length, with a shrug of his shoulders, Dick turned. Having taken his bow and quiver from David, who could not conceal his indecent joy at the utter humiliation of Ambrosio, whom he hated with a truly British hate, he walked slowly to where Hugh sat upon his horse.

"The jest is done, master, and now for good earnest, since 'tis your turn. The Saints save me such another cow hunt in this hell's heat. Had I killed him at once I should be cooler now, but it came into my mind to let the hound live. Indeed, to speak truth, I thought that I heard the voice of Murgh behind me, saying, 'Spare,' and knew that I must obey."

"I hope he will say nothing of the sort to me presently," answered Hugh, "if he is here, which I doubt. Why, what is it now? Those gold-coated marshals are talking again."

Talking they were, evidently at the instance of Cattrina, or his counsellors, who had raised some new objections, which Sir Geoffrey stepped forward to explain to them. But Hugh would not even hear him out.

"Tell the man and all whom it may concern," he said in an angry voice, "that I am ready to fight him as he will, on horse or on foot, with lance or sword or axe or dagger, or any or all of them, in mail or without it; or, if it pleases him, stripped to the shirt. Only let him settle swiftly, since unless the sweat runs into my eyes and dims them, it seems to me that night is coming before it is noon."

"You are right," answered Sir Geoffrey, "this gathering gloom is ominous and fearful. I think that some awesome tempest must be about to burst. Also it seems to me that Cattrina has no stomach for this fray, else he would not raise so many points of martial law and custom."

Then wiping his brow with a silken handkerchief he returned to deliver the message.

Now Hugh and Dick, watching, saw that Cattrina and those who advised him could find no further loophole for argument. They saw, moreover, that the Doge grew angry, for he rose in his seat, throwing off his velvet robe of office, of which it appeared that he could no longer bear the weight, and spoke in a hard voice to Cattrina and his squires. Next, once more the titles of the combatants were read, and their cause of combat, and while this went on Hugh bade Dick bind about his right arm a certain red ribbon that Eve had given him, saying that he wished to fight wearing his lady's favour.

Dick obeyed, muttering that he thought such humours foolish and that a knight might as well wear a woman's petticoat as her ribbon. By now, so dim had the light grown, he could scarce see to tie the knot.

Indeed, the weather was very strange.

From the dark, lowering sky above a palpable blackness sank downward as though the clouds themselves were falling of their own weight, while from the sea great rolls of vapour came sweeping in like waves. Also this sea itself had found a voice, for, although it was so calm, it moaned like a world in pain. The great multitude began to murmur, and their faces, lifted upward toward the sky, grew ghastly white. Fear, they knew not of what, had got hold of them. A voice cried shrilly:

"Let them fight and have done. We would get home ere the tempest bursts."

The first trumpet blew and the horses of the knights, which whinnied uneasily, were led to their stations. The second trumpet blew and the knights laid their lances in rest. Then ere the third trumpet could sound, suddenly the darkness of midnight swallowed all the scene.

Dick groped his way to Hugh's side. "Bide where you are," he said, "the end of the world is here; let us meet it like men and together."

"Ay," answered Hugh, and his voice rang hollow through his closed visor, "without doubt it is the end of the world, and Murgh, the Minister, has been sent to open the doors of heaven and hell. God have mercy on us all!"

So they stayed there, hearkening to the groans and prayers of the terrified multitude about them, Dick holding the bridle of the horse, which shook from head to foot, but never stirred. For some minutes they remained thus, till suddenly the sky began to lighten, but with no natural light. The colour of it, of the earth beneath and of the air between was a deep, terrible red, that caused all things to seem as though they were dyed in blood. Lighter and lighter and redder and redder it grew, the long stand and the pavilions became visible, and after them the dense, deep ring of spectators. Many of these were kneeling, while others, who could find no space to kneel, held their hands upstretched toward heaven, or beat their breasts and wept in the emotional fashion of the country.

Yet not on them were the eyes of Hugh and Grey Dick fixed, but rather on a single figure which stood quite alone in the midst of that great arena where Cattrina and his horse should have been, where they had been indeed but a little while before. The figure was clothed in a red and yellow cap shaped like a cock's-comb, in black furs, a yellow robe and white gloves and sandals. Yonder it stood, fantastic, fearful, its bare and brawny arms crossed upon its breast, its head bowed as though it contemplated the ground. There was not an eye of all the tens of thousands of those who were present that did not see it; there was not a voice that did not break into a yell of terror and hate, till the earth shook with such a sound as might reverberate through the choked abyss of hell.

"The fiend! The fiend! The fiend!" said the shout. "Kill him! Kill him! Kill him!"

The figure looked up, the red light shone upon its stony face that seemed one blotch of white amidst its glow. Then it stooped down and lifted from the sand a knight's lance such as Cattrina had held. It raised the lance and with it pointed four times, east and west and north and south, holding it finally for a while in the direction of the tribune, where sat the Doge with all his noble company, and of Venice beyond. Lastly, with a quick and easy motion, it cast the lance toward the sky, whence it fell, remaining fixed point downward in the earth. Then a tongue of mist that had crept up from the sea enveloped it, and when that mist cleared away the shape was gone.

Now the red haze thinned, and for the first time that morning the sun shone out in a sickly fashion. Although their nerves were torn by the unnatural darkness and the apparition that followed it, which all saw, yet none quite believed that they had seen, the multitude shouted for the combat to proceed.

Once more Hugh laid his lance in rest, thinking that Cattrina was there, although he could not see him.

Then the third trumpet rang out—in that silence it sounded like the blast of doom—and Hugh spurred his horse forward a little way, but halted, for he could perceive no foe advancing against him. He stared about him, and at last in a rage threw his lance to a squire, and, turning his horse, galloped to the tribune. There he pulled it to his haunches and shouted out in a great voice:

"Where is Cattrina? Am I to be fooled, who appear here as the champion of the King of England? Where is Cattrina? Produce Cattrina that I may slay him or be slain, or, Chivalry of Venice, be forever shamed!"

The Doge rose, uttering swift commands, and heralds ran here and there. Knights and captains searched the pavilions and every other place where a mounted man might hide. But they never found Cattrina, and, returning at length, confessed as much with bowed heads.

The Doge, maddened by this ignominy, seized the great gold chain upon his beast and burst it in two.

"Cattrina has fled!" he shouted. "Or Satan himself has carried him away! At the least let his name be erased from the Golden Book of Venice, and until he prove himself innocent, let no noble of Venice stretch out to him the hand of fellowship. Men of Venice, for you Cattrina and his House are dead."

"Will none take up his cause and fight for him?" asked Hugh through Sir Geoffrey, and presently, at the Doge's command, the challenge was repeated thrice by the herald. But to it no answer came. Of this afterward Hugh was glad, since it was Cattrina's life he sought, not that of any other man. Then Hugh spoke again, saying:

"I claim, O Illustrious, that I be written down as victor in this combat to the death, bloodless through no fault of mine."

"It shall be so written, noble Hugh de Cressi," said the Doge. "Let all Venice take notice thereof."

As the words left his lips the solid earth began to heave and rock.

At the first heave Hugh leaped from his horse, which screamed aloud and fled away, and gripped hold of Grey Dick. At the second, the multitude broke out into wild cries, prayers and blasphemies, and rushed this way and that. At the third, which came quite slowly and was the greatest of them all, the long stand of timber bent its flags toward him as though in salute, then, with a slow, grinding crash, fell over, entangling all within it beneath its ruin. Also in the city beyond, houses, whole streets of them, gabled churches and tall towers, sank to the earth, while where they had been rose up wreathed columns of dust. To the south the sea became agitated. Spouts of foam appeared upon its smooth face; it drew back from the land, revealing the slime of ages and embedded therein long-forgotten wrecks. It heaped itself up like a mountain, then, with a swift and dreadful motion, advanced again in one vast wave.

In an instant all that multitude were in full flight.

Hugh and Dick fled like the rest, and with them David, though whither they went they knew not.

All they knew was that the ground leapt and quivered beneath their feet, while behind them came the horrible, seething hiss of water on the crest of which men were tossed up and down like bits of floating wood.

CHAPTER XV

THE DEATH AT WORK

Presently Hugh halted, taking shelter with his two companions behind the stone wall of a shed that the earthquake had shattered, for here they could not be trodden down by the mob of fugitives.

"The wave has spent itself," he said, pointing to the line of foam that now retreated toward the ocean, taking with it many drowned or drowning men. "Let us return and seek for Sir Geoffrey. It will be shameful if we leave him trapped yonder like a rat."

Dick nodded, and making a wide circuit to avoid the maddened crowd, they came safely to the wrecked stand where they had last seen Sir Geoffrey talking with the Doge. Every minute indeed the mob grew thinner, since the most of them had already passed, treading the life out of those who fell as they went.

From this stand more than three fourths of those who were seated there had already broken out, since it had not fallen utterly, and by good fortune was open on all sides. Some, however, tangled in the canvas roof, were still trying to escape. Other poor creatures had been crushed to death, or, broken-limbed, lay helpless, or, worse still, were held down beneath the fallen beams.

Several of these they freed, whereon those who were unharmed at once ran away without thanking them. But for a long while they could find no trace of Sir Geoffrey. Indeed, they were near to abandoning their search, for the sights and sounds were sickening even to men who were accustomed to those of battlefields, when Dick's quick ears caught the tones of an English voice calling for help. Apparently it came from the back of the Doge's tribune, where lay a heap of dead. Gaily dressed folk who had fallen in the flight and been crushed, not by the earthquake, but by the feet of their fellows. These blackened and disfigured men and women they dragged away with much toil, and at last, to their joy, beneath them all found Sir Geoffrey Carleon. In another few minutes he must have died, for he was almost suffocated.

Indeed he would certainly have perished with the others had he not been thrown under a fixed bench, whence one leg projected, which, as they could see at once, was crushed and broken. They drew him out as gently as they could and gave him water to drink, whereof, mercifully for them all, since by now they were utterly parched with thirst, they had discovered a large silver pitcher full, standing in the corner of a little ante-chamber to the tribune. It was half hidden with fragments of fine dresses and even jewels torn from the persons of the lords and ladies.

"I thank you, friends," he said faintly. "I prayed them to keep seated, but they went mad and would not listen. Those behind trod down those in front, till that doorway was choked and I was hurled beneath the bench. Oh, it was terrible to hear them dying about me and to know that soon I must follow! This, had it not been for you, I should have done, for my leg is crushed and there was no air."

Then, having drunk and drunk until even their raging thirst was satisfied, they found a plank. Laying Sir Geoffrey on it, they departed from that human shambles, whence the piteous cries of those still imprisoned there, whom they could not reach, pursued them horribly.

Thus, slowly enough, for there were but three of them, two hampered by their mail, they bore Sir Geoffrey across the Place of Arms. Save for the dead and dying, and some ghoul-like knaves who plundered them, by this time it was almost deserted.

Indeed, a large band of these wretches, who had emerged like wolves from their lairs in the lowest quarters of the great city, catching sight of the gold chain Sir Geoffrey wore, ran up with drawn daggers to kill and rob them.

Seeing them come Grey Dick slipped the black bow from its case and sent an arrow singing through the heart of the one-eyed villain

HIL

who captained them. Thereon the rest left him where he fell and ran off to steal and slay elsewhere. Then without a word Dick unstrung the bow and once more laid hold of an end of the plank.

They came to the mouth of that street where the bravoes had waylaid them on the previous night, only to find that they could not pass this way. Here most of the houses were thrown down, and from their ruins rose smoke and the hideous screams of those who perished. It was this part of Venice, the home of the poorer folk, which suffered most from the earthquake, that had scarcely touched many of the finer quarters. Still, it was reckoned afterward that in all it took a toll of nearly ten thousand lives.

Turning from this street, they made their way to the banks of a great canal that here ran into the harbour, that on which they had been rowed to the Place of Arms. Here by good luck they found a small boat floating keep uppermost, for it had been overturned by the number of people who crowded into it. This boat they righted with much toil and discovered within it a drowned lady, also an oar caught beneath the seat. After this their dreadful journey was easy, at least by comparison. For now all the gloom had rolled away, the sun shone out and a fresh and pleasant wind blew from the sea toward the land.

So, at last, passing many sad and strange scenes that need not be described, they came safely to the steps of the ambassador's beautiful house which was quite uninjured. Here they found several of his servants wringing their hands and weeping, for word had been brought to them that he was dead. Also in the hall they were met by another woe, for there on a couch lay stretched the Lady Carleon smitten with some dread sickness which caused blood to flow from her mouth and ears. A physician was bending over her, for by good fortune one had been found.

Sir Geoffrey asked him what ailed his wife. He answered that he did not know, having never seen the like till that morning, when he had been called in to attend three such cases in houses far apart, whereof one died within ten minutes of being struck.

Just then Lady Carleon's senses returned, and opening her eyes she saw Sir Geoffrey, whom they had laid down upon another couch close to her.

"Oh, they told me that you were dead, husband," she said, "crushed or swallowed in the earthquake! But I thank God they lied. Yet what ails you, sweetheart, that you do not stand upon your feet?"

"Little, dear wife, little," he answered in a cheerful voice. "My foot is somewhat crushed, that is all. Still 'tis true that had it not been for this brave knight and his squire I must have lain where I was till I perished."

Now Lady Carleon raised herself slightly and looked at Hugh and Dick, who stood together, bewildered and overwhelmed.

"Heaven's blessings be on your heads," she exclaimed, "for these Venetians would surely have left him to his doom. Ah, I thought that it was you who must die to-day, but now I know it is I, and perchance my lord. Physician," she added after a pause, "trouble not with me, for my hour has come; I feel it at my heart. Tend my lord there, who, unless this foul sickness takes him also, may yet be saved."

So they carried them both to their own large sleeping chamber on the upper floor. There the surgeon set Sir Geoffrey's broken bone skilfully enough, though when he saw the state of the crushed limb, he shook his head and said it would be best to cut it off. This, however, Sir Geoffrey would not suffer to be done.

"It will kill me, I am sure, or if not, then the pest which that ship, Light of the East, has brought here from Cyprus, will do its work on me. But I care nothing, for since you say that my wife must die I would die with her and be at rest."

At sunset Lady Carleon died. Ere she passed away she sent for Hugh and Dick. Her bed by her command had been moved to an open window, for she seemed to crave air. By it was placed that of Sir Geoffrey so that the two of them could hold each other's hand.

"I would die looking toward England, Sir Hugh," she said, with a faint smile, "though alas! I may not sleep in that churchyard on the Sussex downs where I had hoped that I might lie at last. Now, Sir Hugh, I pray this of your Christian charity and by the English blood which runs in us, that you will swear to me that you and your squire will not leave my lord alone among these Southern folk, but that you will bide with him and nurse him till he recovers or dies, as God may will. Also that you will see me buried by the bones of my child—they will tell you where."

"Wife," broke in Sir Geoffrey, "this knight is not of our kin. Doubtless he has business elsewhere. How can he bide with me here, mayhap for weeks?"

But Lady Carleon, who could speak no more, only looked at Hugh, who answered:

"Fear nothing. Here we will stay until he recovers—unless," he added, "we ourselves should die."

She smiled at him gratefully, then turned her face toward Sir Geoffrey and pressed his hand. So presently she passed away, the tears running from her faded eyes.

When it was over and the women had covered her, Hugh and Dick left the room, for they could bear no more.

"I have seen sad sights," said Hugh, with something like a sob, "but never before one so sad."

"Ay," answered Dick, "that of the wounded dying on Crecy field was a May Day revel compared to this, though it is but one old woman who has gone. Oh, how heavily they parted who have dwelt together these forty years! And 'twas my careless tongue this morning that foretold it as a jest!"

In the hall they met the physician, who rushed wild-eyed through the doorway to ask how his patients fared.

"Ah!" he said to them in French when he knew. "Well, signors, that noble lady has not gone alone. I tell you that scores of whom I know are already dead in Venice, swept off by this swift and horrible plague. Death and all his angels stalk through the city. They say that he himself appeared last night, and this morning on the tilting ground by the quay, and by God's mercy—if He has any left for us—I can well believe it. The Doge and his Council but now have issued a decree that all who perish must be buried at once. See to it, signors, lest the officers come and bear her away to some common grave, from which her rank will not protect her."

Then he went to visit Sir Geoffrey. Returning presently, he gave them some directions as to his treatment, and rushed out as he had rushed in. They never saw him again. Two days later they learned that he himself was dead of the pest.

That night they buried Lady Carleon in her son's grave, which Dick had helped to prepare for her, since no sexton could be bribed to do the work. Indeed these were all busy enough attending to the interment of the great ones of Venice. In that churchyard alone they saw six buryings in progress. Also after the priest had read his hurried Office, as they left the gates, whence Lady Carleon's bearers had already fled affrighted, they met more melancholy processions heralded by a torch or two whereof the light fell upon some sheeted and uncoffined form.

"'Twixt earthquake and plague Murgh the Helper is helping very well," said Grey Dick grimly, and Hugh only groaned in answer.

Such was the beginning of the awful plague which travelled from the East to Venice and all Europe and afterward became known by the name of the Black Death. Day by day the number of its victims increased; the hundreds of yesterday were the thousands of the morrow. Soon the graveyards were full, the plague pits, long and deep, were full, and the dead were taken out to sea by shiploads and there cast into the ocean. At length even this could not be done, since none were forthcoming who would dare the task. For it became known that those who did so themselves would surely die.

So where folk fell, there they lay. In the houses were many of them; they cumbered and poisoned the streets and the very churches. Even the animals sickened and perished, until that great city was turned into an open tomb. The reek of it tainted the air for miles around, so that even those who passed it in ships far out to sea turned faint and presently themselves sickened and died. But ere they died they bore on the fatal gift to other lands.

Moreover, starvation fell upon the place. Though the houses were full of riches, these would scarce suffice to buy bread for those who remained alive. The Doge and some of his Council passed laws to lighten the misery of the people, but soon few heeded these laws which none were left to enforce. The vagabonds and evil-minded men who began by robbing the deserted houses of jewels, money and plate, ended by searching them for food and casting aside their treasures as worthless dross. It was even said that some of them did worse things, things not to be named, since in its extremities nature knows no shame. Only if bread and meat were scarce, wine remained in plenty. In the midst of death men—yes, and women—who perhaps had deserted their wives, their husbands or their children, fearing to take the evil from them, made the nights horrible by their drunken blasphemies and revellings, as sailors sometimes do upon a sinking ship. Knowing that they must die, they wished to die merry.

Sir Geoffrey Carleon lived a long while after the death of his wife. When he passed away at last, ten days or so later, it was painlessly of the mortification of his broken limb, not of the pest, which went by him as though it knew that he was already doomed.

All this time Hugh, Grey Dick, and David Day nursed him without ceasing. Indeed with the exception of a woman so ancient and shrivelled that nothing seemed able to harm her any more, no one else was left in the great palazzo, for all the rest of the household had perished or fled away. This woman, who was the grandmother of one of the servants, now dead of the plague, cooked their food. Of such provision fortunately there was much laid up in the storerooms for use in the winter, since Lady Carleon had been a good and provident housewife.

So those three did not starve, although Sir Geoffrey would touch little of the salted stuff. He existed on a few fruits when they could get them, and after these were gone, on wine mingled with water.

At length came the end. For two days he had lain senseless. One night, however, David, who was watching in his chamber, crept into the room where Hugh slept hard by and told them that Sir Geoffrey was awake and calling them. They rose and went to him. By the light of the moon which shone in at the open window, that same window through which Lady Carleon had looked toward England ere she passed away, they saw him lying quietly, a happy smile upon his face.

"Friends," he said in a weak voice, "by the mercy of God, I go out of this hell to heaven, or so I think. But, if indeed this be not the end of the world, I hope that you who have lived so long will continue to live, and I have sent for you to bless you and to thank you both. In yonder case are certain papers that have to do with the King's business. I pray you deliver them to his Grace if you can and with them my homage and my thanks for the trust that he has reposed in me. Tell him what I have not written in the letters"—and here he smiled faintly—"that I think that few of his creditors in Venice will trouble him at present, though afterward their heirs, if they have left any, may do so. Say, too, to the Doge, who, I believe, still lives, that I send him my good wishes and respects. Also that I grieve that I have not been able to hand him my letters of recall in person, since the King who summons me sends none.

"So much for business, but there are two things more: I have no relatives living save my wife's sister. Therefore, Sir Hugh and Captain Richard, I have made you my joint heirs with her; my testament duly signed and witnessed is in that case with the other papers. My wealth is not great. Still there are certain land and manors in England, a sum of money placed with a merchant in London, whose name you will find written in the testament, my plate and gold coin here, though the former you may not be able to move. Therefore I charge you to bury it and return for it later on, if you can. It is of value, since all my life I have collected such trinkets. I beg you to make provision also for this good lad, David, should he be spared."

He paused a while, for he was growing very weak, then added:

"Another thing is that I ask you, if it be possible, to row my body out to sea and there sink it in deep water, deep, clean water, far from this place of stench and pestilence, for I would not lie in the common pit at last. Now kneel down and pray for my passing soul, since there is no priest to give me absolution, and I must seek it straight from God. Nay, thank me not. I have done with the world and its affairs. Kneel down and pray, as I pray for you, that you may be spared on earth and that we may meet again in heaven, where my wife and others await me."

They obeyed, weeping, yes, even Grey Dick wept a little. Presently when they looked up they saw that Sir Geoffrey was dead, dead without pain or sorrow. Of the first he had suffered none for days, and the second was far from him who wished to die.

Leaving the ancient woman in charge of the house, which she barred and bolted, next morning they took a boat, and the three of them rowed the body of the old knight a league out into the quiet sea. There, after a brief prayer, they cast him into the deep, weighted with stones, so that he might never rise again.

Then they returned, not too soon, for they found thieves in the act of breaking into the house, probably in search of food. These miserable, half-starved men they spared, though they could have killed them easily enough. They even gave them a pouch full of biscuit and dried meat ere they dismissed them. This they did quickly, since one of them, as they could see, was already stricken by the plague and had not long to live. When they were gone, the old woman being out of the house, whence she had fled on hearing the robbers, they collected all Sir Geoffrey's and his lady's jewels and plate, of which there was much, for he lived in state in Venice, as became an ambassador. These they buried in three large iron boxes beneath the flagstones of the cellar, the safest place that they could find. Having thrown the excavated earth into the canal under cover of the dark, they replaced these stones and strewed dust over them.

Wondering whether it would ever be their lot to look upon these chests and their contents again, they left the cellar, to find the old woman knocking at the back door of the house, whither she had returned, frightened by the sights and sounds in the city. They bade her bring them food, which they needed much who had laboured so hard on that sorrowful day, and after they had eaten took counsel together.

"Seeing that all three of us are still in health, as if there is anything in the promises of Murgh we should remain, is it not time, master," asked Grey Dick, "that we left this accursed Venice? Now that Sir Geoffrey is gone, there is naught to keep us here."

"One thing I have to do first," answered Hugh, "and it is to learn whether Sir Edmund Acour, lord of Cattrina, is dead or living, and if living where he hides himself away. While Sir Geoffrey lay dying we could not leave him to make search, but now it is otherwise."

"Ay, master, though I think you'll find the task hard in this hive of pestilence and confusion."

"I have heard that the plague is at work in Cattrina's palace," broke in David, "but when I asked whether he were there or no, none could tell me. That is not a house where you'll be welcomed, Sir Hugh."

"Still I will make bold to knock at his doors to-morrow," answered Hugh. "Now let us seek what we all need—sleep."

So on the following morning shortly after sunrise Hugh and Grey Dick, guided by David, took boat and rowed through most fearful scenes and sounds to the Palazzo Cattrina, a splendid but somewhat dilapidated building situated in a part of the city that, like itself, had seen more prosperous times. The great doors of the place set in a marble archway stood half open. Over them were cut the cognizance of the floating swan, and beneath, in letters of faded gold, the titles of Acour, de Noyon, and Cattrina. No wonder they were open, since the porter's lodge was occupied only by a grisly corpse that lay rotting on the floor, a heavy key in its hand. The courtyard beyond was empty and so, save for a dead horse, were the stables to the right. Passing up the steps of the hall that also stood open, they entered.

Here the place was in confusion, as though those who dwelt there had left in haste. The mouldering remains of a meal lay on the broad oak table; a great dower-chest inlaid with ivory, but half filled with arms and armour, stood wide. A silver crucifix that had hung above was torn down and cast upon the floor, perchance by thieves who had found it too heavy to bear away. The earthquake had thrown over a carved cabinet and some bowls of glazed ware that stood upon it. These lay about shattered amidst shields and swords thrown from the walls, where pictures of saints or perchance of dead Cattrinas hung all awry. In short, if an army had sacked it this stately hall could scarce have seemed more ruined.

Hugh and Dick crossed it to a stairway of chestnut wood whereof every newel-post was surmounted by the crest of a swan, and searched the saloons above, where also there was wreck and ruin. Then, still mounting the stair, they came to the bed-chambers. From one of these they retreated hastily, since on entering it hundreds of flies buzzing in a corner advised them that something lay there which they did not wish to see.

"Let us be going. I grow sick," exclaimed Hugh.

But Dick, who had the ears of a fox, held up his hand and said: "Hark! I hear a voice."

Following the sound, he led his master down two long corridors that ended in a chapel. There, lying before the altar, they found a man clad in a filthy priest's robe, a dying man who still had the strength to cry for help or mercy, although in truth he was wasted to a skeleton, since the plague which had taken him was of the most lingering sort. Indeed, little seemed to be left of him save his rolling eyes, prominent nose and high cheekbones covered with yellow parchment that had been skin, and a stubbly growth of unshaven hair.

Dick scanned him. Dick, who never forgot a face, then stepped forward and said:

"So once more we meet in a chapel, Father Nicholas. Say, how has it fared with you since you fled through the chancel door of that at Blythburgh Manor? No, I forgot, that was not the last time we met. A man in a yellow cap ripped off your mask in a by-street near the Place of Arms one night and said something which it did not please you to hear."

"Water!" moaned Nicholas. "For Christ's sake give me water!"

"Why should I give you water in payment for your midnight steel yonder in the narrow street? What kind of water was it that you gave Red Eve far away at Blythburgh town?" asked Dick in his hissing voice which sounded like that of an angry snake.

But Hugh, who could bear no more of it, ran down to the courtyard, where he had seen a pitcher standing by a well, and brought water.

"Thank God that you have come again," said the wretched priest, as he snatched at it, "for I cannot bear to die with this white-faced devil glaring at me," and he pointed to Grey Dick, who leaned against the chancel wall, his arms folded on his breast, smiling coldly.

Then he drank greedily, Hugh holding the pitcher to his lips, for his wasted arms could not bear its weight.

"Now," said Hugh, when his thirst was satisfied, "tell me, where is your master, Cattrina?"

"God or the fiend can say alone. When he found that I was smitten with the plague he left me to perish, as did the others."

"And as we shall do unless you tell me whither my enemy has gone," and Hugh made as though to leave the place.

The priest clutched at him with his filthy, claw-like hand.

"For Christ's sake do not desert me," he moaned. "Let one Christian soul be near me at the last ere the curse of that wizard with the yellow cap is fulfilled on me. For the sake of Jesus, stay! I'll tell all I know."

"Speak then, and be swift. You have no time to spare, I think."

"When the darkness fell there in the Place of Arms," began Nicholas, "while you knights were waiting for the third blast of the trumpet, Cattrina fled under cover it."

"As I thought, the accursed coward!" exclaimed Hugh bitterly.

"Nay, to be just, it was not all cowardice. The wizard in the yellow cap, he who showed himself to the people afterward and called down this Black Death on Venice, appeared to him in the darkness and said something to him that turned his heart to water. I think it was that if he stayed, within five short minutes he'd be dead, who otherwise, if he fled, had yet a breathing space of life. So he went."

"Ay. But whither, man? Whither?"

"Here to his house, where he disguised himself and bade me prepare to travel with him. Only then the sickness took me and I could not. So he went with some of his people, riding for Avignon."

"What to do at Avignon?"

"To obtain the confirmation of his marriage with the lady Eve Clavering. It has been promised to him by certain cardinals at Court who have the ear of his Holiness the Pope."

"Ah, I thought it! What more?"

"Only this: tidings reached him that the lady Clavering, with the old Templar, Sir Andrew Arnold, journeys to Avignon from England, there to obtain the dissolution of their marriage with Sir Edmund Acour, Count de Noyon, Lord of Cattrina. In Avignon, however the cause may go, Cattrina purposes to snare and make her his, which will be easy, for there he has many friends and she has none."

"Except God!" exclaimed Hugh, grinding his teeth.

"And Sir Andrew Arnold," broke in Dick, "who, like some others, is, I think, one of His ministers. Still, we had better be riding, master."

"Nay, nay," cried Nicholas in a hoarse scream. "Tarry a while and I'll tell you that which will force the Pope to void this marriage. Yes, it shall be set in writing and signed by me and witnessed ere I die. There is ink and parchment in yonder little room."

"That's a good thought," said Hugh. "Dick, fetch the tools, for if we try to move this fellow he will go farther than we can follow him."

Dick went and returned presently with an ink-horn, a roll of parchment, pens and a little table. Then Hugh sat himself down on the altar rail, placing the table in front of him and said:

"Say on. I'll write, since you cannot."

Now Nicholas, having before his glazing eyes the vision of imminent judgment, briefly but clearly told all the truth at last. He told how he had drugged Red Eve, giving the name of the bane which he mixed in the milk she drank. He told how when her mind was sleeping, though her body was awake, none knowing the wickedness that had been wrought save he and Acour, and least of all her father, they had led her to the altar like a lamb to the slaughter, and there married her to the man she hated. He told how, although he had fled from England to save his life, Acour had never ceased to desire her and to plot to get her into his power, any more than he had ceased to fear Hugh's vengeance. For this reason, he said, he had clad himself in the armour of another knight at Crecy, and in that guise accepted mercy at Hugh's hand, leaving de la Roche to die in his place beneath that same hand. For this reason also he had commanded him, Nicholas, to bring about the death of Hugh de Cressi and his squire beneath the daggers of assassins in the streets of Venice, a fate from which they had been saved only by the wizard in the yellow cap, whom no steel could harm.

"The black-hearted villain!" hissed Dick. "Well, for your comfort, holy priest, I'll tell you who that wizard is. He is Death himself, Death the Sword, Death the Fire, Death the Helper, and presently you'll meet him again."

"I knew it, I knew it," groaned the wretched man. "Oh! such is the end of sin whereof we think so little in our day of strength."

"Nay," broke in Hugh, "you'll meet, not the minister, but Him whom he serves and in His hand are mercies. Be silent, Dick, for this wretch makes confession and his time is short. Spare the tool and save your wrath for him who wielded it. Go now and fetch David Day that he may witness also."

So Dick went, and Nicholas continued his tale, throwing light into many a dark place, though there was little more that Hugh thought worthy of record.

Presently David came and started back in horror at the sight of that yellow tortured face set upon a living skeleton. Then the writing was read and Nicholas, held up by Dick, set his signature with a trembling hand to this his confession of the truth. This done they signed as witnesses, all three of them.

Now Hugh, whose pity was stirred, wished to move Nicholas and lay him on a bed in some chamber, and if they could, find someone to watch him till the end. But the priest refused this charity.

"Let me die before the altar," he said, "where I may set my eyes upon Him whom I have betrayed afresh," and he pointed to the carved ivory crucifix which hung above it. "Oh! be warned, be warned, my brethren," he went on in a wailing voice. "You are all of you still young; you may be led astray as I was by the desire for power, by the hope of wealth. You may sell yourselves to the wicked as I did, I who once was good and strove toward the right. If Satan tempts you thus, then remember Nicholas the priest, and his dreadful death, and see how he pays his servants. The plague has taken others, yet they have died at peace, but I, I die in hell before I see its fires."

"Not so," said Hugh, "you have repented, and I, against whom you have sinned perhaps more than all, forgive you, as I am sure my lady would, could she know."

"Then it is more than I do," muttered Grey Dick to himself. "Why should I forgive him because he rots alive, as many a better man has done, and goes to reap what he has sown, who if he had won his way would have sent us before him at the dagger's point? Yet who knows? Each of us sins in his own fashion, and perchance sin is born of the blood and not of the will. If ever I meet Murgh again I'll ask him. But perhaps he will not answer."

Thus reflected Dick, half to David, who feared and did not understand him, and half to himself. Ere ever he had finished with his thoughts, which were not such as Sir Andrew would have approved, Father Nicholas began to die.

It was not a pleasant sight this death of his, though of its physical part nothing shall be written. Let that be buried with other records of the great plague. Only in this case his mind triumphed for a while over the dissolution of his body. When there was little left of him save bone and sinew, still he found strength to cry out to God for mercy. Yes, and to raise himself and cast what had been arms about the ivory rood and kiss its feet with what had been lips, and in his last death struggle to drag it down and pant out his ultimate breath beneath its weight.

So there they left him, a horrible, huddled heap upon which gleamed the ivory crucifix, and went their way, gasping, into the air.

CHAPTER XVI

AT AVIGNON

Hard upon two months had gone by when at length these three, Hugh, Grey Dick, and David Day, set eyes upon the towers of stately Avignon standing red against the sunset and encircled by the blue waters of the Rhone. Terrible beyond imagination had been the journey of these men, who followed in the footsteps of Murgh. They saw him not, it is true, but always they saw his handiwork. Death, death, everywhere death, nothing but death!

One night they supped at an inn with the host, his family and servants, twelve folk in all, in seeming health. When they rose in the morning one old woman and a little child alone remained; the rest were dead or dying. One day they were surprised and taken by robbers, desperate outcasts of the mountains, who gave them twenty-four hours to "make their peace with heaven"—ere they hanged them because they had slain so many of the band before they were overpowered.

But when those twenty-four hours of grace had elapsed, it would have been easy for them to hang all who remained of those robbers themselves. So they took the best of their horses and their ill-gotten gold and rode on again, leaving the murderers murdered by a stronger power than man.

They went through desolate villages, where the crops rotted in the fields; they went through stricken towns whereof the moan and the stench rose in a foul incense to heaven; they crossed rivers where the very fish had died by thousands, poisoned of the dead that rolled seaward in their waters. The pleasant land had become a hell, and untouched, unharmed, they plodded onward through those deeps of hell. But a night or two before they had slept in a city whereof the population, or those who remained alive of them, seemed to have gone mad. In one place they danced and sang and made love in an open square. In another bands of naked creatures marched the streets singing hymns and flogging themselves till the blood ran down to their heels, while the passers-by prostrated themselves before them. These were the forerunners of the "Mad Dancers" of the following year.

In a field outside of this city they came upon even a more dreadful sight. Here forty or fifty frenzied people, most of them drunk, were engaged in burning a poor Jew, his wife and two children upon a great fire made of the staves of wine-casks, which they had plundered from some neighbouring cellars. When Hugh and his companions came upon the scene the Jew had already burned and this crowd of devils were preparing to cast his wife and children into the flames, which they had been forced to see devour their husband and father. Indeed, with yells of brutal laughter, they were thrusting the children into two great casks ere they rolled them into the heart of the fire, while the wretched mother stood by and shrieked.

"What do you, sirs?" asked Hugh, riding up to them.

"We burn wizards and their spawn, Sir Knight," answered the ringleader. "Know that these accursed Jews have poisoned the wells of our town—we have witnesses who saw them do it—and thus brought the plague upon us. Moreover, she," and he pointed to the woman—"was seen talking not fourteen days ago to the devil in a yellow cap, who appears everywhere before the Death begins. Now, roll them in, roll them in!"

Hugh drew his sword, for this sight was more than his English flesh and blood could bear. Dick also unsheathed the black bow, while young David produced a great knife which he carried.

"Free those children!" said Hugh to the man with whom he had spoken, a fat fellow, with rolling, bloodshot eyes.

"Get you to hell, stranger," he answered, "or we'll throw you on the fire also as a Jew in knight's dress."

"Free those children!" said Hugh again in a terrible voice, "or I send you before them. Be warned! I speak truth."

"Be you warned, stranger, for I speak truth also," replied the man, mimicking him. "Now friends," he added, "tuck up the devil's brats in their warm bed."

They were his last words, for Hugh thrust with his sword and down he went.

Now a furious clamour arose. The mob snatched up burning staves, bludgeons, knives or whatever they had at hand, and prepared to kill the three. Without waiting for orders, Dick began to shoot. David, a bold young man, rushed at one of the most violent and stabbed him, and Hugh, who had leapt from his horse, set himself back to back with the other two. Thrice Dick shot, and at the third deadly arrow these drunken fellows grew sober enough to understand that they wished no more of them.

Suddenly, acting on a common impulse, they fled away, every one, only leaving behind them those who had fallen beneath the arrows and the sword. But some who were so full of wine that they could not run, tumbled headlong and lay there helpless.

"Woman," said Hugh when they had departed, "your husband is lost, but you and your children are saved. Now go your ways and thank whatever God you worship for His small mercies."

"Alas! Sir Knight," the poor creature, a still young and not unhandsome Jewess, wailed in answer, "whither shall I go? If I return to that town those Christian men will surely murder me and my children as they have already murdered my husband. Kill us now by the sword or the bow—it will be a kindness—but leave us not here to be tortured by the Christian men according to their fashion with us poor Jews."

"Are you willing to go to Avignon?" asked Hugh, after thinking awhile.

"Ay, Sir Knight, or anywhere away from these Christians. Indeed, at Avignon I have a brother who perchance will protect us."

"Then mount my horse," said Hugh. "Dick and David, draw those two youngsters from the tubs and set them on your beasts; we can walk."

So the children, two comely little girls of eight and six years of age, or thereabout, were dragged out of their dreadful prisons and lifted to the saddle. The wretched widow, running to the bonfire, snatched from it her husband's burnt-off hand and hid it in the bosom of her filthy robe. Then she took some of the white ashes and threw them toward that city, muttering curses as she did so.

"What do you?" asked Hugh curiously.

"I pray, sir, to Jehovah, the God of the Jews, that for every grain of these ashes He may take a life in payment for that of my murdered husband, and I think that He will listen."

"Like enough," answered Hugh, crossing himself, "but, woman, can you wonder that we Christians hold you sorcerers when we hear such prayers from your lips?"

She turned with a tragic motion, and, pointing to the bones of her husband smouldering in the fire, answered:

"And can you wonder, sir, that we wretched creatures utter such prayers when you, our masters, do such deeds as this?"

"No," answered Hugh, "I cannot. Let us be going from this shambles."

So they went, a melancholy procession if ever there one was seen upon this earth. As the three Englishmen marched behind the horses with their weeping burdens Grey Dick reflected aloud after his fashion.

"Jew and Christian!" he said. "The Jews killed one Man who chanced to be a God, though they knew it not, and ever since the Christians have killed thousands of the Jews. Now, which is the most wicked, those Jews who killed the Man Who was a God, because He said He was a God, or those Christians who throw a man into a fire to burn before his wife's and children's eyes? A man who never said that he was a god, but who, they said, put poison into their wells, which he did not do, but which they believed he did because he was one of the race that thirteen hundred years ago killed their God? Ah, well! Jew and Christian, I think the same devil dwells in them all, but Murgh alone knows the truth of the matter. If ever we meet again, I'll ask him of it. Meanwhile, we go to Avignon in strange company, whereof all the holy priests yonder, if any of them still live, to say nothing of the people, may demand an account of us."

So spoke Dick as one who seeks an answer, but neither of his companions gave him any.

On they went through the ruined land unpursued, although they had just brought sundry men to their deaths. For now neither law nor justice was left and those killed who could and those died who must, unwept and unavenged. Only certain travellers, flying they knew not whither, flying from doom to doom, eyed them with hate and loathing because of their companions. Those who consorted with Jews must, they thought, be the enemies of every Christian soul.

Well was it for them perhaps that the early winter night was closing in when they reached the wonderful bridge of St. Bénézet, now quite unguarded, since a worse foe reigned in Avignon than any that it could fear from without. They crossed it, unnoted, for here none lingered in the gloom and rain save one poor woman, who called out to them that all she loved were dead and that she went to seek them. Then, before they could interfere, she scrambled to the parapet of the bridge and with a wild cry leapt into the foaming waters that rushed beneath.

"God forgive and rest her!" muttered Hugh, crossing himself. The others only shrugged their shoulders. Such dreadful sights fed their eyes daily till they learned to take little note of them.

In a deserted place on the farther side of the bridge they halted, and Hugh said to the Jewish widow:

"Woman, here is Avignon, where you tell us there are those who will befriend you, so now let us part. We have done what we can for you and it is not safe either for you or for us that we should be seen together in this Christian city."

"Sir, you speak well," she answered. "Be pleased ere we separate, to meet no more perchance, to tell me your names that I may remember them and hand them down among my people from generation to generation."

So he told her, and thrust onto her a gift of money and the most of such food as remained to them. Then the poor woman lifted up her arms and said:

"I, Rebecca, daughter of Onias and wife of Nathan, call down on you, Hugh de Cressi, Richard Archer and David Day, and on your children forever, the blessings of Jehovah, because you have rescued the widow and her children from the fire and avenged the murder of the husband and the father. O God of my people, as Thou didst save Lot and his house from the flames of Sodom, so save these true-hearted and merciful men! Turn from them the sword of Thy wrath when it smites the sinful cities! Cast the cloak of Thy protection about them and all they love! Prosper their handiwork in peace and in war, fulfil their desire upon their enemies, and at last let them die full of years and honour and so be gathered into Thy eternal bosom! Thus prayeth Rebecca, the daughter of Onias, and thus shall it be."

Then, leading her children, she turned and vanished into the darkness.

"Now," said Dick when she had gone, "although they were spoken by a Jew whom men call accursed because their forefathers, fulfilling prophecy, or some few of them, wrought a great crime when the world was young and thereby brought about the salvation of mankind, as we believe, those are among the most comfortable words to which my ears have listened, especially such of them as dealt with the fulfilling of our desire upon our enemies in war. Well, they are spoke, and I doubt not registered in a book which will not be lost. So, master, let us seek a lodging in this city of Avignon, which, for my part, I do with a light heart."

Hugh nodded, and his heart also was lightened by those words of blessing and good omen. Mounting their horses, they took a street that led them past the great Roches des Doms, on the crest of which stood the mighty palace of the Popes, as yet unfinished, but still one of the vastest buildings they had ever seen. Here on the battlements and in front of the gateway burned great fires, lit by order of his Holiness to purify the air and protect him and his Court from the plague.

Leaving this place on their right they rode slowly along one of the principal streets of the town, seeking an inn. Soon they found one, a large place that had a sign on which three shepherds were painted, and turned to enter its gateway. But, when they saw them, out of that gateway rushed a mob of frantic people waving swords and cudgels, and saying that they would have no strangers there to bring the Death among them.

"Let us go on," said Hugh, "for here it seems we are not welcome."

So they went and tried three other inns in turn. At two of them they met with a like greeting, but the doors of the third were closed and the place was deserted. Then, for a crowd began to gather round them, wearily enough they turned up another street at hazard. Thus they wended their way back toward the great central rock, thinking that there they might find some more hospitable tavern.

Following this new street, they reached a less crowded suburb of the town, where large dwellings stood in their own gardens. One of these, they saw by the flare of some of those fires which burned all about the city in this time of pestilence, seemed to be a small castle. At least it had a moat round it and a drawbridge, which was down. Seeing that lamps burned in its windows, Hugh, who was worn out with their long journeyings, took a sudden resolution.

"Doubtless some knight dwells in this fine house," he said to his companions. "Let us go up and declare our names and degree and by virtue of them claim the hospitality which is our right."

"Be it so," grumbled Dick. "We cannot be worse treated there than we were at the inns, unless the owner adds arrows to the swords and cudgels."

They rode across the drawbridge to the gateway of the little castle, which was open, and finding no one there, through a small courtyard to the door, which also was open.

David dismounted and knocked on it, but none answered.

"An empty house belongs to no one," said Dick; "at any rate in these times. Let us enter."

They did so, and saw that the place was sumptuously appointed. Though ancient, it was not large, having, as they afterward discovered, been a fortification on an outer wall now demolished, which had been turned to the purposes of a dwelling. Leaving the hall out of which opened the refectory, they mounted a stone stair to the upper chambers, and entered one of them.

Here they saw a strange and piteous sight. On a bed, about which candles still burned, lay a young woman who had been very beautiful, arrayed in a bride's robe.

"Dead of the plague," said Hugh, "and deserted at her death. Well, she had better luck than many, since she was not left to die alone. Her dress and these candles show it."

"Ay," answered Dick, "but fear took the watchers at last and they are fled. Well, we will fill their place, and, if they do not return to-morrow, give her honourable burial in her own courtyard. Here be fine lodgings for us, master, so let us bide in them until the rightful owners cast us out. Come, David, and help me raise that drawbridge."

Fine lodgings these proved to be indeed, since, as they found, no house in Avignon was better furnished with all things needful. But, and this will show how dreadful were the times, during these days that they made this their home they never so much as learned the name of that poor lady arrayed in the bride's dress and laid out upon her marriage bed.

In the butteries and cellar were plentiful provisions of food. Having eaten of it with thankfulness, they chose out one of the bed-chambers and slept there quite undisturbed till the morning sun shone in at the window-places and awoke them. Then they arose, and, digging a shallow grave in the courtyard with some garden tools which they found in a shed, they bore out the poor bride, and, removing only her jewels, which were rich enough, buried her there in her wedding dress. This sad duty finished, they washed themselves with water from the well, and breakfasted. After they had eaten they consulted as to what they should do next.

"We came here to lay a certain cause before his Holiness," said Hugh. "Let us go up to the palace, declare our business and estate, and ask audience."

So, leaving David in charge of the house, which they named the Bride's Tower because of the dead lady and the little keep which rose above it, and of the horses that they had stalled in the stable, they went out and made their way to the great entrance of the Pope's palace. Here they found the gates shut and barred, with a huge fire burning behind them.

Still they knocked until some guards appeared armed with cross-bows, and asked their business. They said they desired to see his Holiness, or at least one of his secretaries, whereon the guards asked whence they came. They replied from Italy, and were told that if so they would find no entrance there, since the Death had come from Italy. Now Hugh gave his name and stated his business on hearing which the guards laughed at him.

"Annulment of a false marriage!" said their captain. "Go lay your petition before Death, who will do your business swiftly if he has not done it already. Get you gone, you English knight, with your white-faced squire. We want no English here at the best of times, and least of all if they hail from Italy."

"Come on, master," said Dick, "there are more ways into a house than by the front door—and we won't want to leave our brains to grease its hinges."

So they went away, wondering whither they should betake themselves or what they could do next. As it chanced, they had not long to wait for an answer. Presently a lantern-jawed notary in a frayed russet gown, who must have been watching their movements, approached them and asked them what had been their business at the Pope's palace. Hugh told him, whereon the lawyer, finding that he was a person of high degree, became deferential in his manner. Moreover, he announced that he was a notary named Basil of Tours and one of the legal secretaries of his Holiness, who just now was living without the gates of the palace by express command in order to attend to the affairs of suitors at the Papal Court during the Great Sickness. He added, however, that he was able to communicate with those within, and that doubtless it might be in his power to forward the cause of the noble knight, Sir Hugh de Cressi, in which already he took much interest.

"There would be a fee?" suggested Dick, looking at the man coldly.

Basil answered with a smirk that fees and legal affairs were inseparable; the latter naturally involved the former. Not that he cared for money, he remarked, especially in this time of general woe. Still, it would never do for a lawyer, however humble, to create a precedent which might be used against his craft in better days. Then he named a sum.

Hugh handed him double what he asked, whereon he began to manifest great zeal in his case. Indeed, he accompanied them to the fortified house that they had named the Bride's Tower, which he alleged, with or without truth, he had never seen before. There he wrote down all particulars of the suit.

"Sir Edmund Acour, Count de Noyon, Seigneur of Cattrina?" he said presently. "Why I think that a lord of those names had audience with his Holiness some while ago, just before the pest grew bad in Avignon and the gates of the palace were ordered to be shut. I know not what passed on the occasion, not having been retained in the cause, but I will find out and tell you to-morrow."

"Find out also, if it pleases you, learned Basil," said Hugh, "whether or no this knight with the three names is still in Avignon. If so, I have a word or two to say to him."

"I will, I will," answered the lantern-jawed notary. "Yet I think it most unlikely that any one who can buy or beg a horse to ride away on should stay in this old city just now, unless indeed, the laws of his order bind him to do so that he may minister to the afflicted. Well, if the pest spares me and you, to-morrow morning I will be back here at this hour to tell you all that I can gather."

"How did this sickness begin in Avignon?" asked Grey Dick.

"Noble Squire, none know for certain. In the autumn we had great rains, heavy mists and other things contrary to the usual course of nature, such as strange lights shining in the heavens, and so forth. Then after a day of much heat, one evening a man clad in a red and yellow cap, who wore a cloak of thick black furs and necklaces of black pearls, was seen standing in the market-place. Indeed, I saw him myself. There was something so strange and dreadful about the appearance of this man, although it is true that some say he was no more than a common mountebank arrayed thus to win pence, that the people set upon him. They hurled stones at him, they attacked him with swords and every other weapon, and thought that they had killed him, when suddenly he appeared outside the throng unhurt. Then he stretched out his white-gloved hand toward them and melted into the gloom.

"Only," added Basil nervously, "it was noted afterward that all those who had tried to injure the man were among the first to die of the pest. Thank God, I was not one of them. Indeed I did my best to hold them back, which, perhaps, is the reason why I am alive to-day."

"A strange story," said Hugh, "though I have heard something like it in other cities through which we have passed. Well, till to-morrow at this hour, friend Basil."

"We have learned two things, master," said Dick, when the lawyer had bowed himself out. "First, that Acour is, or has been, in Avignon, and secondly, that Murgh the Messenger, Murgh the Sword, has been or is in Avignon. Let us go seek for one of the other of them, since for my part I desire to meet them both."

So all that day they sought but found neither.

Next morning Basil reappeared, according to his promise, and informed them that their business was on foot. Also he said that it was likely to prove more difficult than he anticipated. Indeed, he understood that he who was named de Noyon and Cattrina, having friends among the cardinals, had already obtained some provisional ratification of his marriage with the lady Eve Clavering. This ratification it would now be costly and difficult to set aside.

Hugh answered that if only he could be granted an audience with his Holiness, he had evidence which would make the justice of his cause plain. What he sought was an audience.

The notary scratched his lantern jaws and asked how that could be brought about when every gate of the palace was shut because of the plague. Still, perhaps, it might be managed, he added, if a certain sum were forthcoming to bribe various janitors and persons in authority.

Hugh gave him the sum out of the store of gold they had taken from the robbers in the mountains, with something over for himself.

So Basil departed, saying that he would return at the same hour on the morrow, if the plague spared him and them, his patrons, as he prayed the Saints that it might do.

Hugh watched him go, then turned to Dick and said:

"I mistrust me of that hungry wolf in sheep's clothing who talks so large and yet does nothing. Let us go out and search Avignon again. Perchance we may meet Acour, or at least gather some tidings of him."

So they went, leaving the Tower locked and barred, who perchance would have been wiser to follow Basil. A debased and fraudulent lawyer of no character at all, this man lived upon such fees as he could wring without authority from those who came to lay their suits before the Papal Court, playing upon their hopes and fears and pretending to a power which he did not possess. Had they done so, they might have seen him turn up a certain side street, and, when he was sure that none watched him, slip into the portal of an ancient house where visitors of rank were accustomed to lodge.

Mounting some stairs without meeting any one, for this house, like many others, seemed to be deserted in that time of pestilence, he knocked upon a door.

"Begone, whoever you are," growled a voice from within. "Here there are neither sick to be tended nor dead to be borne away."

Had they been there to hear it, Hugh and Dick might have found that voice familiar.

"Noble lord," he replied, "I am the notary, Basil, and come upon your business."

"Maybe," said the voice, "but how know I that you have not been near some case of foul sickness and will not bring it here?"

"Have no fear, lord; I have been waiting on the healthy, not on the sick—a task which I leave to others who have more taste that way."

Then the door was opened cautiously, and from the room beyond it came a pungent odour of aromatic essences. Basil passed in, shutting it quickly behind him. Before him at the further side of the table and near to a blazing fire stood Acour himself. He was clothed in a long robe and held a piece of linen that was soaked in some strong-smelling substance before his nose and mouth.

"Nay, come no nearer," he said to the clerk, "for this infection is most subtle, and—be so good as to cast off that filthy cloak of yours and leave it by the door."

Basil obeyed, revealing an undergarment that was still more foul. He was not one who wasted money on new apparel.

"Well, man," said Acour, surveying him with evident disgust and throwing a handful of dried herbs upon the fire, "what news now? Has my cause been laid before his Holiness? I trust so, for know that I grow weary of being cooped up here like a falcon in a cage with the dread of a loathsome death and a handful of frightened servants as companions who do nothing but drone out prayers all day long."

"Yes, lord, it has. I have it straight from Clement's own secretary, and the answer is that his Holiness will attend to the matter when the pest has passed away from Avignon, and not before. He adds also that when it does so, if ever, all the parties to the cause, by themselves or by their representatives, must appear before him. He will give no ex parte judgment upon an issue which, from letters that have reached him appears to be complicated and doubtful."

"Mother of Heaven!" exclaimed Acour, "what a fool am I to let you in to tell me such tidings. Well, if that is all you have to say the sooner I am out of this hateful city the better. I ride this afternoon, or, if need be, walk on foot."

"Indeed," said Basil. "Then you leave behind you some who are not so frightened of their health, but who bide here upon a very similar errand. Doubtless, as often happens to the bold, they will find a way to fulfil it."

"And who may these be, fellow?"

"A bold and warlike knight, a squire with hair like tow and a face that might be worn by Death himself, and a young English serving man."

Acour started up from the chair in which he had sat down.

"No need to tell me their names," he said, "but how, by hell's gate, came de Cressi and his familiar here."

"By the road, I imagine, lord, like others. At least, a few days ago they were seen travelling toward the bridge of St. Bénézet in the company of certain Jews, whom, I am informed, they had rescued from the just reward of their witchcraft. I have a note of all the facts, which include the slaying of sundry good Christians on behalf of the said Jews."

"Jews? Why, that is enough to hang them in these times. But what do they here and where do they lodge?"

"Like your lordship they strive to see the Pope. They desire that an alleged marriage between one Sir Edmund Acour, Count of Noyon and Seigneur of Cattrina, and one lady Eve Clavering, an Englishwoman, may be declared null and void. As they have been so good as to honour me with their confidence and appoint me their agent, I am able to detail the facts. Therefore I will tell you at once that the case of this knight de Cressi appears to be excellent, since it includes the written confession of a certain Father Nicholas, of whom perhaps you have heard."

"The written confession of Nicholas! Have you seen it?"

"Not as yet. So far I have been trusted with no original documents. Is it your will that I should try to possess myself of these? Because, if so, I will do my best, provided—" and he looked at the pocket of Acour's robe.

"How much?" asked Acour. The man named a great sum, half to be paid down and half on the delivery of the papers.

"I'll double it," said Acour, "if you can bring it about that these insolent Englishmen die—of the pest."

"How can I do that, lord?" asked Basil with a sour smile. "Such tricks might work backward. I might die, or you. Still these men have committed crimes, and just now there is a prejudice against Jews."

"Ay," said Acour, "the Englishmen are sorcerers. I tell you that in Venice they were seen in the company of that fiend of the yellow cap and the fur robe who appears everywhere before the pest."

"Prove it," exclaimed Basil, "and the citizens of Avignon will rid you of their troubling."

Then they debated long together and the end of it was that Basil departed, saying that he would return again on the morrow and make report as to certain matters.

CHAPTER XVII

A MEETING

Hugh, Grey Dick, and David, trudged up and down through the streets of Avignon. All that long day they trudged seeking news and finding little. Again and again they asked at the inns whether a knight who bore the name of Acour, or de Noyon, or Cattrina, was or had been a guest there, but none whom they asked seemed to know anything of such a person.

They asked it of citizens, also of holy priests, good men who, careless of their own lives, followed biers or cartloads of dead destined to the plague pit or the river that they might pronounce over them the last blessings of the Church. They asked it of physicians, some few of whom still remained alive, as they hurried from house to house to administer to the sick or dying. But all of these either did not answer at all or else shrugged their shoulders and went on their melancholy business. Only one of them called back that he had no time to waste in replying to foolish questions, and that probably the knight they sought was dead long ago or had fled from the city.

Another man, an officer of customs, who seemed half dazed with misery and fear, said that he remembered the lord Cattrina entering Avignon with a good many followers, since he himself had levied the customary tolls on his company. As for how long it was ago he could not say, since his recollection failed him—so much had happened since. So he bade them farewell until they met in heaven, which, he added, doubtless would be soon.

The evening drew on. Wearily enough they had trudged round the great Roche des Doms, looking up at the huge palace of the Pope, where the fires burned night and day and the guards watched at the shut gates, that forbidden palace into which no man might enter. Leaving it, they struck down a street that was new to them, which led toward their borrowed dwelling of the Bride's Tower. This street was very empty save for a few miserable creatures, some of whom lay dead or dying in the gutters. Others lurked about in doorways or behind the pillars of gates, probably for no good purpose. They heard the footsteps of a man following them who seemed to keep in the shadow, but took no heed, since they set him down as some wretched thief who would never dare to attack three armed men. It did not occur to them that this was none other than the notary Basil, clad in a new robe, who for purposes of his own was spying upon their movements.

They came to a large, ruinous-looking house, of which the gateway attracted Grey Dick's sharp eyes.

"What does that entrance remind you of, master?" he asked.

Hugh looked at it carelessly and answered:

"Why, of the Preceptory at Dunwich. See, there are the same arms upon the stone shield. Doubtless once the Knights Templar dwelt there. Sir Andrew may have visited this place in his youth."

As the words left his lips two men came out of the gateway, one of them a physician to judge by the robe and the case of medicines which he carried; the other a very tall person wrapped in a long cloak. The physician was speaking.

"She may live or she may die," he said. "She seems strong. The pest, you say, has been on her for four days, which is longer than most endure it; she has no swellings, and has not bled from the lungs; though, on the other hand, she is now insensible, which often precedes the end. I can say no more; it is in the hands of God. Yes, I will ask you to pay me the fee now. Who knows if you will be alive to do so to-morrow? If she dies before then I recommend you to throw her into the river, which the Pope has blessed. It is cleaner burial than the plague pit. I presume she is your grand-daughter—a beautiful woman. Pity she should be wasted thus, but many others are in a like case. If she awakes give her good food, and if you cannot get that—wine, of which there is plenty. Five gold pieces—thank you," and he hurried away.

"Little have you told me, physician, that I did not know already," said the tall hooded figure, in a deep voice the sound of which thrilled Hugh to his marrow. "Yet you are right; it is in the hands of God. And to those hands I trust—not in vain, I think."

"Sir," said Hugh addressing him out of the shadow in which he stood, "be pleased to tell me, if you will, whether you have met in this town a knight of the name of Sir Edmund Acour, for of him I am in search?"

"Sir Edmund Acour?" answered the figure. "No, I have not met him in Avignon, though it is like enough that he is here. Yet I have known of this knight far away in England."

"Was it at Blythburgh, in Suffolk, perchance?" asked Hugh.

"Ay, at Blythburgh in Suffolk; but who are you that speak in English and know of Blythburgh in Suffolk?"

"Oh!" cried Hugh, "what do you here, Sir Andrew Arnold?"

The old man threw back his hood and stared at him.

"Hugh de Cressi, by Christ's holy Name!" he exclaimed. "Yes, and Richard the archer, also. The light is bad; I did not see your faces. Welcome, Hugh, thrice welcome," and he threw his arms about him and embraced him. "Come, enter my lodgings, I have much to say to you."

"One thing I desire to learn most of all, Father; the rest can wait. Who is the sick lady of whom you spoke to yonder physician—she that, he thought, was your grand-daughter?"

"Who could it be, Hugh, except Eve Clavering."

"Eve!" gasped Hugh. "Eve dying of the pest?"

"Nay, son: who said so? She is ill, not dying, who, I believe, will live for many years."

"You believe, Father, you believe! Why this foul plague scarce spares one in ten. Oh! why do you believe?"

"God teaches me to do so," answered the old knight solemnly. "I only sent for that physician because he has medicines which I lack. But it is not in him and his drugs that I put my trust. Come, let us go in and see her."

So they went up the stairs and turned down a long passage, into which the light flowed dimly through large open casements.

"Who is that?" asked Hugh suddenly. "I thought that one brushed past me, though I could see nothing."

"Ay," broke in the lad David, who was following, "and I felt a cold wind as though some one stirred the air."

Grey Dick also opened his lips to speak, then changed his mind and was silent, but Sir Andrew said impatiently:

"I saw no one, therefore there was no one to see. Enter!" and he opened the door.

Now they found themselves in a lighted room, beyond which lay another room.

"Bide you here, Richard, with your companion," said Sir Andrew. "Hugh, follow me, and let us learn whether I have trusted to God in vain."

Then very gently he opened the door, and they passed in together, closing it behind them.

This is what Hugh saw. At the far end of the room was a bed, near to which stood a lamp that showed, sitting up in the bed, a beautiful young woman, whose dark hair fell all about her. Her face was flushed but not wasted or made dreadful by the sickness, as happened to so many. There she sat staring before her with her large dark eyes and a smile upon her sweet lips, like one that muses on happy things.

"See," whispered Sir Andrew, "she is awakened from her swoon. I think I did not trust in vain, my son."

She caught the tones of his voice and spoke.

"Is that you, Father?" she asked dreamily. "Draw near, for I have such a strange story to tell you."

He obeyed, leaving Hugh in the shadow, and she went on:

"Just now I awoke from my sleep and saw a man standing by my bed."

"Yes, yes," Sir Andrew said, "the physician whom I sent for to see you."

"Do physicians in Avignon wear caps of red and yellow and robes of black fur and strings of great black pearls that, to tell truth, I coveted sorely?" she asked, laughing a little. "No, no. If this were a physician, he is of the sort that heals souls. Indeed, now that I think of it, when I asked him his name and business, he answered that the first was the Helper, and the second, to bring peace to those in trouble."

"Well, daughter, and what else did the man say?" asked Sir Andrew, soothingly.

"You think I wander," she said, interpreting the tone of his voice and not his words, "but indeed it is not so. Well, he said little; only that I had been very ill, near to death, in truth, much nearer than I thought, but that now I should recover and within a day or two be quite well and strong again. I asked him why he had come to tell me this. He replied, because he thought that I should like to know that he had met one whom I loved in the city of Venice in Italy; one who was named Hugh de Cressi. Yes, Father, he said Hugh de Cressi, who, with his squire, an archer, had befriended him there—and that this Hugh was well and would remain so, and that soon I should see him again. Also he added that he had met one whom I hated, who was named the lord of Cattrina, and that if this Cattrina threatened me I should do wisely to fly back to England, since there I should find peace and safety. Then, suddenly, just before you came in, he was gone."

"You have strange dreams, Eve," said Sir Andrew, "yet there is truth in their madness. Now be strong lest joy should kill you, as it has done by many a one before."

Then he turned to the shadow behind him and said, "Come." Next instant Hugh was kneeling at Eve's bedside and pressing his lips upon her hand.

Oh! they had much to say to each other, so much that the half of it remained unsaid. Still Hugh learned that she and Sir Andrew had come to Avignon upon the Pope's summons to lay this matter of her alleged marriage before him in person. When they reached the town they found it already in the grip of the great plague, and that to see his Holiness was almost impossible, since he had shut himself up in his palace and would admit no one. Yet an interview was promised through Sir Andrew's high-placed friends, only then the sickness struck Eve and she could not go, nor was Sir Andrew allowed to do so, since he was nursing one who lay ill.

Then Hugh began to tell his tale, to which Eve and Sir Andrew Arnold listened greedily. Of Murgh, for sundry reasons, he said nothing, and of the fight from which Acour had fled in Venice before the earthquake but little. He told them, however, that he had heard that this Acour had been or was in Avignon and that he had learned from a notary named Basil, whom he, Hugh, had retained, that Acour had won from the Pope a confirmation of his marriage.

"A lie!" interrupted Sir Andrew. "His Holiness caused me to be informed expressly that he would give no decision in this cause until all the case was before him."

As he said the words a disturbance arose in the outer room, and the harsh voice of Grey Dick was heard saying:

"Back, you dog! Would you thrust yourself into the chamber of the lady of Clavering? Back, or I will cast you through the window-place."

Sir Andrew went to see what was the matter, and Hugh, breaking off his tale, followed him, to find the notary, Basil, on his knees with Grey Dick gripping him by the collar of his robe.

"Sir Knight," said Basil, recognizing Hugh, "should I, your faithful agent, be treated thus by this fierce-faced squire of yours?"

"That depends on what you have done, Sir Lawyer," answered Hugh, motioning to Dick to loose the man.

"All I have done, Sir Knight, is to follow you into a house where I chanced to see you enter, in order to give you some good tidings. Then this fellow caught me by the throat and said that if I dared to break in upon the privacy of one whom he called Red Eve and Lady Clavering, he would kill me."

"He had his orders, lawyer."

"Then, Sir Knight, he might have executed them less roughly. Had he but told me that you were alone with some lady, I should have understand and withdrawn for a while, although to do so would have been to let precious moments slip," and the lean-faced knave leered horribly.

"Cease your foul talk and state your business," interrupted Sir Andrew, thrusting himself in front of Hugh, who he feared would strike the fellow.

"And pray, who may you be?" asked the lawyer, glancing up at the tall figure that towered above him.

Sir Andrew threw back his hood, revealing his aged, hawk-like countenance, his dark and flashing eyes and his snow-white hair and beard.

"If you would learn, man," he said, in his great voice, "in the world I was known as Sir Andrew Arnold, one of the priors of the Order of the Templars, which is a name that you may have heard. But now that I have laid aside all worldly pomp and greatness, I am but Father Andrew, of Dunwich, in England."

"Yes, yes, I have heard the name; who has not?" said the lawyer humbly; "also you are here as guardian to the lady Eve Clavering, are you not, to lay a certain cause before his Holiness? Oh! do not start, all these matters came to my knowledge who am concerned in every great business in Avignon as the chief agent and procurator of the Papal Court, though it is true that this tiding has reached me only within the last few minutes and from the lips of your own people. Holy Father, I pray your pardon for breaking in upon you, which I did only because the matter is very pressing. Sir Hugh de Cressi here has a cause to lay before the Pope with which you may be acquainted. Well, for two days I have striven to win him an audience, and now through my sole influence, behold! 'tis granted. See here," and he produced a parchment that purported to be signed by the Pope's secretary and countersigned by a cardinal, and read:

"'If the English knight, Sir Hugh de Cressi, and his squire, the captain Richard, will be in the chamber of audience at the palace at seven of the clock this evening' (that is, within something less than half an hour), 'his Holiness will be pleased to receive them as a most special boon, having learned that the said Sir Hugh is a knight much in favour with his Grace of England, who appointed him his champion in a combat that was lately to be fought at Venice.'"

"That's true enough, though I know not how the Pope heard of it," interrupted Hugh.

"Through me, Sir Knight, for I learn everything. None have so much power in Avignon as I, although it often pleases me to seem poor and of no account. But let that pass. Either you must take this opportunity or be content not to see his Holiness at all. Orders have been issued because of the increase of this pest in Avignon, that from to-night forward none shall be admitted to the palace upon any pretext whatsoever; no, not even a king."

"Then I had best go," said Hugh.

"Ay," answered Sir Andrew, "and return here with your tidings as soon as may be. Yet," he added in a low voice to Grey Dick, "I love not the look of this scurvy guide of yours. Could not your master have found a better attorney?"

"Perhaps," answered Dick, "that is if one is left alive in Avignon. Being in haste we took the first that came to hand, and it seems that he will serve our turn. At least, if he plays tricks, I promise it will be the worse for him," and he looked grimly at the rogue, who was talking to David Day and appeared to hear nothing.

So they went, and with them David, who had witnessed the confession of Father Nicholas. Therefore they thought it best that he should accompany them to testify to it if there were need.

"Bid my lady keep a good heart and say that I will be with her again ere long," said Hugh as they descended the stairs in haste.

Following the guidance of Basil, they turned first this way and then that, till soon in the gathering darkness they knew not where they were.

"What was the name of the street in which Sir Andrew had his lodging?" asked Hugh, halting.

"Rue St. Benezet," answered Basil. "Forward, we have no time to lose."

"Did you tell Sir Andrew where we dwelt, master?" said Dick presently, "for I did not."

"By my faith, Dick, no; it slipped my mind."

"Then it will be hard for him to find us if he has need, master, in this rabbit warren of a town. Still that can't be mended now. I wish we were clear of this business, for it seems to me that yon fellow is not leading us toward the palace. Almost am I minded—" and he looked at Basil, then checked himself.

Presently Dick wished it still more. Taking yet another turn they found themselves in an open square or garden that was surrounded by many mean houses. In this square great pest-fires burned, lighting it luridly. By the flare of them they saw that hundreds of people were gathered there listening to a mad-eyed friar who was preaching to them from the top of a wine-cart. As they drew near to the crowd through which Basil was leading them, Hugh heard the friar shouting:

"Men of Avignon, this pest which kills us is the work not of God, but of the Jew blasphemers and of the sorcerers who are in league with them. I tell you that two such sorcerers who pass as Englishmen are in your city now and have been consorting with the Jews, plotting your destruction. One looks like a young knight, but the other has the face of Death himself, and both of them wrought murders in a neighbouring town to protect the Jews. Until you kill the accursed Jews this plague will never pass. You will die, every one of you, with your wives and children if you do not kill the Jews and their familiars."

Just then the man, rolling his wild eyes about, caught sight of Hugh and Dick.

"See!" he screamed. "There are the wizards who in Venice were seen in the company of the Enemy of Mankind. That good Christian, Basil, has brought them face to face with you, as he promised me that he would."

As he heard these words Hugh drew his sword and leapt at Basil. But the rogue was watching. With a yell of fear he threw himself among the crowd and there vanished.

"Out weapons, and back to back!" cried Hugh, "for we are snared."

So the three of them ranged themselves together facing outward. In front of them gleamed Grey Dick's axe, Hugh's sword and David's great knife. In a moment the furious mob was surging round them like the sea, howling, "Down with the foreign wizards! Kill the friends of the Jews!" one solid wall of changing white faces.

A man struck at them with a halbert, but the blow fell short, for he was afraid to come too near. Grey Dick leapt forward, and in a moment was back again, leaving that man dead, smitten through from skull to chin. For a while there was silence, since this sudden death gave them pause, and in it Hugh cried out:

"Are blameless men to be murdered thus? Have we no friends in Avignon?"

"Some," answered a voice from the outer shadow, though who spoke they could not see.

"Save the protectors of the Jews!" cried the voice again.

Then came a rush and a counter-rush. Fighting began around them in which they took no share. When it had passed over them like a gust of wind, David Day was gone, killed or trodden down, as his companions thought.

"Now, master, we are alone," said Grey Dick. "Set your shoulders against mine and let us die a death that these dogs of Avignon will remember."

"Ay, ay!" answered Hugh. "But don't overreach, Dick, 'tis ever the archer's fault."

The mob closed in on them, then rolled back like water from a rock, leaving some behind. Again they closed in and again rolled back.

"Bring bows!" they cried, widening out. "Bring bows and shoot them down."

"Ah!" gasped Dick, "that is a game two can play, now that I have arm room."

Almost before the words had left his lips the great black bow he bore was out and strung. Next instant the shafts began to rush, piercing all before them, till at the third arrow those in front of him melted away, save such as would stir no more. Only now missiles began to come in answer from this side and from that, although as yet none struck them.

"Unstring your bow, Dick, and let us charge," said Hugh. "We have no other chance save flight. They'll pelt us under."

Dick did not seem to hear. At least he shot on as one who was not minded to die unavenged. An arrow whistled through Hugh's cap, lifting it from his head, and another glanced from the mail on his shoulder. He ground his teeth with rage, for now none would come within reach of his long sword.

"Good-bye, friend Dick," he said. "I die charging," and with a cry of "A Cressi! A Cressi!" he sprang forward.

One leap and Dick was at his side, who had only bided to sheath his bow. The mob in front melted away before the flash of the white sword and the gleam of the grey axe. Still they must have fallen, for their pursuers closed in behind them like hunting hounds when they view the quarry, and there were none to guard their backs. But once more the shrill voice cried:

"Help the friends of the Jews! Save those who saved Rebecca and her children!"

Then again there came a rush of dark-browed men, who hissed and whistled as they fought.

So fierce was the rush that those who followed them were cut off, and Dick, glancing back over his shoulder, saw the mad-eyed priest, their leader, go down like an ox beneath the blow of a leaded bludgeon. A score of strides and they were out of the range of the firelight; another score and they were hidden by the gloom in the mouth of one of the narrow streets.

"Which way now?" gasped Hugh, looking back at the square where in the flare of the great fires Christians and Jews, fighting furiously, looked like devils struggling in the mouth of hell.

As he spoke a shock-headed, half-clad lad darted up to them and Dick lifted his axe to cut him down.

"Friend," he said in a guttural voice, "not foe! I know where you dwell; trust and follow me, who am of the kin of Rebecca, wife of Nathan."

"Lead on then, kin of Rebecca," exclaimed Hugh, "but know that if you cheat us, you die."

"Swift, swift!" cried the lad, "lest those swine should reach your house before you," and, catching Hugh by the hand, he began to run like a hare.

Down the dark streets they went, past the great rock where the fires burned at the gates of the palace of the Pope, then along more streets and across an open place where thieves and night-birds peered at them curiously, but at the sight of their drawn steel, slunk away. At length their guide halted.

"See!" he said. "There is your dwelling. Enter now and up with the bridge. Hark! They come. Farewell."

He was gone. From down the street to their left rose shouts and the sound of many running feet, but there in front of them loomed the Tower against the black and rainy sky. They dashed across the little drawbridge that spanned the moat, and, seizing the cranks, wound furiously. Slowly, ah! how slowly it rose, for it was heavy, and they were but two tired men; also the chains and cogs were rusty with disuse. Yet it did rise, and as it came home at last, the fierce mob, thirsting for their blood and guessing where they would refuge, appeared in front of it and by the light of some torches which they bore, caught sight of them.

"Come in, friends," mocked Grey Dick as they ran up and down the edge of the moat howling with rage and disappointment. "Come in if you would sup on arrow-heads such as this," and he sent one of his deadly shafts through the breast of a red-headed fellow who waved a torch in one hand and a blacksmith's hammer in the other.

Then they drew back, taking the dead man with them, but as they went one cried:

"The Jews shall not save you again, wizards, for if we cannot come at you to kill you, we'll starve you till you die. Stay there and rot, or step forth and be torn to pieces, as it pleases you, English wizards."

Then they all slunk back and vanished, or seemed to vanish,

down the mouths of the dark streets that ran into the open place in front of the dwelling which Hugh had named the Bride's Tower.

"Now," said Dick, wiping the sweat from his brow as they barred the massive door of the house, "we are safe for this night at least, and can eat and sleep in peace. See you, master, I have taken stock of this old place, which must have been built in rough times, for scarce a wall of it is less than five feet thick. The moat is deep all round. Fire cannot harm it, and it is loop-holed for arrows and not commanded by any other building, having the open place in front and below the wide fosse of the ancient wall, upon which it stands. Therefore, even with this poor garrison of two, it can be taken only by storm. This, while we have bows and arrows, will cost them something, seeing that we could hold the tower from stair to stair."

"Ay, Dick," answered Hugh sadly, "doubtless we can make a fight for it and take some with us to a quieter world, if they are foolish enough to give us a chance. But what did that fellow shout as to starving us out? How stand we for provisions?"

"Foreseeing something of the sort, I have reckoned that up, master. There's good water in the courtyard well and those who owned this tower, whoever they may have been, laid in great store, perchance for the marriage feast, or perchance when the plague began, knowing that it would bring scarcity. The cupboards and the butteries are filled with flour, dried flesh, wine, olives and oil for burning. Even if these should fail us there are the horses in the stable, which we can kill and cook, for of forage and fuel I have found enough."

"Then the Pope should not be more safe than we, Dick," said Hugh with a weary smile, "if any are safe in Avignon to-day. Well, let us go and eat of all this plenty, but oh! I wish I had told Sir Andrew where we dwelt, or could be sure in which of that maze of streets he and Red Eve are lodged. Dick, Dick, that knave Basil has fooled us finely."

"Ay, master," said Dick, setting his grim lips, "but let him pray his Saint that before all is done I do not fool him."

CHAPTER XVIII

THE PLAGUE PIT

Seven long days had gone by and still Hugh and Grey Dick held out in their Tower fortress. Though as yet unhurt, they were weary indeed, since they must watch all night and could only sleep by snatches in the daytime, one lying down to rest while the other kept guard.

As they had foreseen, except by direct assault, the place proved impregnable, its moat protecting it upon three sides and the sheer wall of the old city terminating in the deep fosse upon the fourth. In its little armoury, among other weapons they had found a great store of arrows and some good bows, whereof Hugh took the best and longest. Thus armed with these they placed themselves behind the loopholes of the embattled gateway, whence they could sweep the space before them. Or if danger threatened them elsewhere, there were embrasures whence they could command the bases of the walls. Lastly, also, there was the central tower, whereof they could hold each landing with the sword.

Thrice they had been attacked, since there seemed to be hundreds of folk in Avignon bent upon their destruction, but each time their bitter arrows, that rarely seemed to miss, had repulsed the foe with loss. Even when an onslaught was delivered on the main gateway at night, they had beaten their assailants by letting fall upon them through the machicoulis or overhanging apertures, great stones that had been piled up there, perhaps generations before, when the place was built.

Still the attacks did not slacken. Indeed the hate of the citizens of Avignon against these two bold Englishmen, whose courage and resource they attributed to help given to them by the powers of evil, seemed to grow from day to day, even as the plague grew in the streets of that sore-afflicted city. From their walls they could see friars preaching a kind of crusade against them. They pointed toward the tower with crucifixes, invoking their hearers to pull it stone from stone and slay the wizards within, the wizards who had conspired with the accursed Jews even beneath the eyes of his Holiness the Pope, to bring doom on Avignon.

The eighth morn broke at length, and its first red rays discovered Hugh and Dick kneeling side by side behind the battlements of the gateway. Each of them was making petition to heaven in his own fashion for forgiveness of his sins, since they were outworn and believed that this day would be their last.

"What did you pray for, Dick?" asked Hugh, glancing at his companion's fierce face, which in that half light looked deathlike and unearthly.

"What did I pray for? Well, for the first part let it be; that's betwixt me and whatever Power sent me out to do its business on the earth. But for the last—I'll tell you. It was that we may go hence with such a guard of dead French as never yet escorted two Englishmen from Avignon to heaven—or hell. Ay, and we will, master, for to-day, as they shouted to us, they'll storm this tower; but if our strength holds out there's many a one who'll never win its crest."

"Rather would I have died peacefully, Dick. Yet the blood of these hounds will not weigh upon my soul, seeing that they seek to murder us for no fault except that we saved a woman and two children from their cruel devilries. Oh! could I but know that Red Eve and Sir Andrew were safe away, I'd die a happy man."

"I think we shall know that and much more before to-morrow's dawn, master, or never know anything again. Look! they gather yonder. Now let us eat, for perhaps later we shall find no time."

The afternoon drew on toward evening and still these two lived. Of all the hundreds of missiles which were shot or hurled at them, although a few struck, not one of them had pierced their armour so as to do them hurt. The walls and battlements or some good Fate had protected them. Thrice had the French come on, and thrice they had retreated before those arrows that could not miss, and as yet bridge and doors were safe.

"Look," said Dick as he set down a cup of wine that he had drained, for his thirst was raging, "they send an embassy," and he pointed to a priest, the same mad-eyed fellow who preached in the square when the notary Basil led them into a trap, and to a man with him who bore a white cloth upon a lance. "Shall I shoot them?"

"Nay," answered Hugh; "why kill crazed folk who think that they serve God in their own fashion? We will hear what they have to say."

Presently the pair stood within speaking distance, and the priest called out:

"Hearken, you wizards. So far your master the devil has protected you, but now your hour has come. We have authority from those who rule this city and from the Church to summon you to surrender, and if you will not, then to slay you both."

"That, you shameless friar," answered Hugh, "you have been striving to do these many days. Yet it is not we who have been slain, although we stand but two men against a multitude. But if we surrender, what then?"

"Then you shall be put upon your trial, wizards, and, if found guilty, burned; if innocent, set free."

"Put upon our trial before our executioners! Why, I think those fires are alight already. Nay, nay, mad priest, go back and tell those whom you have fooled that if they want us they can come and take us, which they'll not do living."

Then the furious friar began to curse them, hurling at them the anathemas of the Church, till at length Dick called to him to begone or he would send an arrow to help him on the road.

So they went, and presently the sun sank.

"Now let us beware," said Dick. "The moon is near her full and will rise soon. They'll attack between times when we cannot see to shoot."

"Ay," answered Hugh, "moreover, now this gateway is no place for us. Of arrows there are few left, nor could we see to use them in

HL

the dark. The stones too are all spent and therefore they can bridge the moat and batter down the doors unharmed."

"What then?" asked Dick. "As we cannot fly, where shall we die?"

"On the roof of the old tower, I think, whence we can hurl ourselves at last and so perhaps escape being taken alive, and torment. Look you, Dick, that tower is mounted by three straight flights of steps. The first two of these we'll hold with such arrows as remain to us—there are three and twenty, as I think—and the last with axe and sword. Listen! They come! Take a brand from the hall hearth and let us go light the flambeaux."

So they went and set fire to the great torches of wood and tallow that were set in their iron holders to light the steps of the tower. Ere the last of them was burning they heard their enemies ravening without.

"Listen!" said Hugh as they descended to the head of the first flight of stairs. "They are across the moat."

As he spoke the massive doors crashed in beneath the blows of a baulk of timber.

"Now," said Hugh, as they strung their bows, "six arrows apiece here, if we can get off so many, and the odd eleven at our next stand. Ah, they come."

The mob rushed into the hall below, waving torches and swords and hunting it as dogs hunt a covert.

"The English wizards have hid themselves away," cried a voice. "Let us burn the place, for so we are sure to catch them."

"Nay, nay," answered another voice, that of the mad friar. "We must have them beneath the torture, that we may learn how to lift the curse from Avignon, and the names of their accomplices on earth and in hell. Search, search, search!"

"Little need to search," said Grey Dick, stepping out on to the landing. "Devil, go join your fellow-devils in that hell you talk of," and he sent an arrow through his heart.

For a moment there followed the silence of consternation while the mob stood staring at their fallen leader. Then with a yell of rage they charged the stair and that fray began which was told of in Avignon for generations. Hugh and Dick shot their arrows, nor could they miss, seeing what was their target; indeed some of those from the great black bow pinned foe to foe beneath them. But so crowded were the assailants on the narrow stair that they could not shoot back. They advanced helpless, thrust to their doom by the weight of those who pressed behind.

Now they were near, the dead, still on their feet, being borne forward by the living, to whom they served as shields. Hugh and Dick ran to the head of the second flight and thence shot off the arrows that remained.

Dick loosed the last of them, and of this fearful shaft it was said that it slew three men, piercing through the body of one, the throat of the second and burying its barb in the skull of the third on the lowest step. Now Dick unstrung his bow, and thrust it into its case on his shoulder, for he was minded that they should go together at the last.

"Shafts have sung their song," he said, with a fierce laugh; "now it is the turn of the axe and sword to make another music."

Then he gripped Sir Hugh by the hand, saying:

"Farewell, master. Oh, I hold this a merry death, such as the Saints grant to few. Ay, and so would you were you as free as I am. Well, doubtless your lady has gone before. Or at worst soon she will follow after and greet you in the Gate of Death, where Murgh sits and keeps his count of passing souls."

"Farewell, friend," answered Hugh, "be she quick or dead, thus Red Eve would wish that I should die. A Cressi! A Cressi!" he cried and drove his sword through the throat of a soldier who rushed at him.

They fought a very good fight, as doubtless the dead were telling each other while they passed from that red stair to such rest as they had won. They had fought a very good fight and it was hard to say which had done the best, Hugh's white sword or Dick's grey axe. And now, unwounded still save for a bruise or two, they stood there in the moonlight upon the stark edge of the tall tower, the foe in front and black space beneath. There they stood leaning on axe and sword and drawing their breath in great sobs, those two great harvestmen who that day had toiled so hard in the rich fields of death.

For a while the ever-gathering crowd of their assailants remained still staring at them. Then the leaders began to whisper to each other, for they scarcely seemed to dare to talk aloud.

"What shall we do?" asked one. "These are not men. No men could have fought as they have fought us for seven days and at last have slain us like sparrows in a net and themselves remained unhurt."

"No," answered another, "and no mortal archer could send his shaft through the bodies of three. Still it is finished now unless they find wings and fly away. So let us take them."

"Yes, yes," broke in Grey Dick with his hissing laugh, "come and take us, you curs of Avignon. Having our breath again, we are ready to be taken," and he lifted his axe and shook it.

"Seize them," shouted the leader of the French. "Seize them!" echoed those who poured up the stairs behind.

But there the matter ended, since none could find stomach to face that axe and sword. So at length they took another counsel.

"Bring bows and shoot them through the legs. Thus we shall bring them living to their trial," commanded the captain of the men of Avignon. He was their fourth captain on that one day, for the other three lay upon the stairs or in the hall.

Now Hugh and Dick spoke together, few words and swift, as to whether they should charge or leap from the wall and have done with it. While they spoke a little cloud floated over the face of the moon, so that until it had gone the French could not see to shoot.

"It's too risky," said Hugh. "If they capture us we must die a death to which I have no mind. Let us hurl our weapons at them, then leap."

"So be it," whispered Dick. "Do you aim at the captain on the left and I will take the other. Ready now! I think one creeps near to us."

"I think so, too," Hugh whispered back, "I felt the touch of his garments. Only he seemed to pass us from behind, which cannot be."

The cloud passed, and once again they were bathed in silver light.

It showed the men of Avignon already bending their bows; it showed Hugh and Grey Dick lifting axe and sword to hurl them. But between them and their mark it showed also a figure that they knew well, a stern and terrible figure, wearing a strange cap of red and yellow and a cape of rich, black fur.

"O God of Heaven! 'tis Murgh the Helper," gasped Hugh.

"Ay, Murgh the Fire, Murgh the Sword," said Dick, adding quietly, "it is true I was wondering whether he would prove as good as his word. Look now, look! they see him also!"

See him they did, indeed, and for a moment there was silence on that crowded tower top where stood at least a score of men, while their fellows packed the hall and stair below by hundreds. All stared at Murgh, and Murgh stared back at them with his cold eyes. Then a voice screamed:

"Satan! Satan come from hell to guard his own! Death himself is with you! Fly, men of Avignon, fly!"

Small need was there for this command. Already, casting down their bows, those on the tower top were rushing to the mouth of the stair, and, since it was blocked with men, using their swords upon them to hew a road. Now those below, thinking that it was the English wizards who slew them, struck back.

Presently all that stair and the crowded hall below, black as the mouth of the pit, for such lights as still burned soon were swept away, rang with the screams and curses and stifled groans of the trodden down or dying. In the pitchy darkness brother smote brother, friend trampled out the life of friend, till the steep steps were piled high and the doorways blocked with dead. So hideous were the sounds indeed, that Hugh and Grey Dick crossed themselves, thinking that hell had come to Avignon, or Avignon sunk down to hell. But Murgh only folded his white-gloved hands upon his breast and smiled.

At length, save for the moaning of those hurt men who still lived, the dreadful tumult sank to silence. Then Murgh turned and spoke in his slow and icy voice:

"You were about to seek me in the fosse of this high tower, were you not, Hugh de Cressi and Richard Archer? A foolish thought, in truth, and a sinful, so sinful that it would have served you well if I had let you come. But your strait was sore and your faith was weak, and I had no such command. Therefore I have come to others whose names were written in my book. Ay, and being half human after all—for does not your creed tell you that I was born of Sin? I rejoice that it is given to me to protect those who would have protected me when I seemed to stand helpless in the hands of cruel men. Nay, thank me not. What need have I of your thanks, which are due to God alone! And question me not, for why should I answer your questions, even if I know those answers? Only do my bidding. This night seek whom you will in Avignon, but to-morrow ere the dawn ride away, for we three must meet again at a place appointed before this winter's snows are passed."

"O dread lord of Death, one thing, only one," began Hugh.

But Murgh held up his white-gloved hand and replied:

"Have I not said that I answer no questions? Now go forth and follow the promptings of your heart till we meet again."

Then gliding to the head of the stair he vanished in the shadow.

"Say, what shall we do?" asked Hugh in amazed voice.

"It matters little what we do or leave undone, master, seeing that we are fore-fated men whom, as I think, none can harm until a day that will not dawn to-morrow nor yet awhile. Therefore let us wash ourselves and eat and borrow new garments, if we can find any that are not soiled, and then, if the horses are still unharmed, mount and ride from this accursed Avignon for England."

"Nay, Dick, since first we must learn whether or no we leave friends behind us here."

"Ay, master, if you will. But since yonder Murgh said nothing of them, it was in my mind that they are either dead or fled."

"Not dead, I pray, Dick. Oh, I am sure, not dead, and I left living! When Red Eve and I met, Murgh had been with her and promised that she would recover and be strong," answered Hugh bravely, although there was a note of terror in his voice.

"Red Eve has other foes in Avignon besides the pest," muttered

Grey Dick, adding: "still, let us have faith; it is a good friend to man. Did not yonder Helper chide us for our lack of it?"

They forced a way down the dead-cumbered tower stair, crawling through the darkness over the bodies of the fallen. They crossed the hall that also was full of dead, and of wounded whose pitiful groans echoed from the vaulted roof, and climbed another stair to their chamber in the gateway tower. Here from a spark of fire that still smouldered on the hearth, they lit the lamps of olive-oil and by the light of them washed off the stains of battle, and refreshed themselves with food and wine. These things done, Dick returned to the hall and presently brought thence two suits of armour and some cloaks which he had taken either from the walls or from off the slain. In these they disguised themselves as best they could, as de Noyon had disguised himself at Crecy.

Then, having collected a store of arrows whereof many lay about, they departed by the back entrance. The great front doorway was so choked with corpses that they could not pass it, since here had raged the last fearful struggle to escape. Going to the little stable-yard, where they found their horses unharmed in the stalls, although frightened by the tumult and stiff from lack of exercise, they fed and saddled them and led them out. So presently they looked their last upon the Bride's Tower that had sheltered them so well.

"It has served our turn," said Hugh, glancing back at it from the other side of the deserted square, "but oh, I pray heaven that we may never see that charnel-house again!"

As he spoke a figure appeared from the shadow of a doorway, and ran toward them. Thinking it was that of some foe, Dick lifted his axe to cut him down, whereon a voice cried in English:

"Hold! I am David!"

"David!" exclaimed Hugh. "Then thanks be to God, for know, we thought you dead these many days."

"Ay, sir," answered the young man, "as I thought you. The rumour reached the Jews, among whom I have been hiding while I recovered of my hurts, that the Mad Monk and his fellows had stormed the tower and killed you both. Therefore I crept out to learn for myself.

Now I have found you by your voices, who never again hoped to look upon you living," and he began to sob in his relief and joy.

"Come on, lad," said Grey Dick kindly, "this is no place for greetings."

"Whither go you, sir?" asked David as he walked forward alongside of the horses.

"To seek that house where we saw Sir Andrew Arnold and the lady Eve," answered Hugh, "if by any chance it can be found."

"That is easy, sir," said David. "As it happens, I passed it not much more than an hour ago and knew it again."

"Did you see any one there?" asked Hugh eagerly.

"Nay, the windows were dark. Also the Jew guiding me said he had heard that all who dwelt in that house were dead of the plague. Still of this matter he knew nothing for certain."

Hugh groaned, but only answered:

"Forward!"

As they went David told them his story. It seemed that when he was struck down in the square where the crazy friar preached, and like to be stabbed and trampled to death, some of the Jews dragged him into the shadow and rescued him. Afterward they took him to a horrid and squalid quarter called La Juiverie, into which no Christian dare enter. Here he lay sick of his hurts and unable to get out until that very afternoon; the widow Rebecca, whom they had saved, nursing him all the while.

"Did you hear aught of us?" asked Dick.

"Ay, at first that you were holding Dead Bride's Tower bravely. So as soon as I might, I came to join you there if I could win in and you still lived. But they told me that you had fallen at last."

"Ah!" said Dick, "well, as it chances it was not we who fell, but that tale is long. Still, David, you are a brave lad who would have come to die with us, and my master will thank you when he can give his mind to such things. Say, did you hear aught else?"

"Ay, Dick; I heard two days ago that the French lord, Cattrina, whom Sir Hugh was to have fought at Venice, had left Avignon, none knew why or whither he went."

"Doubtless because of the plague and he wished to go where there was none," answered Dick.

But Hugh groaned again, thinking to himself that Acour would scarcely have left Avignon if Eve were still alive within its walls.

After this they went on in silence, meeting very few and speaking with none, for the part of the great city through which they passed seemed to be almost deserted. Indeed in this quarter the pest was so fearful that all who remained alive and could do so had fled elsewhere, leaving behind them only the sick and those who plundered houses.

"One thing I forgot to say," said David presently. "The Jews told me that they had certain information that the notary knave Basil was paid by the lord Cattrina to lead us to that square where the fires burned in order that we might be murdered there. Further, our death was to be the signal for the massacre of all the Jews, only, as it chanced, their plan went awry."

"As will Basil's neck if ever I meet him again," muttered Grey Dick beneath his breath. "Lord! what fools we were to trust that man. Well, we've paid the price and, please God, so shall he."

They turned the corner and rode down another street, till presently David said:

"Halt! yonder is the house. See the cognizance above the gateway!"

Hugh and Dick leapt from their horses, the latter bidding David lead them into the courtyard and hold them there. Then they entered the house, of which the door was ajar, and by the shine of the moon that struggled through the window-places, crept up the stairs and passages till they reached those rooms where Sir Andrew and Eve had lodged.

"Hist!" said Dick, and he pointed to a line of light that showed beneath the closed door.

Hugh pushed it gently and it opened a little. They looked through the crack, and within saw a man in a dark robe who was seated at a table counting out gold by the light of a lamp. Just then he lifted his head, having felt the draught of air from the open door. It was the notary Basil!

Without a word they entered the room, closing and bolting the door behind them. Then Dick leapt on Basil as a wolf leaps, and held him fat, while Hugh ran past him and threw wide the door of that chamber in which Eve had lain sick. It was empty. Back he came again and in a terrible voice, said:

"Now, Sir Notary, where are the lady Eve and Sir Andrew her guardian?"

"Alas, Sir Knight," began the knave in a quavering voice, "both of them are dead."

"What!" cried Hugh supporting himself against the wall, for at this terrible news his knees trembled beneath him, "have you or your patron Cattrina murdered them?"

"Murdered them, Sir Knight! I do murder? I, a Christian and a man of peace! Never! And the noble lord of Cattrina, Count de Noyon! Why, he wished to marry the lady, not to murder her. indeed he swore that she was his wife."

"So you know all these things, do you, villain?" said Grey Dick, shaking him as a terrier shakes a rat.

"Sir Knight," went on the frightened fellow, "blame me not for the acts of God. He slew these noble persons, not I; I myself saw the lovely lady carried from this house wrapped in a red cloak."

"So you were in the house, were you?" said Grey Dick, shaking him again. "Well, whither did they carry her, thief of the night?"

"To the plague pit, good sir; where else in these times?"

Now Hugh groaned aloud, his eyes closed, and he seemed as though he were about to fall. Grey Dick, noting it, for a moment let go of the notary and turned as though to help his master. Like a flash Basil drew a dagger from under his dirty robe and struck at Dick's back. The blow was well aimed, nor could an unprotected man on whom it fell have escaped death. But although Basil did not see it because of Dick's long cloak, beneath this cloak he wore the best of mail, and on that mail the slender dagger broke, its point falling harmless to the ground. Next instant Dick had him again in his iron grip. Paying no further heed to Hugh, who had sunk to the floor a huddled heap, he began to speak into the lawyer's ear in his slow, hissing voice.

"Devil," he said, "whether or no you murdered Red Eve and Sir Andrew Arnold the saint, I cannot say for certain, though doubtless I shall learn in time. At least a while ago you who had taken our money, strove to murder both of us, or cause us to be torn in pieces upon yonder square where the fires burned. Now, too, you have striven to murder me with that bodkin of yours, not knowing, fool, that I am safe from all men. Well, say your prayers, since you too journey to the plague pit, for so the gatherers of the dead will think you died."

"Sir," gasped the terrified wretch, "spare me and I will speak—"

"More lies," hissed Dick into his ear. "Nay, go tell them to the father of lies, for I have no time to waste in hearkening to them. Take your pay, traitor!"

A few seconds later Basil lay dead upon the floor.

Grey Dick looked at him. Kneeling down, he thrust his hands into the man's pockets, and took thence the gold that he had been hiding away when they came upon him, no small sum as it chanced.

"Our own come back with interest," he said with one of his silent laughs, "and we shall need monies for our faring. Why, here's a writing also which may tell those who can read it something."

He cast it on the table, then turned to his master, who was awakening from his swoon.

Dick helped him to his feet.

"What has passed?" asked Hugh in a hollow voice.

"Murgh!" answered Dick, pointing to the dead man on the floor.

"Have you killed him, friend?"

"Ay, sure enough, as he strove to kill me," and again he pointed, this time to the broken dagger.

Hugh made no answer, only seeing the writing on the table, took it up, and began to read like one who knows not what he does. Presently his eyes brightened and he said:

"What does this mean, I wonder. Hearken."

"Rogue, you have cheated me as you cheat all men and now I follow her who has gone. Be sure, however, that you shall reap your reward in due season. "de Noyon."

"I know not," said Dick, "and the interpreter is silent," and he kicked the body of Basil. "Perhaps I was a little over hasty who might have squeezed the truth out of him before the end."

"'Her who is gone,'" reflected Hugh aloud. "'Tis Red Eve who is gone and de Noyon is scarcely the man to seek her among passed souls. Moreover, the Jews swear that he rode from Avignon two days ago. Come, Dick, let that carrion lie, and to the plague pit."

An hour later and they stood on the edge of that dreadful place, hearing and seeing things which are best left untold. A priest came up to them, one of those good men who, caring nothing for themselves, still dared to celebrate the last rites of the Church above the poor departed.

"Friends," he said, "you seem to be in trouble. Can I help you, for Jesus' sake?"

"Perchance, holy Father," answered Hugh. "Tell us, you who watch this dreadful place, was a woman wrapped in a red cloak thrown in here two or three days gone?"

"Alas, yes," said the priest with a sigh, "for I read the Office over her and others. Nay, what are you about to do? By now she is two fathoms deep and burned away with lime so that none could know her. If you enter there the guards will not let you thence living. Moreover, it is useless. Pray to God to comfort you, poor man, as I will, who am sure it will not be denied."

Then Dick led, or rather carried, Hugh from the brink of that awesome, common grave.

CHAPTER XIX

THE DOOM

It was the last night of February, the bitterest night perhaps of all that
sad winter, when at length Hugh de Cressi, Grey Dick, and David
Day rode into the town of Dunwich. Only that morning they had
landed at Yarmouth after a long, long journey whereof the perils and
the horrors may be guessed but need not be written. France, through
which they had passed, seemed to be but one vast grave over which
the wail of those who still survived went up without cease to the cold,
unpitying heavens.

Here in England the tale was still the same. Thus in the great
seaport of Yarmouth scarcely enough people were left alive to inter the
unshriven dead, nor of these would any stay to speak with them,
fearing lest they had brought a fresh curse from overseas. Even the
horses that they rode they took from a stable where they whinnied
hungrily, none being there to feed them, leaving in their place a writing
of the debt.

Betwixt Yarmouth and Dunwich they had travelled through
smitten towns and villages, where a few wandered fearfully, distraught
with sorrow or seeking food. In the streets the very dogs lay dead and
in the fields they saw the carcasses of cattle dragged from the smokeless
and deserted steadings and half hidden in a winding-sheet of snow.
For the Black Plague spared neither man nor beast.

At the little port of Lowestoft they met a sullen sailorman who
stood staring at the beach whereon his fishing boat lay overturned
and awash for lack of hands to drag it out of reach of the angry sea.
They asked him if he knew of how it fared with Dunwich.

By way of answer he cursed them, adding:

"Must I be forever pestered as to Dunwich? This is the third time of late that I have heard of Dunwich from wandering folk. Begone thither and gather tidings for yourselves, which I hope will please you as well as they do me."

"Now, if I were not in haste I would stay a while to teach you manners, you foul-mouthed churl," muttered Grey Dick between his teeth.

"Let the fellow be," said Hugh wearily; "the men of Lowestoft have ever hated those of Dunwich, and it seems that a common woe does not soften hearts. Soon enough we shall learn the truth."

"Ay, you'll learn it soon enough," shouted the brute after them. "Dunwich boats won't steel Lowestoft herrings for many a year!"

So they rode on through Kessland, which they reached as night was closing in, through Benacre and Wrentham, also past houses in which none seemed to dwell.

"Murgh has been here before us, I think," said Dick at length.

"Then I hope that we may overtake him," answered Hugh with a smile, "for I need his tidings—or his rest. Oh! Dick, Dick," he added, "I wonder has ever man borne a heavier burden for all this weary while? If I were sure, it would not be so bad, for when earthly hope is done we may turn to other comfort. But I'm not sure; Basil may have lied. The priest by the pit could only swear to the red cloak, of which there are many, though few be buried in them. And, Dick, there are worse things than that. Perchance Acour got her after all."

"And perchance he didn't," answered Dick. "Well, fret on if you will; the thing does not trouble me who for my part am sure enough."

"Of what, man, of what?"

"Of seeing the lady Eve ere long."

"In this world or the next, Dick?"

"In this. I don't reckon of the next, mayhap there we shall be blind and not see. Besides, of what use is that world to you where it is written that they neither marry nor are given in marriage, but are as the angels? You'll make no good angel, I'm thinking, while as for the lady Eve, she's too human for it as yet."

"Why do you think we shall see her on earth?" asked Hugh, ignoring these reflections.

"Because he who is called the Helper said as much, and whatever he may be he is no liar. Do you not remember what Red Eve told you when she awoke from that dream of hers, which was no dream? And do you not remember what Sir Andrew told you as to a certain meeting in the snow—pest upon it!" and he wiped some of the driving flakes from his face—"Sir Andrew, who is a saint, and, therefore, like Murgh, can be no liar?"

"If you think thus," said Hugh in a new voice, "why did you not say so before?"

"Because I love not argument, master, and if I had, you would ever have reasoned with me from Avignon to Yarmouth town and spoilt my sleep of nights. Oh! where is your faith?"

"What is faith, Dick?"

"The gift of belief, master. A very great gift, seeing what a man believes is and will be true for him, however false it may prove for others. He who believes nothing, sows nothing, and therefore reaps nothing, good or ill."

"Who taught you these things, Dick?"

"One whom I am not likely to forget, or you, either. One who is my master at archery and whose words, like his arrows, though they be few, yet strike the heart of hidden truth. Oh, fear not, doubtless sorrow waits you yonder," and he pointed toward Dunwich. "Yet it comes to my lips that there's joy beyond the sorrows, the joy of battle and of love—for those who care for love, which I think foolishness. There stands a farm, and the farmer is a friend of mine, or used to be. Let us go thither and feed these poor beasts and ourselves, or I think we will never come to Dunwich through this cold and snow. Moreover," he added thoughtfully, "joy or sorrow or both of them are best met by full men, and I wish to look to your harness and my own, for sword and axe are rusted with the sea. Who knows but that we may need them in Dunwich, or beyond, when we meet with Murgh, as he promised that we should."

So they rode up to the house and found Dick's friend, the farmer,

lying dead there in his own yard, whither his family had dragged him
ere they determined to fly the place. Still, there was fodder in the
stable and they lit a fire in the kitchen hearth and drank of the wine
which they had brought with them from the ship, and ate of the
bacon which still hung from the rafters. This done, they lay down to
sleep a while. About one in the morning, however, Hugh roused Dick
and David, saying that he could rest no more and that something in
his heart bade him push on to Dunwich.

"Then let us follow your heart, master," said Dick, yawning. "Yet
I wish it had waited till dawn to move you. Yes, let us follow your
heart to good or evil. David, go you out and saddle up those nags."

For Dick had worked late at their mail and weapons, which now
were bright and sharp again, and was very weary.

It was after three in the morning when at length, leaving the
heath, they rode up to Dunwich Middlegate, expecting to find it shut
against them at such an hour. But it stood open, nor did any challenge
them from the guardhouse.

"They keep an ill watch in Dunwich now-a-days," grumbled Dick.
"Well, perchance there is one here to whom they can trust that
business."

Hugh made no answer, only pressed on down the narrow street,
that was deep and dumb with snow, till at length they drew reign
before the door of his father's house, in the market-place, the great
house where he was born. He looked at the windows and noted that,
although they were unshuttered, no friendly light shone in them. He
called aloud, but echo was his only answer, echo and the moan of the
bitter wind and the sullen roar of the sea.

"Doubtless all men are asleep," he said. "Why should it be otherwise
at such an hour? Let us enter and waken them."

"Yes, yes," answered Dick as he dismounted and threw the reins
of his horse to David. "They are like the rest of Dunwich—asleep."

So they entered and began to search the house by the dim light of
the moon. First they searched the lower chambers, then those where
Hugh's father and his brothers had slept, and lastly the attics. Here

they found the pallets of the serving-folk upon the floor, but none at rest upon them.

"The house is deserted," said Hugh heavily.

"Yes, yes," answered Dick again, in a cheerful voice; "doubtless Master de Cressi and your brothers have moved away to escape the pest."

"Pray God they have escaped it!" muttered Hugh. "This place stifles me," he added. "Let us out."

"Whither shall we go, master?"

"To Blythburgh Manor," he answered, "for there I may win tidings. David, bide you here, and if you can learn aught follow us across the moor. The manor cannot be missed."

So once more Hugh and Dick mounted their horses and rode away through the town, stopping now and again before some house they knew and calling to its inmates. But though they called loudly none answered. Soon they grew sure that this was because there were none to answer, since of those houses many of the doors stood open. Only one living creature did they see in Dunwich. As they turned the corner near to the Blythburgh Gate they met a grey-haired man wrapped up in tattered blankets which were tied about him with haybands. He carried in his hand a beautiful flagon of silver. Doubtless he had stolen it from some church.

Seeing them, he cast this flagon into the snow and began to whimper like a dog.

"Mad Tom," said Dick, recognizing the poor fellow. "Tell us, Thomas, where are the folk of Dunwich?"

"Dead, dead; all dead!" he wailed, and fled away.

"Stay! What of Master de Cressi?" called Hugh. But the tower of the church round which he had vanished only echoed back across the snow, "What of Master de Cressi?"

Then at last Hugh understood the awful truth.

It was that, save those who had fled, the people of Dunwich were slain with the Sword of Pestilence, and all his kin among them.

They were on the Blythburgh Marshes, travelling thither by the shortest road. The moon was down and the darkness dense, for the snow-clouds hid the stars.

"Let us bide here a while," said Grey Dick as their horses blundered through the thick reeds. "It will soon be sunrise, and if we go on in this gloom we shall fall into some boghole or into the river, which I hear running on our left."

So they halted their weary horses and sat still, for in his wretchedness Hugh cared not what he did.

At length the east began to lighten, turning the sky to a smoky red. Then the rim of the sun rising out of the white-flecked ocean, threw athwart the desolate marsh a fierce ray that lay upon the snows like a sword of blood. They were standing on the crest of a little mound, and Dick, looking about him, knew the place.

"See," he said, pointing toward the river that ran near by, "it is just here that you killed young Clavering this day two years ago. Yonder also I shot the French knights, and Red Eve and you leapt into the Blythe and swam it."

"Ay," said Hugh, looking up idly, "but did you say two years, Dick? Nay, surely 'tis a score. Why," he added in a changed voice, "who may that be in the hollow?" and he pointed to a tall figure which stood beneath them at a distance, half-hidden by the dank snow-mists.

"Let us go and see," said Dick, speaking almost in a whisper, for there was that about this figure which sent the blood to his throat and cheeks.

He drove the spurs into his tired horse's sides, causing it to leap forward.

Half a minute later they had ridden down the slope of the hollow. A puff of wind that came with the sun drove away the mist. Dick uttered a choking cry and leapt from his saddle. For there, calm, terrible, mighty, clothed in his red and yellow cap and robe of ebon furs, stood he who was named Murgh the Fire, Murgh the Sword, Murgh the Helper, Murgh, Gateway of the Gods!

They knelt before him in the snow, while, screaming in their fright, the horses fled away.

"Knight and Archer," said Murgh, in his icy voice, counting with the thumb of his white-gloved right hand upon the hidden fingers of his left. "Friends, you keep your tryst, but there are more to come. Have patience, there are more to come."

Then he became quiet, nor dared they ask him any questions. Only at a motion of his arm they rose from their knees and stood before him.

A long while they stood thus in silence, till under Murgh's dreadful gaze Hugh's brain began to swim. He looked about him, seeking some natural thing to feed his eyes. Lo! yonder was that which he might watch, a hare crouching in its form not ten paces distant. See, out of the reeds crept a great red fox. The hare smelt or saw, and leaped away. The fox sprang at it, too late, for the white fangs closed emptily behind its scut. Then with a little snarl of hungry rage it turned and vanished into the brake.

The hare and the fox, the dead reeds, the rising sun, the snow— oh, who had told him of these things?

Ah! he remembered now, and that memory set the blood pulsing in his veins. For where these creatures were should be more besides Grey Dick and himself and the Man of many names.

He looked toward Murgh to see that he had bent himself and with his gloved hand was drawing lines upon the snow. Those lines when they were done enclosed the shape of a grave!

"Archer," said Murgh, "unsheath your axe and dig."

As though he understood, Dick obeyed, and began to hollow out a grave in the soft and boggy soil.

Hugh watched him like one who dreams, wondering who was destined to fill that grave. Presently a sound behind caused him to turn his head.

Oh! certainly he was mad, for there over the rise not a dozen yards away came the beautiful ghost of Eve Clavering, clad in her red cloak. With her was another ghost, that of old Sir Andrew Arnold, blood running down the armour beneath his robe and in his hand the hilt of a broken sword.

Hugh tried to speak, but his lips were dumb, nor did these ghosts take any heed of him, for their eyes were fixed elsewhere. To Murgh they went and stood before him silent. For a while he looked at them, then asked in his cold voice:

"Who am I, Eve Clavering?"

"The Man who came to visit me in my dream at Avignon and told me that I should live," she answered slowly.

"And who say you that I am, Andrew Arnold, priest of Christ the God?"

"He whom I visited in my youth in far Cathay," answered the old knight in an awed whisper. "He who sat beside the pool behind the dragon-guarded doors and was named Gateway of the Gods. He who showed to me that we should meet again in such a place and hour as this."

"Whence come you now, priest and woman, and why?"

"We come from Avignon. We fled thence from one who would have done this maiden grievous wrong. He followed us. Not an hour gone he overtook us with his knaves. He set them on to seize this woman, hanging back himself. Old as I am I slew them both and got my death in it," and he touched the great wound in his side with the hilt of the broken sword. "Our horses were the better; we fled across the swamp for Blythburgh, he hunting us and seeking my life and her honour. Thus we found you as it was appointed."

Murgh turned his eyes. Following their glance, for the first time they saw Hugh de Cressi and near him Grey Dick labouring at the grave. Eve stretched out her arms and so stood with head thrown back, the light of the daybreak shining in her lovely eyes and on her outspread hair. Hugh opened his lips to speak but Murgh lifted his hand and pointed behind them.

They turned and there, not twenty paces from them, clad in armour and seated on a horse was Edmund Acour, Count de Noyon, Seigneur of Cattrina.

He saw, then wheeled round to fly.

"Archer, to your work!" said Murgh, "you know it."

Ere the words had left his lips the great black bow was bent and ere the echoes died away the horse, struck in its side by the keen arrow, sank dying to the ground.

Then Murgh beckoned to the rider and he came as a man who must. But, throwing down the bow, Grey Dick once more began to labour at the grave like one who takes no further heed of aught save his allotted task.

Acour stood before Murgh like a criminal before his judge.

"Man," said the awful figure addressing him, "where have you been and what have you done since last we spoke together in the midday dark at Venice?"

Now, dragged word by slow word from his unwilling lips, came the answer of the traitor's heart.

"I fled from the field at Venice because I feared this knight, and you, O Spirit of Death. I journeyed to Avignon, in France, and there strove to possess myself of yonder woman whom here in England, with the help of one Nicholas, I had wed, when she was foully drugged. I strove to possess myself of her by fraud and by violence. But some fate was against me. She and that aged priest bribed the knave whom I trusted. He caused a dead man and woman dressed in their garments to be borne from their lodging to the plague pit while they fled from Avignon disguised."

Here for a moment Grey Dick paused from his labours at the grave and looked up at Hugh. Then he fell to them again, throwing out the peaty soil with both hands.

"My enemy and his familiar, for man he can scarcely be," went on Acour, pointing first to Hugh and then to Dick, "survived all my plans to kill them and instead killed those whom I had sent after them. I learned that the woman and the priest were not dead, but fled, and followed them, and after me came my enemy and his familiar. Twice we passed each other on the road, once we slept in the same house. I knew them but they knew me not and the Fate which blinded me from them, saved them also from all my plots to bring them to their doom. The woman and the priest took ship to England, and I followed in another ship, being made mad with desire and with jealous rage, for there I knew my enemy would find and win her. In the darkness before this very dawn I overtook the woman and the priest at last and set my fellows on to kill the man. Myself I would strike no blow, fearing lest my death should come upon me, and so I should be robbed of her. But God fought with His aged servant who in his youth was the first of knights. He slew my men, then fled on with the woman, Eve of Clavering. I followed, knowing that he was sore wounded and must die, and that then the beauty which has lured me to shame and ruin would be mine, if only for an hour. I followed, and here at this place of evil omen, where first I saw my foe, I found you, O Incarnate Sword of Vengeance."

Murgh unfolded his bare arms and lifted his head, which was sunk upon his breast.

"Your pardon," he said gently, "my name is Hand of Fate and not Sword of Vengeance. There is no vengeance save that which men work upon themselves. What fate may be and vengeance may be I know not fully, and none will ever know until they have passed the Gateway of the Gods. Archer the grave is deep enough. Come forth now and let us learn who it is decreed shall fill it. Knights, the hour is at hand for you to finish that which you began at Crecy and at Venice."

Hugh heard and drew his sword. Acour drew his sword also, then cried out, pointing to Grey Dick:

"Here be two against one. If I conquer he will shoot me with his bow."

"Have no fear, Sir Thief and Liar," hissed Grey Dick, "for that shaft will not be needed. Slay the master if you can and go safe from the squire," and he unstrung his black bow and hid it in its case.

Now Hugh stepped to where Red Eve stood, the wounded Sir Andrew leaning on her shoulder. Bending down he kissed her on the lips, saying:

"Soon, very soon, my sweet, whom I have lost and found again, you will be mine on earth, or I shall be yours in heaven. This, then, in greeting or farewell."

"In greeting, beloved, not in farewell," she answered as she kissed him back, "for if you die, know that I follow hard upon your road. Yet I say that yonder grave was not dug for you."

"Nay, not for you, son, not for you," said Sir Andrew lifting his faint head. "One fights for you whom you do not see, and against Him Satan and his servant cannot stand," and letting fall the sword hilt he stretched out his thin hand and blessed him.

Now when Acour saw that embrace his jealous fury prevailed against his fears. With a curse upon his lips he leapt at Hugh and smote, thinking to take him unawares. But Hugh was watching, and sprang back, and then the fray began, if fray it can be called.

A wild joy shining in his eyes, Hugh grasped his long sword with both hands and struck. So great was that blow that it bit through Acour's armour, beneath his right arm, deep into the flesh and sent him staggering back. Again he struck and wounded him in the shoulder; a third time and clove his helm so that the blood poured down into his eyes and blinded him.

Back reeled Acour, back to the very edge of the grave, and stood there swaying to and fro. At the sight of his helplessness Hugh's fury seemed to leave him. His lifted sword sank downward.

"Let God deal with you, knave," he said, "for I cannot."

For a while there was silence. There they stood and stared at the smitten man waiting the end, whatever it might be. They all stared save Murgh, who fixed his stony eyes upon the sky.

Presently it came. The sword, falling from Acour's hand into the grave, rested there point upward. With a last effort he drew his dagger. Dashing the blood from his eyes, he hurled it with all his dying strength, not at Hugh, but at Red Eve. Past her ear it hissed, severing a little tress of her long hair, which floated down on to the snow.

Then Acour threw his arms wide and fell backward—fell backward and vanished in the grave.

Dick ran to look. There he lay dead, pierced through back and bosom by the point of his own sword.

For one brief flash of time a black dove-shaped bird was seen hovering round the head of Murgh.

"Finished!" said Dick straightening himself. "Well, I had hoped to see a better fight, but cowards die as cowards live."

Leaning on Red Eve's shoulder Sir Andrew limped to the side of the grave. They both looked down on that which lay therein.

"Daughter," said the old man, "through many dangers it has come about as I foretold. The bond that in your drugged sleep bound you to this highborn knave is severed by God's sword of death. Christ have pity on his sinful soul. Now, Sir Hugh de Cressi, come hither and be swift, for my time is short."

Hugh obeyed, and at a sign took Eve by the hand. Then, speaking very low and as quickly as he might for all his life was draining from him through the red wound in his side, the old priest spoke the hallowed words that bound these two together till death should part them. Yes, there by the graveside, over the body of the dead Acour, there in the red light of the morning, amidst the lonely snows, was celebrated the strangest marriage the world has ever seen. In nature's church it was celebrated, with the grim, grey Archer for a clerk, and Death's own fearful minister for congregation.

It was done and with uplifted, trembling hands Sir Andrew blessed them both—them and the fruit of their bodies which was to be. He blessed them in the name of the all-seeing God he served. He bade them put aside their grief for those whom they had lost. Soon, he said, their short day done, the lost would be found again, made glorious, and with them himself, who, loving them both on earth, would love them through eternity.

Then, while their eyes grew blind with tears, and even the fierce archer turned aside his face, Sir Andrew staggered to where he stood who in the Land of Sunrise had been called Gateway of the Gods. Before him he bent his grey and ancient head.

"O thou who dwellest here below to do the will of heaven, to thee I come as once thou badest me," he said, and was silent.

Murgh let his eyes rest on him. Then stretching out his hand, he touched him very gently on the breast, and as he touched him smiled a sweet and wondrous smile.

"Good and faithful servant," he said, "thy work is done on earth.

Now I, whom all men fear, though I be their friend and helper, am bidden by the Lord of life and death to call thee home. Look up and pass!"

The old priest obeyed. It seemed to those who watched that the radiance on the face of Murgh had fallen upon him also. He smiled, he stretched his arms upward as though to clasp what they might not see. Then down he sank gently, as though upon a bed, and lay white and still in the white, still snow.

The Helper turned to the three who remained alive.

"Farewell for a little time," he said. "I must be gone. But when we meet again, as meet we shall, then fear me not, for have you not seen that to those who love me I am gentle?"

Hugh de Cressi and Red Eve made no answer, for they knew not what to say. But Grey Dick spoke out boldly.

"Sir Lord, or Sir Spirit," he said, "save once at the beginning, when the arrow burst upon my string, I never feared you. Nor do I fear your gifts," and he pointed to the grave and to dead Sir Andrew, "which of late have been plentiful throughout the world, as we of Dunwich know. Therefore I dare to ask you one question ere we part for a while. Why do you take one and leave another? Is it because you must, or because every shaft does not hit its mark?"

Now Murgh looked him up and down with his sunken eyes, then answered:

"Come hither, archer, and I will lay my hand upon your heart also and you shall learn."

"Nay," cried Grey Dick, "for now I have the answer to the riddle, since I know you cannot lie. When we die we still live and know; therefore I'm content to wait."

Again that smile swept across Murgh's awful face though that smile was cold as the winter dawn. Then he turned and slowly walked away toward the west.

They watched him go till he became but a blot of fantastic colour that soon vanished on the moorland.

Hugh spoke to Red Eve and said:

"Wife, let us away from this haunted place and take what joy we can. Who knows when Murgh may return again and make us as are all the others whom we love!"

"Ay, husband won at last," she answered, "who knows? Yet, after so much fear and sorrow, first I would rest a while with you."

So hand in hand they went till they, too, grew small and vanished on the snowy marsh.

But Grey Dick stayed there alone with the dead, and presently spoke aloud for company.

"The woman has him heart and soul," he said, "as is fitting, and where's the room between the two for an archer-churl to lodge? Mayhap, after all, I should have done well to take yonder Murgh for lord when I had the chance. Man, or god, or ghost, he's a fellow to my liking, and once he had led me through the Gates no woman would have dared to come to part us. Well, good-bye, Hugh de Cressi, till you are sick of kisses and the long shafts begin to fly again, for then you will bethink you of a certain bow and of him who alone can bend it."

Having spoken thus in his hissing voice, whereof the sound resembled that of an arrow in its flight, Grey Dick descended into the grave and trod the earth over Acour's false and handsome face, hiding it from the sight of men forever.

Then he lifted up the dead Sir Andrew in his strong arms and slowly bore him thence to burial.

THE END

THE ESSENTIAL ADVENTURE LIBRARY

The Essential Adventure Library features the world's best adventure novels. Travel through time and space, from ancient Egypt to medieval Europe, from the deepest mysteries of Africa to a South Seas island paradise. **Call 1-888-7XLIBRIS (1-888-795-4274) to order your next book today!**

Every novel features heart-pounding action, exotic mysteries, and epic fantasies. The **"All-Adventure"** series includes the following works of **H. Rider Haggard**:

"The Brethren" is an elite group of medieval knights during the time of the Crusades. Sir Godwin is mortally wounded in battle, his spirit is denied entrance to Heaven, and he is sent back to Earth to redeem himself. Joining the Brethren, Godwin travels to the Middle East on a Holy Quest. History, religion, and adventure come together in this unforgettable epic.

"Cleopatra" Deep in an ancient Egyptian tomb, three papyrus scrolls are discovered containing the secret history of Cleopatra! Narrated by Harmachis, the rightful heir to Egypt's throne, this never before told tale brings history's most seductive enchantress to life. Can Harmachis fulfill his destiny or will Cleopatra destroy him? Epic legends, fantastic adventure, and compelling romance combine to answer history's greatest mystery.

"King Solomon's Mines / Long Odds" Allan Quatermain is about to embark on the most dangerous hunt of his career. His new employers, Sir Henry Curtis and Captain John Good, have a map drawn by a dying Portuguese prospector. It reveals a route across the great desert, past a fearsome range of mountains, to the greatest treasure in all Africa, the lost diamond mines of King Solomon himself! Also included in this volume is the rare novella of "Long Odds"-another adventure story featuring the legendary hunter, Allan Quatermain.

"Morning Star / Moon of Israel" brings together two amazing adventures in ancient Egypt. In "Morning Star", a royal prince faces many extreme challenges to win the throne and the heart of his beloved. "Moon of Israel" features the biblical tale of Exodus and brings to life the excitement and mystery of long-ago religions and cultures. Greed, betrayal, and ultimately, redemption are the themes of these two powerful novels.

"Queen Sheba's Ring" A ring from antiquity or an elaborate hoax? One of the lost adventure novels of H. Rider Haggard, "Queen Sheba's Ring" features Middle-Eastern mysticism and a secret society descended from ancient Abyssinians. History, myth, and romance mix in this satisfying adventure.

"Red Eve" Journey back in time to the Dark Ages of Europe. This occult historical novel presents a fascinating account of a time when superstition ruled the Earth. Meet the Black Plague as a personified presence with supernatural powers. This compelling tale is another one of Haggard's lost adventure novels.

"She Who Must Be Obeyed" Ayesha is She-Who-Must-Be-Obeyed, a 2,000-year-old queen who rules a fabled lost city deep in a maze of African caverns. She has the occult wisdom of Isis, the eternal youth and beauty of Aphrodite, and the violent appetite of a lion. Journey on an exotic expedition to a far-off locale shadowed by magic, mystery, and death.

"Wanderer's Necklace" Former lives are recalled as Olaf, a fierce Nordic warrior, cheats death, finds a mystical necklace and a powerful sword, and sets sail to the ends of the earth. Battling to protect a Byzantium princess, Olaf finds his way to Egypt where he hopes to unravel a cunning mystery. Mythology and fantasy intertwine in this compelling adventure.

"When the World Shook" Three Englishmen are marooned on a mysterious South Seas island. A local legend tells of the powerful god who has been sleeping for centuries. Can suspended animation revive the lost civilization of Atlantis? Who is the elusive woman whose appearance is identical to our hero's dead wife? Find the answers in this exotic adventure of spirit travel, reincarnation, and the occult powers of a lost city.

"World's Desire" turns to Homer's "Odyssey" for inspiration and a starting point in ancient Greece. This novel chronicles the further adventures of Odysseus and Helen of Troy in far-off lands. Heroic fantasy and classical mythology form the basis of this action-filled tale.

"The Yellow God: An Idol of Africa" One of the lost adventure novels of H. Rider Haggard, "The Yellow God" is both a spell-binding mystery and an exotic, action-filled adventure. Sir Robert Aylward has a mysterious gold mask in his possession and to unlock its secrets will bring death! Travel from England to Africa to find the truth. This fantasy adventure features talismans, a lost race, reincarnation, and vampirism.

Call 1-888-7XLIBRIS (1-888-795-4274) to order your next book today! For more information on these titles and for a complete list of all Essential Library editions, please visit our website **www.EssentialLibrary.com.**

THE ESSENTIAL HORROR LIBRARY

The Essential Library presents "**All Gothic Horror**," a multi-volume series featuring the most spine-tingling tales of classic terror. Step through everyday reality and encounter the supernatural for yourself. **Call 1-888-7XLIBRIS (1-888-795-4274) to order your next book today!**

Selected gothic horror titles include:

"**All Gothic Horror 1: The Boats of the Glen Garrig & The House on the Borderland**" by William Hope Hodgson This book brings together in one volume the first two novels of Hodgson's "Trilogy" which was an important influence on H.P. Lovecraft. Fast-paced adventure combines with the supernatural to create "The Boats of Glen Garrig." "The House on the Borderland" is an ancient and crumbling estate, overrun by wild gardens. There resides a man who has a most unusual story to tell—a story that blends horror, fantasy, and science fiction. As acclaimed horror writer T. E. D. Klein says, "Never has a book so hauntingly conveyed a sense of terrible loneliness and isolation."

"**All Gothic Horror 2: The Ghost Pirates & Carnacki, the Ghost Finder**" by William Hope Hodgson This book concludes Hodgson's Trilogy with "The Ghost Pirates" which tells the captivating tale of the ship "Mortzestus", an unlucky vessel haunted by "too many shadows". The unifying theme seems to be the dreadful forces that lurk just beneath the veneer of what we, in immense folly, believe to be "reality". Malign forces may surface at any moment to drag us to destruction or worse. As an added bonus, the chilling account of "Carnacki The Ghost Finder" is also included. As a beautifully written work of pure imagination, Hodgon's novels have few equals, and have been compared to the writings of Poe, Machen, and Blackwood.

"All Gothic Horror 3: The Complete Purcell Papers" by Joseph Sheridan Le Fanu Brought together in one volume, this is an anthology of supernatural tales, as recorded by a parish priest in southern Ireland. These recollections represent the legacy of the late Francis Purcell, P. P. of Drumcoolagh. This collection of 9 short stories/ novellas include "The Last Heir of Castle Connor," "The Strange Event in the Life of Schalken the Painter," and "Billy Malowney's Taste of Love and Glory." Horror can take many forms. A creeping sense of doom. A pit of fear. The unseen terror which lurks just out of sight. The Purcell Papers documents the most astonishing and terrifying tales of old Europe. Are you brave enough to find out for yourself?

Call 1-888-7XLIBRIS (1-888-795-4274) to order your next book today! For more information on these titles and for a complete list of all Essential Library editions, please visit our website **www.EssentialLibrary.com.**

THE ESSENTIAL
NON-FICTION LIBRARY

The Essential Library also features compelling and easy-to-read non-fiction classics. From history to biography to exotic travel, you can find the best true-life experiences here. **Call 1-888-7XLIBRIS (1-888-795-4274) to order your next book today!**
Selected non-fiction titles include:

"Early Australian Voyages" by John Pinkerton This book a captivating account of true-life stories of courage and daring. Meet the brave explorers who were the first to cross the uncharted seas.

"Eight Years Wandering in Ceylon" by Samuel Baker Explore nineteenth century Sri Lanka and immerse yourself in an exotic bygone world.

"The Essential Shakespeare: A Guide to 19 Plays" This book provides a narrative guide to the plots of Shakespeare's greatest plays. The text has been updated and summarized, while retaining all of the wit, wonder, comedy, and tragedy that can only be Shakespeare.

"The Great Astronomers" by R. S. Ball Meet some of the greatest scientific minds of the ages: Copernicus, Galileo, Kepler, and Issac Newton. Unearth the origins of astronomy with Ptolemy and the ancient Greeks. Explore the moon with Tycho Brahe. Help Edmund Halley discover the greatest comet of all time. All these astronomers and many more are part of the captivating saga of man's eternal quest to master the heavens.

"Memoirs of Extraordinary Popular Delusions & the Madness of Crowds, Volumes 1 & 2" by Charles MacKay How often do you come across a book that can explain most everything? This complete edition demonstrates that the madness and confusion of crowds knows no limits, and has no temporal bounds. Here are astonishing and entertaining tales of thievery, greed and madness. This informative, funny collection encompasses a broad range of manias and deceptions from haunted houses and the prophecies of Nostradamus to speculative investment excess. Charles MacKay explains it all in this complete two-volume edition.

Call 1-888-7XLIBRIS (1-888-795-4274) to order your next book today! For more information on these titles and for a complete list of all Essential Library editions, please visit our website **www.EssentialLibrary.com.**

THE ESSENTIAL MYSTERY LIBRARY

The Essential Mystery Library features the world's best mysteries, detective stories, and suspense novels. The centerpiece is *The Essential Rinehart Collection*, a ten-volume set of Mary Roberts Rinehart's best works.

Call 1-888-7XLIBRIS (1-888-795-4274) to order your next book today! Selected titles include:

"Caught in the Net" by Emile Gaboriau features a gang of thieves trapped in a web of deceit. Emile Gaboriau is a French author who has written compelling and atmospheric detective novels. Most of his tales are set in nineteenth century Paris and feature vividly realized characters who experience love, loss, joy and betrayal.

"Other People's Money" by Emile Gaboriau examines what happens when money and murder meet. High finance is the backdrop to this atmospheric detective novel set in France. Can you solve the crime before time runs out?

"The Mystery of Oricval" by Emile Gaboriau takes the reader down the proverbial garden path and who knows what awaits at the end? Is the French countryside as peaceful as it seems? The compelling characters and intricately plotted mystery will keep you riveted through the stunning conclusion.

"Sleuth of St. James Street" by Melville Post Marquis read the secret message in his emotionless drawl: "The American is destroyed, and his accursed work is destroyed with him. Send the news to Bangkok and west to Burma. The treasures of India are saved." So begins, "The Sleuth of St. James Street"—a riveting Victorian mystery adventure.

The Essential Rinehart Collection brings together the best works of Mary Roberts Rinehart, the famed mystery writer. Here are the volumes published to date:

"Volume 1: The Circular Staircase / The Man in Lower Ten" In "The Circular Staircase," an aunt takes a summer house and finds it has occupants she never bargained for. "The Man in Lower Ten" is a legal thriller where the clues incriminate three entirely different people and the innocent fight for justice.

"Volume 2: When A Man Marries / The Window At the White Cat" "When A Man Marries," his troubles begin! The old nursery rhyme holds true for Jimmy Wilson. On the anniversary of his divorce, his friends gather to cheer him up. Only everything goes deadly wrong. "The Window At The White Cat" deals with high-level corruption and turns on some astonishing coincidences.

"Volume 3: Where There's A Will / The Case of Jennie Brice / The After House" Three of her novels, all set in the early 1900's, are collected here for the first time. Each story features a cast of memorable characters, mysterious happenings and leads up to an astonishing conclusion!

"Volume 4: Long Live The King" Once, in a small European kingdom, a long time ago, there lived Prince Ferdinand William Otto—a young boy longing for adventure. One day he runs away from home and sets into motion events that will change the course of history.

"Volume 5: The Amazing Interlude / The Street of Seven Stars" Set during World War I, "The Amazing Interlude" is both a haunting romance and a mystery. A young woman, Sara Lee, joins the Red Cross, travels to Europe, and changes her life forever. "The Street of Seven Stars" is an atmospheric mystery set in long-ago Austria.

"Volume 6: The Bat / Bab, A Sub-Deb" Mary Roberts Rinehart is at the top of her form in "The Bat," an innovative retelling of "The Circular Staircase." Someone—or something—is trying to frighten Cornelia Van Gorder to death! "Bab, A Sub-Deb" is the author at her most experimental—a writing assignment that leads to tragedy and murder.

"Volume 7: Dangerous Days" The darkening storm of the first World War threatens to tear apart the lives of a group of friends. At the eye of the storm is Clayton Spencer, an ambitious businessman, who must risk everything to be with the woman he loves.

"Volume 8: A Poor Wise Man" There were bad times coming. The old peaceful quiet days were gone, for age and obstinacy had met youth and the arrogance of youth, and it was to be a battle. Birth, death, and renewal are the themes that Mary Roberts Rinehart tackles in this emotional and thought-provoking novel set during the first World War

"Volume 9: Sight Unseen / The Confession" In "Sight Unseen" the Neighborhood Club, a group of six friends, decide to hold a séance for fun-only to have a blood-curdling crime reenacted before their eyes. Soon, they are hot on the trail of a murderer. "The Confession" is a grim but powerful portrait of a woman's guilt, depression and mental breakdown.

"Volume 10: The Breaking Point" Elizabeth Wheeler lives in a small town, sings in the church choir, and dreams of a man who will sweep her off her feet. Instead, she is thrust into a series of events beyond her control leading to passion, madness, betrayal, and ultimately, murder! Can she ever set thing right?

Call 1-888-7XLIBRIS (1-888-795-4274) to order your next book today! For more information on these titles and for a complete list of all Essential Library editions, please visit our website **www.EssentialLibrary.com.**

THE ESSENTIAL LIBRARY

The Essential Library is a book series, which features engaging and approachable literary works drawn from the fields of poetry, drama, and comedies. **Call 1-888-7XLIBRIS (1-888-795-4274) to order your next book today!** Selected titles include:

"The Complete Poems of Andrew Lang, Volumes 1 & 2" Andrew Lang was a noted Scottish scholar and writer of the nineteenth century. He wrote five books of poetry, which have been consolidated into two volumes. Lang chose to liken his poetry to the grass of Parnassus-wild flowers at the foot of the mountain. His poetical work is at times wild and natural yet also elegant and timeless.

"The Diary of a Nobody" by George & Weedon Grossmith This comic novel presents the details of English suburban life through the anxious and accident-prone character of Charles Porter—whose diary chronicles his daily routine. The small minded but essentially decent suburban world he inhabits is both hilarious and painfully familiar.

"The Essential Odyssey: The Adventures of Ulysses" For more than 2,500 years, Homer's Odyssey has been the definitive saga of the archetypal survivor. Through intelligence and courage, Ulysses overcomes what seem to be insurmountable forces, imposed by gods and men alike, to regain home and family after a separation of twenty years. This book is a narrative of Homer's epic poem, which preserves all of the suspense-filled adventure while updating the language to be more accessible to today's modern reader.

"The Lunatic At Large / Count Bunker" by J. Storer Clouston Two unique comedic masterpieces, "Lunatic at Large" and its sequel, "Count Bunker" are presented together for the first time. It all began with a letter: "One of my most esteemed patients is in an extremely unstable mental condition. I have strongly recommended quiet and change of scene, and at my suggestion he is to be sent abroad under the care of a medical attendant. I have now much pleasure in offering you the post . . ." So begins the adventures of a lunatic at large!

Call 1-888-7XLIBRIS (1-888-795-4274) to order your next book today! For more information on these titles and for a complete list of all Essential Library editions, please visit our website **www.EssentialLibrary.com.**